SECRET SKY

WINDSTORM
PRESS

PRAISE FOR SECRET SKY

Secret Sky is a deeply moving book and it will stay with you forever. It's gentle and lyric, and it's dark and hard. It's an intelligent novel, generously sprinkled with beautiful, subtle humor, and written by a natural storyteller. What a treat!

—J.F. Kaufmann, author of *The Langaer Chronicles*

J.P. McLean captures your attention and you're hooked before you flip the first page. Before too long, she skillfully manages to have you question what you once thought impossible. A thoroughly enjoyable read that had me looking forward to her second book, long before I was through with the first.

—Island Gals Magazine

PRAISE FOR THE GIFT LEGACY

" A profoundly intelligent story of a captivating young woman whose victories and struggles with a unique gift will grab your every emotion.
—Jennifer Manuel, award-winning author of
The Heaviness of Things That Float

" JP McLean possesses her own unique gift: the ability to bewitch her readers with her boundless imagination.
—Elinor Florence, Globe and Mail bestselling author of
Bird's Eye View

" Riveting mash-up of urban fantasy, mystery and new adult—seamlessly woven together with a steamy love story.
—Roxy Boroughs, award-winning author of
The Psychic Heat series

" JP McLean is the mistress of unpredictability. So many twists and turns, so many surprises.
—Charlie Bray, author of *The Trouble with Celebrity*

" A superbly crafted fantasy thriller.
—Diana Stevan, author of *A Cry from the Deep*

" McLean's expertly drawn world is filled with intriguing characters and near-familiar settings that draw you into this compelling read.
—Katherine Prairie, author of
the Alex Graham thriller series

" It has everything you're looking for in a contemporary fantasy: masterfully crafted characters, exciting plot, believable magic.
—J.F. Kaufmann, author of The Langaer Chronicles

" A well written, superbly executed thrilling read!
—Pat McDonald, British crime author

TITLES BY JP MCLEAN

THE GIFT LEGACY

Secret Sky

Hidden Enemy

Burning Lies

Lethal Waters

Deadly Deception

Wings of Prey

THE GIFT LEGACY COMPANION

Lover Betrayed (Secret Sky Redux)

To Darline & Scarlett

SECRET SKY

THE GIFT LEGACY
BOOK 1

Jo-Anne P McLea

JP MCLEAN

Secret Sky
The Gift Legacy ~ Book 1
First Canadian Edition

Copyright © 2018 by JP McLean
All rights reserved.

Previously published as *The Gift: Awakening*

ISBN
978-1-988125-27-5 (Paperback)
978-1-988125-28-2 (MOBI)
978-1-988125-29-9 (EPUB)
978-1-988125-30-5 (PDF)

Edited by Nina Munteanu
Copy edit by Rachel Small
Book cover designed by JD&J with stock imagery
provided by Oleg Gekman © 123RF.com
Author photograph by Crystal Clear Photography

Excerpt from *Hidden Enemy* copyright © 2018 by JP McLean

Excerpt from *Lover Betrayed* copyright © 2019 by JP McLean

Cataloguing in Publication information available
from Library and Archives Canada

WINDSTORM PRESS
BRITISH COLUMBIA, CANADA
WWW.WINDSTORMPRESS.COM

For MD—thanks for the L&S, patience and for picking up the slack. I could never fly this high without you.

The greatest gift is a portion of thyself.

—Ralph Waldo Emerson

CHAPTER ONE

Can you tell me your name?"

"*Emelynn*," I answered, closing my eyes to dampen the cresting wave of nausea.

"She's nonresponsive."

No, I'm not. I forced my eyes open. His face was a blur. "*My name's Emelynn*," I repeated but, oddly, I couldn't hear my voice.

"Did you find any ID?"

Nearby, a siren wailed. Had it rained? The damp air smelled of worms and wet earth. I lost the fight with my eyelids.

"No, and no sign of her shoes or transportation either. Are you ready to move her?"

"Yes, she's immobilized and secure. On three ..."

The world tilted at a dangerous angle. Flashing lights throbbed, breaching my shrouded eyes.

"Female, early twenties, BP's ninety-eight over fifty ..." The man's voice trailed off as I melted into the pleasant reprieve of a quiet darkness.

I liked the soft, fuzzy quality of the darkness. I felt comfortable there, but loud voices and harsh lights dragged me back and dumped me into a boisterous room. The clatter hurt my ears. I desperately wanted to shush these people, but that would be rude. A hazy face pressed in, but my eyes wouldn't focus. The man behind the face flicked a sharp light in my eye ... so ... inconsiderate.

"Can you tell me what day it is?" he asked, as if I were an idiot.

It's ... hmm ... what day was it? And why couldn't I move? I felt an overwhelming desire to curl up and go back to sleep. The man finally let me close my eyes. I pulled against whatever held me in its grip, but I didn't have the strength to fight it.

"Let's get a CT scan, spine and head, stat, and run a panel in case we have to go in."

Even with my eyes closed, the room was too bright and filled with a cacophony of electronic beeps, bells and the sharp voices of people who wouldn't stop shouting. I wanted to ask them to leave me alone, but my voice wouldn't come. They jostled me and I dipped into that blissful darkness again—the one that pushed away all the noise.

The darkness soothed me until the man with the snap-on gloves interrupted the calm again, his sharp light piercing my eye like a knitting needle. "Can you tell me what city you live in?"

Did he think I didn't know? I almost said Toronto, but that wasn't right, was it? Didn't I just move to Summerset ... or was that a dream? Why was I so confused? God, my head hurt.

"Any change?" I heard him ask.

Was he talking to me?

"No. She's still hypotensive, but stable."

I guess not.

"Pupils are equal and reactive," he said, and then I heard him sigh. "It's been six hours. Do we know who she is yet?"

"*My name's Emelynn,*" I said in defeat because I knew he couldn't hear me.

"No, the police searched the park. No purse, no ID."

"What was she doing in the park at that hour?" one of them asked.

"The police haven't ruled out that she might have been dumped there, but she was wearing workout gear so she could have been hit while jogging."

"It would have been late for a jog in the park, wouldn't it?"

"Maybe she works shifts?" the other voice offered.

Listening to their conversation exhausted me. Before I could figure out what it meant, the darkness claimed me again and that's exactly where I wanted to be.

If only they would let me stay there, but they were relentless with their light. This time when the stabbing light woke me, the thought that perhaps I was dying flitted through my mind. Was I supposed to go toward the light? Maybe I wasn't doing it right.

The pain didn't reach me in the dark, but I slept fitfully and had the oddest dream. It was the dead of night and a powerful storm was gathering strength. The gusting winds blew across the crests of angry waves, creating whitecaps that seemed to glow in the dark. Towering cedars and firs rained needles as they bowed to the wind. The great crooked trunks of old arbutus trees groaned and twisted, spewing glossy leaves into the breeze. And I had a bird's-eye view of it all as I watched the storm unfold—below me.

Home was here in the dream, somewhere. I sensed it calling out to me, drawing me toward its warmth and safety. I knew the small cottage so well, but I couldn't find it. The storm would stop if I could just get inside, but the wind blew me out over the treetops, farther and farther away. And then I was falling ... falling ... falling through the night sky, careening out of control, crashing through the tree canopy until that blissful darkness put an end to the terrible fall.

The pointy light woke me again. "Can you tell me your name?" the man asked, peeling back my eyelids and flicking that damn light.

"Emelynn," I said, relieved to hear the sound of my voice. But the relief was short-lived. My head exploded in agony when I turned away from the light.

As the pain hit a crescendo, I heard him remark "I'm losing her" and I surrendered into the peaceful darkness again.

"Emelynn," the man said the next time he woke me with the flicking light. "Emelynn, don't struggle—we've immobilized your head. Do you know where you are?"

I squinted, straining to bring the face behind the glasses into focus. "The hospital?"

"Good. That's good, Emelynn. I'm Dr. Coulter. You've had an accident."

"What accident?" Car accident? I don't have a car. No, wait, I think I do have a car. Why was this so hard?

"You don't remember?" He pressed his lips into a thin line and furrowed his brow.

I tried, but the dream was all I could think of. "Did I fall?"

"We don't know. We were hoping you could tell us."

"My head hurts."

"You have a concussion. I can't give you anything for it yet. Can you tell me what you were doing in Sunset Park last night?"

"I live there," I said, but that wasn't right either. Why was I so mixed up? I'd figure it out later, I thought, as sleep once again tugged at me.

He seemed to share my confusion. "We'll talk again later."

I folded into the darkness when it came for me. Perception was all mixed up in the dark making it difficult to sort out what was real and what wasn't.

When the darkness faded, it revealed an airport scene that looked vaguely familiar. I drifted toward a young couple with a little girl and watched as the man leaned in to kiss the woman.

"I love you," he said, pulling away.

My heart stopped when I saw the man's face.

He turned to the little girl and mussed her hair. "Be good for your mother. I'll only be gone a few days."

Oh, god, no. I knew what this was. I had to stop him. "No! Don't go!"

He put his big tackle box on the luggage cart beside the bag that I knew held his fishing rods. "I'll be back Tuesday. Don't forget about those peanut butter cookies you promised me." He smiled down at her, then turned and walked out to the float plane tied to the dock.

"No!" I cried as he leaned forward, ducking into the plane, oblivious to my presence. "Please," I begged. Then I heard someone calling my name.

"Emelynn. Emelynn, that's right, look at me. I'm over here," said a woman in scrubs who moved her face into my line of vision. I blinked up at the nurse.

"It was a dream, that's all, dear. You have a concussion. Your head is braced so try not to fight it. You were thrashing in your sleep." She adjusted the blankets and checked the IV.

Pain returned with my awakening and ramped up quickly. It wasn't just my head anymore. My entire left side was on fire. A moan escaped my throat. "I'll get Dr. Coulter," the nurse said, hurrying from the room.

Time crawled while I played a miserable little game of Which Body Part Hurts More. There was no clear winner.

Dr. Coulter arrived at a gallop. He and the nurse succinctly exchanged statistics at a rapid-fire clip. BP? One oh six over sixty. Urine? Clear. Orientation? Improving. With a clipboard in hand, he checked on a number of beeping machines before he looked at me.

"Can you tell me your name?" He put the clipboard down with a clatter and pulled that damn penlight out of his breast pocket.

"Emelynn," I answered, as he held my eyelid captive.

"Good," he said, distracted by his light-flicking exam. "Do you have a last name, Emelynn?"

"Taylor," I responded with trepidation. What kind of trouble had I gotten myself into?

He repeated the light exam with my other eye. "Very good," he said, and then he finally saw me, not just my eyes.

"Where do you live?" he asked.

"Cliffside Avenue," I replied.

He smiled warmly. "Glad to hear you've moved out of the park."

"Excuse me?" He made no sense, and my head throbbed in time with the beat of my heart.

"During one of our previous discussions, you said you lived in Sunset Park. I'm just happy to see that your memory is coming back. What do you remember about your accident?"

"Accident," I said, mulling over the question, holding out for some clues. He wasn't offering any and my dreams were all mixed up with reality. Had I dreamt that I'd fallen through the trees or was that real? My head kept pounding. I drew my right hand up and followed the path of the tube sticking out of the back of it up to a dripping IV bag.

"Late Monday or early Tuesday?" he continued, bringing my attention back to his question.

"I'm sorry, I don't remember," I said, distracted now. "How long have I been here?"

"You came in on a 911 call at"—he checked the notes on the clipboard—"oh-one-thirty on Tuesday."

I tried to process the information.

"That's one thirty in the morning. You were found in Sunset Park. Do you remember why you were in the park at that hour?"

"The park is right beside my house." I tried to recall the details that would make sense of this scenario, but they escaped me, and the pain made concentration difficult. "I don't remember."

"Okay. Let's give it a few more hours. Memory loss isn't uncommon with this type of brain injury. It may be temporary."

"*May* be?"

"It's still early. We need to give it more time."

"It feels like I've been here for days."

"I'm sure it does. We've been waking you on the hour since you arrived. It's standard procedure for concussions. Unfortunately, your blood pressure is still too low and you've been unconscious more than not during your stay here in the ICU, so we're not done yet. How's your pain?" he asked. "On a scale of one to ten."

"Nine hundred," I said, closing my eyes. "What happened to me?"

"I don't know, but it was particularly hard on your left side." I heard him pick up the clipboard again. "You've got ten stitches in the back of your head plus seven or eight in your left ankle, and a whole host of contusions and abrasions including some nasty-looking road rash on your face, but I don't think it'll scar." He flipped up a sheet of paper. "There's no evidence of sexual assault but you sustained an injury to your kidneys. The blood has already cleared from your urine, so we'll remove the catheter in the next few hours."

I heard him set the clipboard down on the table again, and I opened my eyes when he took my hand. "I can give you something for the pain, but I'm afraid it won't help much," he said. "It's important that we're able to rouse you at regular intervals for the next six hours or so. Do you think you can hang in there?"

"Do I have a choice?"

He gave me a crooked smile. "I'll order your meds and check on you in a few hours."

The nurse returned with a needle and stuck it into the IV line. "I'll wake you in an hour," she said.

I don't remember falling asleep. A thick fog rolled in around me. I dreamt again but not of the family at the airport or the terrifying fall through the tree canopy.

... I saw a little girl wearing green gumboots and a puffy purple jacket over pink fleecy pyjamas. She tottered around the edge of a large, wet lawn, looking for something. Her face lit up when she spied a brightly coloured egg in the bird bath. She gathered it up then ran squealing toward a couple. The man stood behind the woman with his arms wrapped around her. They sported adoring grins as they stood guard over a basket already laden with similar prizes, nestled in the bottom. I realized it was me in that puffy jacket. I wouldn't have been more than three or four years old.

The scene disappeared in a heartbeat when the nurse woke me. I'd been sleeping for an hour. It felt like seconds. When she left, the fog returned.

... I was nine or ten years old and beachcombing with my father. He had that tool in his hand, the one he used to break open fist-sized geodes searching for the crystals hidden inside. I heard him call me and when

I got close, he turned over a flat piece of shale rock and laughed as I squealed and ran away from the tiny crabs that scrambled to find fresh cover.

My heart quickened as the nurse woke me and the memory faded. She assured me it had been an hour. The thick fog came back, pulling me under.

... A blonde-haired woman in a wide-brimmed hat whispered my name. She held her hands palm out, inviting me to a game of patty cake, and I lifted my hands to mirror hers. She spoke in a quiet voice, repeating a haunting refrain. She kept watch over her shoulders, and when the dark shadows approached, she vanished.

The nurse woke me again. I had dipped in and out of fog so often I felt disoriented. "What time is it?" I asked.

"Just after six in the morning," she said, pumping up the blood pressure cuff. "Wednesday." She paused to listen to her stethoscope. "You're in the ICU, and I'm happy to report that your blood pressure is improving." The Velcro made a ripping noise as she removed the cuff.

"Good morning, Emelynn," Dr. Coulter said as he crossed behind the nurse to retrieve the clipboard. "Your vitals are looking better. How's your pain level?"

"It hasn't improved with time," I said, forcing a smile.

"Have you remembered any more details about your accident?" he asked with a hopeful expression on his face.

"No," I lied. The lie came easily; I was good at lying. I'd been hiding my secrets for so long that I didn't even flinch as the lie rolled off my tongue.

Dr. Coulter raised his chin and glared down his nose. "Well, keep trying. You're out of the danger zone, so I'll give you something more for the pain now. Maybe you'll remember more after you've rested." He frowned in disappointment as he left my room.

He didn't believe me but he didn't press me either, which was a good thing: I could fill the room with what I was withholding. Because unfortunately, I now remembered all of it ... every last detail.

The nurse administered a shot of something into my IV line and within minutes I floated on a cloud of bliss as the pain melted away and darkness welcomed me back—with a vengeance.

CHAPTER TWO

I found myself back on the memory roller coaster, and this trip through the past was in high definition.

...I was back on the beach in my favourite patch of sand. Nanny Fran waved from inside the patio door. The familiar musical opening of *The Young and the Restless* wafted down. She didn't worry about my safety; Dad had waterproofed me from an early age.

Building sandcastles was one of my favourite pastimes and I'd progressed considerably since my plastic-sand-pail days. I decorated the towers with treasures I found in flotsam the tide brought in. Bits of brightly coloured glass or delicate sheets of frilly seaweed made each day's masterpiece unique. But regardless of how many turrets and great halls there were, I always dug a moat to protect the castle walls. Of course, it went without saying that there would be at least one princess in residence and depending on the day, either a prince or a dragon who would swoop in to play the hero.

I saw a woman picking her away along the shore. She wore a long, flowing sundress with a huge hat that shaded her face and shoulders. She kept her head down, but as she got closer, I noticed her watching me when she thought I wasn't looking.

She stopped a few feet away from me. "Hi," she said, tilting her head to the side and twirling a large feather between her thumb and forefinger. "Here," she said, offering the plume. "It'll make a nice banner." She gestured to the high turret on which I had just put the finishing touches. I squinted up at her and accepted her feather, poking it into the sandy tower.

She adjusted the brim of her hat so I could see her eyes. "My name's Jolene. What's yours?" she asked with a hint of a smile on her face. Her voice was soft, like the pale blue of her eyes.

"It's Emelynn, Emelynn Taylor, but most people call me Em."

"Your castle-building skills are impressive for such a young girl, Emelynn. How old are you? Ten? Eleven?"

"No," I said, with the indignation of a preteen. "I'm twelve."

"Oh, my apologies," she offered with a guarded chuckle. "Do you live here?" She nodded toward the stairs that led to the cottage.

She spoke in such a quiet voice that I felt obliged to answer in a whisper, fearful anything louder would blow her away. "Yeah," I said. "Where do you live?"

"I'm not from here." Her thin smile vanished and she hunched her shoulders, scanning the horizon.

Blonde hair peeked out from under her hat. My own hair was brown, like my mother's, but my father liked to tease me and say it was red, especially in the sun.

Jolene tensed up and stepped away. "I'll visit again," she said, leaving in a rush.

She did visit again—always careful in her approach and never staying long enough to sit down. Sometimes she'd bring bits of beach treasure for my castles. One time she asked about my mother, another time about my father. She offered weak smiles in response, as if a big one might exhaust her. And she kept looking over her shoulder, like she was expecting someone.

On the last day I ever saw her, she finally sat down beside me on my small patch of sand. She wrapped her arms around her knees and pulled them close to her chest.

Looking off to the horizon she said, "I have to leave soon."

She was tense again, guarded. "Are you going home?" I asked.

"I'd like to give you something before I go," she said, not answering my question.

"Oh?"

"A *gift*," she said, drawing her eyebrows together. "A very special *gift*, Emelynn." But she didn't look very happy about it.

"For me?"

"Yes, for you, but first I need you to promise me something."

"What?"

"Promise that you'll keep the gift a secret."

"Why?" I asked, confused.

"People won't understand," she said. "Can you promise me?"

I should have been more suspicious. As soon as I agreed, Jolene released a heavy sigh that relaxed her shoulders. The worry lines in her forehead faded and she smiled. Not the weak smiles I had seen, but a genuine, from-the-heart kind of smile, like Nanny Fran's.

She inhaled deeply and closed her eyes for a long moment. When she reopened them, the sadness I had sensed in her eyes before was gone, replaced by a strange radiance.

She extended her hands to mine so that each of our fingertips touched—including our thumbs—quite a feat given the length of her graceful fingers compared to mine. When she was satisfied that our hands were in the right position, she caught my gaze. I found I couldn't look away from her. A tear escaped her eye as she spoke to me and the wind picked up. Her voice sounded like a prayer, but I didn't understand the meaning behind the lofty words. It didn't appear that she expected a reply, so I just returned her gaze and listened.

When I awoke on that small patch of soft sand, Jolene had disappeared and I thought perhaps her visit had been a dream. She hadn't left a secret gift after all and I was getting cold. I knew Nanny Fran would frown on my disappointment about a gift that hadn't materialized, so I never mentioned it to her.

But a few days after Jolene left, I learned her visit was no dream. I knew because that night, when the sun set, darkness didn't follow. I remember that night well, waiting for the dark that never came.

It should have been black as a witch's hat outside. Yet I could see as clear as if it were midday. The nightlight had a different quality; it had a blue cast rather than the golden quality of daylight.

This wasn't a minor adjustment—it was profound. The night came alive. There were no shadows for fear to lurk in; no dark corners for monsters to hide in; and no night for scary things to go bump in. Now I knew why Jolene had warned me that people wouldn't understand. *I* didn't understand. A whole new world opened up to me and it was absolutely unbelievable.

I didn't tell a soul.

Given the brevity of our encounter, I would never have imagined that her acquaintance would figure so largely in my life.

Jolene's face was a gossamer spectre in my mind, and I watched it fade to nothing. She's not really here, I thought. That was a long time ago. The drug-induced fog was weak enough for me to be aware that this was just a memory, but I didn't want to remember any more. Jolene embodied the beginning of the end of "Normal." I knew what came next. I fought against the fog, struggling to break its grip.

Gradually the darkness abated. I opened my eyes, taking in the glass partition and the bank of machines that beeped beside me. The drug they'd given me was waning. I drifted lightly in and out of sleep, but there were no more dreams.

Eventually, the drug lost its hold on me completely and my head began to keep time to my heart again. The nurse removed my catheter. When she returned, it was midafternoon and I was fully awake. She helped me use the bathroom then settled me back in bed.

Shortly after that, I was moved out of the ICU. The new room was much quieter even with the erratic snores that escaped from two of the four beds.

Despite a few nagging gaps, most of what happened the night of my accident came back to me. Luckily, I'd remembered enough of the conversations I'd overheard while semi-conscious to patch together a believable story because the truth was not an option.

I was ready for Dr. Coulter's questions when he found me. He wore fashionable reading glasses that he removed when he finished looking at my chart. I guessed his age at around fifty. His blond hair, greying at the temples, was cut short and lay flat to his head like straight hair does.

"How did you sleep?" he asked, sliding his glasses into the breast pocket of his white coat. His penlight made an unwelcome appearance.

"It didn't feel much like sleep—more like a whirlwind trip through the Land of Oz," I said.

"Yes, I'm afraid morphine has a tendency to do that. How's the pain today?" he asked, as he examined my eyes.

"Better." I appreciated that my head hurt less. Either that or I was getting used to a whole new level of pain.

"I'm glad." He studied my face while he contemplated his next question. "Have you figured out what happened in Sunset Park on Monday night?"

"Not all of it," I offered. His question felt like a challenge. "I went for a run. The park is beside my house."

"Awfully late for a run, wasn't it?" he countered.

"I needed to clear my head," I said, tossing it back to him.

"You weren't wearing shoes when they found you."

Was he taunting me? Why was he pressing this? What did it matter to him? "Yeah, that's weird. Like I said, I don't remember all of it."

"You didn't see who or what hit you." It wasn't a question.

"No, I didn't."

He stared down at his hands, leaving dead air between us. "That's feasible," he finally said.

Feasible? What a curious choice of word.

He abruptly changed the subject. "Is there someone at home who can watch over you for the next twenty-four to forty-eight hours?"

"No, I live alone."

"Do you have a friend or relative who could stay with you?"

"No, I just moved here. I don't know anyone. But don't worry about me—I'm used to looking after myself."

"I've no doubt, but that might be difficult to do if you lose consciousness again. Normally, I'd release you into your family's care at this point, but given your circumstances, I'll keep you overnight." He picked up my chart and made some notes. "There are two police officers outside who would like to speak with you. I'll send them in."

I was ready for the police; it was Dr. Coulter who confused me. He acted as though he knew more about me than he should. I couldn't figure out if that really was the case, or if the hit to my head had messed with my instincts.

Constable Tao Wong took copious notes, while Constable Chris Mendel asked the questions. She informed me that a police photographer had documented my injuries in Emerg after I'd been stabilized. The photos were necessary, she assured me, in the event the person responsible for my injuries was ever caught. They assigned me a case number and I signed some papers before they went to check on my house to make sure it was secure.

It was early evening when they left. Dread wafted over me as I looked at the clock and thought of the empty evening hours ahead of me—entirely too many in which to contemplate the position I'd put myself. No one was going to find a person or vehicle responsible for my injuries: this mess was entirely self-inflicted.

My "Grand Plan," the one I'd moved halfway across the country to implement, had failed miserably. It was a devastating blow. The quiet cottage with its isolated beach was the perfect setting. All I had to do was figure out how to control Jolene's gift, which had taken on a life of its own; a life that threatened to expose my secret; a life that forced me to hide, shun friends and endure the constant threat of bodily harm.

I had thought the plan would work. It was my best effort and I'd been so certain of its success that I'd not considered the possibility of any other outcome. Normally, I prided myself on my "glass half full" attitude, but looking down the length of my battered body in the hospital bed was a sobering reminder that I'd failed. Jolene's gift was still in control, crushing my hopes for a normal life, for friends and for freedom from the fear that ruled my life.

I fell asleep with tears on my face, wallowing in self-pity. It wasn't a good sleep. Did anyone ever sleep well in a hospital? Staff came and went at all hours, and unfamiliar noises roused me regularly.

Morning arrived with another new nurse, who removed my IV and changed my dressings. It was the first opportunity I'd had to get a look at the extent of the damage. It wasn't pretty unless purple and blue were two of your favourite colours.

"I'm afraid your clothes were cut off in Emerg," she said, "but I found some scrubs for you." She handed me the thin green garments, neatly folded. On top sat a pair of pink flip-flops. "Those, I pulled from the lost-and-found," she said with a conspiratorial wink.

She helped me dress and the process drained me. I lay back down and waited for Dr. Coulter, who arrived in his white coat just before noon.

"The police officers who spoke to you yesterday are waiting down the hall," he said, moving to the side of the bed. "They kindly offered to take you home. Let's do a final check," he said, pulling out that damned penlight again.

He waved it in front of my eyes then checked my blood pressure. "The nurse changed your dressings?"

"Yes."

"All right then. You're ready to go." He handed me a prescription. "It's for Tylenol 3. You can fill it at the pharmacy downstairs. It'll get you through the worst of the pain, but don't overdo it."

"Thank you."

"Come back to Emergency right away if you develop blurred vision or difficulty with motor coordination." He fished out a business card and handed it to me. "Phone my office to make an appointment in ten days to have those stitches removed."

He stood, heading to the door, but turned before leaving. "Be careful, Emelynn—you could have been killed in that accident, or worse." He gestured to the card in my hand. "Call me if you have any more problems with ... jogging ... or whatever it was you were doing." Then he was gone.

What an odd parting remark.

The constables were mindful of my injuries as they helped me into the back seat of their patrol car. Patients holding IV poles and smoking cigarettes stared. I felt like a criminal and wanted to tell them I was just getting a lift home. Instead, I slouched down and looked away.

The fresh air was a shock after being indoors for so long. Even if I hadn't seen the white-capped mountains crouching in the distance, I would have known I was on the west coast from the heady scent of blossoms and fresh-mown grass that permeated the air.

A week ago, I had taken a taxi along a similar route from Vancouver International Airport to Summerset, a small suburb about thirty minutes south of Vancouver. I had been struck, as I was now, by the expanse of greenery flowing past the car windows. It was a stark contrast to the concrete grey of Toronto, where I had lived for the past ten years. This city dripped green: thick lawns, overflowing flower gardens and fat hedgerows. Cherry and magnolia trees bloomed everywhere and those were just the blossoms that I recognized from the back seat of the car. It was beautiful—I had forgotten how very many shades of green there were.

Constable Wong's voice startled me. "We have no leads in your case yet, no witnesses, and no reports of other similar attacks."

"Oh," I said. "That's good—that there have been no more reports." I knew full well that there wouldn't be any other reports.

We turned onto Cliffside Avenue and headed to the last driveway on the right. My house sat at the southernmost end of the cul-de-sac, which ended where Sunset Provincial Park started. An old willow tree grew in the corner where the park boundary met the cul-de-sac marking the end of the street. The park's trees delineated the southern edge of the property. A berm of native shrubs provided privacy from the road.

Anyone looking at my house would see a modest but handsome Arts and Crafts-style bungalow, set back into the far edge of about two acres of land amid a scattered handful of mature trees. A gravel driveway ran straight through the property from the street effectively dividing the lawn; one-third on the garage side, two-thirds on the house side. At the house, the driveway widened into a large loop that afforded cars an easy drive around and back out to the road.

What the casual observer might not notice is that this ordinary bungalow hid a spectacular setting. It wasn't immediately evident unless you knew the neighbourhood. Tall fir and cedar trees filled out the back edge of the lot, behind the house, all along a ridge. If you listened carefully, you could hear the rhythmic wash of waves. If you missed the sound of waves, you might catch a whiff of briny air or pungent seaweed in the ocean breeze.

"The back patio door was unlocked last night, but the keys were where you said they'd be, so we secured it." They followed the driveway around the top of the loop, pulling up close to the front porch.

The driver turned the car off. "Please stay here, Ms. Taylor. We'll make another circuit of the house and perimeter," she said as both constables got out of the car. They used my key to go into the house.

The circuit wouldn't take long. The small bungalow followed a basic centre hall design with rooms running symmetrically off either side. The small bedroom on the right was the one that I'd used as a child. The home's only bathroom separated my former bedroom from the larger one I now claimed, which had an ocean view.

The left side of the house followed a similar layout. The first room on the left could have been a small third bedroom but my father had turned it into his study. The galley kitchen abutted his study and a counter ran the width of the kitchen, separating it from the dining room. We used the counter as a breakfast bar, and three stools still stood underneath it on the dining-room side. Our dining-room table sat on the other side of the breakfast bar, and beyond that was the living room, delineated by the back of my mother's pale blue sofa. It faced a small coffee table and two comfortable chairs in a matching gingham pattern. The chair in the corner had a coordinating ottoman. The living room was a little bigger than my bedroom, and both rooms had sliding glass doors that opened onto a deck, which extended the width of the house.

The constables returned a short time later. "Someone's been in the house, but it looks like they had a key," Constable Wong said. "They left you a note." He handed me a piece of paper.

Sorry we missed you—must have had our wires crossed. We'll teach you the ropes next visit.

C&G

"Do you know what that's about?"

"Yes. Charles and Gabby Wright. They've looked after the place for years. They were going to teach me how to use the mower. Guess I missed them."

Satisfied with the explanation, they helped me out of the car and up to the porch. The cottage's unfinished cedar siding had weathered to a chalky grey patina. It contrasted nicely with the freshly painted navy door and white trim. The smell of paint still hung in the air and if you looked, you could see tiny white drips dotted along the grass beneath the siding.

"Don't hesitate to call the station if you remember any more details. The phone number is right here." Constable Wong pointed it out on the form he handed me. "They'll ask for your case number, which is on the top, right-hand side."

"Thanks again," I said. "I'll call if I remember anything." I gave them a polite smile and watched their car complete the loop then drive away.

I was left alone on the porch: a bittersweet homecoming this time around.

There was something very special about this house. My father had bought it many years ago when there were only a few neighbours. At that time, the homes along Cliffside were just cottages because no one was interested in living this far out of the city. He had not yet met my mother, so the small house suited him well. He often spoke of the lovely elderly couple who had sold him their cottage when it got to be too much for them to keep up.

The neighbourhood had changed considerably since then. Sunset Provincial Park bounded both the southern and most of the eastern edge of the property, and those forested areas remained undeveloped. However, every single lot north of ours now boasted a home large enough to make ours look like a coach house.

I stepped through the door and locked it behind me before heading to the kitchen. I dropped Charles and Gabby's note on the hall table beside the vase of flowers that still had a day or two of life left in them. They'd left the flowers and a plate of cookies a week ago to welcome me home. Sadly, the cookies were just a delicious memory.

The couple had been hired to maintain the cottage and grounds during our family's long absence, and they'd kept us filled in on the changing neighbourhood over the years.

I chuckled, thinking back to how upset I'd been when I first learned that these strangers would be in our house. At the time, I felt I'd been unfairly yanked away from the only home I'd ever known and dumped in Toronto, so I resented them. Of course, I didn't understand that they weren't actually living in the cottage.

Now, I realized how lucky we were to have found them. Not only had they kept the yard neat and tidy, but they also seemed to have stopped time from touching the house. It was in perfect condition, gleaming both inside and out. They'd even stocked the fridge with a few basics, for which they refused to let me reimburse them. That thoughtfulness endeared them to me and made my homecoming complete.

But today, the only thing that was going to improve my homecoming was another painkiller. I put the kettle on and removed the cap from the Tylenol 3. It wasn't exactly a gingersnap, but it was going to go down just as nicely with a cup of orange pekoe.

My body ached as if I'd gone a few rounds in a UFC cage and lost—badly. But the physical pain wasn't the worst of it. It was the weight of my failure that hurt the most. I'd had such high hopes for the Grand Plan and now both my hopes and the plan were a smoking ruin. How had that happened so quickly?

It was exactly one week ago today that I arrived here on the coast. In those seven short days, I'd attempted everything I could think of to bring Jolene's gift under control. Now I was fresh out of ideas and low on optimism. Jolene's gift had always been dangerous, but my ill-conceived plan had turned a dangerous situation into a deadly one in the pause between heartbeats.

Not for the first time, I wished I'd never met Jolene. She didn't know me or my family, so why me? Did she know what she had done to me? To my life?

I turned on some music and shuffled back to the kitchen to tip the water from the whistling kettle over the tea bag at the bottom of a gigantic mug. I settled into a deck chair with my feet stretched out stiffly in front of me. This was where I belonged, where I felt safe, my sanctuary—the one place in the world where I didn't have to worry about floating away. I warmed my hands on the mug of tea and turned my gaze beyond the deck to the beach below: the beach where I'd met Jolene.

In warm weather, my father and I would wander together along this beach. He never tired of showing me the wonders of living by the sea. I thought he was the smartest man alive. He knew all about the sea birds and mammals that shared our shore. We visited the small tidal pools and wondered at the beauty of the colourful sea creatures trapped within.

This wasn't a warm, sandy beach with endless white sand and turquoise water—the kind you see in advertisements for Caribbean getaways. This beach was unkind. The waters were cool at best, and sand was limited to patches of mottled brown and grey deposits that filled in the gaps between shale rock or sandstone flagstones. Football-sized rocks were plentiful and strewn about the shore in a haphazard fashion making hiking this stretch of beach an ankle-twisting prospect.

But this was my beach, the beach of my youth. It was an extension of the house by the simple fact that it was connected to it by a staircase that dropped off the north end of the deck upon which I now sat contemplating my tea.

Though I hadn't set foot in the cottage for more than ten years, it wrapped its arms around me like a warm blanket. It reinforced for me what a good idea it had been to return. I felt more at home here than I had in years of living in Toronto. Tonight I needed the warmth and consolation of it.

My parents had been happy in this cottage, and I spent the first twelve years of my life in it. My dad was in his last year of a pediatric residency when he met my mother. The flame of their love was a slow but intense burn. My mother was a behavioural research Ph.D. They knew each other for two years before they went on a formal date, but from that day forward, they were never apart. Laura moved into the cottage and married Brian when she became pregnant with me. They were madly, unfashionably in love.

After I came along, they found Nanny Fran. She was my parents' solution to the school's inconvenient habit of sending me home in the evenings, for the weekends and for the ever-increasing number of Pro-D days—not to mention the entire months of July and August.

Lucky for me, I loved Nanny Fran. Every time I catch the scent of wintergreen, I'm reminded of the green mints she carried in her apron pockets. She made the best grilled-cheese sandwiches and acted out the characters in my favourite bedtime stories no matter how many times I requested the same ones and no matter that I was far too old for the charade.

But good things never last. It all started to unravel after Jolene's visit. Normally I put Herculean effort into not remembering those last few months we spent in Summerset. But I was vulnerable tonight and didn't have the strength to keep the dreadful memories at bay.

That fateful summer of Jolene's visit morphed into fall. It was a sunny day in late October when we piled into the car to drive Dad to the airport. He'd been looking forward to the trip for weeks. It was just a short getaway, he'd said—a few days to recharge his batteries. My father was going on what he called the "ultimate" fishing experience, the pinnacle of relaxation, at a remote fishing camp in the Queen Charlottes.

My mother and I watched the small float plane taxi out onto the Fraser River then lift off and disappear. He would be gone four days.

He never came home.

The small plane and all five people on board were lost at sea, and to this day neither the plane nor the bodies have been found.

Within days of his funeral, it became painfully obvious that his absence was going to be too much for my mother. She reached out to her colleagues and found herself short tracked for a position in Toronto.

I didn't want to leave our cottage. Dad was going to find his way home, I just knew it, and I was furious at my mother for abandoning him. I remember struggling against her as she tugged me through the Vancouver airport with Nanny Fran in tow. The tears rolled down my face as the luggage disappeared on a conveyor belt while I clung to Nanny Fran. It was a horrible goodbye.

We left Summerset that day and moved to a condo in Toronto; all the familiar people and places of my life were torn away. That's when my mother became Laura to me.

Laura threw herself into her new role at the University of Toronto's behavioural sciences research lab. She found safe harbour amid the sterile labs. I lost her there. My father had left us, and though he hadn't intended to, he'd taken my mother with him.

CHAPTER THREE

I t pained me to remember those days. I sipped my tea, vaguely aware that the wind had calmed down now that the sun was setting. Dampness crept in with the cooler night air, and the memories tumbled out, unimpeded.

My early days in Toronto were a blur. One day blended into the next without any discernible events to distinguish the days. I buried my head in the proverbial sand and drifted along in a numb state of grief and depression. Laura did some burying of her own—in her job, and Nanny Fran was thousands of miles away. I hated that we had traded the beautiful green of the coast for a dirty-grey sea of concrete. I didn't belong in Toronto.

The grieving was complicated by my youth; there was so much I didn't understand. By nature I was shy, and the grief made me withdrawn. I dreaded the prospect of making new friends, in a new school, halfway through the term, in a new city.

My first day at Jesse Ketchum Public School proved just how painful that experience would be. Mrs. Norris had prepped the class for my arrival. I knew it the instant I crossed the threshold: no one looked me in the eye. Instead, feet shuffled and books were rearranged. When I settled into my seat midway down the aisle two over from the window, Peggy Gilcrest confirmed my worst suspicion. She leaned over and assured me that I was going to be okay because her grandfather had died last year and she was okay. I wanted to crawl into a hole and die.

My father's death was still a raw, gaping wound, and the only way I got through each day without breaking down into a sobbing mess was by keeping sympathy-laden intruders at bay. After all, they hadn't known my father and didn't know me, so why would they be sorry? Feigning distraction or pretending I couldn't hear their kind remarks became second nature.

My new classmates seemed confused by my indifference, but that soon changed. Their confusion turned into derision, and later, avoidance. But I didn't care; numb felt better than heartache. After a while, I actually liked that they ignored me. It gave me the solitude I craved, which, in hindsight, was probably not a good thing.

Of course, I thought my coping mechanism was working quite nicely. It gave me all the alone time I needed. I might have continued like that for years if it hadn't been for the fact that I started sleepwalking. At first, it was just once every three or four weeks, so nothing too alarming. Then it started happening more frequently. My mother stepped in when she discovered me sleeping on the kitchen counter one morning, with my head propped against the flour canister and my legs sprawled out over the stovetop. That was the catalyst that set off a round of visits to doctors and eventually, a shrink.

It was the shrink who explained the grieving process to me. I guess it was helpful to know there were proper steps involved, and that most people went through these same steps in their own time, though I don't remember going through denial or bargaining. The final step was supposed to be acceptance, the Holy Grail of grieving. I, however, seemed to be stuck vacillating between anger and depression.

My frame of mind didn't bode well for my education or making new friends. The school held me back a year to make up for the months lost to mourning, and then I watched the few faces I recognized move on to high school without me.

Being known as the girl who'd been "held back a year" pretty much sealed my fate at the school—I was the least-popular student. Needless to say, I wasn't invited to join the "in-crowd," and even the "out-crowd" wasn't showing much interest. It was just easier to avoid them all.

When I finally made it to high school, my grief had lost its sharp edge. Thoughts of my father and our life as it used to be at the cottage waned. I was able to appreciate the stunning fall colours. It was one of the few times Toronto trumped the coast. The brilliant reds, vivid oranges and neon yellows of the maples and oaks turned treed streets into kaleidoscopes of colour. But it didn't quite make up for my absent mother.

High school offered up a fresh batch of schoolmates who drifted by, leaving no impression at all. I just couldn't find traction with the Goths or the geeks or the preppy set. I'd kept everyone at bay for so long, I couldn't figure out how to connect.

I knew all the alone time wasn't healthy, but I considered it better than the alternative. After all, the most important people in my life had left me, one way or another. I wasn't up for repeating the experience with new friends.

My self-imposed isolation eventually drew the attention of the school counsellor, Mr. Picatta. After repeated "helpful" suggestions, I joined the photography club, mostly to get him off my back. The club turned out to be a good fit, and I met a friend. Julie Mathias seemed to struggle with her social skills as much as I did. I knew that only because I'd heard the other girls talking about her in the cafeteria. It wasn't very nice.

Julie and I hit it off in a low-key kind of way by working together on photo-club projects. We were both quiet and shy; both average students; both sitting on the outside looking in. Julie was aware of how she was viewed by the other girls and it grated on her. She'd grown up with them, so it was a particularly cruel rejection. I had nothing invested, so their avoidance of me didn't bother me as much.

We didn't talk about the hard stuff, although I knew her mother was an alcoholic and she knew my father had died in a plane crash. Toward the end of the school year, Mr. Gregory set up a night shoot for the photography club. Naturally, Julie and I paired up to do it together.

That was the night I decided to tell Julie about my night vision. It was the first time I'd told anyone about Jolene's gift. She didn't believe me, of course. Who would? Despite what I thought was clear, undeniable proof, she couldn't confirm what I could see in the dark. After that, she didn't want anything more to do with me.

She made that point perfectly clear when she told the other girls, the very ones who had spurned her, about what she called my "make-believe world." I quickly became fodder for the nasty girls' gossip mill and tumbled a few more rungs down the popularity ladder. That was the last time I tried to tell anyone.

After my first year of high school, the sleepwalking abated, which eased my mother's mind. I learned to be vigilant with the lights in the condo, turning them on when darkness fell. Of course, it was never dark for me, but people were quick to question your sanity if they found you wandering around in the shadows.

A gust of wind brought my thoughts back to the present. The memories had drained me. I rose stiffly from the deck chair with my cold tea. The Tylenol 3s had finally kicked in. Even though it was early, I climbed into bed. For the first time since I'd moved back to the cottage, I experienced the loneliness and isolation that I'd hoped I'd left in Toronto. It was a familiar but unwelcome feeling. I fell asleep with a heavy heart.

I did, however, sleep deeply. The second call to my cellphone came in just after 9:00 a.m. I'd let them both go to voice mail. Unfortunately, after the second call, I was wide awake. Physically, I felt better than I had at this time yesterday, but the improvement was relative.

I dragged my stiff, achy body out of bed and limped into the kitchen. I tossed some grounds in the ancient coffee maker. The crotchety old machine had been a pleasant find, my first morning in the cottage. I remember how relieved I'd been to hear the first drops of water gurgle into the filter. For me, coffee in the morning was an absolute necessity, but my bevy of choice in the afternoons was good old orange pekoe.

While the coffee brewed, I checked my messages. The first was from Charles. They were going to be in my neighbourhood today and would stop by to organize another lawn mower lesson. I would have to think up a good story to explain my injuries because if they heard the official police version, they would surely tell my mother, and I didn't want her worrying long distance.

The second message was from Dr. Coulter—not his office, but Dr. Coulter directly, which surprised me. Maybe here on the west coast, doctors personally checked up on their ER patients. When I called him back, I was dumped into voice mail. I left him a message assuring him of my good health, and then went in search of comfortable clothing. I dug around until I found my old sweatpants and an oversized sweatshirt, and then I gingerly pulled a thick pair of rubber-soled sock-style slippers over the stitches on my left ankle.

My stomach rumbled, reminding me that I hadn't eaten dinner last night. I poured a bowl of Corn Flakes and tottered to the sofa. I managed to sit without spilling anything, but it might not have registered even if I had. My surroundings, the cereal, even the coffee existed in a fuzzy melancholic shroud today. I blamed my depression on all the memories I'd dug up yesterday.

Perhaps a visit to the beach would perk me up. Drinking my morning coffee on the beach was a routine I endeavoured to entrench by repeating each morning the weather allowed. I swallowed a painkiller and poured a heater into my coffee. A basket holding a few rolled towels sat on the floor by the patio door. I grabbed one and put two soft weights into my sweatpants pockets. Holding my pants up with one hand and my coffee in the other, I headed to the stairs at the north end of the deck. It was a slow, careful descent to the beach, where I claimed a soft spot in front of the closest beached log. The pungent smell of seaweed filled the air. I rarely saw other people down here and this morning was no exception. Not a surprise, considering the nearest public access was a two-kilometre hike north.

I pulled my knees up and rested my back against the driftwood, letting the peace sink in. This was heaven on earth and just being here in this place did more for me than the Tylenol. A thick cloud bank hung low on the horizon making the air feel cooler than it was.

Seagulls flew overhead calling noisily to each other, and smaller shorebirds flitted in and out of the scrub brush close to shore. Sea fleas jumped around my ankles, but soon my presence was ignored and the tiny bugs and dime-sized crabs came out of hiding to resume their quest for food.

This was where I used to build my sandcastles. This beach, the cottage—these were the elements of my past that I loved the most. This is where Normal was for me, or at least where it used to be. Nothing had been normal since Jolene's visit or since we moved away. Coming back here had been part of the Grand Plan: my plan to find my way back to Normal, back to happy.

The remoteness of this stretch of beach ensured a certain amount of privacy, a critical element of the plan. However, the rocky composition of the beach directly in front of the cottage didn't suit my purpose. The beach that did meet my requirements surrounded a well-protected cove about a kilometre farther south of here. It was comprised mostly of sand with a few large rocks, but none of the football-sized tripping hazards that stippled the beach in front of the cottage.

Although I was in no hurry to visit that beach again any time soon, it occurred to me that I had a perfectly good pair of Rocket Dogs, a few soft weights and about fifty feet of rope that I should try to recover. Oh, and my favourite hoodie. The ocean would likely have claimed the shoes, but if the tides hadn't been too high, the hoodie might have survived. At least the rope would still be there. It was tied around a rock and the soft weights wouldn't have washed away.

I thought about waiting until tomorrow, but with each new tide, the hope of finding my belongings ebbed. Besides, maybe the walk would loosen my muscles and speed the Tylenol delivery. I got up and headed south, picking my way carefully among the rocks. Just shy of my destination, I realized that it was too far a hike for this stage of my recovery, but I'd come too far to turn back.

On the hottest summer days, my father would take me on this very walk. He would hold my hand and help me along until we got to the sandy cove, then he would hike me up onto his shoulders and take off at a gallop with me giggling and holding on to his head for dear life. He would make like an airplane, reaching up to take my hands in his and stretching them out for wings. The sense of being out of control would make me squeal and laugh even louder.

"You're Amelia Earhart, daredevil flying ace," he'd say, swooping left then right. The roller-coaster ride might have frightened me but I knew Dad would never let me fall. Remembering it now split my face into a wide smile.

I didn't meet anyone along the way, though I did see footprints in the sand above the high-tide mark near the big rock, where I should have found my rope. Yet it and my weights were gone, and so were my sneakers and hoodie. In fact, there was no evidence that I had ever been here. I guess I'd left it too long and the tide had pulled it all out to sea.

I rested against the boulder, searching for the sun that hid behind the clouds. My body appreciated the lull. The ocean sounded different here, the waves softer against the sand than against the rocks in front of the cottage. I thought about my father as I looked across the sand. What would he think if he knew what I used this beach for these days? Would it frighten him as much as it did me?

With a heavy sigh, I pushed off from the rock and started for home. The physical aches and pains would fade, I reminded myself as I picked my way over the rocks. Then I'd be able to look at things more objectively. I rested again on a beached log before I headed up the stairs to the cottage. Lunch was another Tylenol with a bowl of Campbell's cream of mushroom soup.

I was lying on the sofa reading Ken Follett's *Pillars of the Earth* when the doorbell softly chimed—too softly. I'd have missed it if I'd had the music on. It was probably Charles and Gabby. I rehearsed my story as I walked to the door, pulling my hair around my face to hide as much of the road rash as I could.

They would have ridden their bicycles, their normal mode of transportation. I opened the door and, sure enough, two bikes rested on kickstands just beyond the porch.

Their smiling faces dissolved under a cloud of alarm the moment they caught a glimpse of my face.

"Oh my, Emelynn, what happened?" Gabby asked. Concern spread across her face as she loosened the strap of her helmet. "Are you all right?"

"I'm fine. It looks much worse than it is," I lied, mindful of their connection with my mother.

"We can come back," Charles said, grimacing.

"No, really, I'm okay. Come on in. Can I get you anything?"

Gabby removed her helmet and finger-combed her short dark hair. My guess put her at about forty, which had been a surprise when we first met. For years, I'd pictured her as a plump sixty-year-old, but she had an athletic build, and both she and Charles appeared fit, though he had a bit of a paunch. Charles reminded me of my grade ten biology teacher. He wore binoculars around his neck, kept a magnifying glass in his pocket and constantly took notes on a small notepad. He was a few inches taller than Gabby, and close to her in age, but had more grey in his hair.

They traded glances before accepting my invitation then followed me down the hall. Seeing my painful gait, they ushered me directly to the sofa. Gabby poured them each a glass of water.

"How did this happen?" Charles asked, gesturing from my head to my toes.

"It was a stupid accident. You know me, I'm so clumsy," I said, fully aware that they barely knew me. "I wasn't paying attention the other day on the beach and jammed my foot between the rocks—you know, the ones just out front there? Anyway, I twisted my ankle and fell, mostly on my face," I said. "I should have called you yesterday to cancel our lesson. I'm sorry."

"Don't be, it was one of our regularly scheduled days anyway. We can do the lesson next time—that is, if you're feeling up to it," Gabby said, handing Charles a glass.

"Sure, that would be great."

"Is your mother on her way?" Gabby asked.

"Oh no, it's not that bad. I haven't even told her yet."

"I'm sure she'd want to know anyway."

"It's just a few bumps and bruises and this ugly scrape," I said, gesturing to my face. "I don't want her to worry. Besides, there's nothing she can do that would be better than the Tylenol 3s the doctor prescribed." I hesitated, gauging her reaction. She was only slightly appeased. I added, "But you're right—I'll tell her," and that seemed to satisfy her.

Charles sat back and looked me over, frowning. I must have looked worse than I thought, and it was impossible to hide the pain that pinched my face. I needed to get another painkiller in me. Clearly, I wouldn't be making the martyr short list. I changed the subject. "So, what are you two planning to do in the yard maintenance department this afternoon?"

"Next stop is a dethatching job, and then an eight-foot cedar hedge needs a haircut. But the real prize today is that Mrs. Stuart over on Elm Street has finally agreed to let us photograph her lovely home. It was built in 1891 and is a prime example of Queen Anne architecture."

"I didn't know you were interested in architecture," I remarked.

"Oh, yes," Gabby said. "The history of this neighbourhood is fascinating, and I'm sure you've noticed, it's especially rich in old character homes."

"Why do you think we jumped at the chance to take care of your place?" Charles said. "Yours is one of the original cottages in this area and it's certainly the oldest Arts and Crafts home here. It's got sturdy bones, this one." He looked around with unmistakable admiration.

No wonder the cottage looked so good. They really cared about the place and it showed. I liked them more and more all the time.

"It's nice to see someone living in it again," Gabby said, leaning forward to pat my hand. "But don't let Charles fool you. He's more interested in the birdwatching from here than he is in the architecture, isn't that so, Charles?"

Charles shot Gabby a look of disapproval, which Gabby shooed away with a wave of her hand. He cleared his throat and asked, "So how about you—what's on your agenda today?"

"Definitely not dethatching, whatever that is, or mowing lawns for that matter. I think another Tylenol and maybe a nap," I said.

"That's probably a good plan," Charles said, and he and Gabby rose to leave.

I waved goodbye to them at the front door just as my cellphone rang.

Call display showed it was Dr. Coulter. "Good morning," he started. "May I speak with Emelynn Taylor?"

"This is Emelynn."

"It's Dr. Coulter. How are you?"

"About as good as can be expected," I replied. "My head hurts and I ache all over, but apparently I'm going to make it."

He chuckled at that. "Are the Tylenol 3s helping?"

"Yes, thanks, they are, and they don't bring on the crazies like morphine."

"Have you had any problems with double or blurred vision?"

"No, but I'll go to the ER if I do," I responded, remembering his predischarge instructions.

"Okay, good. Do you still have my contact information?"

"Yes," I said, and then my curiosity got the best of me. "Do you always personally follow up with your patients?"

"Not often. But I do with the ones who don't have family or friends here. I also wanted to remind you to call to make an appointment to have those stitches out."

"Oh, right. I'll get in touch next week," I assured him. "Thanks for calling," I said before we hung up.

I swallowed a painkiller then crawled back into bed. I was generally a fairly upbeat person, but the accident had been a real setback. I'd had setbacks before—endless times. Some days, my life seemed an incessant march of one step forward, two steps back, but none of the other bumps in the road had been quite as life threatening as this one. That's what scared me.

The fear factor had been ramping up steadily ever since Jolene's visit. The night vision was a fender-bender compared to the head-on collision that resulted from the death of my father. Then there was the fateful move to Toronto resulting in one social faux pas after another, but even those disasters weren't the pinnacle. The prize that sent my life over the cliff was a little something extra I discovered about Jolene's gift.

I was in Mrs. Swan's innocuous human health class studying sleep patterns. We had just finished a section on REM sleep when the next topic was introduced—abnormal sleep patterns. This included a number of disorders, but the one that caught my attention was sleepwalking. My senses went on high alert.

I remember glancing nonchalantly around the classroom, hoping that no one had observed my unusual interest in the topic. I felt like I had "sleepwalker" stamped on my forehead, but no one seemed to be looking at me and pointing.

Later that same night, lying on my bed, I couldn't stop thinking about that class. A storm swirled around in my head spewing out images that made me uneasy; sleepwalking, Laura shaking me awake, confusion, the dream. It always started with the dream.

In the dream, I floated inches above my bed with the sheets draped over me. I'd had the same dream dozens of times after I moved to Toronto. But that night, a shiver ran through me, chilling me to the bone. I remember bolting upright, shocked at my sudden realization: it had not been a dream. Of that fact, I'd been absolutely certain. Sleepwalking had not been my problem, it never was. No, my *problem* was much more complicated. I actually did float above my bed. I didn't sleepwalk, I drifted. I drifted until I bumped into something, and then I would float down and settle on whatever surface was below me at the time. That would be the place my mother would discover me the next morning.

The realization shattered my comfortably numb existence, and though I had no idea what this new development was, I had no doubt who was responsible for it: Jolene.

CHAPTER FOUR

In the months that followed, I looked for answers on the Internet, careful of prying eyes and always erasing my search history. If a website even hinted at night vision, levitation or weightlessness, I pursued it down to the last footnote.

I spent countless hours wading through endless lists of Google hits. A few legitimate sites referenced infrared technology or mechanical means to achieve weightlessness, but those sites didn't explain what was happening to me. The vast majority of them touched on demonic possession, shamans, cults, witchcraft, trances, mystical rapture, aliens and space invaders. Not exactly the kind of company I wanted to be in.

My research on Jolene offered only a dead end. I didn't know her full name or where she lived. I knew absolutely nothing about her. For all I knew, she *was* an alien.

When I got frustrated with my progress on the Internet, I researched the old-fashioned way: in person, at the library. Unfortunately, those results proved just as fruitless. A sane person would have considered the lack of any corroborating material and dropped the entire notion.

I thought about telling my mother, but what exactly would I say. "Hey Mom, I think I can float?" I couldn't do it on demand so there was no proof, no tangible evidence of any kind. She was a scientist; she would need something more concrete than mere words if I expected her to believe me, and after what I'd read on the Internet, she'd probably have me committed.

In hindsight, I wish I'd told her about it back in the beginning.

Instead, I'd kept my affliction a secret. It started off nobly enough, but the secret had turned into a guilty burden with a life of its own.

In the absence of answers, I carried on as normally as I could. I remained vigilant about turning the lights on at night, and I filled my life with distractions. Reading helped—it was easy to escape inside the pages of a book, but it wasn't enough. I started a new job at my mother's lab.

Cleaning the lab animals' cages wasn't much of a job, but I needed the money for university. I felt sorry for the critters locked in their miniature jail cells going nowhere on their exercise wheels. It eased my conscience to make their lives a bit better.

But the lab job wasn't enough of a distraction, so I took on a volunteer position at the SPCA. I manned the phones and greeted the walk-in traffic, and whenever I could, I took the shelter dogs on walks.

The distraction routine worked for a while. Then, just when I started thinking I could tuck the memories of floating into a distant corner of my mind, I was rudely yanked back into chaos.

I'd been in bed reading, completely absorbed in a book, when I reached for my bedside water glass. I extended my arm on autopilot and cracked my hand into the headboard. Startled, I looked to see what I'd hit and was momentarily disoriented. The glass should've been right there at my fingertips, but I had to look down to find it. My fingertips hovered two feet above my water glass—*I* hovered two feet above my water glass. I let out a gasp then fell straight down onto my bed. My head knocked the headboard on the way down. My paperback thumped into my chest and my arm smacked the edge of the bedside table, upsetting the water glass. I remember thinking I was going to have a bruise. I lay still for a long time.

When I regained my senses, I swung my feet over the side of the bed and righted the water glass. I tried to make sense of it. My skin tingled all over. I ran my fingers over a small lump developing on the back of my head. Strangely, I'd had no awareness of the floating while it was happening. How long had I been up there?

I lay back down and tried to recreate the float. I squeezed my eyes closed and concentrated on weightless thoughts, floating thoughts. It didn't work. I remained firmly planted on the bed. Gravity didn't even think about leaving me. Was I losing my mind? I didn't think so, but maybe all crazy people felt that way. If it weren't for the lump on my head, I might have been able to chalk it up to an active imagination.

It happened again a few weeks later. I was on my bed again, lost in a book. But unlike the first time, I became aware of the weightlessness before the shock of it set in and sent me tumbling. I was able to breathe and I turned my head from side to side. What a strange feeling it was. I tried to sit up but did more of a forward roll. I dropped my book to the bed and reached my toes to the floor.

A few upward flaps of my arms and I was back on solid ground. As soon as my toes touched the floor, the force of my weight returned. I stood still, completely overwhelmed. That odd tingling sensation wafted over my skin again. I had to remind myself to breathe.

Now what? Were the men in white coats on their way? Should I ask my mother to prepare the XL cage for me? Whatever this thing was, it was evolving at an alarming pace. It had gone from a remembered dream to real episodes in a matter of weeks.

I remember the ominous weight that suffocated me when I realized there was no escape: I couldn't ignore it, I couldn't run away from it, and I certainly couldn't trust anyone who might find out about it. They'd think I was crazy and send me to a rubber room. Hell, maybe I was crazy, but I couldn't imagine anything worse than being locked up. I'd be stuck running on a big wheel, day after day, and never get out.

While I was at university, the frequency of episodes increased steadily. When it occurred within the confines of the condo, it wasn't too bad. I could drift only so far and I rarely gained the full height of the ceilings. If I didn't panic when I became aware of the float, I could manoeuvre myself down without injury. But sometimes, it caught me unawares. On those occasions, inevitably, panic would set in and I'd drop like a stone. Those drops hurt like hell. If I didn't hit something hard on the way down then the floor did the damage. The only saving grace was that my mother was rarely home, so she never got a first-hand glimpse.

Outside the condo, the fear of discovery became nerve-racking. It wasn't a matter of if, but when. The when happened on a cold October day. I was in Starbucks seated at the front window with a mug in my hand, admiring the cherry reds of the maple leaves that overhung the sidewalk. When I realized that I'd lifted off, I instantly sacrificed the mug in favour of grasping the table edge. The coffee burned my leg, but fortunately, no one looked until they heard the mug hit the floor. That odd tingly sensation was back under my skin and, though I didn't under-stand it, I now associated it with the floating episodes.

At least that time I was in a confined space. I was terrified of it happening outdoors, but predictably, it did.

I'd been walking an SPCA dog, a Dalmatian named Dotty. We came around a bend in the path through the park and I wandered over to a bench to rest. A horse chestnut dropped out of the tree above me, landing on the aluminum slat of the bench with a sudden *thwap*. The noise startled me and I lost my hold on gravity. Thankfully, I didn't lose my hold on Dotty's leash. Being deaf, Dotty wasn't startled, but she wasn't blind, and she bolted when she caught sight of my using her leash like an anchor chain.

She didn't get very far. I might have been light as air to pull behind her, but it was only a six-foot leash. I smashed into the first tree she rounded and painfully bounced off it then down to the gravel path before the drag of my weight forced her to stop. My chin and collarbone took the brunt of the impact, and my right arm was wrenched from the pull of the leash, but the most painful injury was the scrape that extended from my elbow to my hip.

Dotty looked confused but wasn't hurt, though I'm sure her neck took a cruel tug when I landed. The only good news was that no one seemed to have witnessed the fiasco.

After the Dotty experience, I grew desperate for some way to keep my hold on gravity, and hence my sanity. I isolated myself and quickly learned about the joy of added weight in my pockets.

My first forays into the world of extra weight started in the canned goods section of a Sobeys grocery store. Soup was good, but not heavy enough—it took too many cans to make me safe. The larger cans were bulky and awkward, but my sanity was worth the sacrifice.

I was carting a knapsack of tomato juice around Toronto's Eaton Centre when I came across workout weights. I fitted myself out with a set of three-pound strap-on ankle weights and two-pound neon-green wrist weights. After the first week, I discovered that wearing the leg weights all day put too much stress on my knees. The resulting pain eventually forced me to give them up.

The wrist weights were better, but painful in an entirely different way. Toward the end of my first year of university, as I crammed for an art history final in the student lounge, the growing quiet around me made me look up. The students seated closest were staring at my shirt sleeves, which had errantly inched up to reveal the neon wrist weights. I quickly tugged my sleeves down, but the damage had been done. That's when I learned that a minor fashion faux pas was as quick a route as any to social banishment.

The embarrassment of that episode sent me back to the Internet to look for alternatives. The search turned up soft divers' weights. They were blessedly black, small and easy to handle. I found a dive shop on Yonge Street, close to the Davisville subway station, that sold them.

I started off carrying so much weight that I was in constant danger of losing my pants. The threat of a public disrobing forced me to find suitable clothing that usually involved large, reinforced pockets. The result was a bad version of grunge that left people wondering about my fashion sense. Winter became my favourite season, and not because of the fluffy white stuff. Giant purses and book bags were my saviours in the warm, humid months of summer.

As time wore on and the floating incidents continued, I changed my mindset from considering this a gift to considering it an embarrassing burden.

I spent my university days hiding, dressing badly and never attending any social functions involving heels or summer clothing. I regularly injured myself in panic-induced drops and despite my best proactive measures, I was often covered in scrapes and bruises.

The episodes persisted, and so did my search for any scrap of information I could find. Levitation, floating, flying, soaring, hovering—I investigated them all. Most of what I found fit into the you-must-be-a-serious-wacko category. Either that or I was a comic book character and just didn't know it.

I became proficient in my quest to hide and control my condition. The methods I used were simple: pack extra weight, turn the lights on at night and avoid people.

Most people relish the memories of their university days, the humorous sorority antics, drinking parties or endless love affairs. My days were spent combating the embarrassing scenarios that my slowly evolving "gift" inflicted upon me. I was happy to see the end of university. I made it out without being discovered and that was a bigger relief than graduating.

Unfortunately, the complications of Jolene's gift made my world feel awfully small. I'd been wandering around the condo in Toronto wondering how on earth I was going to cope with Jolene's legacy in a work situation, when the idea of moving back to the cottage in Summerset occurred to me. The more I thought about it, the more perfect it felt.

My mother's generous graduation gift of six months of paid living expenses tipped the scale. I loved my mother but living with her meant maintaining the charade 24/7. I needed a break from the constant threat of discovery. Something had to change before I lost my mind.

No one knew me at the cottage. It was isolated and only steps away from private outdoor space that I could use to experiment and possibly, hopefully, learn how to control this thing.

The Grand Plan slowly took shape. I didn't know how I would do it, but one thing I knew for sure—it was imperative that I develop a way to cope that wasn't so cumbersome and isolating.

I woke momentarily disoriented, but sharp pain from a post-nap stretch reminded me exactly where I was. My head started drumming out my heartbeat. I glanced at the bedside clock. I'd slept the whole afternoon away. I piled the pillows behind me and sat up, looking out the patio door to the Pacific. I never closed the curtains; the view was too spectacular to cover and no one could see in up here anyway.

It was still light outside but the clouds hadn't cleared. Unfortunately, the effect of the painkiller had. I took another one with a gulp of water. My sock pulled uncomfortably at the stitches. I peeled it back to take a look. The stitches were neon blue with spiky cut ends. I reached around the back of my head. The hair around the stitches there felt stiff. My fingers came away with flakes of dried blood. Mottled patches of black and blue decorated my left side.

My Grand Plan had failed, and miserably. Where would I go from here? Should I try to overhaul the plan, or should I abandon it?

Overhauling the Grand Plan was the harder route and there was no guarantee it would work. Abandoning the plan was easier in terms of effort spent, and it was certainly quicker. All I had to do was tell someone. Of course, that also meant telling my mother. She would be terribly hurt that I'd kept this from her. And once I divulged my secret, I'd lose control over what happened. Hopefully, my mother's hurt and disappointment wouldn't prevent her from advocating for me no matter what institution I ended up in.

While I considered my options, I remembered something else— when I moved here, I'd promised myself I was going to change more than my address. I'd vowed to master this gift and regain my life.

The optimist in me held out hope. I may have nearly killed myself, but I'd also rediscovered the cottage and the beach. I was getting to know Charles and Gabby and I'd already found a doctor. Hell, I'd only been here three weeks. I still had five months left of my mother's funding and money in the bank from my job. Abandoning the plan at this point would be tantamount to giving up. That wasn't me. I'd come too far to walk away after a bump in the road; well, maybe it was a crater, but I decided to not let this setback be the end of my hopes. Positive thoughts were what I needed right now.

When, not if, I gained control of this condition, I would find my way back to Normal, perhaps make a friend or two. Maybe even find a man who would look at me twice. I might be a freak, but I was a grown woman and, freak or not, I didn't want to be a virgin forever. This move was my chance—my fresh start—and it wasn't over yet.

I glanced at the bedside clock again: six thirty. It would be nine thirty in Toronto. I reached for the phone and dialled my mother.

Laura and I were quite different. She was driven by science and research. Her life was orderly, predictable. Mine was the polar opposite. I was driven by uncertainty and secrecy. Fear of discovery was my motivator. My life was as far removed from order and predictability as you could get. The only things we had in common were our green eyes, fair complexions and self-imposed isolation: hers at work, mine at home.

"How are you, sweetheart?" she answered, obviously consulting her call display.

This was her usual opening line and it was my opportunity to slip the injury info in, and then quickly move on with other gossipy tidbits to distract her.

"I could be better."

Which prompted the expected "Oh?" followed by "What happened?"

For years, I'd blamed my bumps and bruises on clumsiness or not paying enough attention to my surroundings. Although it provided a good cover story, I got a little tired of the constant reprimands.

"I fell again," I lied. "Out on the beach this time—on those rocks out front."

"Did you hurt yourself?"

"I twisted my ankle and needed some stitches, but the worst of it was landing on my face."

"Ouch, Emelynn," she said, poised on the edge of the expected and oft-repeated admonishment. "You have to be more careful."

"Yes, I know. But at least I found a nice doctor, and you know how hard they are to come by." It was a bit of an inside joke, coming from the daughter of two doctors.

"Well if you're making jokes, your injuries can't be too bad."

"I'm fine, really. Hey, guess who I saw today?" I then launched into my diversionary update on Charles and Gabby.

"I miss you," she said before we hung up.

She did, I knew that, but she was pragmatic and knew that when I graduated I would be making my own way in the world. She worked such long hours that we hardly ever saw one another when we lived together. I suppose it was just the fact that she knew I had moved that caused her to miss me.

Once she was on board with the idea of my moving, she made it easy; we worked out the details in less than an hour. It had all happened so quickly. The cottage was furnished, so I just had to pack my personal belongings. I boxed and shipped what didn't fit into the two large suit-cases that travelled with me. When I crossed the cottage's threshold, I felt that I had truly come home.

It seemed strange at first, claiming the master bedroom that used to be my parents' as my own, but it made sense. Then I wandered around the house, room by room, letting the memories wash over me. I took my time, reminding myself where all the light switches were so I would be prepared when I had to keep up the illusion of darkness.

On my second day here, the boxes arrived. I hooked up the Bose music system and put on KT Tunstall. I turned up the volume and sang along with "Black Horse and the Cherry Tree," dancing around the room in a state of bliss.

Had it only been a week since I'd unpacked? I glanced at the Bose with a smile and turned it on. As music filled the room, I headed for the fridge. A quick rummage produced nothing I felt like eating, or more accurately, nothing I felt like cooking. The Flying Wedge had proven to be an excellent substitute. I pulled their menu from the junk drawer and ordered a "Popeye" for delivery. That particular pizza had spinach and feta, which was almost health food.

I wandered to the built-in bookshelf and picked up a framed photo of my parents. It was one of only three family photos that I'd brought with me. The picture had been taken at an outdoor café in Seattle during their honeymoon. Brian had his arms wrapped around Laura and their faces reflected blissful devotion. I definitely took after my mother. Though my hair was lighter than hers with an auburn tinge to it, there was no doubt that I was her daughter. I set the photo back on the bookcase and picked up another one.

This one had been taken by a professional in connection with Dad's work. He looked very much the doctor in it. It wasn't how I thought of him, though. I rarely saw him wearing the white coat. It was an old photo—probably from the mid-eighties because Dad's face was free of the worry lines that accompanied a life with family responsibilities. Of course, I always thought of him as handsome, but there wasn't a particular feature I could point to. He had medium-brown hair and pale blue eyes with a straight, average-sized nose and unremarkable chin. It was a pleasant face, and his genuine smile garnered trust—a good asset in his profession treating children.

I traded the photo for my favourite one. Looking at it was like seeing an old friend after a long absence. My mother had taken this shot of him. She was expecting me at the time, and they were taking a fishing trip before I came along and complicated their lives. Dad wore a saggy old canvas hat littered with fishing lures and sported a silly-ass grin. I wondered if the grin was because of the pathetically tiny fish he dangled or the woman taking the picture. He was undeniably happy in this photo and it warmed my heart.

The doorbell rang and its soft two-tone chord reminded me that I needed to get someone to look at it to crank up the volume. Maybe Charles knew someone. The familiar tone took me back to the times my father and I played nicky nicky nine doors on my very unappreciative mother. I don't think she ever forgave him for teaching me that game.

I took my smile to the front door to greet the pizza delivery man. The "Popeye" smelled promising and, once again, I was not disappointed in the Flying Wedge. After I'd eaten, I heated a mug of ginger ale—something my mother used to do for me when I had an upset stomach. Now it was something I did for myself whenever I needed comfort. I claimed my usual seat on the deck. The sun was quite low on the horizon, but it hadn't slipped away yet.

The Pacific was quiet tonight. Slowly, the golden hue of daylight was replaced by the blue hue of the night. With the change of light, I thought of Jolene. Her strange gift had brought me back to this house. For some inexplicable reason, Jolene's gift and my father's death were forever intertwined in my mind.

Tears welled up and overflowed but weren't accompanied by the racking sobs that for many years set my grief apart from mere physical pain. I returned to the living room, picked up my favourite photo of Dad in his fishing hat and smiled through my tears. This was the face I needed to see when I got out of bed in the morning. I moved it to my bedside table.

The professional photo, I took down to his study and set on the desk. It felt good, as if I were bringing him home. I couldn't help but think that Dad would have approved. One of his most prized possessions was a painting, which still hung above the desk. It was a dramatic seascape that I remember him looking at with a tender smile on his face. No wonder my mother didn't take it with us to Toronto—she was not about to keep any reminder of the ocean that had taken him away from us.

I wandered back through the house and out onto the deck. Dad was on my mind as I leaned on the railing and stared out at the beach. I replayed treasured memories over and over in my head, afraid that if I didn't, they would be lost. My memories were all I had left of him.

I stayed there, wrapped in my memories until the coolness of the night forced me indoors. I locked up and swallowed another painkiller before I slipped into bed.

Sometimes visiting these memories made me dream about him. I closed my eyes, hoping. It was usually the same dream—us walking along the beach and Dad cracking a giant geode to reveal a palm-sized crystal that was clear and colourless, and warm to the touch when he laid it in my hand.

CHAPTER FIVE

Dad's face remained etched in my mind when I woke the next morning. I loved that dream. It felt like a soothing embrace from the father I still missed. I almost expected to see the crystal lying next to the silly fishing photo of him that smiled back at me from the bedside table.

I swung my legs out and the ensuing aches provided a sharp reminder that the painkillers were no longer in my system. I downed another one with a glass of orange juice then tucked two soft weights into my housecoat's pockets and headed down to the beach.

If I hadn't been watching my step, I would have missed the foot-prints in the sand. Someone had been in front of the cottage. The edges of the prints weren't sharp, but I would have noticed them if they had been here yesterday. The rocks made it impossible to follow the trail, but whoever it was had spent some time right here at the bottom of the steps. I felt a chill go through me.

Since I'd been back, I'd only seen people on the beach twice and they had both been neighbours. Even though the beach was public pro-perty, no one came this close to the houses—it was considered impolite. Or it used to be.

I was glad I'd locked the patio door last night, and I started rethinking my no curtain in the bedroom policy, too.

Suddenly my new morning-on-the-beach ritual didn't seem so appealing. I returned to the house and walked down the hall to check the mailbox. I tightened my robe's belt and opened the front door. The scent of freshly cut lawn greeted me. Bees buzzed among the roses in the small garden beds on either side of the porch. They ignored me as I checked the mailbox, which was empty.

I looked over to the garage which sat on the southern edge of the property at a ninety-degree angle to the house. Its doors and trim had been painted to match the house. The double garage doors were padlocked when I'd arrived. I'd tried to see inside by pressing my face to the window. Despite cupping my hands around my eyes to block the sun's glare, it had been impossible to see more than vague shapes through the thick coat of dirt caked to the inside of the glass.

That was the day after I'd arrived from Toronto. It was the day I'd met Charles and Gabby. I'd asked them about the garage keys, and as I recalled that conversation, a big smile spread across my face.

"They're in here," Charles had said as he pulled open a drawer in the kitchen. He withdrew a ring of keys and tossed it to me.

"Let me show you," he said as he led us outside.

I unlocked the garage doors and he demonstrated how to prop the left side open by wedging a well-used stick between the door and the ground. Dim light spilled into the opening, and the first thing I laid eyes on was my dad's old MGB.

My face lit up. I had forgotten all about the little red convertible. Even my mother hadn't mentioned it. Charles watched my reaction carefully. The plates had expired in 2002 and the tires had been flat for so long that the rubber had cracked and gaped open in spots.

Charles quickly identified which keys unlocked it. The car had two bucket-style front seats and no back seat to speak of. The dust was so thick I couldn't tell if the ragtop was canvas or leather.

Charles and Gabby were uncharacteristically quiet. They knew about the car, of course; they were in and out of the garage with the lawn mower and other garden tools all the time.

"You look surprised," Charles said with puzzled amusement.

"I'd forgotten." Something else of my father's. Dare I hope that I might be able to drive it? I shot an expectant look at Charles and he grinned back at me.

Guessing at my speculation he said, "I think it's salvageable, but the old girl's going to need a lot of work and some TLC to get her running again." He was sure it had never been properly prepared for storage. He was right, it hadn't: it had been abandoned.

"I'm useless around cars, but I know someone who isn't. Would you like me to ask him to swing by to take a look?"

I took a moment to think about it and then said, "Sure, I'd like that." I had a driver's licence, but only limited driving experience and I'd never owned a car. The possibilities were enticing.

Cheney Meyers was the mechanic whom Charles had mentioned. The first time I met Cheney, it was eight in the morning; I had just gotten out of bed. I hadn't washed my face or brushed my teeth when the doorbell chirped. I answered the door without so much as having put a comb through my hair. I pulled my housecoat closed and cracked open the front door a half inch. "Can I help you?" I asked, mortified.

He did a good job not looking uncomfortable, which I'd clearly made him with my barely-open-door greeting. "I hope so," he said, then introduced himself as the friend of Charles who had come to see me about the car. I hadn't expected Charles to act quite so quickly.

Cheney wore a plaid shirt and blue jeans that day. He was taller than I was, but not by much because I didn't have to look up too far to meet his eyes through the crack in the door. Cheney had thick, brown hair and lovely blue eyes. Though I wasn't very good at guessing ages, I put him in the twenty-five to thirty category. He most certainly fit comfortably in the handsome category.

He took the keys that I offered and strolled to the garage. Meanwhile, I raced through my bathroom and dress routines, careful, as always, to make sure I had soft weights in the hidden pockets of my jean jacket before I joined Cheney at the garage.

He had the car hood propped up on a strut and was poking around in the engine shaking his head. When he saw me approach, he pulled a rag out of his back pocket in what looked like a well-worn habit. "I think it's fixable, but it needs a lot of work," he said. He leaned against the car, slowly wiping his hands on the dirty rag.

When he asked how long it had been stored, his voice took on an unmistakable tone; I knew admonishment and I felt it coming on.

"Ten years," I said, but then, with a practiced habit of my own, I diverted him. "Since my father passed away." It worked. He changed tack and, instead of a lecture, he ran off a list of repairs that he estimated would cost "more than a grand, less than three." It was probably foolish of me to ask the mechanic who would make money repairing the car if it was worth fixing, but I did.

"Sure," he said. "It's not a performance machine or anything, but it's a funky little ride. I'd fix it if it were mine." It was that last comment that convinced me to do it. I let him take the MGB with him.

That was last Sunday, which should have been a day off for him. We signed some paperwork at the dining room table and I encouraged him to linger while he admired the view from the deck, and I admired the view of him. We found lots to talk about. Neither of us had travelled much and we liked a lot of the same music. He was down-to-earth, comfortable in his own skin—easy company.

The next day, Cheney returned. It was Monday, also one of his days off. This time it was ten in the morning, but the previous night had been a particularly late one on the beach and I was stiff and sore. Once again, I was barely out of bed when Cheney rang.

I remember he actually cringed when I opened the door, but I didn't take him up on his offer to come back another time. He waited on the porch until I returned a few minutes later, dressed, hair pulled back, and teeth brushed. Cheney wore jeans again with a long-sleeved jersey shirt and smelled of aftershave, which I hadn't noticed the day before. I hadn't overestimated his good looks or his physical attributes. I almost wished he weren't so handsome. What must he think of me after finding me in the state he had, two days in a row?

His estimate for the work was just shy of $2,000 and he offered to start right away. He and his father were both mechanics and partners in Meyers Motors. They thought they could have the car ready in about two weeks. I gave him the green light.

That was almost a week ago. I looked away from the now empty garage and took my smile back inside the house. I must remember to thank Charles for the introduction, I thought, as I made a plan.

Cheney said I could check in on his progress any time, and I hoped he would be true to his word. Unfortunately, every time Cheney saw me, I looked terrible. For a moment, I let myself think that he might not notice the road rash on my face, but one look in the mirror dispelled that wishful thought. My face actually looked worse today; the purple bruising had started to turn weird shades of brown and yellow around the edges. But I couldn't do anything about that, and spending time with Cheney sure beat dwelling on my aches and the Grand Plan's untimely demise.

I shook my jeans out of the dryer and struggled into them, then pulled on a lightweight sweater. I donned my jean jacket, complete with weights, tucked my ID and a twenty in my pocket along with bus fare and locked the door behind me.

I headed down the driveway past a feathery Japanese maple,

flowering dogwood and a deep pink magnolia. Towering old fir trees grew close to the street. North of us, the neighbour had planted a laurel hedge, which served as a dense divider between our properties. The ten-minute walk to the bus stop took twenty.

The bus arrived in a puff of diesel exhaust that would have choked and killed a small mammal. I asked the driver to let me know when we reached Fourth Avenue, which was as close as I could get to Cheney's shop on this route. He nodded as I paid the fare and then, with a hiss and lurch, the big diesel was back into traffic.

We travelled along Deacon Street, a major corridor in Summerset comprised of both commercial and residential sections. We swayed past a section of Deacon known as "the strip." It was a popular shopping area I had recently become reacquainted with, though I still felt more like a tourist than a local. Before too long, the driver bellowed, "Fourth Avenue!" One of the good things about riding the bus was that they never got lost, unlike me, who had absolutely no sense of direction. I nodded my thanks and disembarked into another puff of foul-smelling exhaust.

I headed down Fourth Avenue, which intersected Stafford Street close to Meyers Motors, continuing the snail's pace I had set when I left the house. I may have been feeling better, but the soreness wasn't gone and the stitches in my ankle pulled a bit with each step, just to remind me they were still there. The distraction of Cheney would be worth the discomfort, I thought, looking forward to seeing him again.

From a block away, I spotted the shop's old-fashioned sign hanging from a tall black pole on the corner of the property. The tow truck Cheney had used to transport the MGB was parked out front. A silver compact was hoisted in the air occupying one of the two bays, but Dad's little red car was nowhere to be seen. The garage was deserted, as was the cluttered reception area to the right.

I headed around the back of the shop and spotted a collection of tires neatly lined up beside an assortment of spare parts. A formerly white nylon tarp stretched over a series of metal hoops constituting a temporary shelter. The front end of the MGB stuck out of it with its hood propped up. I recognized Cheney bent over it.

I cleared my throat. "Excuse me." Cheney straightened and came around the front of the car. He smiled at first but abruptly lost the grin on closer inspection. Yup, third time was the charm all right.

"I'm sorry, I should have called first," I said.

"It's okay. What happened to you?" he asked as he came closer.

I supplied him with my now rehearsed story, and quickly changed the subject. "How are you making out with the car?"

"Good, but we've got a ways to go yet." He pointed out the car's new tires and battery. "Most of the other parts have arrived and we've made a good start at getting them installed. It'll be another five or six days though." He adopted a concerned expression. "Let's go in the office so you can sit down."

I trailed after him back to the office. He held the door open then led me to one of the two red vinyl chairs in the corner. He was handsome despite the baggy coveralls that I knew hid an impressive physique. His sky-blue eyes were rimmed with long thick lashes any woman would envy.

"Can I get you something?" he asked. "We have wicked coffee." I guess I looked skeptical enough that he felt the need to point out the Keurig machine that sat on top of a small bar fridge across the room. "It's no trouble. We even have cream," he said. "Real cream."

"Sure," I said, and he dug out some mugs.

He slipped one into the machine and poured water in the top. "Do you take sugar?"

"No, just cream."

"My dad's here somewhere. He and your friend, Charles, go way back. I'll introduce you as soon as he comes around."

I didn't relish the thought of explaining my bruises to someone else, but I let it go and watched Cheney. When the machine finished sputtering, he brought me the mug.

"You're right. It's good," I said.

He made a second cup and came to sit beside me. "I hope you don't mind me saying this, Emelynn, but you look kind of beat up for someone who tripped over a rock on the beach."

Maybe my story wasn't as good as I'd thought, but I couldn't change it now. "Yeah, I'm dismally uncoordinated and I bruise easily. It looks worse than it is," I said, repeating my familiar refrain. Once again, I diverted the conversation as best I could and asked him about his family.

"I grew up in Kitsilano," he said. "We moved here when I was fifteen." He was an only child and had lost his mother to cancer a few years ago. "I live with my dad not too far from here," he added.

We settled into comfortable conversation until our coffees were gone.

"Well, I'd better get going," I said. "I've taken up enough of your time." I stood just as his dad walked in. That this was Cheney's father was obvious. He could easily have been mistaken for a shorter, more compact, older brother to Cheney.

"Dad, this is Emelynn. You know, the MGB. Charles's friend," he said by way of introduction.

"Jack," he said, extending a greasy hand out of habit before he yanked it back. "Sorry, hazard of the trade." He reached for the rag in his hip pocket the same way Cheney had.

I could tell the moment he really saw me. He became still and turned his head to check in with Cheney. He had adopted the same pained expression Cheney wore when he first saw my bruises.

Thanks to my new and improved good looks, another awkward moment was hanging in the air. "I was just leaving," I said, making my way to the door. "Nice to meet you, Jack."

"Cheney, why don't you take her home?"

"Yeah, sure." Cheney followed me out and I didn't argue as he led me to the passenger side of the big tow truck. I couldn't tell if he was being a gentleman or just anticipating that it would be a struggle for me to get into the truck's cab, but he stayed close until I was seated, then closed my door before going around to the driver's side.

The truck's interior smelled like a garage. Oily car parts spilled from the bench seat onto the floor. Cheney climbed in the driver's side. "Don't mind the mess," he said, reaching down to turn the key. The truck roared to life.

"Sorry," I mumbled, embarrassed that he'd caught me looking at the clutter. "What's that?" I asked, pointing to a gadget that was suctioned to the windshield.

"It's a GPS. Are you familiar with them?" he asked. I shook my head. He turned it on and showed me how it worked.

Given my lack of directional sense, one of these units could free me from the Land of the Lost. I was sold. "I'm going to look into getting one of those."

He turned right on Deacon. "I'll help you pick one out if you like."

We slipped into the flow of traffic. "Your dad seems real nice," I said.

"Yeah, he is," Cheney replied. "He's had a tough time of it since Mom died, but he's hanging in there." He changed lanes. "Are you seeing anyone right now?"

My heart bounced. "No," I replied. I could have expanded on the no—not now, not ever, not possible—but shut my inner self up.

He looked over at me. "No?" he said, sounding surprised, which was nice. "Well, if you're interested, maybe you'd like to go to a movie sometime?"

He'd caught me off guard, and I hedged. "Thanks. Maybe when I'm feeling better." As nice as the offer was, I just couldn't make the leap. Not now.

He parked at the front porch then came around to help me down from the truck's cab. After some purse diving, I found the keys and opened the front door. He reached across me to push the door open but didn't move out of my way. I sensed him gauging my reaction to his closeness and then he bent his head down and kissed me. The shock rocked me right down to my toes.

"I hope you think about letting me take you out," he said. His smile released a swarm of butterflies in my stomach.

He turned back to his truck while I stood on the porch with my mouth open. I was still standing there dumbstruck when he drove off.

I went inside, dropped my purse and jacket en route to the sofa, and sat down. My scattered thoughts played like bumper cars in my head.

I already felt overwhelmed in my efforts to rein in this gift. I had nothing left to offer. Cheney was a distraction I had no right to be interested in—though I was, and I hadn't been too subtle about it either or he wouldn't have kissed me. I was attracted to him—who wouldn't be? Under different circumstances, I'd have liked to get to know him better, much better. I was almost twenty-two years old and I'd never had a relationship with a man. The level of energy involved in keeping my condition a secret precluded that option.

Until my floating was under control, I needed to put Cheney out of my mind and refocus my attention on the thing that mattered the most. The sooner I learned how to control this albatross of a gift, the sooner I'd be able to get on with the business of living my life; a *real* life full of normal things like dating and friends and clothing without reinforced pockets. Then, maybe, I could think about Cheney.

CHAPTER SIX

L ife in the cottage carried on. Every morning, I spent some time on
the beach and each day my headache and body pains faded a little.
Today marked the tenth day since my accident. I'd brought
my book to the beach but was having trouble concentrating. My appointment with Dr. Coulter was today and that made me think about the
accident. I recalled an old quote that went something like "Those who
don't remember history are condemned to repeat it." My accident was
not the kind of history I could afford to repeat. I closed my book and
reviewed the accident in detail.

I'd put the Grand Plan into action the day after I arrived in BC,
purchasing a fifty-foot length of yellow nylon rope from the local
hardware store. That night, as soon as darkness fell, I donned my dark
clothing, put my hair into a ponytail and walked to the sandy beach
where I made my first clandestine attempt.

In hindsight, it seemed foolish, but at the time I thought that if I
could get enough momentum behind me, I'd be able to force the float. I
tied one end of the rope to my ankle; the other I secured around a large
rock. That gave me fifty feet of sprinting room before I got to the rock
and another fifty feet beyond it. I'd hoped it would be enough distance
to give me the momentum I needed to lift off. The rope was my tether,
my safety line. If I was successful, I'd need the rope to pull myself back
down to the beach.

I ditched the soft weights and set to work. But it was harder than I
thought to achieve any speed running on sand. I tried with shoes and
without; in stocking feet; in bare feet. I face-planted into the sand—more

than once; rope-burned not one but both ankles; and failed to manage a single float or hover of any kind.

I'd gone home unsuccessful that first night, but not defeated. I returned the following night to try my next bright idea. It still involved the rope, but this time I'd convinced myself that the float might happen with a bit of a head start. I would jump from a height. The first attempt was from a rock that stood about a metre off the ground. After several jarring jumps with no sign of weightlessness, I went in search of a higher perch.

A gnarly old tree root with a good length of tree still attached proved a good alternative and gave me almost twice as much height as the rock. Unfortunately, dropping from that height only served to punish my joints. The float remained elusive, and I gave up when my knees finally called it quits.

The walk back to the cottage after that second night felt like a funeral march. That was the first time I'd allowed myself to dip into the possibility of failure and I could hardly breathe at the thought. It wasn't just a move across the country that I had invested in this; my whole future was at stake. Any hope of normalcy or happiness was inexorably tied to gaining control over Jolene's legacy.

Each failure made it harder to slap on a happy face and keep going. But that's what I had to do, so I'd tamped down my disappointment. Not learning how to control this thing was simply not an option. I had to remain positive and that's the attitude I'd brought to my third night of covert activity on that sandy beach.

I gave the first two nights' efforts one more try, but neither the sprints nor the drops from the big rock or the tree root produced results. My knees ached and my ankles were raw with rope burns, but I had one more bright idea: combining speed with a leap. With my blood flowing, I'd warmed enough to ditch the hoodie. Bare feet had proven the most effective in the sand, so I removed my shoes and socks and added them to the pile of discards.

Over and over again, I sprinted down the beach, leaping into the air at the last moment. My ankles protested, but I stuck with it. Each time I fell, I charged again. I repeated the exercise until my lungs couldn't suck in air fast enough. I doubled over. Despite my efforts, gravity remained stubbornly, persistently and absolutely intact.

I'd failed. Despair reared its ugly head and choked me. I reached down frantically fighting to loosen the knot of rope around my ankle.

The moment I was free of it, I straightened and screamed my frustration into the night at the top of my lungs. I stamped my feet and screamed again. This was never going to happen for me. It was utterly hopeless. I was going to be a freak for the rest of my life.

When the tears finally came, I dropped to the sand and gave myself over to the thickening misery. It was easier than fighting it. I curled into a ball and let despair reign. The tears kept coming. I was so tired of the effort it took to keep up a positive attitude. It sucked what little life I had right out of me.

Eventually, the tears dried up. I rolled onto my back and gazed at the storm clouds hanging low overhead. The wind was picking up momentum pushing the clouds across the night sky. This could be as good as my life ever got. Maybe I should walk into that frigid water and put myself out of my misery. The water was about eight degrees Celsius, colder than my fridge. Hypothermia could be my friend. And that happy little thought was just the icing on my pathetic cake.

Utterly exhausted, I closed my eyes and concentrated on what was comforting and familiar: the steady, rhythmic lap of the ocean and the light, fish-infused scent of the damp air. A soothing numbness crept over me, blotting out the pain of my failure and the ache in my heart before claiming the noise in my head. I resigned myself to the complete lack of sensation.

How much time passed, I would never know. Gusting winds roused me. I remember being angry at the intrusion. I didn't want the perfect numbness to end. But the wind howled around me. I opened my eyes to the storm clouds and reality sank in. I had to go home, regroup, see if I could salvage anything positive from the ruins of the night.

I gave a brief thought to the tingling sensation that danced across my skin before I rolled over. Then all rational thought scattered as I realized the beach was five storeys below me. The effort to turn over had sent me into a slow roll that I wasn't able to stop or control. I'd rolled down gentle grassy hills as a child, but this didn't compare—it was like rolling down Grouse Mountain. I didn't even have time to be afraid of the gut-wrenching height before the gusting wind pushed me up and over the trees at the top of the cliff. The beach disappeared behind me as the wind twisted and turned me over, blowing me farther into the park.

Panic flared. I looked frantically about for salvation. I had never been this high before. I flapped my arms, but that just changed my sideways roll into a head-over-heels tumble. I had less control than a leaf caught in a gust of wind and no manner of flailing about seemed to help—it only made my flight more erratic.

Between gusts, the wind would let up and my flight would slow. When I could focus again, I saw that my trajectory was roughly parallel to the treetops. I tried to find something, anything, to grab. I extended my arms and finally managed to snag the tip of an arbutus tree. The motion spun me around, sending me sailing into branches lower down in the tree canopy. I smelled the sharp aromatic scent of fresh cedar as I tumbled, snapping limbs on my descent.

I watched the ground closing in and the gravel path rushing up, but I was powerless to slow the inevitable. I closed my eyes before impact and came to in the hospital.

It seemed like such a little mistake, but it could have killed me. I lifted my fingers out of the sand and brushed them off, squinting up at a bright sky that promised a warm day. Needless to say, the Grand Plan needed some work. I shifted the heavy book. For instance, I now knew that I should never ever release the rope before I put weights in my pocket. I'd also learned that neither momentum nor height would jump-start a float of any kind. That left concentrating my efforts on passive methods that had worked in the past—when distracted, while sleeping, or when startled.

How I would do that, I had no idea and I wasn't ready yet anyway. I still had stitches that needed to be removed and if I didn't get moving, I'd be late for my appointment with Dr. Coulter.

I pushed myself up out of the sand and headed back to the cottage. Ten days post-accident and my aches and pains were happily just twinges in the background. The headache was still there but dulled to the point that Tylenol 3 would be overkill.

I grabbed my coat, tucked the weights into the inside pockets and swung my knapsack over my shoulder.

The big smelly bus was right on time, a pleasant change from my experience with Toronto's public transit system—not the smelly part, the on-time part.

One bus transfer and a short stroll later, I found myself on a well-treed street in an older neighbourhood. The homes here were dignified, the yards manicured. The doctor's office was in the converted attached garage of a large old house.

When I stepped inside, I saw another man waiting. "Good morning," I said. He looked up from his magazine and nodded. His appointment must have been after mine because Dr. Coulter took me first.

"Emelynn," he said with just a glance at his other patient before he ushered me ahead of him into a small examination room. According to the framed certificates on the wall, Dr. Coulter's given name was Avery. "Good to see you again. Why don't you hop right up there." He indicated the paper-draped examination table.

I hardly recognized him in this setting, out of his white lab coat. He wore jeans and a V-neck pullover with the sleeves pushed up. The only obvious nod to his profession was the stethoscope hanging around his neck. He was much taller than I remembered, over six feet anyway. The only other times I'd seen him, I'd been lying in a hospital bed so his height hadn't registered.

"The scrapes on your face are healing nicely. How are you feeling otherwise?"

"Much better, thanks."

He gently inspected my contusions and scrapes. I watched the stethoscope dangle as he worked and caught a memory. Something about his movements or maybe it was his casual dress reminded me of another doctor: my father. If he were alive, they'd be about the same age.

He misted my ankle with antibacterial spray then snipped and removed the neat row of stitches. He repeated the process on the back of my head. It didn't hurt. He checked my blood pressure and reflexes then made a final check of my pupils with his penlight.

"You'll live," he declared with a smirk on his face that made me smile. His comfortable manner was disarming. "Have you made any progress yet figuring out how you came to be a barefoot torpedo in the park a week ago?"

"Torpedo?" I asked, raising an eyebrow.

He laughed. "Have you got a better description?"

I appreciated his sense of humour if not the descriptor. "I guess I was in the wrong place at the wrong time." He had been kind to me and I liked him, so I didn't want to have to lie to him. The smile on his face told me he wasn't going to make me, which was a relief. I gathered my things then extended my hand. "Thank you, Dr. Coulter."

He took my hand between both of his and looked me in the eye to make sure he had my attention. "Don't lose my card and please try to be more careful. If you get in trouble again, call me."

I got the impression he wasn't referring to medical trouble. I left his office bewildered by his comments. It was the second time he'd left me feeling as if he knew more about me or the accident than he let on. He couldn't know about my secret, so clearly my paranoia was showing. I decided to chalk his comments up to a quirky personality.

The bus chugged along Deacon Street. I disembarked along the strip and took a moment to get my bearings. I felt like a grown-up in a dollhouse; the stores seemed so much smaller to me now than when I was a child.

Larger stores such as the Safeway and Shoppers Drug Mart engulfed entire blocks on the south side of the street. None of those stores had been here ten years ago. The north side was home to about four blocks of old boutique-style storefronts. This part of the strip had a small-town feel to it that resonated with me. Some of the shops looked familiar from years ago, but quite a few had been newly renovated.

Behind me to my left was a pet store with a window display of comical dog outfits. If you didn't look closely, you'd assume it was a baby boutique. To my right was Dimitri's Deli, which attracted lineups at noon, and Time Again, a consignment clothing store. The familiar Starbucks logo was here and so was the Scotiabank with an instant teller out front, but what I was looking for was Cottage Wines.

I found it one block down. I didn't know a lot about wine, but I did know what I liked, at least as far as the reds were concerned. Argentinian Malbecs were my current favourites, having recently edged out Chilean Merlots.

On my way back to the bus stop, I detoured to Rumbles, a bookstore I'd been meaning to check out. I depressed the old-fashioned thumb latch on the door handle and opened the door to the tinkle of a brass bell. The door didn't close on its own—I turned around and shut it. Immediately I liked the place; it was unpretentious and cluttered.

A woman with curly dark hair sat behind a counter to the left. She looked up and nodded hello then returned to reading her book. She had a fifties-era look about her that had everything to do with the eyeliner, the crisp cotton blouse, and the wide, matching hair band. The small store was crammed with books. I inhaled the familiar new-book aroma of fresh paper and glued bindings, with a sprinkle of dust thrown in. A scattering of well-worn chairs graced the space, but the emphasis here was unmistakably on books. It was an old store with stacks that reached to the ceiling.

I wandered up and down the aisles caressing book spines with my fingers, tilting my head to read the titles. Ken Follett's newest tome, *Fall of Giants*, caught my eye and I picked it up to read the dust jacket. Though I was tempted to buy it, it was heavy and I hadn't yet finished his *Pillars of the Earth*. Besides, I'd already packed two bottles of wine in the knapsack and still needed to pick up some milk and a few other groceries. These were the unfortunate limits when travelling with a knapsack on public transportation.

The clerk saw me hesitate and asked, "Can I help you find something?" We were the only two people in the place, and I headed back to the front of the store. The woman was about my age.

"No, but thanks," I replied. "I have too many other things to pick up." I shrugged to indicate my knapsack and added, "Not enough room in here today."

She removed her glasses and studied my face. "My name's Molly," she said, and I wondered if I had something on my face. I looked down at the name tag that spelled out her name.

"I'm Emelynn," I replied, returning the courtesy. "You've got a great store here."

"Emelynn Taylor?" she asked. A wide smile spread across her face, lighting up her eyes. "Molly Connolly," she said, pointing excitedly to herself.

"Molly?" I took a step back and looked at her. "It really is you. What a nice surprise." We had been friends in elementary school but I hadn't seen her since I left for Toronto. "Is this your store?"

"No, I just work here. You look great, well, except for that bruise." She looked as if she expected an explanation but quickly moved on. "How many years has it been?" she asked, estimating the time in her head. "I bet it's at least ten."

"You're right."

"Wow ... it's good to see you. What brought you back to the old neighbourhood?"

"I live here now—just moved back."

"You and your mom still have that place down on Cliffside?"

"Yeah, that's where I'm living. You remember it?"

"Sure. That place brings back memories. Remember when your Nanny Fran took us to see the Woodwards' Christmas display? How old were we? Seven?"

"Gosh, yeah," I said, remembering the window into Santa's workshop. I pictured the big man nodding his head up and down, rubbing his fat tummy in circles over and over again. He watched over the elves who hammered and painted, their arms repeating the motions endlessly. "It was grade two. Remember how exciting it was to be downtown in Vancouver?"

The bell over the door sang out the arrival of a delivery man backing through the door with a hand truck stacked with boxes. Molly glanced over. "Hi, Sal. Just put them here behind the counter."

"Sorry, Emelynn. I've got to check this order before I sign off on it. Will you come back? I'd love to catch up."

"Sure, that'd be nice. I'm in the neighbourhood all the time." I scooted to the door and held it wide for the delivery man.

"Great," she said. "I'm here Tuesday to Saturday."

"I'll see you soon," I said, closing the door behind me.

I headed for the Safeway, smiling and shaking my head. Molly Connolly. Who'd have thought?

Later that night, when dusk arrived and daylight exchanged itself for blue, I ambled out to the deck and leaned against the railing. Dusk was my favourite time of night. I enjoyed the privacy that near darkness provided. Gazing down the beach, I spotted someone approaching from the north. By the gait, I guessed it was a man.

I watched him pick his way among the rocks at the water's edge. He glanced up once, but I hadn't turned on the lights in the cottage so felt safe that in the fading light he couldn't see me. He carried on, heading south.

The following morning dawned brilliantly, though a tad chilly. I proved myself incapable of multi-tasking when I managed to spill milk over the rim of my bowl of Cheerios while checking email. What a mess. At least the milk hadn't hit the laptop.

After I cleaned up, I tucked my book under my arm then headed down the stairs to the beach. With not a soul in sight and just the company of seagulls and crabs, I settled in to read.

Running into Molly last night had been bittersweet. She was a reminder of what my life might have been like if it hadn't been for Jolene's interference. I wanted to rekindle our friendship, but a relationship with Molly wouldn't be any different than one with Cheney in terms of my condition and the deception involved in keeping the secret.

There was a difference though. It was subtle, granted—but different. I wasn't starting a relationship with Molly: it was already there. We shared a history. Maybe I was justifying it to myself, but I felt hopeful and the added bonus was that Molly hadn't had a front row seat to my Toronto humiliations. I opened my book, happy at the thought that I was on my way back to Normal.

I read until my bladder suggested a trip back up the stairs. I headed to the bathroom then took a shower and dressed. My cellphone rang and I scrambled to find it.

"Hey Emelynn, it's Cheney. Are you going to be home soon?"

"I'm home right now," I said.

"Oh, I guess you didn't hear the doorbell."

"Sorry. I was in the shower," I said, heading for the front door.

"Then I'm glad I waited."

I opened the heavy door and my heart skipped a beat at the sight of the shiny red MGB parked in my driveway. Cheney leaned against it looking like the cover of a women's edition of *Car and Driver*.

He watched me approach, beaming with pride. So he should be; the car looked spectacular. It was polished to a high gloss and the ragtop was a deep, rich black.

"Hi," he said. "I was beginning to think I'd have to leave without seeing you."

I stood speechless, not sure which looked better to me, the car or Cheney. I let out a sigh. At least the car was mine.

"You're looking considerably healthier than the last time I saw you." He reached out to touch my cheek where the bruise was faded to pale yellow. His touch electrified me and I had to step back. I couldn't afford to be electrified by him. Not now anyway.

He quickly withdrew his hand. I had to be more careful about sending him mixed messages. Despite the awkwardness that had bloomed between us, he took the time to show me every inch of the car, going over the work that he and his dad had done so beautifully to restore the MGB.

I let the details consume my attention and oozed appreciation, but it didn't change a thing. I sensed him pulling back from the sting of my rejection.

I tried to convince myself that this was best. It wasn't the time to encourage a new relationship. I had bigger problems. If he knew about them, he'd thank me rather than feel spurned. In fact, he'd run screaming in the opposite direction, wishing he'd never met me.

He got behind the wheel and started the engine. It coughed a cloud of smoke. Cheney finally smiled, looking faintly amused but not apologetic. "That's just the nature of MGBs," he said. "It doesn't affect the performance."

He made sure I knew how to shift the gears then turned the ignition off and got out. He handed me the keys. "Let me know if you have any trouble with it. MGBs can be finicky, but this one seems uncharacteristically good." He hesitated, not sure what to do next.

I shot my hand out to shake his. "Thanks so much. I really appreciate the care you've taken with it." He nodded then stepped away and headed back to his tow truck. Then he was gone.

Cheney was the closest I'd ever come to having a real date. He was a catch, too: sweet and kind—he even had his own business. His good looks were just the sprinkles on an already well-iced cupcake, and now he was gone. What a crappy twist of fate that he came along when he did. I retreated into the house to sulk.

I couldn't hold on to the possibility of Cheney. It put too much pressure on resolving my condition, and if there was one thing I was absolutely certain about, it was that I didn't need any more pressure there.

Cheney would be yet another dream I would have to watch float by the wayside while I worked on controlling Jolene's gift. He could anchor miserably alongside fashion sense, school friends and social skills.

So what was I doing moping around the house? It was time to put the Grand Plan back in action. To do that, I needed to replace the rope, which would be a lot easier now that I had a car. There was no sense in wasting a trip either, so I loaded the recycling into the tiny car and got behind the wheel. I turned the key in the ignition and it sparked to life. My eye was drawn to the rear-view mirror as a cloud of smoke curled up behind the vehicle.

The little red car was an indulgence and I felt spoiled. I headed out to find the mom-and-pop hardware store that had supplied the first coil of rope—the rope that now floated out on the Pacific somewhere.

Driving a stick was going to take some getting used to. I apologized to both my dad and Cheney in equal measure as I ground a gear or two making my way to Deacon Street then down to Anderson's Hardware. A strap of bells sang out my entry. I said hello to the man behind the counter. He reeled off fifty feet of rope then carefully burned the ends to keep them from unravelling. He labelled my neatly coiled yellow bundle, then led me to the till and rang it up.

I tossed the rope behind the driver's seat then drove to Starbucks and ordered a chai latte. While the barista frothed the milk, I snagged a thumb-worn *Vancouver Province* newspaper and took it and my latte to a sidewalk table. It was a perfect spot to people-watch and take in the late morning activity. I flipped through the paper until my milky treat was gone, and then abandoned my prime outdoor table.

The barista told me where to find the closest recycling bins. I drove the car a block to unload the flattened cardboard and had the car pointed for home before I remembered Molly. Rumbles was just around the corner. It would be fun to share the news of Dad's car's resurrection with someone who had known him.

I pulled up outside Rumbles and stayed in the driver's seat until I caught Molly's attention and waved her outside. There was no one in the store. She jumped off her stool and came out to the curb.

"This is your dad's old car?" she asked, circling and admiring. I opened the door and climbed out. She'd borrowed her wardrobe from the fifties again, wearing pale blue capris with a coordinating sweater set.

"Yeah, I got it back from the shop this morning," I said, caressing the ragtop. "What do you think?"

"Sweet." I knew there was a reason I'd stopped here. She peppered me with questions and compliments in such quick succession I couldn't get the answers out fast enough. I followed her circles around the car. When she finally slowed down, I had to remind myself that we hadn't seen one another in ten years. Our old friendship had just bubbled to the surface.

"I have a brilliant idea. How would you like an opportunity to show off your car and have a good time to boot?" she asked with a hopeful twinkle in her eye. "There's a new restaurant in Seaside. I've only been once before, but it was really good. You and I could drive up there, have dinner and catch up."

Seaside was another small tourist town about a twenty-minute drive north. "That's a great idea," I said. I hadn't been to a restaurant since the move. "When do you get off work?"

"Six thirty. I know it's a little early for dinner, but the restaurant won't be busy then. We can take our time."

"That sounds perfect," I said, settling behind the wheel. "See you at six thirty," I called over my shoulder as I pulled my car out onto Deacon Street. *My car*—now that was going to take some getting used to.

When I got home, I stashed the coil of rope in the hall closet, deciding to put off that daunting adventure until tomorrow night. My phone call to my mother went to voice mail. I had too much news for a voice message so I composed an email instead, telling her all about reconnecting with Molly, and Cheney's delivery of the MGB. It was a night for celebrating.

Molly was waiting outside Rumbles when I pulled up. She jumped in and off we drove. I hadn't been to Seaside in years, but Molly knew the way. The picturesque little town tweaked vague memories of sand pails and flip-flops. We found parking close to the restaurant and the hostess seated us right away.

We split an appetizer of calamari and started down the long road of catching up. The restaurant lived up to Molly's billing. The ahi tuna melted in my mouth, while Molly raved about her catch of the day—ling cod.

The first impression that Molly presents is one of reserve, shyness even, but scratch the surface and an infectious enthusiasm shines through. She was different from the girl I remembered, but she would likely say the same of me. The reserve was a reflection of her maturity but the enthusiasm was the Molly I remembered.

"Mom, Dad and the twins moved to the Sunshine Coast when I finished high school," she said. "I could have gone with them, but I was keen to move out when I got accepted into Emily Carr. Mom and Dad helped me find a two-bedroom condo close to Granville Island." She looked wistful, remembering good times. "Four of us ended up living there. It was cramped, but we had a blast."

"How long have you worked at the bookstore?"

"Rumbles? Almost a year. The owners are nice and they're flexible with time off. Plus, the store's usually quiet so I get to indulge my reading habit. They even let me include some of my own book recommendations when I'm making up the orders. I found an apartment about a half hour's bus ride from there."

Molly's dark, curly hair and milky white skin were courtesy of her Scottish father. Her round face and wide-set eyes were a credit to her mother, who was descended from First Nations. She had happy light-brown eyes and curves that she carried beautifully.

"How about you, Emelynn? You're being awfully quiet."

She was right. As much as I loved hearing all about what she'd been up to, I couldn't share the interesting bits of my life. There wasn't a patch big enough to convincingly cover the lies and secrets. Instead, she got a glossed-over version of my time in Toronto.

"Are you ever going to tell me how you got that bruise on your face?"

"It's nothing," I said, dismissing her concern. "I had a fight with the rocks on the beach. They won."

She chuckled at that and I moved on, telling her about Charles and Gabby and finding Dad's car. I even put in a plug for Cheney, having established that she didn't have a man in her life.

It proved impossible not to go on again about the MGB. "You know," I said, "Meyers Motors isn't that far from Rumbles—just down Fourth Avenue at Stafford."

"I don't even have a driver's licence," Molly said. "So a car's not anywhere near the top of my shopping list."

"I don't know. It might be worth getting one just to meet Cheney," I said, letting that hang in the air a few seconds, for both our benefits. Telling Molly about Cheney felt like releasing him. Not that he had ever been mine, but the possibility had been mine, even if just for a brief moment.

"Oh?" was the only opening I needed from Molly to set that balloon afloat. She was already impressed with his work on the car, so I filled in the few other details I knew about his partnership with his dad at Meyers Motors. Though he worked and lived fairly close to the bookstore, Molly didn't recognize him from my description. Maybe bookstores weren't his thing.

"I'm sensing there's something wrong with this Cheney guy," Molly said, frowning. "Otherwise, why would an unattached girl such as you be so anxious to pawn him off? What's he got—six fingers on one hand or a giant bum for a nose?"

"Ah, poor Cheney," I said, laughing. "And I'm not pawning him off. I'm just not looking for a man in my life right now, and I hate to see a good one go to waste." With that said, I had done all I could. I'd planted the Cheney seed. The rest was up to her.

After we drained the life out of the Cheney topic, she told me about her interest in fashion design, and I told her about my SPCA volunteer work. We finished dessert and still hadn't run out of things to talk about, but it was close to nine and we fell under increasing pressure to let the waiter turn over the table.

We got back into the MGB still reminiscing. She fed me directions to her apartment. I pulled up front.

"That was fun," she said, getting out.

"Yeah, I had a good time."

"Let's do it again soon."

"I'd like that," I said, then waited until she had the apartment door open before I waved goodbye and pulled away.

Predictably, I took a wrong turn and got lost. I blamed it on the newness of driving and getting used to the car. After all, why beat myself up when I had new excuses at my disposal. Eventually, I found my way back to Deacon. From there, I knew my way home.

I backed into the garage, thinking it was a tight squeeze. Had my dad thought the same? Would he have reassured me that I'd get used to it with practice? It was a bit of a contortionist's trick wiggling out of the seat without dinging the car door against the work bench, but I managed. As I straightened up, I spied a collection of fishing rods mounted on the wall to the left of the window. They had been my dad's pride and joy. In a far recess of my memory, I recalled that each of the rods had a particular specialty though I couldn't recall the details. Dad would be so pleased if I cleaned them up. I promised myself I'd do that real soon.

It was after ten when I closed the front door. I dropped my keys on the hall table and headed to the kitchen—more specifically, to the red wine. Tonight seemed like a perfect night to indulge in a glass. After all, I had two things to toast: my new car and my renewed friendship with Molly.

I poured a glass of red and sauntered outside to the deck. A carpet of stars twinkled overhead, inspiring me to venture down the stairs to the beach. As I approached the bottom step, I caught sight of a man about twenty yards away. He'd startled me but I didn't give myself away. I knew he couldn't see me in the dark.

So why was he walking in my direction? Maybe he'd caught my movement coming down the stairs. I kept perfectly still hoping he'd pass by. Something about him seemed off to me. I couldn't quite put my finger on it, but the skin on the back of my neck tightened and my instincts screamed, run!

It was too late. He knew I was there and he continued his deliberate walk, straight toward me. Our eyes met for the briefest of moments and the glimpse zapped me like an electric shock. I jerked my gaze away, gasping for air. What the hell? What just happened?

I grabbed the railing with my free hand and he rushed to close the distance between us. "Are you all right?" he asked in an innocent voice that didn't ring true. He searched my face until once again, he looked directly into my eyes.

There was no warning. His gaze riveted me in place and this time I couldn't break his strange hold. As soon as his eyes locked on mine, I was lost. My body trembled uncontrollably and I felt my knees buckle. He reached out and touched me. I couldn't catch my breath. The last thing I saw were his pale hazel eyes. Then my world went black.

CHAPTER SEVEN

I don't know how much time passed before I felt myself rouse. The surface I lay on felt soft, comfortable even. It swayed in a gentle rocking motion. Not an unpleasant effect, just unexpected. I opened my eyes and tensed; I wasn't alone. Sitting on a chair beside me was the man from the beach who'd taken my breath away. He leaned against the wall with his feet propped on the bed reading a *Pacific Yachting* magazine. He hadn't yet noticed that I was conscious.

Black, curly hair fell into his eyes, as if he'd missed his last two dates with his barber. But his hair was his only soft feature. The lines of his face were straight and sharp, his square jaw freshly shaved and punctuated with a cleft in his chin. I put his age at about thirty. He wore a long-sleeved knit shirt that clung to him leaving no doubt that he was lean and muscled.

"Welcome back," he said, his voice smooth and calm. "How are you feeling?"

Really? He was going for polite? What a stupid question. I slowly drew away from him, pulling the soft faux fur cover with me. We were on a boat. I glanced around, noting the richly toned, polished wood on the ceiling and in the built-in dressers on both sides of the room.

"Who are you?" I asked.

"Someone you should have met a long time ago." He lowered the magazine. "My name's Jackson Delaney."

Yeah, sure it was. "What do you want with me?" I asked, glad my voice didn't quiver.

"Nothing," he said, looking me straight in the eye. I quickly broke the contact, remembering all too well what those pale eyes could do.

Nothing? If I weren't so scared, I'd laugh. Then another, more frightening thought occurred to me: maybe he was crazy.

"I'm just trying to keep you safe," he said, setting the magazine aside.

"Safe?" I snorted. "You *kidnapped* me to keep me *safe*?" Immediately I regretted my derisive tone. If he was crazy, I didn't want to set him off.

"Safe," he repeated, as if saying it twice would make me believe him.

What the hell did *safe* even mean to a kidnapper? "I didn't know I wasn't," I said, more cautious this time.

"I'm aware of that. That's why you're here."

His cryptic answers were maddening, but what choice did I have but to play his stupid game. "I don't understand."

"Yes, I'm sure you don't. There's much you don't understand, Emelynn. We have a lot to talk about—"

I cut him off, my anger finally breaching caution. "How do you know my name? Where are we?"

"We're on my ship," he said, sounding bored. "I brought you here last night," he added—it seemed I was trying his patience.

"Why?"

He held up his hand to stop any further interruption. "I'm sure you have a lot of questions, which I promise to answer. But right now, I'd like a coffee. What about you?" He swung his feet off the bed and stood, ignoring my anger, as if I were a bothersome fly he could shoo away.

"I don't want a damn coffee. I want answers."

He acted as though I hadn't spoken. "There's a head starboard." He gestured around a corner. "Freshen up then meet me up top."

He walked to the door, ducked under the frame then disappeared up some steps in the corridor outside. The man moved with confidence and purpose, like someone used to being in charge.

I didn't give a damn about his answers. I tossed aside the warm cover and took in the thick white comforter underneath and pillows as soft as clouds. Was he the one who had laid me down here? Put that cover over me? Goosebumps crawled across my skin at the thought of what he could have done to me. He hadn't hurt me, but then again, maybe that was still on his agenda. I needed to get off this boat.

I stood, swaying with the gentle rocking of the boat, and yanked

JP McLean

open every drawer searching for something—anything—to use as a weapon. Empty. They were all empty. A padded storage bench sat at the foot of the bed. I rifled through it, pulling out more bedding, but found nothing suitably sharp or heavy. I slid the closet door open and found rain slickers on flimsy plastic hangers. Useless!

I searched the head with similar results unless the supply of tiny soaps, miniature tubes of toothpaste and small bottles of shampoo could be used as missiles. I looked down at the bottles in my hand and a maniacal laugh escaped. I could whack him with a plastic hanger or pummel him with tiny toiletries. What a choice. Things were not looking good in the weapon department.

I splashed water on my face and brushed my teeth, which knocked the edge off my slumber. I had a horrible feeling I'd need to be alert to escape the man who called himself Jackson.

I left the bedroom, skirted the steps, and found a hallway with two more doors on either side and another at the far end. They were all locked. With nowhere else to search, I returned to the steep stairs and started up. A blinking red light on a small security camera caught my eye. Great—he was watching me.

I found myself on another level of a boat that would most definitely fit in the "large" category. Two more locked doors stood on either side of a short hallway, which emptied out into a kitchen area that looked scrubbed clean. More security cameras winked their red lights at me. Ignoring them, I pulled on what I hoped was a knife drawer, but it wouldn't open. I tried several more with the same result. The tidy living room area beyond was furnished with two white leather sofas and matching chairs. Two tall captain's chairs faced forward, secured to the floor. Mounted behind the one on the right was a large, spoked, steering wheel, but I saw no sign of the man.

I turned back toward the kitchen. A bathroom door on the left was unlocked and vacant. I headed through the hall off the kitchen where I'd seen a door that led outside. The day was overcast. I walked outside and found myself under cover at the rear of the boat beside a table with four chairs. A small sink and bar fridge hid like stowaways behind another staircase.

I took the stairs up to a spacious upper deck. Even though it was overcast, the bright white of the fibreglass reflected enough light to force me to squint. The deck was open to the sky at this end but covered at the opposite end, where I found him. He faced me, sitting on a sofa at the far end of the covered space. The furniture was identical to the seating downstairs, except here it was navy blue. Behind Jackson were two more captain's chairs and another huge steering wheel with a bank of controls. I would never have imagined you could steer one boat from two locations.

Land loomed off in the distance. It was too far to swim to and I couldn't identify any landmarks. Where were we? He watched my approach and gestured for me to sit opposite him.

I avoided looking directly at his eyes and slowly made my way to the sofa. Neither of us wore shoes. As I got closer, my eyes roamed over a collection of familiar belongings laid out on the large coffee table in front of him. He never took his eyes off me as I took in the disconcerting collection.

I dropped to the sofa. Displayed in front of me were my soft weights, coiled rope, favourite hoodie and black Rocket Dogs.

Jackson, or whatever his name was, pushed a cup toward me and poured coffee from a thermos. "Cream?"

I reached for the cup, nodded yes, and finally took my eyes off my belongings. I looked at him, but his face gave nothing away. Who was this man? It felt as if he were playing some kind of game with me, but why? Had he witnessed my accident that night on the beach?

The coffee was warm and oddly comforting. I tucked my legs up under me. Just what did he actually know? "What's all this stuff?" I asked.

He raised his eyebrows. "It's too late for that, Emelynn. Your reaction gave you away the moment you laid eyes on it." He sat back against the sofa and put his feet up on the table.

My scalp crawled. "What do you want?"

"I told you. Nothing."

This cryptic game of his was wearing thin. "So ... you kidnapped me to return my things?"

He ignored my comment and studied me, as if measuring my reaction or trying to figure something out.

Finally, he spoke. "You and I have something in common: something important."

I drew my brows together, confused.

He swung his feet off the table, stood and came around behind me. I turned on the sofa to follow his movement. He strolled out from under the covered roof section, looked over to make sure I was watching, and then, without any obvious effort or warning, he drifted up off the deck, hovering a few feet in the air.

My mouth dropped open, which seemed to satisfy him. He floated back down to the deck as though nothing at all had happened. He returned to the sofa and put his feet up on the table.

"I thought that would save us a lot of time and denial," he said as he brushed some curls out of his eyes and picked up his cup.

I stared at him, dumbfounded, and then closed my mouth. There was a smugness to his grin—he'd enjoyed the effect of the shock he'd delivered. He sat comfortably in the ensuing silence, while I grappled with what I'd just witnessed.

When I found my voice, I asked, "How did you know about me?"

"Dr. Coulter. He knew the minute he examined you at the hospital. Avery keeps an eye out for our kind."

"Our *kind*?"

"Yes, Fliers."

"Fliers." I tried the word out loud. "Is that what I am, a Flier?"

"Well," he gestured toward my belongings resting between us on the coffee table. "Maybe not a very good one, but yes."

So it was this man's footprints I had seen when I went to retrieve my things. "What exactly is a Flier?" I asked.

"We're ordinary people who have an extraordinary gift: a talent, so to speak. It's as rare and inexplicable as clairvoyance or telepathy. The gift allows us to throw off gravity as easily as an overcoat."

"That's impossible." I shook my head, dismissing the notion.

"It is possible. We're living proof."

"But how can that be?" The concept flew in the face of all reasonable thought. "What you're suggesting contradicts Newton's law of gravity and who knows how many other scientific imperatives."

He looked at me with a mix of frustration and determination while he mulled over his thoughts.

"Did you know that until 2005, scientists couldn't explain how bumblebees were able to fly? *Theoretically*, their stubby little wings made flight an aerodynamic impossibility."

"Regardless, that doesn't prove the possibility of what you're suggesting."

"My point is, bumblebee flight remained a mystery for hundreds of years. It's not unlike the puzzle of the Pyramids. *Theoretically*, the Pyramids shouldn't exist. Science tells us that it is impossible for the

Egyptians to have constructed them with the tools and skills they had available at the time. Yet those tombs have stood for centuries thumbing their pointy noses at us.

"Nor can scientists quantify the power of positive thinking or the placebo effect and no one has ever definitively solved the mystery of the Bermuda Triangle. There are lots of things in this world that we don't understand, Emelynn, or that can't be explained by science. But that doesn't mean they don't exist. Science will catch up and figure it out some day."

If Jackson's aim was to turn my world upside down then he got an A for his efforts. And he might have shaken my foundations, but I was still grounded. This levitation thing could easily be an optical illusion, a magician's trick. It was going to take a whole lot more than words to convince me.

"How did Dr. Coulter know I was a Flier?" I asked, hesitating on the last word.

"Your eyes," he responded. "We have eyes that don't refract light in the usual manner. It's what allows us to see in the dark."

"So Dr. Coulter is also a Flier?" I asked, again hesitating on the last word. It felt surreal to finally have a label for my condition.

"Well, he has night vision but he can't fly, which is highly unusual. He's the only one I know like that, and he's also the reason you're here. He asked me to watch out for you. I was waiting in his office the day you went to get your stitches out."

I looked over at him and could finally place his face in Dr. Coulter's office.

"I've been keeping an eye on you since your accident, and believe me, babysitting you is not what I want to be doing with my time. Your being here was not part of my plan. I only intervened because you left me no choice when you bought more rope yesterday. I didn't want you to kill yourself, which you seem doggedly intent on doing."

"You've been watching me? You're the man I saw on the beach." The thought of someone watching me was beyond creepy. "You're the one who was loitering at the foot of my stairs." I raised my voice as outrage pushed indignation aside.

"You never saw me and I certainly wasn't hanging around your stairs, but yes, I've been watching your movements. I'm sorry if that upsets you, but we needed to know more about you."

"You kidnapped me!"

He leaned forward. "Yes," he said, unapologetic. "And you may not choose to believe me right now, but it's for your own good. We're trying to keep you safe."

I didn't know what was more creepy—the watching me part, the casual acceptance of kidnapping part, or the *we* part he'd referred to more than once.

"I *did* see you on the beach. The night before last. You were walking south, close to the water. You even looked up to the deck. I saw you."

"It wasn't me. I wasn't on foot when I checked on you, so you can skip the accusation."

"Then who was it who left footprints at the foot of my stairs?"

"You live on a public beach," he said, his own indignation showing. "It could have been anyone."

He had a point. I softened my tone. "How did you know what I was planning to do with the rope?"

Jackson leaned back into the sofa, relaxing again. "The night of your accident Avery phoned me with the few details he learned from the paramedics. I flew out there. It didn't take me long to find your things on the beach. Rope burns on your ankles, rope on the beach. I put two and two together. It wasn't that difficult."

Dr. Coulter hadn't mentioned the rope burns; I thought he hadn't noticed them. Jackson refilled our coffee cups.

"So, what have you learned about me?" I asked.

"Your name is Emelynn Taylor, born June '89, no siblings. We don't know anything about your father. You've been living with your mother, Laura Aberfoyle. You graduated from U of T with a BA last month and moved here a few weeks ago. The Flier community in the GTA has never heard of you or your mother."

Had he just recited that laundry list of my life's details from memory? That this stranger knew so much about me left me uneasy. And who was this *we* he kept referring to?

"Well, you've certainly done some digging." We sat in silence a while longer. "You keep referring to *we*—who are the *we*?"

"Fliers. There aren't a lot of us so we keep track of one another, watch out for one another." He swung his feet to the floor and stood. "Let's go below to the galley and get something to eat. I'm famished," he said. "Perhaps I can tell you more about Fliers over a meal and then, if you're up for it, maybe you'll fill in some blanks for me." With that said, he started for the staircase.

I stared after him. Was he kidding? He disappeared below, and I shook my head. It wasn't like I had anything else to do. I got up and trailed behind him.

Jackson moved as though he knew what he was doing in the kitchen, or "galley," as he called it. I watched him open with apparent ease the very drawer that wouldn't open for me earlier.

"Yeah, about that—you have to lift up on the front of these drawers to pull them out," he said. It was not-so-subtle confirmation that the cameras weren't just decorations. "Keeps them from jumping open on their own when the ship's underway."

"You're awfully confident that I won't find a way to escape," I said as he pulled out pans, bowls and utensils.

"I'm not holding you here, Emelynn. You can leave any time you want." He turned his back to me and laid bacon strips in a heavy pan. I guess I didn't look like the knife-wielding type. He turned back around and cracked an egg into a cup of milk, beat it with a fork then added it to a bowl of flour. He was making pancakes—from scratch. He didn't even look at a recipe.

"If there was any other way to manage this situation, I'd have found it." He turned the bacon with a fork then poured batter into bubbling butter in another pan. I think *this situation* meant me. He set out two plates on the bar along with butter and syrup.

I didn't think kidnap etiquette obliged the victim to help so I strolled around the room and watched. "Sit," he said, pointing to one of the stools under the bar. He piled pancakes on both plates then added a few strips of crispy bacon to each before sitting down.

As much as I didn't want to enjoy the meal, there was no denying the pancakes tasted great and I was starving. He finished eating before me then sat in silence, waiting. When I put my fork down he cleared away the dishes then pushed the sleeves of his sweater up to his elbows. I watched the tendons and muscles of his forearms dance as he wiped the counters down. He was easy to watch—could have made the cover for *Kidnapper GQ*.

I trailed him over to the living room area, where we sat across from each other exactly as we had done earlier on the top deck. The tufted white leather sofas and matching chairs were arranged around a low glass coffee table. I looked past him to the ocean beyond, thinking life really was stranger than fiction. As if my life wasn't complicated enough—how was I supposed to absorb this new twist?

Jackson drew a deep breath, attracting my attention. "Fliers are a tight-knit group. Someone should have known about you, but you weren't on anyone's radar either here or in Toronto. That's why we were so surprised to learn about you."

"How many of you are there?"

"*We* number in the thousands at best." I felt the gentle sway of the boat; it served as a constant reminder that I was out of my element. "For the most part, we live in more temperate climates so there are more of us on the west coast and in the southern states than there are east or farther north. Here in the Lower Mainland, including you, there are thirteen of us."

"I wouldn't be so quick to count me among your numbers," I said, putting a snarky bite on his assumption. "So far I've learned that you've spied on me, dug up personal information about me and, oh yes, you kidnapped me. Those aren't exactly attributes of a group that I want to belong to."

Jackson laughed out loud. "Well, I see it quite differently. You were doing your best to kill yourself or bring yourself to the attention of someone who would do it for you. We took pity on you and brought you here to safety. Now I've fed you and I'm trying to teach you something about your rather unique situation." He was genuinely amused, which fired my anger.

"I don't think the police would agree with your assessment," I challenged. It wiped the smirk off his face and he got quiet again.

"You're right. They wouldn't. I shouldn't have been so flippant. I'm sorry."

His apology dropped my anger down a notch.

"Maybe I could have handled things differently, but now that you're here, aren't you curious? Don't you want to know more about your gift and the people you share it with?"

I *was* curious. I'd spent half my life looking for these answers, but I didn't trust him. I crossed my arms and stared at him in silence.

"I can see that you and I have to build some trust—mend some fences, so to speak."

Was that even possible, I wondered?

"Go on, ask me a question," he said, sitting forward, presenting an eager face.

"What's your name?"

"Jackson Delaney—I already told you that. Ask me something else."

"Prove it," I said, and his eager face disappeared under furrowed brows.

He hesitated, then pulled out his wallet and handed me his driver's licence.

It was his photo all right, and his name really was Jackson. Jackson Matthew Delaney. Born 1982. "You're a long way from home," I said, noting his New Orleans address.

"Yes, I am." He held out his hand for the licence. With a solemn look on his face, he returned his wallet to his pocket and leaned back again.

He hadn't lied. Maybe I could stick around long enough to get some answers. "How did you learn about your condition?" I asked. He took a deep breath that sounded a lot like relief.

"I was born this way so I've always known about my *condition* as you so oddly put it. My parents were both Fliers."

I heard the past tense. "They've passed away?"

"Yes, they're both gone now."

"I'm sorry," I said out of habit before I thought how absurd it was to be offering him sympathy. He didn't seem to notice the absurdity and acknowledged the sentiment with a nod of his head.

"Those of us who are born with the gift have night vision from the moment we're born. We've never known what it's like to be night blind. Flight comes later. Usually around puberty, so it differs for everyone, but by fifteen or sixteen, most born Fliers are fully functioning."

"If you're not born a Flier, how else can you become one?" I asked, though I already knew of at least one other way.

"You can be given the gift," he said, then raised his eyebrows questioningly. When I didn't respond he continued. "Or you can steal it. But, regardless of whether it's given or stolen, the person relinquishing the gift forfeits everything: the night vision, the ability to fly, sometimes even more than that." He leaned forward. "The process isn't predictable, so when the transition goes badly, it leaves the donor weak and vulnerable. About half the time, it kills them. Flier history is full of these cautionary tales so, as you can imagine, we don't take too kindly to those who steal the gift."

He sat back, studying me with his chin jutted forward in silent accusation. I said nothing and he continued. "That's why it was important for us to know more about you. Obviously, you weren't a born Flier—you're too old to be as inept as you are. Fortunately for you, neither your history nor our observations of your behaviour led us to believe you stole it. That leaves us to assume that someone gifted it to you. Am I right?"

Did I trust Jackson enough to have this conversation with him? He had kidnapped me, but he hadn't harmed me—yet. He had also said I could leave any time, though how I would accomplish that I had no idea. But I couldn't ignore the fact that he was the only link I'd ever had to discovering more about Jolene's gift. The truth was, I needed him more than he needed me right now, and he already suspected most of what I could add to the conversation anyway.

"Yes, I think so, but I was quite young at the time. I don't remember it very clearly."

"Tell me what you do remember," he asked, leaning forward again, his elbows on his knees, giving me his full attention.

"I was twelve and living in that house you kidnapped me from. I was alone, playing on the beach ..." Saying it out loud felt wrong.

"Go on," he urged.

"I've never told anyone this before."

"That's good. It probably kept you safe. Go on."

But I didn't continue. If keeping quiet about it had kept me safe, then it was probably best that I stay that way.

"Do you remember how Dr. Coulter found you?" he asked. "Your belongings I recovered from the beach?" He leaned in until I couldn't avoid his eyes. "You're not safe out there anymore. I can help you."

Was he right? Maybe he could help me. "A woman named Jolene 'gave me the gift' as you put it. The night vision showed up a few days later. That part's never changed. My dad died a few months after Jolene's visit and then my mother moved us to Toronto."

Jackson frowned. "I don't understand. How could you have had the gift since you were twelve years old and still be so unskilled at flying?"

For some reason, his comments raised my hackles. "Well, unlike you, I didn't have my parents to show me the ropes, and I couldn't tell them. Jolene was very clear that I keep it a secret."

He raised his hand. "Hold up a minute. Where was Jolene?"

I shrugged. "I don't know."

"So what's your connection to her? Is she a family friend?"

"No. I'd never met her before that summer, and I haven't seen her since. Didn't really think about her again until high school when the floating thing started to happen."

"*Floaty* thing?" He said it as if I'd insulted him.

"Floating," I said, correcting him. "Believe me, it wasn't a happy discovery. It got worse when I was at university. The episodes became more frequent and I couldn't predict when they were going to happen. It was inconvenient not to mention embarrassing. That's why I moved back here—why I've been practicing on the beach. I'm trying to learn how to control this thing. You have no idea how difficult it's been for me."

"Well, that explains a lot."

"It does?"

"Yes, except for Jolene." He looked past me, frowning. "Why would she gift you and then not put any support in place for your transition?" He looked back to me. "No wonder you got into trouble—you're lucky you haven't killed yourself."

He studied his clasped hands mulling something over. "I'll do some digging around and see what I can find on Jolene. Do you know her last name?"

"No. She would have been thirty-five or forty at the time, but I might be off about her age. She was pretty with blonde wavy hair." I sat back and thought about Jolene. Could she really have died from giving me her gift? It was unsettling to think about. "Why would a Flier choose to give the gift away?"

"Most of the cases I've heard of involve Fliers who are suffering from a terminal illness. The gifting is always formally documented, so there isn't any question about intent. Like I said, there are repercussions to stealing the gift."

Actually, he hadn't mentioned repercussions, but I was glad that whoever "they" were had been convinced that Jolene had given me the gift.

I felt like the conversation had come to an end. "So, where do we go from here? Will you take me home now?"

"I could," he said, "but I don't think that's a good idea."

"Why not?"

"You're a Flier, Emelynn, and there are people out there who might figure that out. Given your antics, that isn't exactly a stretch. They would be more than happy to get their hands on you. Take my word for it—that would not be a pleasant experience."

"Forgive my skepticism, but I find that a little hard to believe."

"Do you?" he said, straightening. Anger edged his voice. "It's happened before, many times. The latest disappearance happened three months ago when one of the New Orleans covey went missing. We still haven't found her and she's an exceptionally skilled Flier, not to mention intelligent and painfully careful. If they can get her, they can certainly get you."

"Jackson, I don't know what you want me to say. You don't look like a nutbar, but you did kidnap me. You've been spying on me and you kind of creeped me out last night. Granted, you haven't hurt me, at least not yet, but how do I know you're not one of those people you told me I should be so worried about?"

"Hurt you!" He sighed heavily, shaking his head. "You'd know by now if I was your goddamn enemy." He paced in front of me and raked his hands through his hair. "Why the hell did I let Avery talk me into taking you on?" I watched him pull his phone out of his back pocket. "You"—he pointing at me in exasperation—"stay here."

As if I was going anywhere? He turned and headed up top. Could I really be thinking he had a nice butt in those faded jeans? What the hell was wrong with me? That butt was attached to the man who'd abducted me.

This time I didn't follow him.

CHAPTER EIGHT

Twenty minutes later the sound of voices startled me; I hadn't heard another boat arrive, not even one close by. They talked for a while then I heard footfalls descending the stairs. I moved to the side of the room with my back against the wall. Jackson appeared first, followed by a shorter, sturdy man and a tiny woman with short red hair and bright eyes. She reminded me of a pixie except for the fact she was dressed in black from head to foot. The man was dressed similarly. He ran his fingers through brown, windblown hair in a futile attempt to tame it.

Jackson approached with the two in tow. "Eden Effrome, Alex Krause, this is Emelynn Taylor." They looked normal enough. "I've filled Eden and Alex in and they've agreed to help us out." From the look on her face, it seemed this was the last place Eden wanted to be.

I addressed her directly. "Did he tell you he kidnapped me?"

She looked back to Jackson. "Yes, he filled us in."

"And you're okay with that?" I said, the accusation unmistakable as I stared into her troubled eyes.

She shook her head. "You're putting us all in danger, Emelynn. I know you weren't aware of it at the time, but you are." She had difficulty keeping eye contact. "I wish we'd been more subtle with you," she said as she shot Jackson some daggers, "but with one Flier still missing, we couldn't take a chance. We don't have the manpower to go searching for two of you."

"How am I putting you all in danger?" The leap from my being in danger to their being in danger made no sense.

Alex answered. "You're connected to us now, Emelynn, whether you like it or not. If they find you, they'll dig around looking for others. They'll uncover Avery first. Those records are public. Once they find him, they'll find the rest of us. But they might find your family first. That wouldn't turn out well for them. The people we're talking about aren't nice."

Eden nudged Alex. "We're not trying to scare you, Emelynn," she said, trying to soften Alex's words. "Maybe we haven't gotten off to a good start, but we need you to understand the situation we're in. We need you to grasp the serious repercussions your actions have on all of us."

I heaved a sigh. Their logic might have been feasible if I believed the scenario they had described. Either that or Stockholm syndrome was setting in. "I think I need to sit down," I said, and headed to the sofa to gain some balance against the sway of the boat. The three Fliers joined me. "Forgive my naïveté, but exactly who would want to steal this flying thing and why on earth would they want it?" If some schmuck wanted to take this nightmare off my hands, I'd be first in line. Their stunned reaction had me rethinking my question before I'd closed my mouth.

Eden looked to Alex, who answered the question. "Is it so hard to see the allure? The thrill, the power, to say nothing of the freedom?" He rubbed his forehead, letting his words hang in the air. "Fliers are taught from an early age to be unerringly discreet about their gift, so it's unusual for an outsider to learn about us, let alone learn the particulars of how to steal the gift, but it happens. Naturally, the Tribunal is a fairly effective deterrent; no one wants to be in their crosshairs."

Jackson took over. "But the bigger threat comes from people far more dangerous and secretive than rogue thieves. We've long suspected that our own military has had us in their sights, and I can guarantee you if they suspect we exist then the organized crime circuit also suspects. All they need is the physical evidence to prove it.

"These aren't the kind of people that the Tribunal Novem can just eliminate and be done with. These are powerful groups that would love nothing more than to turn us into guinea pigs—see what we can do, and then try to bottle it."

My sane inner voice shook her head. "Oh, come on." Did they think we were in a conspiracy movie? Their stone-faced facades gave me pause. Maybe it was best to keep my thoughts to myself. I plastered a "you don't say" look on my face.

I think Eden was the first to buy my acquiescence. She did her best to lighten what had become an all too serious conversation. "The gift isn't all doom and gloom, Emelynn. There's a reason it's referred to as a gift. Jackson asked us here to help explain our predicament, but we can also show you the upside to all this."

She turned to Alex and Jackson. "I know it's daylight, but I think we should risk a demonstration. Emelynn needs to see what's at stake. We'll be careful," she said, reassuring them both. They nodded.

"Come on." She stood and invited me to join her. "We'll show you."

I followed her up the steps to the upper deck wondering if she and Alex knew Jackson's hovering trick. This time though, I knew what to expect and I'd be watching carefully for clues that would expose the charade. She gestured for me to stand aside. I obliged and walked over to lean against the rail.

Jackson and Alex circled the perimeter, scanning the ocean and sky all around the boat. I arched an eyebrow watching them make a big production out of their surveillance. Who could possibly see us from here?

They took up a position against the rail opposite me. "Okay," Alex said, giving Eden the go ahead.

And then Eden promptly gave me the why behind all their caution. She slipped out of her shoes and, with less effort than a diver on a high board, she took two steps, raised her head, tucked her arms in tight and flung herself into the air. She didn't just hover above the deck as I had expected, nor did she dive down into the water as her motions predicted. Instead, she soared up and over the railing, gracefully arching away from the boat. I watched her fly, and it took my breath away. If there was such a thing as an aerial ballet, she would be the prima ballerina. She made a swimming motion with her arms from time to time as she dipped low to the water then swooped high above us, circling far wide of the boat before looping back down and then up and over the other side. When she cleared the rail behind Jackson, she slowed down, straightened up and landed gracefully, feet first.

Eden's demonstration was simply unbelievable. I stood there thunderstruck, taking in her flushed face, windblown hair and the incredible exuberance she radiated. I felt as though I should clap, but instead I stood there with my mouth open.

Alex didn't wait for me to regain my composure. He took off next and his performance was amazing on a completely different level. He flew with such speed that I lost track of him a few times as he dipped low then soared back much higher than the boat. His flight was quick and athletic, more similar to an Olympic tumbling event than a ballet.

When he returned to the boat he grabbed Eden and spun her around. Jackson watched their affectionate embrace and glanced my way sporting a smile that touched off tiny wrinkles at the corners of his eyes.

"That was impressive," I said, too stunned to stop staring at them. They really could fly. I finally understood their vulnerable predicament, which was more frightening by the prospect that, apparently, I was one of them.

Jackson's voice broke the spell. "There's a good possibility you'll be able to do this too, Emelynn. We don't know for sure, of course. Your development hasn't exactly been typical, but we can try. What do you say?"

"What do I say?" I repeated, incredulously. "I can't fly. I can't even lift off with fifty feet of rope and weights to launch." A seagull screeched overhead as if to emphasize my point. "I think you're overestimating my skills a wee bit."

Jackson chuckled softly. "I think I can help. Do you want to try?"

"How?" I asked.

"If you let me … I can jump-start the process." He studied the cynicism evident on my face. "I've done it before, Emelynn. How do you think I got you here?"

Oh. I hadn't given that disturbing detail any consideration—until now. "Okay, how do we do this then?" I asked just before the voice in my head added, "Welcome aboard the crazy train, Emelynn."

"Come over here." He held his arm out. I joined him. "Turn around." Up close, he was at least half a foot taller than I was. "You need to trust me. I'm going to put my arms around you and when I lift off, you'll lift with me. You don't need to do a thing. Are you ready?"

I hesitated before replying, "All right." Then, as unsure and doubtful as I was, I let this stranger put his arms around me and, incredibly, we lifted off the deck. It was an oddly intimate position for strangers, but given what we were doing, I'm not sure the regular rules of propriety applied. We rose until we hovered over Eden and Alex. I felt that familiar tingling sensation that I associated with floating spread out under my skin.

"How are you doing?" he asked.

"G-Good. My gravity has gone."

"Amazing isn't it?" he said. "If I let go of you now you would stay airborne. If you weren't a Flier, you'd drop straight down. But don't worry, I won't let go. Do you want to circle the ship?"

"Yes," I said, this time without hesitation, and with that, he took me up and over the edge of the boat. I tensed when we cleared the rail and he tightened his grip. He lowered us so we hovered over the water, where a light breeze blew through my hair. I looked down, gauging us to be about ten feet off the surface of that frigid water and shivered. We slowly circled the boat. At the stern, I saw its name, *Aerial Symphony*, spelled out in scroll lettering with "New Orleans" written beneath. We made a full circuit before he headed up and over the rail, gently landing us right where we'd taken off from. The moment he released me, gravity returned.

Eden and Alex awaited my reaction. "That was incredible," I said, hoping I wasn't looking as bewildered as I felt. Wide smiles crept across their faces, the kind that acknowledged a shared secret passion.

"Would you like to learn to do that on your own?" Jackson asked. I think at that moment I would have done anything he asked.

"Yes," I said without pause. "Do you think I can?"

"I don't know, but I think we should try," he replied. "The safest place for us to do that is right here, but not until after dark. There's less chance of someone seeing us then."

"We have to be so careful," Eden added. "We only fly in daylight when we have no other choice. Alex and I will help if you like. We aren't leaving until after dark anyway."

"I'd like that," I replied, but words seemed so inadequate—fireworks would be more appropriate. My thoughts spun out of control. I ended up down the stairs and sitting on the sofa, across from Alex, barely aware we'd moved back to the living room. I had so many questions. They flopped around in my head like fish out of water, too slippery to get a firm hold on.

"Eden?" I sought her out as she gathered up the cold drinks Jackson set out on the counter. "Are your parents Fliers?"

"Yes," she replied, filling glasses with ice from the door of the fridge.

I turned to Alex. "How about yours?"

He stopped flipping through the magazine in his hands. "Yeah, mine too. Actually, you're the first Flier I've met who wasn't born this way."

"How old were you when you started to fly?" I asked, addressing the question to all three of them.

Eden replied first. "I was thirteen, but I was a slow learner. It took a few years to get good enough for my parents to let me fly solo." She sat down beside Alex.

Alex said, "I was fourteen, but I was hell on wheels and there was no holding me back once I got started." Alex patted Eden's thigh and winked at her.

"Jackson?" I asked as he rounded the sofa with the tray of drinks.

"I was like Alex," he said, and gestured toward the tray. "Help yourself." He poured Coke over the ice in his glass then took the drink to the computer and tapped away at the keyboard.

I skipped the icy glass in favour of a bottle of water and cracked off the lid while watching Jackson. What was he doing?

"Emelynn," Eden said, focusing my attention. "I don't mean to pry, but like Alex, I've never met someone who was gifted rather than a born Flier and I'm curious."

"Oh, sure, what do you want to know?"

"Everything. Who, how, when—the whole thing." She and Alex looked expectantly at me from the edges of their seats.

I told them all I knew about Jolene, and just as Jackson had been, they were perplexed by her abandonment of me.

"That can't be how it's supposed to be done," Eden said, more to Alex than to me.

"Can't be," he said, with a shake of his head.

I glanced over my shoulder to see if Jackson was paying attention. From our earlier conversation, I had gotten the impression he knew more about the gifting process, but the computer had his undivided attention.

"How do born Fliers learn to fly?" I asked, unable to picture the process.

"It's like puberty," Eden said. "We didn't really dwell on it when we were growing up. You know it's coming and sometimes it affects you in embarrassing ways, but we all go through it." Eden looked to Alex for his input.

"Yeah, at first you can't control it and you end up flying into stuff. I started indoors until I got control of lifting off and landing, then they let me practice outside. An adult was always there with me until I proved myself. Of course, no self-respecting teenager doesn't test the limits," Alex said with a grin, pulling Eden close.

"Speak for yourself," she said. "I'll have you know I was the poster child for good behaviour."

I was envious. Imagine how different my childhood would have been had I been raised in a similar situation? And what a relief to be able to talk to other people about this burden that I'd been managing on my own for so long.

"The only thing that's never tolerated is behaviour that risks our exposure," Eden said. "That's strictly a no go. Even very young Fliers learn that rule early on."

They were horrified when I told them about the incident in Starbucks and the time in the park walking Dotty. It prompted more questions about Jolene, but I couldn't offer any insight into why she'd targeted me or what had happened to her.

"You must have a fairy godmother," Eden said. "I can't believe you've made it this long without mortal damage. And what if someone had found out about you? You'd have disappeared like the others." Eden furrowed her brow.

"The others?" I asked.

"Yes, eighteen others—three from one family in San Diego," she said, curling into herself. "It's frightening." Alex rubbed her arm soothingly.

"People disappear all the time," I said. "Which is horrible, I know, but what makes you think these Flier disappearances aren't just the everyday kind?" God that sounded harsh, but really, missing people were in the news all the time.

"Some of them might be, it's possible, but we're Fliers." Alex spoke as if I would appreciate his exception, which wasn't the case.

"I'm sorry, Alex, I don't understand."

"Fliers are hard to abduct. You can bind our hands and feet and we can still hover and fly, and you've already had a taste of Jackson's skills, so you know first-hand how much damage we can do when pushed."

I blanched recalling how Jackson had incapacitated me in mere moments. "Oh," I said as the reality of his words sank in, wiping the doubt from my face.

"About two years ago—" Eden started, but Jackson, whose attention had suddenly returned to our conversation, turned in his chair, abruptly cutting her off.

"How about we spare Emelynn the worst-case scenario," he said, holding Eden's gaze with a cautionary expression before turning his attention to me. "I think she knows how important secrecy is to us."

Despite Jackson's smile, and the casual manner he adopted as he walked back to the sofa, tension was evident in the muscles that twitched along his jaw, and his smile didn't touch his eyes.

"Sorry, man," Alex said. Jackson dismissed him with a wave of his hand.

They might have wanted this exchange to disappear, but I was curious now, not only about the missing Fliers, but about why Jackson didn't want me to know the details. And why was Alex apologizing to him? Tension stymied our conversation.

Since no one else spoke, I broke the awkward silence. "How did you two meet?" I asked of Eden and Alex, happy for a lighter topic.

Eden snickered. "That's a funny story. He told you he likes to test limits, right?" she said, smiling at Alex, who rolled his eyes and leaned back against the sofa. "We met in Emerg in Seattle. I was working the night Alex came in. We all thought he was a drug addict on a binge because he showed all the classic signs, but turns out he was just working without a mask—testing the paint-fume limit of an enclosed space." She smirked over her shoulder at him and whispered loudly, "That's what happened to him," which provoked the desired reaction.

He reached forward, wrapped both his hands around her neck and pulled her back to him then licked up the side of her face. "But you love it," he said as she squealed her delight.

Now, not only was I envious of their Flier upbringing, I was also envious of their relationship. I wanted that. God, how I wanted to feel that connection with someone.

We carried on our discussion and I learned that Eden and Alex were both originally from Seattle, where their families still lived. Eden was a nurse and worked shifts at the hospital in Richmond and Alex did custom paintwork, mostly on motorcycles, out of his own small shop. Gradually, the conversation waned and our individual attentions wandered.

Eden and Jackson went into the kitchen to fix us something to eat. I heard Eden ask Jackson where he kept things. As they prepared sandwiches, I strolled over to the extensive bookcase on the wall opposite the TV and ran my fingers along the spines. It was a large and varied collection.

The fiction interests included some classics such as Tolstoy's *War and Peace* and a well-worn copy of Jane Austen's *Pride and Prejudice*. There were also a surprising number of self-help and romance titles alongside Sara Gruen's *Water for Elephants* and John Berendt's *Midnight in the Garden of Good and Evil*. Biographies of American presidents and Canada's Group of Seven mingled with books on art history and architecture. The reference books covered everything from how to identify birds of the Pacific Northwest to the flora and fauna of Texas and Louisiana. Was Jackson responsible for the eclectic collection? I removed a coffee table book on orca and brought it back to the sofa.

Jackson made another swing by the computer before he helped Eden carry the plate of sandwiches and more drinks over to the coffee table. Eden handed Alex a napkin and plate as I helped myself to half a ham and cheese and a bottle of water then sat back, balancing the plate on my lap while I unfurled a napkin.

"I'm not having any luck finding a Flier by the name of Jolene," Jackson said. Ah, so that's what he'd been doing on the computer. "It's a fairly unique name, which made me think it would be easy to find. I've put out some feelers so maybe something will come in later."

"You have a directory of Fliers?" I asked.

"Yeah, something like that," he said, but offered no further explanation as he leaned in to take a sandwich. He swiped at the dark curls that tumbled into his eyes, reminding me of another question.

"What's that thing you do with your eyes, Jackson?" I asked. "What you did to me on the beach last night?" He looked up at me then, and I recalled the debilitating effect of those pale hazel eyes.

Embarrassment crossed his face. "Most Fliers can do that, Emelynn, not just me, though perhaps I've got more options than others." He glanced at Alex, who nodded in agreement. "You, however, being a Flier, shouldn't have been as susceptible as you were."

"So, what is it?" I asked.

"It's complicated," he said, chewing his sandwich and his thoughts. "Basically, it's a manipulation of both the adrenal glands and the nervous system. We use either our eyes or touch, or a combination of the two. What I did was cause an overload in your system. It results in a temporary loss of consciousness—no permanent damage." He looked contrite until he added, "It's a useful skill." Then he just looked cold.

Did he intend to be callous? "Useful skill?" I asked.

"Yes. Having the ability to immobilize someone is like having a built-in stun gun. It gives me an advantage."

"Good to know," I said. His "advantage" left me feeling vulnerable. I changed the subject.

"What's a covey?" I asked. "You mentioned it earlier."

"It's how we refer to groups of Fliers. There's safety in numbers, so we generally associate with a home covey and we'll make ourselves known to local coveys when we travel."

"Are you all members of the local covey?" I asked.

"Eden and Alex are, but I'm just visiting."

"Speaking of that," Alex interjected, "any word on Sandra?"

Jackson shot him a look that was easy to interpret. He didn't want to discuss this in front of me.

I asked Jackson directly, "Is she the one you mentioned earlier who's gone missing?"

Jackson nodded his answer to me then turned back to Alex, shaking his head with a heavy sigh. "Not since last week." Jackson took another bite of his sandwich then continued. "She's still headed north. Her cellphone's off and there's no new activity on her credit cards."

This was enlightening. Evidently, Jackson had the infrastructure in place to perform a pretty extensive monitoring operation. I wondered how you set something like that in motion. It was either fascinating or disturbing, depending on which side you were on. It also went a long way to explaining how he had learned so much about me.

"How do you know that Sandra is heading north?" I asked.

He looked right at me but didn't answer. Alex looked from him to me. Finally, Jackson spoke. "I'm not comfortable talking about Sandra." He set his half-eaten sandwich back on his plate and pushed it away from the edge of the coffee table. He rested his elbows on his knees and rubbed his forehead.

"Can't the police help?" I asked. This couldn't be the first time they'd thought of that, surely.

"Not so far," he said, "and please, Emelynn, I don't want to discuss Sandra."

Clearly, but I didn't understand. "What about this *Tribunal* you mentioned. Can't they help?"

Immediately three sets of eyes shot over to me.

"No, they can't help," Jackson blurted out, more forcefully than I thought necessary. He rose from the sofa, hands on his hips, and exhaled an angry breath.

"O ... kay," I said. Apparently, the Tribunal was off limits.

I was about to ask another question when Jackson raised his hand to stop me. "Emelynn, I know you are interested and curious, but you're going to have to believe me when I say that the less you know, the better. This is a dangerous game and I've already exposed you to more information than I should. Let's just work on getting your flying skills up to par so you can take care of yourself."

Eden was looking at Jackson when she said, "He's right, Emelynn." She hesitated, checking Jackson's reaction carefully before she looked back to me. "Forget about Sandra."

I finished my sandwich and returned to flipping through the orca book.

"Emelynn, why don't you go below to your cabin and get some rest. It's going to be a long night and you'll want to be fresh and sharp." Jackson wasn't being kind. I had just been dismissed.

Taking my cue without argument, I headed out of the room and down the stairs. When I got to the bottom I could hear the three of them talking in my wake. I paused, feigning interest in something under my foot, hoping the ruse would cover my eavesdropping activities from the camera that blinked its attention. They weren't exactly arguing, but unmistakable tension rode their words. Jackson seemed to be admonishing them, but their words were muffled. I gave up and headed to my cabin.

Lying on the bed, I let my thoughts roam. I resented being dismissed like the help. And what was it that Eden had been about to tell me before Jackson cut her off? They didn't trust me and that bothered me more than I wanted it to.

I should be absolutely thrilled for all I'd learned this afternoon. A part of me was, but the euphoric lift was tempered by uneasy feelings of vulnerability. This Flier world wasn't all sweetness and light: Fliers were disappearing. Why were they trying so hard to keep the details from me? Did they suspect Sandra was already captive and spewing secrets, putting us all at risk? What exactly had I stepped into?

I had no doubt they were discussing it right now. Jackson didn't send me down here to rest—he wanted me out of earshot and that only fuelled my curiosity. What were they hiding?

The bed was undeniably comfortable and that rocking sensation had a lulling effect, but my head was spinning. There was no way I was going to be able to turn it off and get to sleep.

CHAPTER NINE

I felt momentarily disoriented when I opened my eyes, astonished that I'd managed to drift off. The tiny porthole windows gave me a glimpse of the darkening sky. It was dusk, that magical time when the blue glow of nightlight replaces the golden glow of daylight. I left the bed, made a quick visit to the head then climbed the stairs, dismally aware that my budding relationship with the three Fliers was hanging by a mistrustful thread.

Eden and Alex sat with their backs to me. Jackson sat across from them. They talked quietly around the coffee table in the living room. "How are you doing?" Jackson asked when I approached.

"Fine thanks. I slept."

"Good. It'll be dark enough to start in another thirty minutes or so." The dismissive edge he'd had in his voice earlier was gone.

Eden turned to face me. "We've been trying to figure out how to teach you the basics, and we think we've come up with a plan."

As much as I wanted to feel connected to Eden and the others, I thought it best to keep them at arm's length. I needed them, so I'd play along, but as soon as I learned how to control this thing, I was out of here.

"Oh?" I said as I sat down. "What did you come up with?" No one seemed to notice my guarded demeanour.

Eden talked and the more detail she revealed about learning to fly, the more fascinated I became. She talked about liftoffs and landings; hovering and manoeuvring; and the effects of wind, speed and resistance. It was both exciting and terrifying.

Their first order of business was getting me to rethink how I would achieve liftoff. According to Eden, it was the most critical element and also the most elusive.

Jackson went over it again. "It's not a physical thing, Emelynn, it's psychological. Forget about your ropes and weights—they aren't remotely connected to the process. Jolene gave you an innate power and it resides deep inside you. You need to find that power and tap into it."

Alex added, "You need to train yourself to mentally throw off your gravity. Once you have it mastered, it takes only a moment of effort."

"I have no idea how to do what you're asking," I said, already frustrated.

"Neither do we," Eden said, "so be patient with us. We all learned to fly like we learned to walk so it's second nature to us. Trying to break it down into 'How-to' steps is tricky."

"If we don't get there right away, don't worry—I can always jumpstart you like I did before," Jackson offered. "But you need to work on it. Like Eden said, it's absolutely paramount."

"It might help if you find something to associate it with," Eden said. "When I was young, I visualized a white feather. I don't know where that came from, but it's always been a part of flight for me. When I visualize that white feather, it pulls the magic right out of me. It's not something I do consciously anymore, but I always know it's there."

Eden smiled reassuringly. "We all had the benefit of years of preparation before we did it. No one expects you to master this in one night, Emelynn."

"Besides," Alex said, "all this great advice will have to sink in before you're able to use it." He winked at me and that helped lighten my mood. "Let's just try to have some fun with it."

We headed up the stairs to the top deck, which Jackson called the "observation deck," and formed a small circle away from cover.

"Here," Jackson said, handing me an elastic hair band. "Tie your hair back." I frowned at him. "So it doesn't get in your face." He motioned impatiently as I complied. How does a guy who doesn't use one come up with a hair elastic? I wondered.

Eden reached over and squeezed my hand. She couldn't have weighed more than a hundred pounds or been more than five feet tall, but that head of spiky red hair made her seem larger than life. "Watch us as we each lift off. We'll go through the motions slowly. With any luck, you'll see something in our liftoffs that will provide a trigger for you."

Jackson went first, making it look absolutely effortless. With his hands straight down at his sides, he tilted his head back and then he was in the air. He stabilized a few feet above the deck, his hair wafting forward in a breeze. He really did need a haircut.

"My turn," Eden said. She put more effort into it. She extended her arms away from her body by a few inches, palms out. She had her chin tucked in and her head down. She lifted her head in a fluid movement at the same time as her palms turned inward and her arms pulled flat into her body, and then she was airborne. She settled into a smooth hover beside Jackson.

"Now me." Alex lifted his head, reached up with his right hand and his whole body followed in one single motion. He, too, made it look easy.

The three of them hovered above the deck, looking down at me.

I returned the collective gaze with apprehension. "Now I suppose you think it's my turn," I said, nervous about the prospect.

"Come on, give it a shot," Alex said.

Ah, what the hell. Nothing was going to change if I just stood here feeling like an idiot.

I tried Jackson's method first. I planted my feet and stood still with my arms down at my sides then raised my head to the heavens, praying that my body would follow suit. But predictably, it didn't.

"So much for Jackson's approach," I said, as I prepared to mimic Eden's.

I planted my feet farther apart, positioning my arms slightly out from my body, palms out, head down, chin in. I even tried to visualize the white feather as I swept my head up and moved my arms in tight to my body. The result wasn't a surprise.

"Two down," I said, and looked hopefully up at Alex.

Again, I planted my feet, lowered my head and positioned my arms. With a fluid movement, I raised my right arm straight above my head at the same time as I swept my head upward. I even jumped, but it didn't help. I exhaled heavily and hung my head.

"Don't sweat it, Emelynn," Jackson said, landing back on the deck. "It'll come, just give it some time. Meanwhile, let's get you up in the air. It's not like we don't have anything else to teach you." He smiled as he came around behind me. "Ready?" I nodded, too disheartened to speak. He wrapped his arms around my waist and lifted me up. The moment cool air brushed the soles of my feet, gravity left me and my spirits lifted instantaneously.

"Will you take me around the boat again?" I asked.

"Sure," he said. "Hold on." I crossed my arms over his as he pulled us up and over the railing. Given the mistrust between us, it shouldn't have felt so good to have his arms around me. He flew faster than before and by the time we'd come full circle, my resolve to keep him at arm's length had crumbled. He brought me back around, facing Eden and Alex, about a metre off the deck. That tingle under my skin was back, in force.

"Now remember, you're a Flier, so when I release you, you'll stay afloat. Here, hold my hand." He unfolded his right arm, holding it out in front of me. I grasped it then he slowly unfurled his other arm, releasing all but my hand into the cool night air.

What do you know—he was right. I held his hand and floated right alongside him. I was jerky though, trying to find my balance. It was like my first time on ice skates. Even the slightest movement produced a new round of lurch and rebalance.

A smile stretched across my face as I looked down past my dangling feet to the deck below. I looked over at Eden and Alex with that wide smile in place and it must have been infectious because they both smiled back in kind.

"So," Jackson said, drawing our attention. "We thought we should start with Flying 101 and teach you some basic manoeuvres. You know how to swim, right?"

"Sure," I said.

"Good, that'll help," Alex said, taking over the lesson. "When young Fliers ... or, I guess I should say, new Fliers, are starting out, they're often taught to make motions that closely mimic swimming. I'll show you what I mean." He made a slow breaststroke motion and I watched his body glide forward in response, just as it would if he were in water. Then he moved his arms straight out in front, hands in the classic "stop" position to slow the motion before turning back to face us.

"A word of caution though," he said. "Up here, away from gravity, motion is extremely sensitive. It doesn't take much effort to produce big results. Watch and see what I mean." This time he put some muscle behind his breaststroke and not only shot ahead but also pitched forward, horizontally, and he kept on going. I watched him twist his shoulder, leaning to the right, and that motion brought him back around to us. He slowed himself using his arms again.

Jackson looked over at me expectantly. "You ready to give it a try?"

I stole a glance at the water below, took a deep breath, and nodded. "Just don't let me fall."

Eden quickly reassured me. "We won't. Alex and I will flank you and Jackson will position himself ahead of you. We'll be your training wheels, okay?"

"Okay," I said, preparing myself as they assumed their positions.

"I'm going to release you now," Jackson said, facing me as he loosened his hand.

When he let go, I started all over again doing the spastic lurch and jerk while they waited patiently for me to find my balance. "All right, I think I'm ready."

Jackson was front and centre, motioning me forward.

I made the tiniest breaststroke imaginable and moved forward—granted, not very far, but even that much was exciting.

"That's a start. Now increase the effort," Jackson said, moving backwards as he continued motioning me forward.

My next breaststroke was stronger and had me moving forward fast enough that Jackson had to reach out and put his hands on my shoulders to slow me down.

"That's good, now a little more." Jackson motioned me on again.

This time, I gave it a solid effort, comfortable that Jackson could stop me if I coasted too far. What a thrill ride. I sailed forward and leaned quite naturally into an almost horizontal position. Jackson was right there, keeping pace then slowing me down.

It wasn't until we stopped that I became aware of how far from the boat we'd travelled, how high we were. I stared down, wide-eyed. My lungs constricted, making it hard to breathe.

"I've got you." Jackson wrapped an arm around me then rapidly moved us back to our starting position over the boat. "Let's take a break." He lowered us to the deck. Alex and Eden were right beside us and I couldn't hide how shaky I was when Jackson released me. "It takes some getting used to," he said. "The height, the movement, all of it."

I looked over to Eden. She and Alex nodded their agreement.

Jackson turned me around and bent his stern face close. "Panic is not your friend up there. It makes you do crazy things, like pinwheel your arms. Big, rapid movements like that are dangerous."

The danger was painfully familiar. I acknowledged his concern with a nod. He straightened up and guided me to the sofas, with Alex and Eden following closely behind.

It was a relief to have something solid under me again. I stretched my feet out to the coffee table and stared up at the cloudless sky. The vast carpet of stars twinkled brightly out here—the happy result of not having to compete with city lights. It was the same when I looked up from the deck of the cottage. The other three started a quiet conversation, but I was lost in my daydreams about the cottage and flying and didn't pay them any mind.

"What do you say, Emelynn?" Jackson said, pulling me away from my thoughts and obviously repeating himself. "You want to give it another try?"

"Sure," I said, and we moved back to our original positions on the boat deck.

Once again, Jackson moved behind me. "Ready?" he asked, and then we were back in the air, Eden and Alex right beside us.

The moment he released me, we started all over again. We ran through the forward movement drill several more times before they thought it was a good idea that I learn how to stop myself.

They persisted. Soon I was using my outstretched arms with my hands bent in the stop position to slow myself. Sometimes, I would assert too much effort with one arm or the other, which would tip me into either Eden or Alex, but I was getting the hang of it.

We moved on to learn how to change direction. This manoeuvre proved the hardest yet. It involved shifting my posture and leaning my shoulder in the direction I wanted to travel. Getting the right amount of momentum was tricky. More than once I sent myself pitching forward. If it weren't for my *training wheels*, I would have tumbled out of the sky.

Alex checked his watch. "It's one in the morning. Let's call it a night." I blinked in disbelief. I'd been so wrapped up in what I was doing, I'd lost track of the time.

Jackson moved behind me, folded his arms around my waist and guided our descent to the boat deck. This time, when he released me, gravity returned—not as I'd become accustomed to, but with a force I wasn't expecting. I would have fallen to my knees if Jackson hadn't anticipated my reaction and gripped my arms.

"Don't be alarmed," he said. "Until you get used to it, gravity will play tricks on you. It comes back with more force the longer you've gone without it. You'll be fine in a moment."

When I was steady, we headed below deck. Jackson rummaged around in the fridge and handed out bottled water.

Eden said, "We need to keep working on the basics, maybe add in some altitude changes."

"I agree," Alex said.

"Let's do some hovering, too. She's holding pretty steady when Jackson lets her go," Eden said. The other two nodded their agreement.

It was strange to hear them talk as if I were in another room. I guess they weren't that far off the mark. Part of me wasn't in the room—it was back at the cottage.

"I hate to bring this up," I said, "but I have to go home. I need to check my email and if I don't call my mother soon, she's going to worry about me."

It was a simple enough request, so their reaction caught me off guard.

"Yes, of course ... but it's too late, tonight," Jackson said. The three of them exchanged conspiratorial glances that chilled me. Evidently, this topic had been discussed earlier, in my absence. "We're too far from shore, and we don't have any way to get you off the ship right now." Jackson's reasons sounded a lot like excuses and I frowned.

"Alex and I will be back tomorrow after dark," Eden said. "We'll go then. How's that?" Eden's eyebrows shot up in a hopeful expression, but I didn't offer agreement. Something about how they were looking at one another, as if I couldn't be trusted, really irked me. If anyone should feel mistrustful, I should.

Jackson said, "In the morning, we'll get your email set up on board and you can call your mom from my phone." The tension in Jackson's jaw was at odds with the relaxed facade he was trying to pull off.

"Tomorrow night, we'll go to your house, you can pack a bag. Then we'll move offshore again so we can continue your training here on the ship, safely out of sight." Jackson presented the plan in such a casual manner, one might think he was graciously accommodating me, but I saw it differently: it was designed to keep me in their sights and under their control.

I'd been right. I needed to keep them at arm's length. I was still a hostage, still at their mercy. What the hell was wrong with me? God, I had told these people, virtual strangers, things I'd never discussed with anyone. When was I going to learn not to reach out? All I ever got in return was my hand slapped.

Eden and Alex gathered their things. "We'll be back tomorrow night, Emelynn," Eden said, forcing a smile. "Wouldn't it be great if you managed a liftoff? You know, give Jackson a break." I'm sure she was trying to dispel the tension my silence had introduced. It didn't work.

Jackson said goodbye to the pair and they left as quietly as they'd arrived. Flying, I presumed.

Jackson disappeared below deck and returned with a T-shirt. He handed it to me. "Something for you to sleep in."

He locked the outside doors and led me back down to the lower level. "That's my stateroom," he said, pointing to a door at the end of the hall. "Just knock if you need anything." He turned to leave but hesitated. "You've made a lot of progress today. Sleep well." He then headed to his room. I heard a click as his door closed.

Talk about a crappy ending to a great day. Crappy because I was pissed off that they didn't trust me, but great because I finally knew what I was.

I undressed and took a quick shower, then pulled on Jackson's T-shirt and climbed into bed. I recognized his scent on the shirt and thought about how many times he'd had his arms around me. I'd never given it a thought before, but now I wondered, when was the last time someone held me, touched me? My mother hugged me when I left Toronto, but before that? I couldn't remember. Was it me? Did I throw off a "don't touch me" vibe?

I listened to the soft slap of water against the hull, mulling over the events of the past thirty-six hours. What did I really know about these people, other than their names? It was obvious they wanted me on a short leash, but why? Did they think I'd escape? Go to the police? I suppose if I were them, it would be a consideration. But was it something darker than that? Fliers were disappearing—they'd said it themselves. Maybe the danger was closer than they'd let on. Jackson hadn't wanted Eden to tell me the details. Were they coddling me? What else were they keeping from me, and why?

So many unanswered questions and there wasn't a thing I could do about it. Eventually, I'd learn the truth. Meantime, I'd do better to concentrate on the positive things—like the fact I now had the answers for which I'd spent years searching. Maybe I'd overreacted and they weren't being unreasonable in the trust department. We'd only known each other a few hours. Maybe a good dose of mistrust was a healthy survival instinct for all of us at this juncture.

Eden seemed nice enough. She was a peacemaker and it was hard not to like that in a person, unless of course she was just spackling over the ugly parts. Her excitement about flying was positively infectious and she'd been kind to me, sympathetic.

Alex was more serious, but once in a while his enthusiasm burst through and when it did, he lit up. But only for brief moments. As soon as he realized his enthusiasm was showing, he pulled that serious mantle back down. With him, I got more of a sense of loyalty: to his covey and to Eden.

Jackson was harder for me to figure out. I had mixed feelings about him; he'd spied on me and kidnapped me, and he didn't trust me. Yet at the same time, he'd made himself vulnerable by revealing his identity and exposing the Flier world to me. Now he was helping me learn how to fly. He was a real contradiction—a tall, dark, brooding, secretive, moody contradiction, who I found oddly compelling.

It occurred to me that my life would never be the same. There was no turning back. I had learned more about Jolene's legacy in the past few hours than I had in the many long years since I'd acquired it. All of my previous efforts to control it had been eclipsed in one evening. Funny how life-altering change can happen in the blink of an eye—especially in the blink of the mesmerizing pale hazel ones I imagined as I drifted off to sleep.

CHAPTER TEN

The new day shone brightly through the small porthole windows. It was after ten by the time I got out of bed. I caught a glimpse of myself in the mirror. Bed-head. My morning laugh, but it didn't seem quite as funny here as it did staring back at me from my own bathroom mirror. I dressed and made my way upstairs. Jackson sat at the computer with his back to me and turned around when he heard me approach. His hair was wet and combed straight back. It changed his look from casual to formal, as if he should be wearing a tux and not yesterday's faded jeans. He would look fabulous in a tux.

"Good morning. How'd you sleep?" he asked, looking at me as if gauging how much my attitude might have thawed overnight. He wore a torso-hugging T-shirt that gathered in folds overlapping the waistband of his jeans.

"Fine, thank you." I was inclined to give him some slack this morning. A good night's rest had helped me gain perspective. We still had trust issues, but the bottom line was that I needed them.

"Coffee's ready," he said, holding his own steaming mug.

I helped myself to a cup and carried it to the sofa. "What are you working on?" I asked, gesturing to the computer.

His expression morphed into annoyance. "Seeing if there's any news," he said, prompting me to think he hadn't slept as well as I had.

Surely he could give me a tad more information than that. "Sandra news?" I prompted. "Jolene news?"

"My San Francisco contacts may have a lead on Jolene's identity, but nothing solid yet. Are you hungry?"

"Sure, I could eat," I said, noticing the change of subject.

We had fruit salad and toast. Our scant breakfast conversation was strained and of the "nothing important" variety—especially nothing about Sandra or any other missing Fliers.

It took a bit of conversational fumbling, but we finally found a topic he was happy to talk about: boats. After he got over the fact that I knew nothing about boating, despite living so close to the ocean, he helped me with some terminology. I learned that the living room is referred to as the salon, bedrooms are staterooms or cabins, and maps are charts. He even taught me a nifty way to remember which side of the boat was port and which was starboard.

"Think of a drunken sailor complaining, 'There's no red port left.' Then you'll remember the left side is port and the port-side navigation light is red."

"Would you like a tour?" He stood and gestured behind the galley.

Those doors had been locked yesterday, so maybe Jackson was making some headway in the trust department. The chartroom was the size of a closet and housed a bank of wide, shallow drawers. Its top lay hidden under large paper charts. More neatly rolled charts poked out from cubbyholes beside the drawers.

He opened the door to the crew quarters. "I hire crew for everything from cooking to fish guiding to piloting, depending on who's with me and where I'm going. The *Symphony*'s 102 feet, so I can't always manage her by myself." Two narrow double bunks crowded the room that also housed a built-in tallboy chest against one wall and a louvred closet door on the other.

He closed the door behind us and we returned to the galley, a term I was having difficulty remembering to use in place of "kitchen." I resumed my barstool seat while he cleaned up. He put the leftover salad back in the fridge then washed our dishes. He seemed preoccupied, having gone quiet as he wiped down the counters then slowly dried the dishes with a painfully thorough tea towel routine.

He didn't look at me when he spoke. "I know we got off to a rocky start, but I hope you now understand why I brought you here."

He wiped the counter—again, stalling. Finally, he looked at me. "I also hope you know that you're safe here and we're not going to hurt you." He continued to fuss unnecessarily. "It's important, Emelynn. You need to learn how to fly and you need to learn quickly. The safest place for you to do that is right here."

Something was troubling him.

"Do you trust me?" he asked, and my intuition twitched. Trust—that was it.

"I'd like to, but if you don't mind, I think I'll hold off on that until I know you better." His eyes grew wide and my intuition vibrated. "In the meantime, I'm willing to give you the benefit of the doubt."

Then it clicked. The tables had indeed turned. I took the direct approach. "You're worried about the phone call to my mother. The one you promised me last night. You're afraid I'll say something." Judging by his reaction, I'd touched the right nerve.

"I won't break my promise. You should call her. She might be worried about you. But I want you to make the call right here."

"Now who's the one with trust issues?" I said, and laughed out loud. He was squirming and though I knew it wasn't gracious, I got more than a little satisfaction from his discomfort.

"Where's the phone?" I asked, holding out my palm across the counter.

He pulled it out of his back pocket and passed it to me, but didn't let go. "You said you'd give me the benefit of the doubt," he reminded me. "I'm counting on you to keep your word." He released the phone but didn't move. As if to emphasize his point, he folded his arms and stood his ground.

I dialled my mother's lab in Toronto, turning my back to him as I slid off my chair and moved toward the sofa. Much to my disappointment, I got her answering machine. I left an upbeat message reassuring her that I was away from the house, but fine. I added, with emphasis, that I would call her again soon. I turned back to make sure Jackson had heard that part and nearly jumped out of my skin. He was right behind me.

"Jesus!" I yelped. "You could have warned me."

"And spoil my fun?" He smirked, clearly pleased with himself. He reached for the phone and I handed it over. "Don't take it personally. I don't trust anyone—learned that the hard way. Let's get underway," he said, pocketing the phone.

He turned away, and I was left wondering who had burned him, and had it been business or personal? I would have asked but knew there was zero chance of an answer.

I tagged behind asking questions about the gadgets and switches he flipped, seemingly at random.

"Why don't you put those dishes away?" he said, forcing a tight smile. He turned his back and went outside to weigh anchor. It was a noisy endeavour. His effort to get me out of his way gave me an opportunity to snoop in the cupboards. His well-stocked galley disproved my preconceived notion of a guy's kitchen offering no more than beer, pickles and, on a good day, cheese.

When he returned, I poured the last of the coffee and handed him his mug. His hair had dried and was once again falling into his eyes. I caught myself thinking that I shouldn't find him so attractive.

"Come on," he said, and I followed him up to the observation deck.

The engines rumbled to life and I strolled to the stern to see what was happening under all the noise. The ocean frothed white and swirled out behind us as the engines revved up. The ride was smoother than I had expected, given our increasing speed. I easily wandered about on the deck with no fear of losing my balance in the boat's movement. Jackson looked at ease in one of the tall captain's chairs, his attention divided between steering and keeping his eye on two different computer screens. I glanced at the compass, noting our southeast bearing.

I reclaimed my coffee and settled onto the forward-facing sofa with my feet tucked under me, looking out at nothing but ocean and a distant land mass. This was almost as good as the view from the deck of the cottage. Thinking about it made me miss it more. A lifetime had passed since I'd landed on the *Symphony*. I looked forward to going home again, back to my sanctuary.

The next hour melted away in our wake as the waves, the birds and the ever-changing horizon competed for my attention. When the boat started to slow, the shore came into view. I could see a vast green space on the far right of the land mass that had to be Sunset Park. If I was right, then the tiny specks to the left of the park were houses.

Twenty minutes later, we had slowed to a crawl. Jackson passed me the binoculars. The tiny specks had grown to the size of matchboxes and indeed one of them was my cottage. It looked so insignificant from here.

Jackson got busy again once we stopped moving. He disappeared below and I soon heard the noise of the anchor. When the engines became quiet, I joined him below.

"Are we ready to go?" I asked. It was just after lunch and I was anxious to go home.

"A few more hours. We need to wait until dark," he said, reminding me.

It was a restless wait. Jackson was quiet and poor company. He looked like a man with a lot on his mind. We passed the time making tuna salad sandwiches and small talk, but I was the one who did most of the talking.

What I really wanted to talk about was Jackson. He knew an awful lot about me and I knew virtually nothing about him. He proved quite adept at deflecting my questions, but I was determined and pressed on through his reticence. It was frustrating, but he finally relented. He had either figured out that I wasn't easily deterred, or it may have had something to do with my bringing up the notion of trust over and over again.

"I was raised in New Orleans," he said. "My parents were both Fliers."

"Have they been gone for long?" I asked.

"Mom died when I was fifteen. Dad passed last year." A heavy sadness settled on his shoulders. His father's death was still a fresh wound. He was quiet for a minute and I thought I'd lost him again but then he straightened up. "Dad left me this ship. He really loved her. We had some great times here and now I've made her my home." That explained the well-stocked kitchen. His face brightened and he looked around the salon with a contented smile on his face.

I pressed on. "Do you have sisters or brothers?"

"No." He spit out the one-word answer. All the animation that had lit his face when he talked about the *Symphony* disappeared. Talk about stepping on a conversational land mine.

And he completely shut me down when I turned my questions to the missing Sandra. I'd asked how she'd been taken and what her connection was to the group here. He clenched his jaw in a stubborn line making it clear I wasn't going to get any more information out of him.

This time, he changed the subject. "Let's get your email access functioning." The muscles in the side of his jaw twitched as he fired up the computer. He had already set up a guest user account. My bet was the guest user on this computer didn't have access to much. "I'll leave you to it," he said, surrendering his chair.

He had given me access to one webmail URL. Wow! I'd have to try not to wear out my welcome. I opened my email account and deleted the usual junk mail offering cheap Viagra and low-interest mortgage loans. Molly had sent an email saying she'd had a great time at dinner in Seaside and wanted to set up another dinner date. I replied with a quick "me too and yes, let's do that again soon." The last one was from my mother. I crafted a reply that would ensure she wouldn't worry about me.

Before I shut it down, I explored Jackson's computer system. I didn't get far. Everything was either password protected or flat out "access denied." He'd been thorough and my woeful computer skills were no match.

It was hours away from darkness and Jackson had made himself scarce. I headed to the sofa and flipped through a magazine, but nothing caught my interest. I had flying on my mind—pretty stiff competition. There was nothing quite like it and I couldn't wait to learn more. Hmm, I thought, looking around. There was enough space right here to practice liftoffs. If it worked, I might bump my head on the ceiling, but no one was around to laugh at me. What the hell.

Standing in a bare patch of floor, I copied Eden's liftoff motions. I gave it a couple of earnest tries before switching to Alex's method. When that was likewise fruitless, I replicated Jackson's moves.

I thought about Eden's white feather. Maybe I needed a talisman. I figured it would have to be something meaningful and probably also represent flight. Trouble was, I was coming up with a great big blank on that front.

Discouraged, I sat down and went back to flipping through the magazine. At least I was going home tonight, and thoughts of the cottage lifted my spirits. I looked forward to getting out of the clothes I'd been wearing for three days straight.

Jackson eventually reappeared. He had those soft creases you get on your face when you first lift your head off the pillow. Maybe his mood had improved with the nap. He had also changed into black jeans with a dark turtleneck. He read a *New Yorker* magazine while we waited for night to fall.

Before too long, we were basking in the bluish glow that signalled darkness. I heard gentle thumps as Alex and Eden boarded the observation deck. Their quiet conversation preceded them. We said our hellos, but I couldn't sit still. I jumped to my feet like a jack-in-the-box, anxious to set out.

"So, what's the plan for getting me home?" I asked as I shifted from one foot to the other. Jackson sighed heavily. He didn't appear eager to get on with leaving the boat.

He spoke like a sergeant major. "I'm going to escort you to shore. Eden will come with us. Alex will stay here. You pack enough clothes for a few more days. We can do laundry here." His staccato proclamations didn't leave a lot of room for alternatives. Apparently, the nap hadn't worked. "We're going to get you in and back out quickly, and then we need to head offshore away from prying eyes."

"Let's go then," I said, and turned toward the stairs. Jackson followed but with considerably less enthusiasm. Eden and Alex were right behind.

Jackson called me over and I turned my back to him as he wrapped his arms around me. It was already a familiar move. We lifted off without any obvious effort and headed up and over the boat's rail. Eden was right beside us.

The night air was cool and damp. Jackson flew faster than he had on our trip around the boat last night. My hair blew into his face and I felt his body jerk as he tossed his head aside to get it out of his way.

He spoke close to my ear. "I should have reminded you to tie your hair back."

"Sorry," I said. "I'll do it when I get home."

We approached the cottage from the south and he landed us on a slab of sandstone. That was my longest flight yet and it had been exhilarating.

Jackson stayed close as he released me. "Brace yourself," he said before he let go. I was glad for the warning. Gravity returned with force. At least this time I knew it was coming, and just like before, after a few moments, I was steady again.

We headed up the steps. Eden rested against the rail of the deck looking out toward where the *Symphony* waited offshore.

The big patio door was unlocked. "You could have at least locked it when you snatched me," I said.

Jackson looked unapologetic. "Let me check it out," he said, stepping inside ahead of me. He quickly scoped out the living room and kitchen then ducked into the bedroom. I watched him leave my room and head down the hall toward the bathroom.

"What a gorgeous view," Eden said before she turned to follow me inside. "No wonder you love this place." She walked to the bookcase and ran her hand over the wood. She looked appreciatively at the plank floor and my mother's furniture. I was pleased that she liked it.

I heard the front door open and caught a glimpse of Jackson leaving. Checking out the yard, I assumed, or whatever else interested him out there.

"We'd better get busy," Eden said. "Do you have an overnight bag?"

"Not really, just my knapsack," I said, and headed to the front hall to find it. I grabbed a pair of yoga pants and a hoodie out of the dryer on the way back. I tossed them onto the bed then rifled through my dresser, adding bras, undies, T-shirts and jeans to the pile. Next, I headed to the bathroom to gather essentials. My big toothed comb was at the top of the list.

Eden sat on my bed shaking her head. "It'll never fit in this little bag." She glanced up offering a sympathetic look.

"It's either that or a honking big suitcase," I said, shrugging an apology. "I don't have anything in between."

"Let's see the suitcase," she said. I pulled one out of the guest-room closet and dragged it down the hall to show her. "That could be a problem."

Jackson took that opportune moment to return to the house. "You can't take that." He pointed to the offending suitcase. "It's almost as big as Eden and she'll have to fly with it."

"You fly carrying me," I protested.

"You shed gravity. That won't."

Eden reluctantly agreed. "I don't think I could do it, Emelynn. You'll have to pare down." Jackson headed to the living room.

I dug through the pile and removed the jeans. Eden reached over to take out the light-coloured T-shirts. "Don't bring anything too bright to fly in." I was left with two sets of dark coloured clothes. I went to the bathroom to change into clean jeans and a T-shirt. I added a nightshirt to the pile and pulled the clean hoodie over my head—one less thing to pack. The rest fit into the knapsack.

My cellphone! Damn, I should have thought of that earlier. They might let me take it, but I didn't want to risk asking. I made a point of looking for my wallet. It wasn't in the kitchen drawer I rummaged through, but the charger was. With Eden still in the bedroom and my back to Jackson, I slipped it into my hoodie pocket and headed to the front hall closet. I donned my jean jacket and stowed the charger into one of the hidden pockets I'd fashioned for weights. I transferred the phone from my purse to the other hidden pocket and breathed a sigh of relief.

I grabbed my wallet and made my way back to Eden in the bedroom. "You done?" she asked.

"Yes, I think so." I fastened the bottom buttons of the jean jacket to secure the hidden pockets. We headed to the living room where Jackson waited.

He stood with his arms crossed, anxiety radiating off him like a heat wave. "Your hair," he said, nodding to the offending curls.

I turned to the bathroom to get a hair elastic. "Sit down, relax." I gestured to the sofa, but Jackson didn't look much like he was about to take a load off.

"We can't stay, Emelynn," he said. Why was he so tense? He was killing any chance I thought I might have to soak in some quality cottage time.

"Let me take your things," Eden offered when I returned. I passed her my knapsack then pulled my hair into a ponytail and joined Jackson at the patio door.

"Do you want to lock it this time?" he asked, and I thought I recognized a brief flash of chagrin on his face. Not a full-out apology, just a wee nod in that direction. Jackson waited for me to get the key into the lock before he followed Eden's red head and my bouncing backpack down the steps. I pocketed the key then trailed behind them.

It was disheartening to realize that leaving the cottage had lightened Jackson's mood. In fact, our moods shifted in opposite directions as we travelled between my cottage and his boat, which made me doubt that he and I were ever going to be on the same page. A disappointing insight, I thought, as I hit the second landing. Then the unthinkable happened; I lost gravity with my last footfall and rebounded upward, unchecked. This wasn't a graceful liftoff like Eden's. I didn't have any weight in my pockets and I panicked, flailing my arms in a vain attempt at control. Terrifying memories of my uncontrolled flight through the park flashed through my mind.

I shrieked and both Eden and Jackson snapped their heads around. Their gaze shot to where I should have been—then followed the sound of my next shriek up into the air. Eden reacted first, vaulting up and reaching out to me. She got hold of my ankle and yanked me down, bowling me into Jackson, who was on her heels. He absorbed my momentum, wrapped his arms around me then landed us safely on the beach. Jackson and Eden tossed quizzical glances back and forth.

"I'm sorry," I muttered. "That was embarrassing."

"Is that what was happening to you before, in Toronto?" Eden asked, her voice shaking. Her anger seemed harsh and out of place. I had told her some of my more embarrassing floating stories last night, and she'd obviously put two and two together.

"Yes, but having weights in my pockets or a heavy book bag over my shoulder kept it in check."

"Weights wouldn't have stopped that," she said, her eyes on fire. "What were you thinking!"

What was I thinking? "Are you kidding me?" I didn't know whether to cry or scream as my own anger boiled over. "You think I like doing that? It scares the crap out of me!"

Eden backed away and lowered her head, taking a deep breath. "I'm sorry," she said, her voice calmer. "I know it's not your fault. You scared me. That's all."

She looked genuinely apologetic, which sent my guilt meter soaring for having raised my voice. "I'm sorry for shouting," I said to her, then turned to include Jackson, who looked at me as if I'd sprouted a second head. "I'm sorry," I repeated emphatically.

Jackson nodded once, but his furrowed brow stayed firmly in place. "We need to get out of here," he said. "Let's go." He twirled his finger directing me to turn around.

We landed back on the boat ten minutes later.

Alex was waiting. "Any trouble?" he asked.

"Not the kind you'd expect," Jackson reported. "You?" Alex shook his head. "Why don't you go unpack your things, Emelynn." He motioned Eden to give me the knapsack. "We won't go too far tonight, but we do need to move farther away from your neighbours."

I had been dismissed again. At least this time, I was happy to go; I needed time to regroup and shake off the tension from that near miss. I headed below, hesitating for a moment at the bottom of the steps to eavesdrop, but their conversation was lost in the night breeze. I didn't need to hear the words to know that I was the topic of their discussion.

The boat engines started up as I closed the cabin door and threw myself onto the bed. Thank god Eden and Jackson had been there tonight. I didn't want to think about what would have happened in their absence or how many times I'd gone down those stairs wearing just my housecoat with four or six pounds of weight in my pockets—in broad daylight. My condition was getting worse. Was I provoking it by being airborne?

The boat was underway. My contraband phone was down to one bar. A quick search of the room revealed an outlet on the far side of the bed. I plugged in the charger and pushed the phone against the edge of the bed where it would be inconspicuous. It took but a minute to tuck my clothes and toiletries away, and then I lay back on the bed waiting for the engines to slow down. When I heard the anchor dropping, I headed back up.

It wasn't even eleven o'clock. I rejoined them in the living room, where they'd gathered. Jackson was at the wheel, shutting down the electronic gadgets.

A pizza sat in the middle of the coffee table. "Help yourself," Alex offered, an empty plate of crumbs in front of him. Eden sat quietly on the opposite sofa.

"Did you make that yourself?" I asked, going for polite conversation as I took a seat beside Eden and slid a slice onto an empty plate. Eden nursed a Coke and didn't look up.

"No, it was delivered," he said, straight-faced. I smiled, appreciating his humour. He watched me turn to check Eden's expression for signs of amusement, but she was off in another world. Jackson, finished with his captain's chores, joined us and helped himself to a plate. Alex's stab at comedy was lost in the ensuing quiet.

Whatever the three of them had been discussing before I arrived undoubtedly concerned me because in short order they were all looking at me. Their undivided attention raised the hairs on the back of my neck.

"What?" I asked, taking another bite.

"We were talking about what happened to you earlier tonight," Eden said. She didn't look angry, just concerned. "The risk of exposing us is only part of it. You could have killed yourself."

When my mouth was clear I apologized—again.

"You don't need to apologize," Alex said. "We just don't know how to help you deal with it."

"I think the unscripted flights will come to an end when you learn how to fly properly," Jackson said as he helped himself to more pizza.

"Well, the sooner that happens, the better," I said, and I meant it. The sooner I learned the ropes, the sooner I could get out of their hair and back to the cottage.

"Given your impromptu side trip tonight," Jackson continued, "we think the most important thing for you to learn next is how to land." They all nodded their agreement.

We polished off the pizza and while Eden cleaned up, we talked strategy. It was telling that they didn't once mention the "paramount" liftoff skill. Apparently, my unscripted flight had shifted the priorities. It had also instilled an unsettling sombre mood. I hated that I was responsible for all of this: their efforts and now their worry.

Back up on the observation deck, the four of us assumed our positions from the previous night but with markedly less enthusiasm. Alex took the lead. "Jackson is going to get you in the air. Once you're away from him and stable, we'll show you how to land."

"You ready?" Jackson asked, managing a weak smile as he came around behind me.

"Sure," I replied. He folded his arms around me and we lifted off. We stopped two metres above the deck surface before Jackson carefully unwrapped his arms to hold me at arm's length. When I stopped wobbling, he released me.

"I don't think I'll ever get tired of this," I said quietly, marvelling at the wonder of being airborne. Eden returned my smile, agreeing with me, but not with the same excitement she'd shown last night. My wild sprint off the deck at the cottage had frightened her. It frightened me too; I just didn't want to admit how much.

"So, landings," Alex said, focusing our attention. "What goes up must come down, right? From this height, with no speed behind you, you need only a feather-light touch of momentum to get down. Don't forget, without gravity, every movement you make will cause an exaggerated reaction. To land from here, all you need to do is raise your arms in a small sweeping motion. Jackson, you're on. Show her how it's done."

Jackson had been rubbing his temples. It reminded me that he hadn't wanted to take me on in the first place. He'd be glad when I was gone. I watched him rotate his arms in a small upward movement and gently drift down to the deck.

"Or," Alex said, "you can drop your upper body by bending at the knees, and that will set you down. Eden, will you do the honours?"

Eden swung her arms above her head and bent her knees, as if she were doing a delicate squat, and then she too drifted down to the deck.

"You ready to try?" Alex asked, looking over to me.

"Here goes," I said with a sigh, choosing the arm rotation method.

For once in my life, the effort paid off without a hitch: I landed like a pro, right where I was supposed to. What a relief.

"You did it," Eden said, exhaling softly. I watched the tension in her shoulders melt away. We all needed a success tonight, and my smooth landing broke the spell of the dark mood.

"Let's do it again," I said, this time with enthusiasm.

Jackson came around behind me. "Ready?" he asked. Even he seemed relieved.

We drilled through the landing procedure dozens of times. It was midnight before we took our first break.

Eden said, "You'll have to repeat this process until it comes to you intuitively." She and Alex retired to the sofas while Jackson and I continued to practice. By the time we called it quits at two in the morning, I had successfully landed from heights of about thirty feet with no broken bones.

After Eden and Alex said goodbye and flew off, Jackson and I headed down to the galley. He handed me a bottle of water and then, just as he had last night, he locked the outside doors. We headed to the lower deck and he escorted me to my cabin. "You're doing great, Emelynn," he said as he laid his hand on my shoulder. "Do you have everything you need in there?" he asked, indicating my room.

"Yes, I'm good," I said, distracted by his hand. He gave my shoulder a reassuring squeeze before turning and heading to his own room.

I closed my door and retrieved my nightshirt. As I reached to turn out the light, I noticed my cellphone. It was now fully charged. It seemed as if days had passed since I'd plugged it in. I thought I'd been so clever to sneak the phone on board. Now I felt less like I'd gotten away with something and more like I was betraying the trust of the very people who were teaching me how to fly.

I checked the phone for messages. There was one from Charles; they needed to push back their scheduled lawn care until next Monday. I tucked the phone away. Even if there was someone I wanted to call, the hour was too late now. Maybe tomorrow.

CHAPTER ELEVEN

y father pressed a perfectly clear, warm crystal into my hand and I looked up at him in wonderment. But the peaceful moment shattered in a menacing growl. Dad's eyes questioned the intrusion—

I jolted awake to the sound of revving engines. It was just past six. The abrupt wake-up call had my heart pounding. I lay back down in an effort to calm my nerves. We'd slept less than four hours. Jackson must have been in a hurry to get out of sight of my house. It felt like overkill.

Jackson was a difficult man to figure out. He was secretive, guarding whatever it was he did on his computer and shutting me down when I asked about Sandra or the other missing Fliers. But he was generous with his time when it came to teaching me to fly, even though it had to be painfully boring for him. He could be dour and moody, but then he'd open up and smile. I didn't know what to make of him, except that he held my attention much more than he should. I liked his arms around me and I still hadn't returned his T-shirt.

With no hope of getting back to sleep, I showered and dressed and headed up top. I snagged two bananas as I passed through the galley and climbed the stairs to the upper deck.

Jackson stood at the wheel looking as though he hadn't taken time to shower or shave. I handed him a banana. "I made breakfast," I said, which put a rare smile on his face. It was a nice smile when he made the effort. I could tell it was real because it stretched all the way to the corners of his eyes, making tiny wrinkles. He wasn't hard to look at, even this early.

We continued moving away from shore. Thirty minutes later, he cut the engines. I could no longer see land.

"Let's go below," Jackson said. He set up the computer for me and then settled himself on one of the sofas under a cozy blanket.

The only email I opened was my mother's. It was in response to the phone message I'd left her yesterday. She told me to have fun. I wondered how I'd explain my absence. How much could I tell her?

I swivelled around to find Jackson asleep. He looked so comfortable curled up in his blanket. I yawned and lay down on the other sofa under a matching blanket and closed my eyes.

I woke in one of those blank *Where am I?* moments you get sometimes when you wake in unfamiliar surroundings. I stretched and rolled over and there was Jackson, sitting on the opposite sofa with his feet on the coffee table, watching me. Something about his look sent a rolling wave of warmth from my toes to the top of my head. I could fall for this guy—this guy I knew next to nothing about. I wondered if he felt the same sparks I did. Probably not. More likely he wondered when I was going to learn how to fly well enough to get off his boat.

"I don't think I've thanked you yet," I said, sitting up.

He pinched his brow. "For what?"

"For last night. If you and Eden hadn't been there, who knows where I'd have ended up."

"It's not your fault."

"I know that, but I'm still sorry you're saddled with me."

"You're one of us, Emelynn. We stick together. I'd like to think you'd do the same for me if I needed your help." He got up and tossed his blanket over the back of the sofa. "I'm going to take a shower."

It was barely noon and Eden and Alex wouldn't be back for hours. I went below to freshen up.

Jackson still hadn't returned when I resurfaced. I hunted through the fridge with lunch on my mind and found cold cuts. I'd just finished plating our sandwiches when Jackson arrived.

"Good timing," I said, offering him a plate. We carried our lunch to the sofa.

It wasn't much, but at least I felt like I was contributing. He flipped on CNN. This was feeling a lot like Normal. It wasn't, of course, but here we were sitting comfortably in the living room watching CNN, eating lunch. Just like thousands of other households. Maybe this was my new Normal.

When the news cycle repeated, he flipped to BBC. Sporadically, Jackson's cellphone would buzz and he'd react, but he didn't enlighten me. I headed to the bookcase and picked up *The Art of Racing in the Rain*. I hadn't read it yet, but it had gotten great reviews. Jackson was back on the computer.

"What do you do for work?" I asked, thinking Jackson infinitely more interesting than the book.

He turned away from the computer to face me. "I took over my dad's business when he passed away."

"What kind of business?" I asked, happy to have him sharing something about himself without a fight.

"Property development."

"What's your role?"

"Making deals, mostly."

"You enjoy it?"

"Yeah, I guess. It keeps the *Symphony* afloat anyway," he said. A smile brightened his face. It wasn't a look I saw often, but talking about the *Symphony* drew it out of him. He turned back to the computer, reabsorbing himself in whatever he was doing. Perhaps that's what he spent so much time doing on the computer—making deals.

Just after darkness fell, Alex and Eden arrived. "How was your day?" Eden asked.

"Good, uneventful," I replied.

Alex had his head buried in the fridge and came out pulling the tab on a Coke. "Are you looking forward to tonight, Emelynn?"

"Yes," I said, and I was—mostly. It was hard not to be excited where flying was concerned, but my lack of results in the whole liftoff area worried me. They had all emphasized the critical nature of that one skill and it had completely eluded me so far.

"Good," Alex said. "Before you know it, you'll be flying."

I didn't share his confidence, but I sure hoped he was right. We chatted for a few minutes then got down to work.

On the observation deck, one by one, each lifted off. They slowed down and exaggerated their movements. Unfortunately, it was wasted effort. I couldn't help thinking of my failed efforts on the beach with the rope and weights. Maybe I'd left it too long and I'd never be able to lift off on my own. It was a discouraging thought.

We reviewed landings and practiced moving forward, increasing speed each time, and then I learned a new manoeuvre: moving backwards.

At eleven o'clock, we took a break and I was already fatigued—not so much from the physical effort, that part I could handle, but from the concentration required. It was a constant drain. I would have been happy to call it quits for the night.

"We've got to head home," Alex said.

Jackson checked his watch. "It's early."

"Yeah, I know, but I've got a new client coming in first thing tomorrow. I want to make a good impression."

"Of course. You've got to take care of business. We'll be okay on our own," Jackson said. "She only needs one spotter anyway."

They left, assuring us they'd be back after sunset tomorrow. Jackson looked over at me with expectation. "You ready to put in some more time?"

"I know I need the practice, but I'm pooped," I replied.

"You said it yourself—you need the practice. Come on." He stood and offered me his hand.

I reluctantly joined him. After his jump-start, Jackson put me through my paces yet again. At that point, I felt fairly good about my progress and I should have stopped then because shortly after that feel-good moment, I made a stupid mistake. I overcorrected a forward roll and sent myself tumbling. My attempt at control flipped me upside down and I went into full panic mode, flailing my arms and setting off a wild spin. Jackson raced in, caught me by a wayward wrist and yanked me around, stopping the hellish ride.

He helped me back to the boat and shushed my apologies, which was kind, but my confidence was shaken.

"No, that one's on me," Jackson said with a dismissive shake of his head. "You told me you were tired but I pushed you anyway. Don't beat yourself up. I should have been closer. Let's just call it a night."

He wasn't getting an argument from me. We headed down the stairs to the galley and he locked the door behind us. "I don't know about you, Jackson, but I'm exhausted. I'm going to bed." I turned and started for the steps. "Good night," I said over my shoulder.

"I'm right behind you," he said.

He walked me to my cabin and lingered in the doorway. "We've all made those mistakes Emelynn. Don't make more of it than it is. You did great tonight. You're learning quickly."

"Thanks. It doesn't feel that way right now though."

"You've made a lot of progress in three days. Just think how far along you'll be in a week." He hesitated a moment longer. "Good night, sleep well," he said, and then he headed down the hall to his own room.

I shut the door and had a hard time getting him out of my head as I shambled through my nighttime bathroom ritual and crawled into bed. Was Jackson thinking about me? I wondered.

We slept until noon. It was overcast and foggy, and the weather lent an oddly claustrophobic air to the boat.

Jackson had cut up some fruit. I found the oatmeal and made us a pot of porridge. We ate companionably, both of us drizzling maple syrup over our warm bowls. I had the distinct impression that it wasn't just me—we were both becoming more comfortable with each other.

"I spoke with Eden this morning," Jackson said as he stood to clear the dishes.

"Oh? Did you tell her about my panic attack?" I asked.

"Eden reminded me we've seen that before. Remember? Back at your place, the night we went to get your stuff?"

I hadn't forgotten.

"We're thinking that maybe we need to address it. You know, see if we can help you deal with these panic attacks or better yet, stop them from setting in. What do you think?"

I took a deep breath, dreading the thought. "It scares me."

"Yeah, I know, but you've got to get a handle on this. Panic is absolutely deadly—you've already landed in the hospital once."

"You're right. Absolutely right. Let's work on it tonight," I said, finally resigning myself to it.

"All right then. Tonight."

We took turns at the computer. I checked my email and he did god knows what. I flipped through magazines but found nothing between the pages interesting enough to distract me from the fear of challenging my panic. It seemed to me to be an insurmountable obstacle, though I supposed I had to start thinking differently if I wanted to overcome it.

The fog didn't abate. It clung stubbornly to the day, blocking out the sun. Jackson stood at the big wheel staring out into the grey mist. "You know," he said, "being socked in like this, we should be safe enough to get in some practice. You feel up to it?"

I looked up from the magazine. "I suppose," I answered, my enthusiasm dampened by last night's tumble.

"After you, then."

I dragged myself up the stairs and when we reached the observation deck, Jackson suggested we start with a liftoff attempt. I mimicked their liftoff moves with exaggerated emphasis but still had no success. Jackson quickly dismissed my grumblings, reminding me it might take time. Patience really is a virtue, I thought; I just wasn't feeling very virtuous.

"Never mind," he said as he came up behind me. "You ready?" he asked, already wrapping his arms around me. I nodded. He lifted us up then slowly released me.

"You're making progress, Emelynn, whether you notice or not. See how steady you are now when I release you? Just a few days ago you'd be rocking and rolling when I let you go."

"Yeah, I guess," I said, pleasantly aware that he was right. "But don't get too far away. I'm really not up for another tumble."

"I'm sorry about last night. I should have stayed closer. I'll be more careful," he said with aching sincerity.

We spent an hour reviewing the moves I already knew. It didn't feel like work at all. It felt an awful lot like playing hooky, and I found myself trying to stifle the laughter that burst out as we goofed around. When we'd exhausted all the moves I'd already learned, he taught me how to move in a hover and, for the first time, I thought, hey, this is easy. It was just a matter of minute movement: more like leaning actually, but with balance.

By the end of the second hour, I felt much more comfortable in the air and we were both ready to take a break. We each claimed a sofa.

"You know," Jackson said, as he reached his hands behind his head, "I've been taking this for granted for so long now that I'd forgotten how much fun it can be." He beamed a megawatt smile and stretched his torso.

"I'm sure it's not as much fun for you as it is for me."

"You might be surprised. This is a little like being a kid again." It was easy to believe him looking at the grin that took up half his face. "I can't wait to show you more moves, but that's nothing—just wait until you're flying."

I liked Happy Jackson so much better than Moody Jackson. I hoped he stayed around for a while.

After a short rest, Jackson had me back in the air and at it again. My confidence improved by the minute and that gave me the boldness I needed to take on his new tricks. He showed me how to do a horizontal twist and a front roll—on purpose!

I didn't screw up once. He kept close, just in case, but the few times

I overcorrected or got going too fast, I was able to manage on my own. Soon, he wasn't leading the action anymore, but following me as I worked through one manoeuvre to the next.

Finally, we called it quits and went below.

"I haven't played like that in years," Jackson said. "I guess I can thank you for giving me an excuse to indulge."

"My pleasure. That was the most fun I've ever had." I couldn't get the grin off my face. The freedom of floating around like that was indescribable. "I wish I had the stamina to do that all day long."

"Let's get a bite to eat," Jackson suggested, and I trailed behind him to the galley. We made a big pot of penne pasta with pesto sauce. I started making a salad and then, as if on cue, Eden and Alex arrived.

"This looks great," Eden said, helping Alex set the table.

"Good thing you made lots," Alex added, rubbing his hands together. "It smells fantastic."

After we sat down to eat, Eden asked how we'd spent our day. It was all the prompting I needed to gush out a descriptive summary of our antics in the fog. Their amusement continued through a full slate of questions. Alex was keen to pry from Jackson all the embarrassing details of my more colourful blunders and, much to my chagrin, Jackson happily obliged. I didn't mind though and laughed along with them. In fact, I couldn't remember the last time I'd laughed so much.

After dinner, we went up top. I was eager to show Eden and Alex my new moves, which looked amateurish compared to theirs, but they were gracious and paid me compliments anyway.

Unfortunately, the fun and games were coming to a close. I could tell they were anxious to get on with tackling my "little" panic problem. We landed and while they strategized, I listened.

Their approach involved invoking a situation that would trigger my panic and then guiding me out of it. "It's important," Eden emphasized when she recognized the anxiety that widened my eyes to dinner-plate proportions.

"It'll be the death of you if you don't get a handle on it," added Jackson.

And so, the next phase of my training began; the scary phase.

CHAPTER TWELVE

J ackson huddled with Eden and Alex to work out the details of a plan I wasn't allowed to hear. Once done, they returned to me.

"Let's head up," Eden said, and we lifted off—I, with the help of Jackson, of course. He had to be getting tired of the routine.

Eden took me higher than ever before. Trepidation set in as we levelled off. Without warning, someone grabbed my ankles and set me spinning then tossed me like a Frisbee. I gasped, immediately losing my sense of up and down. I fought the panic and tried to apply what Jackson had taught me about stopping rolls, but I was spinning too quickly.

Alex shouted, "Spread eagle, Emelynn. Create resistance."

I gulped air, pushing at the panic and stretched out. The spin slowed. My sense of which end was up returned and I felt myself coming out of the rotation and straightened up. Not bad, I thought. I was back under control. As soon as my senses returned, I looked around to get my bearings. The *Symphony* was but a smudge far below and off in the distance. As those facts registered, I had a frightening flashback to my fall in the park.

Panic set in swiftly and gravity returned with a sledgehammer. I went down fast, feet first, backpedalling all the way. Jackson dove after me and grabbed my flailing forearm in a vice-like grip, but not before my soles felt the sting of hitting the water. I reached up with my other hand and held on tight. His face was set in hard lines as he flew us quickly back to the boat deck. We landed hard.

Jackson barked, "Jesus! What the hell were you thinking? You don't take on gravity when you're that high. You'll kill yourself."

Eden and Alex landed right behind us, rushing over. "You okay?" they both asked at once.

Tears ran down my face. I didn't want to cry but I'd scared myself, and Jackson's yelling at me hadn't helped. Eden wrapped an arm around my shoulder and dragged me to the sofa. "It's okay," she cooed. Alex sat down on my other side, rubbing my back as if he were soothing a five-year-old. I felt like an idiot.

Jackson paced. "I'm sorry, Emelynn," he said. "I should have been better prepared. I just never imagined you'd use gravity, of all things—didn't even think you could. That's suicidal."

"Well, it's not like it was intentional!" I shouted back through sobs. "It's automatic. I couldn't stop it."

Jackson squatted in front of me and put his hands on my knees. "It was a panic response: plain and simple. I know it wasn't intentional and it may feel like an automatic reaction, but you *can* stop it. You must. You already know how. You did it just this afternoon. It's in there ... in your head," he said, tapping his finger on my forehead. I swatted his hand away.

He stood and resumed pacing. Speaking to no one in particular, he said, "We have to find a way to reprogram your thinking. Fear triggers your panic. The panic triggers the rush of gravity. So you must think that gravity will mitigate the fear." He didn't expect an answer; he was trying to break the problem down into its component parts: Chapter One of *Problem Solving for Idiots*.

"I suppose during your previous experiences gravity did solve your problems. Well, until you nearly killed yourself in the park." He paused. "Maybe that's the key! If you can connect the pain of that fall with your panic response, maybe you can correct it."

"You know," I said, following his logic, "I did flash back to that fall. I think it was after I realized how high I'd drifted." Water had wicked up to my knees, chilling me.

"Maybe we're trying too hard," Alex said, jumping in. "If we teach Emelynn to invoke the gravity plunge on command, maybe the resulting fall wouldn't cause her to panic. Then she'd be able to stop it." We all looked at him thoughtfully.

"I think you've got a point," Eden said. "It makes sense." She looked at me. "What do you say?"

"That might work," I said. "It's worth a try." I looked over at Jackson. "What do you think?"

"I agree." He got up, motioning for us to follow. "Let's go. We'll return to where we were when you panicked. Alex and I will drop down to act as your safety net if you can't stop yourself. Eden, you talk her through it. Okay?"

We must have all agreed because Jackson wrapped his arms around me and had me up in the air in seconds. I'm not sure if they remembered how new to all of this I was. My skills were beginner at best and my confidence had taken yet another hit.

When we reached the designated spot, Jackson released me, Eden took hold of my hands. "Are you ready?" she asked. I didn't trust my voice not to quiver so I nodded instead then watched Alex and Jackson move away from us.

She still had hold of my hands. "They won't let you get hurt. You can trust them. Now focus. Do you remember how it felt?" she asked. I nodded. "I want you to try to recreate that sensation of taking on your entire body's weight. Grab hold of that weight—let it bowl you over. You'll start to fall, but I want you to let it happen."

I looked away from her, down below. We were awfully high up.

"They'll stop you, don't worry, but the first step is being able to trigger the gravity and then we'll teach you how to stop the fall. We have a lot of vertical room to work with. Do you understand?"

I nodded. It was the best I could do. Eden released my hands and I steadied myself. I looked below to see where Alex and Jackson had situated themselves. From this height, they looked like SimCity stick people. I looked back at Eden, who urged me on.

I drew a deep breath, closed my eyes and let the sensation of gravity roll over me. Turns out, taking on gravity was as easy for me as blinking. I let it hit me in the chest and knock me backwards then straight down. Panic didn't have time to kick in before Jackson and Alex grabbed hold of me. Gravity vanished with their touch, and after confirming that I was okay, they escorted me back up to Eden.

They released me and I steadied myself again. "That was interesting," Eden said. "You take on gravity like it's an old friend."

"Yeah, and isn't that prophetic: the only flying skill that comes naturally to me is falling like a stone." I said it in all seriousness, but infectious laughter percolated around me.

"So all we have to do now is get you to put the brakes on a gravity-fed drop." Jackson sighed, shaking his head. "Okay. Let's go."

Alex and Jackson returned to their positions closer to the water.

"You ready?" asked Eden. I nodded again. "This time, after you're in free fall, shift your body so you're horizontal and then spread eagle to create resistance. That'll slow you down. Alex and Jackson will catch you before you hit water."

I didn't even close my eyes this time. I summoned gravity and it obeyed like a well-trained dog. It hit hard, knocking me backwards again, starting my free fall. I concentrated, keeping my wits about me and as soon as I could, I splayed myself out. I felt the wind resistance slowing my body, but not fast enough. Alex grabbed me before I got wet, and after we'd rearranged ourselves, we headed back up to Eden.

"You and gravity definitely have a thing going on," Eden said as we approached. "I don't see any sign of panic at all. It's almost like turning on your gravity switch has turned off your panic one."

"That's a good thing, right?" I asked, ever hopeful.

"Well, it's an odd thing for sure, but it won't be a good thing until you can stop shy of the water. Let's try again," Alex said. He and Jackson returned once more to their positions below us.

"You ready?" Eden asked. I nodded. This time I had a better result. I still needed help stopping, but I'd added arm movement to increase resistance, which helped slow me even more before I reached Alex and Jackson. I had a smile on my face when they grabbed me.

We repeated the exercise a dozen times and with each attempt, I improved. I was no longer panicking and that left me able to concentrate on functioning instead of just reacting wildly.

Everyone looked tired. "How about we quit while we're still ahead?" I suggested. They agreed. When we got back to the boat Jackson invited Alex and Eden to stay for a glass of wine.

"That's the best invitation I've had all night," Eden said as she took Alex's hand and headed below. Jackson and I followed.

Alex and I headed for the sofas while Eden waited for Jackson to uncork and pour from a bottle of red. Eden carried over two glasses and handed one to Alex as she snuggled into him. Jackson handed me a glass and sat down beside me.

"Cheers," Alex said as we raised our glasses. "I think we reached a milestone today." Alex looked over at me. "We still have to practice a few things, but you've got the basics under your belt. I think we're ready to let you loose."

"We should fly tomorrow night," Eden said with considerable enthusiasm. "No more lessons, just flat out fly."

"I agree," added Jackson, and we raised our glasses again. "To tomorrow." We touched glasses, sealing a pact.

"You're going to love the flying part, Em. There's nothing quite like it," Alex said, a look of distant bliss on his face. "It's what makes it all worthwhile. You'll see." I desperately wanted to believe him.

Eden and Alex finished their wine and said good night.

I drained my own glass and thought longingly about my bed. "It's been an awfully long day," I said. I stood to take my glass to the sink.

"But a productive one," added Jackson, following me.

"I know I'm making headway," I said, rinsing my glass. "And you're all being so patient."

"I feel a 'but' coming on," he said.

"I just wish I was making as much headway with the liftoffs, is all."

"I know," he said, turning to face me. He raised his hands to my shoulders and bent his head forward. "Be patient. It'll come in its own time. Trust me."

His touch lit me up in all kinds of ways, none of them appropriate.

"Let's go to bed," he said as he turned my shoulders to face forward and guided me to the stairs. "You'll be more enthusiastic after you've had your first flight."

But his guiding hands had me thinking I'd be more enthusiastic following him to his bed. What was it about Jackson that had my hormones raging? Sure, he was tall and handsome and—okay, he did have a nice butt, but the jury was still out on his personality. He ran cold as often as he ran hot. He had an incredible, infectious smile, but I didn't often see it. And he was secretive. I shouldn't be so attracted to someone I knew so little about: especially someone who hadn't wanted me on his boat in the first place.

I crawled into bed and tried to shut off my brain. I slept fitfully, dipping in and out of restless dreams but never quite waking. I flew in the dreams and flew hard. I flew high above jagged rocks that lined a frothy ocean shore. I was out of breath and tired, but I couldn't stop. The flight was relentless: fast and frantic.

A great boulder was tied to my ankle with yellow nylon rope. The rope dug into my skin and no amount of shaking loosened either the burden or the rope. Though I struggled desperately, flying against its weight, the boulder dragged me ever closer to the jagged rocks below.

Even in my sleep, I had an awareness of tossing and turning but remained trapped beneath a thin veil of consciousness. I couldn't wake

JP MCLEAN

and I couldn't stop flying. I struggled to the point of exhaustion. I had lost so much altitude that the great boulder began kissing the tops of the rugged peaks below. Every bounce caused the rope to bite into my ankle. A massive rock loomed in my path and my dream skidded into slow motion as I watched, powerless to stop the collision. The boulder at my ankle hit the massive rock with a thunderous boom.

I glanced down as the rock below cleaved in two, split apart … and gasped at the sight. Dozens of crystals, perfectly formed and clear as diamonds, glittered from the freshly exposed rock.

I breached consciousness, waking in a tangle of sweaty bedding and breathing hard. I fought free of the sheets. Goosebumps crawled along my limbs but not because I was cold. The small hairs on the back of my neck stood on end as I slowly unravelled the threads of the dream, finally recognizing its significance.

In a heartbeat, I became singularly focused. I jumped out of bed and threw the cabin door open, vaguely aware that it banged hard against the wall as I pounded down the short hallway, aiming for the stairs. In a blink, I was up that staircase, then through the galley heading out back to get up to the observation deck. The door stuck. I rattled the knob then shoved my shoulder into it until my brain kicked in; it was locked. God knows I'd seen Jackson lock it enough times. I turned the deadbolt, shot through that door and ran to the back deck.

I heard Jackson shout my name as I rounded the corner. I charged up the last set of stairs to the observation deck with focused determination and burst forward, harnessing the storm that had gathered at my core. I reached deep inside my psyche for the smooth, clear crystal. I visualized it pulsing in my palm, glowing warmly. The moment I wrapped my fingers around it, its energy poured into me: the power of the crystal roared into my limbs. Without slowing, I leapt. Gravity snapped free, and I soared into the night sky. Not a gentle liftoff, not a graceful arc, but a lightning quick, powerful trajectory that shot me straight up to the heavens.

I was distantly aware of Jackson's form on the deck below me. My new skills kicked in and I slowed myself down but nothing could quiet the triumphant shout I let loose.

Jackson flew up and closed in quickly, reaching out to grab my forearm. "Whoa there, Em … steady," he said, worry lining his face.

I couldn't stop smiling. There weren't words to describe the overpowering sense of euphoria.

"Well, look at you," he said, a smile replacing his pinched brows. "I guess you figured it out."

"I guess I did," I said, still grinning.

"Do you know how quickly you shot up here?" He moved his face into my line of vision. "You might want to take that speed down a notch next time."

"Uh-huh," I mumbled. The reality of what I'd done started to sink in. That familiar tingling sensation under my skin was now a surging hum of pure energy.

We made a slow, steady descent to the observation deck. He stayed close when he let go of my arm but didn't need to. Gravity was playing nice.

"I should go back to bed," I said, feeling a bit shell-shocked.

"I think that's best," he agreed, and escorted me back to my cabin.

I crawled between the sheets and found the deep sleep that had evaded me earlier.

It was one thirty in the afternoon when I finally woke. I could tell by glancing out the porthole windows that it was foggy again. I stretched and settled back into the pillows.

I felt different. More comfortable, more grounded. It was hard to identify exactly what had changed. I examined my hand, searching for signs of last night's crystal. It wasn't there, but I sensed it within me. I knew with every fibre of my being that if I closed my eyes and called it to me, it would come. And it was powerful. It thrummed within my body, giving me a strength I hadn't known before.

The crystal was the key. Its warm, smooth touch was the very thing that awakened the power of the gift. It didn't matter that it wasn't a physical object. Once the power was coursing through my limbs, there was no stopping its momentum. It was as if some long buried instinct had burst forth, harnessing and concentrating the power into a force strong enough to snap gravity's hold on me.

This was going to take some getting used to.

The crystal was my talisman. It lived in my soul. It had been hiding in distant memories and recurrent dreams. But if Jolene had given me my gift, why did it feel as if my father was the one responsible for the talisman, the missing key that unlocked the gift?

I took a shower then headed up top to find Jackson tucked into the computer. He finished what he was doing, leaned back in his chair and laced his fingers behind his head.

"You slept in," he said, scrutinizing my every move.

I poured a glass of juice. "Yeah, looks like I did. Do you want some?"

He shook his head. "So ... how are you feeling today?" he asked, unconcerned about my health. It was a barefaced fishing expedition.

"Pretty. Damn. Good." I let a smile consume me.

"Yeah, I thought you might be." Jackson chuckled and got up to follow me to the sofa.

"What happened last night, Em? What was it that finally triggered a liftoff?"

It was an innocent enough question, and no doubt, of all people, he was the one who deserved an answer. After all, he'd been the one doing double duty in the liftoff department for the past few days. But I couldn't do it. My instincts whispered to me to keep quiet, to protect this part of me that no one else knew.

"It was a dream I had ..." I said, looking over at him, trying to think up something plausible to tell him. "I was flying but had this rock tied to my ankle ..."

He perched on the edge of the sofa, waiting for me to continue. "The rock dragged me down and I struggled against the weight of it." I paused, and then the lie fell into my lap. "Somehow, I managed to cut the rope, which released the rock and that's when I woke up."

He frowned. "That's it?"

"Yeah, that's it."

"Hmm," he mumbled, reaching for the TV controller.

I couldn't tell if he believed me or not. I turned my attention to the news. Anderson Cooper was interviewing some despot in the Middle East via satellite link. My mind wandered back to last night. I couldn't wait to try another liftoff.

"What would you like for breakfast?" Jackson asked.

"How about I cook this morning," I offered, happy for something to focus on.

"Great." He flipped to BBC.

A quick tour of his fridge produced all the fixings I needed to make scrambled-egg wraps. I added salsa, green onions, sour cream and cheddar. It was one of my better efforts. Jackson agreed.

"It's foggy out again," Jackson said. "If you're up for it, we could get some practice in."

I looked at him and, in a flash, my confidence wavered. This was what I'd wanted, right—a chance to lift off again? Yet, I was terrified.

"What if I can't do it again?" I asked. Anxiety eroded my voice.

Jackson reached over and squeezed my hand. "It's inside you, Emelynn. It's not going anywhere. You did it once—you'll be able to do it again." He had more confidence in me than I did.

"I guess I'm going to have to try it again, sooner or later," I said, taking a deep breath. I just wished I could do it in private. The thought of having an audience for this made me uncomfortable.

Jackson stood and started to clear away the dishes.

"Would you mind, Jackson"—I hesitated, searching for words that wouldn't offend him—"if I did this on my own? Just this one time. I'll be too nervous if you're up there watching me."

He would have looked less pained if I'd punched him in the gut. And then, of course, I felt bad for having asked.

"What if you need help?"

"I'll whistle if I lift off."

"I don't know, Em. You could fall and end up in the water."

"Please?"

He looked at me for a long time from under a furrowed brow. Finally, he relented. "Okay, but I'm not waiting for you to whistle. I'll give you a two-minute head start and then I'm coming up."

I started for the door. "Two minutes," I said.

Jackson glanced down at his watch. "Go. Two minutes." He looked up at me but kept his hand on the watch.

I pulled the back door open and rounded the corner to the stairs, recalling with clarity the power of the crystal that had coursed through my veins earlier. Each footfall took me closer to that power; it hummed just below my skin. I raced up the stairs, reaching within for the crystal as I ran. I didn't feel the urgency I had felt after the dream, but the strength was there, itching to get out, and all my trepidation fell away. I could see it only with my mind's eye, but I sensed its smooth surface and the warmth of its touch. Its power was surging, concentrating: anticipating release.

I hit the observation deck at a sprint and then, as if I'd done it all my life, I took a swift stride forward, harnessed that great source of power inside me and shot up into the sky. Gravity snapped instantly, propelling me high overhead. There were no words for my relief and exhilaration, and I shouted to the heavens. My limbs trembled with power. The hum of it skittered across my skin with such potency that I wouldn't have been surprised if my body threw off a glow.

Two seconds later, Jackson came up after me. He latched onto my arm to help slow me down.

"I thought you were going to whistle!" he yelled.

"I thought you were going to give me two minutes!"

Then the absurdity of the moment hit us and we burst out laughing.

"Come on," Jackson said. "Let's have some fun."

The next few hours whizzed by. It was like going to the county fair and getting on all the rides without having to pay or wait in line. We took several trips out over the water and I didn't suffer a single panic attack. We rolled and we twisted. We flew arcs and circle eights. I cruised through all the manoeuvres: forward, backwards, left and right. I hovered. I sped up and slowed down; I soared high and dropped low. Though it was scary and exciting in equal measure, the freedom was absolute. It was nirvana on steroids and I was hooked.

Exhaustion finally slowed us down and we landed to take a rest.

"Do you realize I haven't had to correct you even once today?" Jackson remarked as we headed to the galley.

"I hadn't, but you're right," I said, thinking how much more relaxed I'd been up there today. Discovering the crystal had unleashed something in me. It was more than just the liftoff—it was the power behind it. It gave me strength and confidence.

Jackson headed for the wine. "I know it's early, but let's celebrate." He poured us each a glass of red. "Here's to independent flight," he said, touching his glass to mine.

He barely got a sip in before his cellphone rang. I could tell he was talking to Alex. "Eden and Alex are bringing dinner," he announced, ending the call. Half an hour later they arrived carrying a big bag of Chinese takeout.

"Wine before dinner," Eden said, eyeing our empty glasses. "What's the occasion?"

"Emelynn has something to celebrate," Jackson said, all smiles. Eden and Alex turned expectant faces my way.

"I lifted off. Twice," I said, feeling like a braggart.

"Fan-fucking-tastic," Alex said, rushing over and spinning me around in a bear hug.

"Congratulations," Eden said, getting in line to give me a hug. "How did it happen? I want every detail."

Still feeling protective, I reiterated the rock and rope story I'd told Jackson earlier. Jackson kept piping up to add details—like how I'd been wearing a nightshirt the first time I went up, and the whole whistle thing—but it was all in fun. He was having a great time, and it felt like we had bonded into a comfortable family unit.

I set the table while Eden unpacked the bag of aromatic aluminum containers. The men joined us and we heaped our plates, chatting amiably, laughing at Alex and Jackson's lame banter. I savoured a bite of ginger fried beef and it hit me, with a bit of a shock, that I was no longer a hostage. As I looked around the table, I realized I now thought of Eden, Alex and even Jackson as friends.

It hadn't occurred to me before but now I understood they had taken a huge risk bringing me here. If I'd overreacted, it could have turned out so much worse—for all of us. They'd made themselves vulnerable by trusting me with their secret, and their control over me decreased in direct proportion to the skills I gained through their lessons. In hindsight, they must have been aware of the dichotomy all along. They had given me the skills I needed to leave—right now if I chose. But I didn't; I knew now that I belonged with them and had more to learn.

Tonight, we were going flying, and we all bristled with excitement. They didn't even give me instructions: a clear break from what had become our routine. The other thing markedly different was the three of them standing back, anticipating my solo liftoff.

Their attention was embarrassing, but there was no getting away from the audience this time. I closed my eyes and took a moment to prepare, blocking out everything around me. I imagined the warmth of the crystal in my palm and let its energy build. When it hit a crescendo, I called that power to me, took a swift stride forward then soared straight up into the sky. God, it was absolutely electrifying. Up here, with the hum of power surging through me, I felt invincible.

Jackson was right behind me and grabbed hold of my arm to slow me down. Eden and Alex were close on our heels. I grinned like an idiot. Jackson looked over to them. "She needs more practice slowing her ascent, but I think she's got the gist of it," he said, laughing.

"Oh, you think," Alex said.

Eden simply said, "Wow."

Jackson was right. I was using much more power than necessary to snap gravity's hold on me, and the resulting ricochet shot me into the air with too much velocity. I needed to temper my enthusiasm and not draw so much power next time.

When we'd all recovered from my command performance, Alex took off flying. Eden followed closely behind. Jackson urged me on next and, after I'd safely moved into a flying position behind Eden, he brought up the rear.

I accelerated, letting my body pitch forward into a horizontal stance, and felt the wind blow my hair back. It was exhilarating. When I got close to Alex, I shouted over the rush of wind in my ears, "You're right, it's the easiest thing I've done yet." He winked with a smile.

I didn't know where we were going, and I didn't care. I tucked in behind Alex and Eden and glimpsed Jackson following behind. We flew up and glided down; dipped and looped back up; rolled around and even flew face-up for a short distance. I discovered I could apply more speed when holding one or both hands over my head as though I were diving. The movements came without thought. I also knew instinctively that I could fly a lot faster. I had to hold myself back because I didn't want to overtake Eden or Alex who, I'm sure, were keeping us at a safe pace. I was having the time of my life.

Too soon, I spotted Jackson's boat ahead in the distance. We must have travelled in a large circle around it. I wasn't ready to stop, but I reluctantly followed them down. Once we'd all landed safely, and I didn't collapse in a rush of gravity, Jackson herded us down below. I talked the whole time; I couldn't shut up. With so much excitement bubbling up out of me, I didn't want to waste time breathing.

I hadn't noticed Jackson pouring drinks. He handed me one and motioned for me to drink. Which I suppose was tantamount to asking me to put a cork in it. I couldn't blame him. I kept the silly grin on my face, accepted the proffered drink, chinked his glass then tasted a sip.

It took my breath away; I coughed and my eyes watered. My reaction made him laugh. "It's a rusty nail," he told me as we settled on the sofas in the same places we'd occupied last night. "I don't suppose I need to ask if you enjoyed tonight's flight," Jackson said with a lovely smirk on his face.

"That was the best," I said, finally coming down to Earth.

"Yes, it was," agreed Jackson.

"Just one note of caution, Emelynn," Alex said, and I turned to him. "Voices travel really well over water, so you should probably curb the talking unless you want someone to overhear you." That seemed to tickle their collective funny bone.

"Is it just my imagination," I asked, "or is there some reason why I seem to fly faster when I've got my arms pointed above my head?" I demonstrated what I meant, assuming my version of a diver's stance.

"No, it's not your imagination," Alex said. "When you streamline your body like that, what you're doing is reducing drag. That allows air to flow more smoothly over your contours and that, in turn, lets you fly faster. It also takes less effort. That's why car manufacturers use wind tunnels to help design their cars."

"Of course," I said, happy to make the connection. Maybe I did have some innate sense of this gift after all.

We talked for another hour or so and they gave me more tips than I could possibly remember.

Finally, Eden and Alex prepared to leave. "I won't see you tomorrow, Emelynn," Eden said. "Though I'd like nothing more than to have another night like this, I'm working nights at the hospital for the next four shifts."

Alex added, "I'm going to give you a few nights off, too. I like to work nights when Eden does, so we can have more time off together."

"Looks like we're on our own for a few days," Jackson said.

Eden fished a piece of paper out of her pocket and handed it to me. "It's my phone number and email. Phone me if you want to get together and do something."

"I'd like that," I said, feeling as if I'd been set free. They left in a whisper.

Jackson fired up his computer and I flicked on the TV. When he had finished doing whatever mystery activity he did on it, he logged off and turned it over to me. I checked my email and sent Molly a quick hello to tell her I'd be in touch soon. I then headed back to the sofa and pulled a blanket over my lap.

"You want another drink?" Jackson asked.

"Sure, I'm not driving—why not?" I watched him drop the ice and amber liquid into our glasses. He handed me one and sat down beside me, putting his feet up on the edge of the coffee table.

"I enjoyed myself tonight," he said. "I think you're going to be a strong Flier. You amaze me with the strides you've made in five days."

"I can't believe it. Feels more like five months." I swallowed a sip of the drink and felt its warmth spread out inside me as it made its way down my throat. The night had been more fun than I'd had in a very long time and I wasn't anxious to see it end. But the real world was knocking at my door. "I guess I'd better head home soon. I'm sure you'd like your spare room back."

He ran his finger around the rim of his glass. "Not really. I'm kind of getting used to having you around." He looked at me with a warmth in his face I hadn't seen before, and clinked his glass against mine. "Here's to many more nights like tonight."

"I'd like that," I said. "Cheers." I took another sip, letting my mind wander to flying and all the wonders of this new world. Maybe when Eden was back on days, Jackson would invite us all back. I hadn't intended to get so quiet, but my thoughts were heavy with speculation and I found myself daydreaming.

Jackson's touch startled me. "Where'd you go?" he asked, reaching out to push my hair away from my face.

His touch electrified me. "Sorry," I said, tilting out of his reach. "It's just … sometimes it's a little overwhelming." I was keenly aware of the lingering heat from his fingers.

"I bet," he said, resting his arm on the sofa behind me.

Was I just imagining that he was making a move?

"I'm sure it's been tough on you, growing up without your father, having to deal with this gift with no guidance. And now, to have this dumped on you—you've done well."

I guess it was just my imagination. I let my mind wander back to flying. I couldn't wait to fly again. Maybe Eden could come to the cottage and we could take off from the deck. Would we have enough room to lift off from there? I wondered where she and Alex lived and where they did their flying. I couldn't wait to get up in the air again.

I was deep in my thoughts when Jackson reached his hand under my chin and turned my face toward his. I hadn't noticed that he'd moved closer, and his touch sent my pulse into the stratosphere. He brushed his thumb against my lower lip then leaned in and touched his lips to mine. It was a gentle kiss, barely there, but it left me breathless. He pulled away to weigh my reaction, and sensing no opposition, he leaned in and kissed me again, with purpose this time. I kissed him back, liking the touch of his lips and the way his tongue played against mine.

Without a lot of comparative experience, I wasn't the best judge, but given the way parts of me tingled that had never tingled like that before, I'd say he was an expert in the kiss department.

Jackson pulled away and took my hand in his. "I wish you didn't have to go."

I was lost for words and way out of my depth. "I can come back another time. We could go flying," I suggested. We quietly sipped our drinks and my world tilted off its axis. I hadn't seen this coming. I'd felt attracted to him but I had thought it was just me.

"I guess we'd better call it a night," Jackson said, breaking the spell. "I'll take you home tomorrow if you'd like."

"I'd like," I said reluctantly as he helped me up off the sofa. We headed to our rooms.

When we got to my door, he pulled me into an embrace that was nothing like when he helped me lift off. This was a full contact, thigh to shoulder, sensual embrace. He kissed me again, deeply—deeply enough to melt all inhibition and hesitation. He breathed "Sweet dreams" into my ear then released me and turned to his own room. I watched his long strides take that nice butt all the way to his cabin.

After I staggered through my door and closed it behind me, I leaned back against it to catch my breath. I went through my getting-ready-for-bed routine on autopilot. When I crawled into bed, I had still not sloughed off the unmistakable tingle that had taken over my body. The more I thought about Jackson, the more aroused I became. I ran my fingers down between my legs to find the little knot of nerves that, given some attention, would help release the tension. A shudder or two later I turned over, hoping I had eased the tension enough to find sleep.

CHAPTER THIRTEEN

The next morning, I found myself reluctant to get out of bed. The encounter with Jackson had me second-guessing everything. I lingered under the covers with the memory of his lips on mine but was apprehensive about seeing him. In the harsh light of day, would he regret kissing me? I stared up at the wood-paneled ceiling. Why was I imagining the worst? Just get your butt out of bed, I thought.

After a long shower, I scrunched my hair to bring out the curl and put on a touch of eyeliner, smudging it like the drugstore saleswoman had shown me. I felt like a giddy schoolgirl with her first crush. I took one last look in the mirror, decided it wasn't going to get any better, and headed up the stairs.

He was in the galley pouring coffee when I arrived. "I heard you coming," he said, explaining his perfect coffee-pouring timing. He immediately dispelled my anxiety by kissing the top of my head as he handed me a mug. I inhaled his clean laundry scent. "How did you sleep?" he asked.

"Good. How about you?"

"It took me a while to fall asleep. I had someone on my mind," he replied, sporting a sexy smile. "I'll make breakfast today. How do bacon and eggs sound?"

"Like heaven," I said, enjoying the fresh coffee aroma wafting up from my mug. First coffee and now breakfast? This was shaping up to be the best morning ever.

After breakfast, I cleared the dishes while he had a turn at the computer. When the galley was clean, I moved to the living room and thumbed through a magazine waiting for him to join me. When he finally did, an awkward silence ensued.

"I guess you'd like me to take you home?" he said.

"If you wouldn't mind. I need to touch base with some people, do some catching up around the cottage."

Jackson remained quiet for a moment. "Okay. You go ahead and pack. I'll meet you up top." He sounded deflated, and a little piece of me dared to hope it was because he would miss me.

I returned to my cabin and heard the engines roar to life followed a short time later by the unmistakable rumble and clank of the anchor being weighed. I did one last check of the head and cabin then lugged my knapsack up the stairs. I left it in the living room, which still sounded better to me than "salon," and headed up top.

Jackson stood at the wheel and we were underway. I squinted into the sun and settled in for the duration. This time, when we got close to shore, I didn't need the binoculars to pick out the cottage. Jackson set the anchor then shut down the engines.

"I'll take you to shore in the dinghy," he said, pointing to the back of the deck below us, where a white Zodiac rested on a ledge behind the galley door. I'd passed the inflatable dinghy every time I climbed the stairs to the observation deck, but inexplicably, I'd never given it a second thought.

"Hmm. Funny how you never offered to take me home in it before."

"Yeah, funny that," he said with a bemused smile.

We descended the stairs to the landing behind the galley. Jackson opened the gate to the Zodiac's platform then deftly released the dinghy's latches. It was attached to cables that extended up to a metal arm mounted on the side of the boat. He worked the levers that controlled the large arm to lift the Zodiac off the platform, and then he swung it over the side of the boat and lowered it to the water. The whole operation unfolded smoothly in mere minutes.

We went below to where Jackson had tied the Zodiac to the stern of the boat and secured the arm's lines. After we donned life vests, he loaded first my knapsack and then me into the front of the dinghy. He settled in at the stern, started the motor then pointed us to shore.

He beached the boat in front of the cottage and after I got out, he pulled it a few feet farther up on the rocks—enough so that the tide wouldn't claim it too quickly. "I'll walk you up," Jackson said, shouldering my knapsack.

The cottage was just as we'd left it, but Jackson insisted I let him check it out. For what, I didn't know, but I wasn't anxious for him to leave. "Take your time," I said, and turned on some music.

"You know, Em," he said as he walked back down the hall, "if I didn't know otherwise, I would have bet that a Flier picked this location. It's perfect. With the exception of that one neighbour to the north, you could fly in and out of here unseen any night."

He was right, and only a week ago I wouldn't have considered that perspective. It gave me a whole new appreciation for the cottage.

We looked out to where the *Symphony* was anchored. It was far enough away that we would need binoculars to read her name.

"I've got some things to do today," Jackson said, turning to face me. "But how do you feel about going flying tonight?"

I jerked my head back. "I would have thought you'd be glad to have a night off," I said, pleased with his invitation.

"I've had too many nights off, and last night put me in the mood for flying. What do you say?" He looked at me expectantly.

I gazed back outside as I mulled over his offer; I was torn. "I'd like that," I said, picking at lint on my sleeve, "but I want to sleep in my own bed tonight."

"Sure," he said without a moment's hesitation. "I can understand that. How about I drop by after dark?"

"Sounds perfect."

"Good." He leaned in and kissed me gently on the lips. "See you tonight then." He squeezed my hand and left. I watched him wrangle the Zodiac back into the water, and then he headed off to where the *Symphony* awaited.

I stood alone in the cottage watching the empty shoreline. The significance of the moment crept up on me: if I truly felt victimized, this was the point when I would call the police. The report of my abduction would be complete with dates and names, including the *Aerial Symphony*. Yes, I could wreak havoc on all of their lives—if I felt that way.

But I didn't. I felt grateful. After years of struggling, I had finally reached my all-consuming goal—to gain control over my condition and reclaim some semblance of a normal life. That was a momentous accomplishment and one I would never have achieved without Jackson's intervention.

He'd extracted me from the pages of the epic tragedy in which I'd been stuck and introduced me to the romantic thriller that could be my new life. In hindsight, my diving weights seemed silly; my secret pockets, overkill; my fear and embarrassment, a bad memory.

I finished unpacking my knapsack and put a load of laundry into the washing machine. My cellphone fell onto the floor with the tangle of dirty clothes. I checked it for messages. Cheney had left one to see how I was making out with the car. I hadn't talked to him since he'd dropped off the MGB in my driveway.

Cheney. Hearing his voice brought me up short. Cheney should have been a no-brainer for me. He was the total package. Wasn't it just last week that I'd pushed him away? Relationships had been out of the question until this flying thing was resolved. Wasn't it resolved now?

So why did it feel like nothing had changed, in the face of absolutely everything having changed? Then it hit me: I couldn't tell anyone. Not my mother; not Molly; not Cheney; no one. Protecting the secret was paramount. I would never be able to share the wonder of flying—the complete sense of freedom and peace that being airborne under your own steam provided.

Over the course of just a few days, my world had changed inexorably. It was no longer the same world that Cheney inhabited. My world orbited miles away from his. That whole "Before Flying" part of my life felt like someone else's. The realization stopped me dead in my tracks. I had to sit down. Was there any hope of going back? Did I even want to?

I stared down at the phone in my hand and laughed. Careful what you wish for, Emelynn, I thought. You wanted Normal, you got it, now deal with it.

I stood and forced myself to focus on the present. Charles and Gabby's bi-weekly yard maintenance schedule was stuck to the fridge. Their earlier phone message indicated they had to reschedule. I made a note to make sure I would be home. Surely they would expect me to be recovered and ready for a lesson in lawn mowing by then.

Then I phoned my mother. I tried her office but it was already early evening in Toronto, and she didn't answer. She wasn't answering at the condo, either, so I left her a message.

A glance in my fridge dictated my next priority. I tossed my purse over my shoulder and headed for the MGB. I had a moment's pause when I realized this was the first time in a decade that I didn't stop to load my pockets with weights before heading out.

The car chugged to life in a puff of smoke and I thought of Cheney's remarks about the nature of MGBs. It brought a smile to my lips. I drove out and headed for Safeway.

After I'd packed the groceries in the car, I pulled up to the curb outside of Rumbles and glanced inside. Molly sat behind the counter. I tooted the horn and she looked out. When I saw her enthusiastic wave, I lit up. I had missed Molly and our uncomplicated friendship. It hurt to think my new secrets might ruin it.

"Where have you been?" she said as soon as the bells over the door tinkled.

"Sorry?" The bookstore was once again bereft of customers—or paying customers anyway.

"It's been days. I know you have an epically bad sense of direction, but even you couldn't have been lost for this long," she said, stifling a smile.

"Aren't you a funny girl."

"If you hadn't shown up soon, I was going to call the authorities and report you missing."

"You're reading the wrong kinds of books," I said with a laugh. "My life isn't that interesting." The comment caught in my throat.

"Let's sit," she said, motioning for me to follow her to the chairs near the front window. "How's the car?" she asked, looking out at the small red convertible that I now called mine.

"Great," I said as we sat down. "But I do need to visit Cheney because I've forgotten how to take the top down."

Molly arched an eyebrow. "Yeah, sure you did," she said, and tilted her head to one side. "What happened to 'I'm not looking for a man in my life right now'?"

"I'm not," I said. A smile crept onto my face.

"No? That smile tells me otherwise. I think you're still interested."

She was partially right. A part of me regretted pushing Cheney away, especially now that so many of the questions that had held me back had been answered. But I'd moved on.

"He's all yours," I said. "Or did you change your mind about his butt nose and extra appendages?"

When our laughter faded, she told me what I'd missed about her twin brothers' latest escapades. They were sixteen now and learning how to drive. My mind wandered as Molly spoke. I felt a huge disconnect. I wanted to tell her everything, and I couldn't. My lies felt like an insult to our friendship. What kind of friend was I?

Eventually, I extracted myself. I gave her a hug goodbye, promising a dinner date and movie sometime soon. Molly grinned through the shop window as I drove off.

I had intended to go home but changed my mind. The disconnect I had felt with Molly was something I would have to get used to. I decided to head to Meyers Motors and get Cheney's help with the soft-top.

"Emelynn, how can I help you?" Jack asked, approaching the car as I got out.

"I'm looking for Cheney."

"Sorry, he's out on a call. Can I help you?"

I was disappointed, but maybe it was for the best. At least I wouldn't have to lie to him ... today, anyway.

Jack was happy to show me again how to lower the ragtop. I thanked him then drove home, enjoying my first trip with the top down and the wind in my hair.

As I unpacked the groceries, my thoughts raced. Seeing Molly eased the disappointment of not seeing Cheney, but it left me unsettled. It had been naive to think that once I had control of the whole floating thing, my life of secrets would be over. I now had a whole new collection of secrets to keep. I was lying by omission every time I opened my mouth to talk to Molly, Cheney or anyone else who wasn't a Flier.

And, at this point in my life, flying was the biggest part of me. I felt like I would explode if I couldn't talk to someone about it—to revel in the excitement and newness of it. I pulled Eden's number out of my bag and dialled.

Much to my relief, she picked up. "Hi, Emelynn, I'm glad you called. You made it home all right?"

"Jackson brought me home in the Zodiac this morning," I said. "He's coming back tonight and we're going flying again."

"Damn!" she said. "I wish I could go with you. Flying never gets old."

Eden and I carried on talking about all things flying. It felt like she was my safety valve and the longer we talked, the more the pressure eased. She told me about her nursing job at the hospital, and I filled her in on the discovery of my dad's car. She talked about Lululemon, a shop that specialized in yoga clothing particularly well suited to flying, and we agreed to go shopping together soon.

There was one other topic on my mind, but I wasn't sure she'd be receptive to me asking. I asked anyway. "How well do you know Jackson?"

"Not that well. We were introduced three months ago through a mutual contact. That's generally how we learn about visiting Fliers."

"What do you think of him?"

"He seems like a decent guy. Avery checked him out through his contacts and they vouched for him. Avery's even having Jackson help train the covey. The man's got skills. You'd be impressed with how diligent he's been about trying to find his covey's missing Flier."

"I'm glad to hear it. He's growing on me, despite the way we met." He was growing on me more than I was willing to let on to Eden.

"I've got to get ready for work."

"I wish you were coming with us tonight," I said.

"Me too. Have fun."

I saved her number to my contacts and went to get ready for my night's adventure.

Jackson arrived just after dark, and this time he didn't need the Zodiac. I'd been sitting on the deck anxiously awaiting his arrival. "Are you ready?" he asked, walking up the stairs.

"Can't wait," I said. "I've been looking forward to this all day."

"Me too, and I have something for you." He held out his hand in a loose fist waiting for me to catch the surprise. He released a tiny electronic gadget into my hand. I raised my eyebrows. "It's an earpiece with a microphone. Now we won't need to shout to each other up there."

He reached over my shoulder to push my hair aside. "You fit it into your ear like this," he said as he gently pushed it in place. "You'll need to adjust it so it's comfortable and pull the mic out a little." I felt for the mic and did as he said, then wiggled the earpiece around until it fit. This would make flying so much more fun.

"Think you can manage a liftoff from here?" He drifted upward, effortlessly as usual, and hovered above the roofline waiting for me to follow. It took more work for me, but each time I lifted off, it got easier, more fluid. I closed my eyes, visualized the crystal in my hand and concentrated on the growing hum under my skin. I called the power forward, broke gravity's hold then lifted off. This time I didn't overdo it. I was in control tonight and although Jackson was prepared, he didn't need to slow my ascent. This was the first time I felt truly independent in flight.

As soon as we cleared the trees, we headed out over the park. He pointed to where I'd had my accident and we circled around to take a look at the sandy beach I'd launched from on that fateful night. Looking at it from my current perspective, I recognized how feeble my effort had been. No wonder Jackson had intervened. That whole episode seemed as if it had happened a million years ago.

"Let's check on the *Symphony*," Jackson suggested, taking the lead and soaring off. I followed each of his dips and rallies. He sped up and I chased him. He dashed left then made a snap turn right and dared me to follow. I loved the challenge and easily kept up to him.

I caught sight of the *Symphony*'s white hull and we slowed down to land on the observation deck. We went below, where I helped myself to a glass of water while Jackson disappeared for a few minutes. He returned to check a panel of dials and lights.

"Everything's good here. You ready to go again?" he asked.

"Sure am," I replied.

He bolted ahead of me, laughing as he ran up the stairs. "Catch me if you can," he shouted with a devilish grin on his face then he leapt into the night and disappeared into the distance.

He'd caught me by surprise, but I was up for a game of follow-the-leader. I quickly called on the crystal to harness the power coursing through my limbs and sped off after him. It was only after I was chasing him that it occurred to me that the whole liftoff process was rapidly becoming second nature.

He'd gone for height and it took a few minutes to catch up. When he saw me approaching, he took evasive action, dipping down and curling left. I had him in my sights though and raced ahead to cut him off. The surprise on his face was worth the extra effort.

I took over the lead, taunting him, daring him to follow. I shot back up, soaring as high as I dared before levelling out. He made the chase look easy, but I wanted to make him earn his kibble so I stepped up the game. He tried to make me laugh by trash talking into my earpiece—something about my momma and a bitch slap. He did succeed in making me laugh, but I was still the one out in front. I twisted and turned, dipped and soared. This was so much fun. He was gaining on me again as he laughed into the earpiece.

"You'll never catch me," I teased, gauging his approach.

I was enjoying the excitement of this cat and mouse game. I knew I had more speed in me; I could feel it pent up, like a coiled spring. The thrill of the game made me push myself. I turned, waiting until Jackson was so close he could have touched me, then whispered, "Come and get me." I arched backwards and dove down, assuming a diving stance as I streamlined my body and let loose that energy that had been pulsing in me. The speed of my escape surprised and thrilled me at the same time. I dipped down, levelled off parallel to the water and poured it on, pushing myself, testing.

The speed was intoxicating, but it came with a price. I learned that lesson when I tried to lift my head out of the triangle formed by my arms; I'd wanted to see where Jackson was. The moment I lifted my head, the wind grabbed it, and my whole body jerked upward. I quickly tucked my head back in and corrected my trajectory.

That scared me. What the hell was I doing? I wasn't experienced or skilled enough to fly this fast. I needed to slow down. At least I knew how to do that. I unclasped my hands and slowly spread my arms. The wind caught my hair and whipped it into my face. It stung my eyes and they teared up, momentarily blinding me. I then made the monumental mistake of moving my hand to clear the hair away. Suddenly, I lost stability and whirled in the wind. I couldn't tell up from down, and the wind whipped me around like a plastic bag in a hurricane.

Panic, my familiar adversary, set in. Before I could stop it, my shoulder slammed into something hard and I flipped into a crude end-over-end cartwheel. It felt like skimming across concrete, but at least it slowed me down. I thought it was a small price to pay before I grasped the reality that the concrete was water—and that water quickly drank me down.

The cold shock of it forced the air from my lungs. Salt water shot up my nose. I gasped for air, desperate to breathe, and sucked even more water into my lungs. The back of my throat burned with each breath that brought more salt water into my mouth. I kicked my legs wildly, forcing my head above water, coughing and spitting. The surface surged and I struggled to tread water as rippling waves broke around me making it impossible to breathe without inhaling great gulps of sea spray. Fear clawed at me as the dark water pulled me under. I fought back, pumping my arms and legs in a vicious battle to push my head to the surface. I gulped more sea spray before the frigid water dragged me under again. I scissored my legs frantically. My limbs were fast becoming leaden weights that I could no longer feel. By some miracle, I broke the surface and seized a watery breath before sinking into the cold depths again. I watched helplessly as the water closed over my head. I kicked but couldn't break the surface. Though agonizingly close, even with my hand outstretched, the surface shimmered just out of reach.

The ache in my lungs would not be denied. I inhaled. Cold, thick fluid filled my lungs. Blackness drifted over me, enveloping me in a profound sense of calm.

The calm was rudely disturbed by a painful grip on my forearm. I felt my body being dragged upward through the water. The friction of the water clutched at my clothes, but the grip on my arm was stronger. The instant I was free of the water, I felt light as air and then it was the wind that clutched at me. Then nothing.

Sharp pain brought me back with a gasp. I lay flat on my back. A shadow hovered over me, pumping my chest.

I coughed and retched. Desperate hands rolled me onto my side, and I spewed impossible amounts of sea water out of my mouth and nose. Salt stung my eyes and burned my throat. I had the worst ice cream headache of my life, and the coughing made the fire in my throat roar.

Jackson frantically shouted, "Emelynn, Emelynn!" He shook my shoulders.

I rasped, "I'm okay."

He pulled me up to a sitting position and wrapped his arms around me, rocking me gently. "I'm so sorry," he whispered over and over. "You flew so fast, I lost sight of you. I didn't think anyone could fly that fast. God, I'm so sorry. I couldn't find you." I was vaguely aware of being back aboard the *Symphony*.

He rubbed my back and cradled my head but despite his best efforts, I was absolutely frozen. My body shook uncontrollably and I thought my teeth would break with their incessant chattering. I couldn't feel my fingers. "Your lips are blue," Jackson said. He picked me up and draped me over his shoulder in a firefighter's hold then carried me down to the cabin I had vacated just hours earlier.

He put me down on the bed then ran into the tiny head. I heard the shower come on. He undressed me, averting his eyes as best he could, and helped me into the shower. The warm water was unexpectedly painful on my skin. I slumped down the wall and sat on the shower floor and let the water wash over me.

I'm not sure how long I sat in the sluice of warm water. Eventually, my circulation returned. I felt my fingers and legs again, but my neck and shoulder ached from the ocean's impact. I slowly stood and carefully shampooed the remaining salt water out of my hair. I washed my body and reached over to turn off the water.

Jackson stood close to the door and held out a large towel. I stepped into the terry cloth. He wrapped it around me and pulled me close. It was warm—he must have run it through the clothes dryer.

He kissed my forehead. "I put a housecoat out for you. I'll go make us something warm to drink," he said, leaving me to finish towelling off. I wrapped my hair in the towel and donned the thick white robe. Jackson must have run it through the dryer too. I pulled it around me, soaking in the warmth then brushed my teeth and combed out my hair.

I felt much better by the time I left the head and made my way up to the living room. Jackson was also wrapped in a plush white robe, and it wasn't until then that it occurred to me he had also been in the frigid water. He must have been just as cold as I had been.

As soon as he saw me come around the corner, he wrapped me in his arms. It felt wonderful to have him hold me, and I had to hush him as he tried to apologize again. He dismissed my concerns about his own cold, wet experience, assuring me he was dry and warm.

Taking my hand, he led me to the white leather sofa. "Here, turn around." He pulled me into his chest as he reclined. I leaned back against him and he tugged the faux fur throw over us. It felt like home, lying here in his arms.

Two snifters sat on the table behind him. He reached for one and handed it to me; he took the other. "Brandy," he said, and I could feel the warmth of it through the thin crystal snifter. He was making a habit of heating things for me. The brandy blazed a trail from my mouth, down my throat and into my stomach, warming me from the inside out.

We lay in silence for a long while, sipping our drinks. When I had emptied the snifter, I passed the glass back to him. "Would you like another?" he asked.

"No, but thanks." I was finally warm. "Thank you, Jackson. Thanks for finding me, for getting me out of there." He hushed me. I felt so protected, so well taken care of. I had come close to dying tonight and now here I was lying safe and comfortable in his arms.

But it wasn't enough—I needed more. I needed to feel alive—not just safe and comfortable. An overwhelming wave of desperate desire washed over me, one I had never felt this strongly before.

As if he could read my mind, Jackson slid his hand under the folds of my robe. My breath hitched and he paused. I didn't stop him. His hand was warm against my bare skin, gently caressing my waist then moving up to brush the underside of my breast before reaching up to cup it fully. He rubbed his thumb over my nipple and my pulse raced in response.

God, yes. This was what I craved—this was what I needed. I heard his breathing deepen. He licked the edge of my ear then pulled my earlobe into the grip of his teeth and gave it a gentle nibble as he gathered my damp hair in his hand and brushed it aside. He traced his lips down my neck to my shoulder, which he was slowly unwrapping. There was no mistaking the direction this encounter was headed, and I was so ready for it.

"Jackson, I need to tell you something," I whispered, and then rushed on before I lost my courage. "I've never done this before."

His hands stopped mid-caress. "Never?" I shook my head. "Ah, damn," he muttered under his breath. Disappointment flooded me.

I felt his hesitation, and put my hand over his, holding him to my breast. "I don't want to stop." He kept still for a long time. My heart thumped loudly.

"Are you sure about this?" he asked, and I exhaled in relief as he slowly resumed his caress. I nodded, not trusting my voice. "I'll be as gentle as I can," he whispered into my ear. I felt his erection stiffening against my back, and then he picked up where he'd left off with the trail of kisses down my neck before licking what I discovered to be a deliciously sensitive area at the base of my neck.

He repositioned himself so he was propped up on his elbow, lying on his side facing me. His pale hazel eyes studied my face. What did this handsome man see in it, I wondered? He bent his head and kissed me, spreading my lips with his mouth before running his tongue along the edge of my teeth. His hands pushed my robe away and I undid his, sliding it off his shoulders as I ran my hands across his collarbone and down his torso. The faintest brush of fine, straight hair dusted his chest.

I traced my hands down the full length of his body, and landed on that perfect butt I had long admired. He hummed his pleasure, enjoying the sensation as much as I was. With renewed urgency he plundered my mouth, exploring it, claiming it. He curled his hips, pressing his erection against my thigh.

I pulled away and he frowned. "You okay?" he asked.

"More than okay. You're just what I need tonight." I grazed my teeth over my lower lip and leaned forward to lick one of his nipples. It puckered under my tongue. He inhaled a sharp breath that sounded like "keep going." I did, flicking it with the tip of my tongue before closing my mouth around it. His hand slipped under my hair at the back of my head and pulled me away.

His lips curled in a sexy smile. "My turn," he said, and kissed my neck, working his way down to my breasts. One after the other, he took each nipple into his mouth, swirled his tongue around the tip, teasing a groan out of me. His tongue was the perfect antidote to the cold Pacific.

His hands coaxed my legs apart and his fingers flitted across my most sensitive apex, pausing for just a moment before sliding back, exploring. I gasped, stiffening as I felt him insert his finger. It hurt but then his thumb found its way back to my apex and the dual effect was sensational. "That's it," he whispered as I relaxed and he started moving his fingers in a rhythm as old as time.

When he stopped, I felt abandoned. He pulled a condom from the pocket of his housecoat and let the robe fall to the floor. The fine dark hairs that covered his chest formed an enticing line down his stomach and continued as far as I could see. Curious, I trailed the dark hair, reaching down to touch his erection. The skin was softer than I'd imagined and so delicate that I could feel every nuance of the stiffness beneath. Did he know he was the first man I'd ever touched? Tentatively, I wrapped my fingers around him. He shuddered and held my hand in place, slowly stroking up and down. His visceral response to my touch made me want more.

He removed my hand to slip the condom on and I had a moment to take in his dark curls and think to myself that this was an important moment—one I'd remember forever. He positioned himself between my legs. "You sure about this?" he asked, rubbing the tip of his erection across my knot of nerves and then just barely inside the edge of my wetness.

"God, yes," I answered.

He propped himself up on his elbows and I saw in his face the strain he was under as he held himself back. "This is going to hurt," he said in a breathy voice. He held my gaze as he pushed into me. I felt pressure. He pulled back a bit then pushed forward, harder, and the pressure turned to pain. I gasped.

He pulled back again and searched my face. I nodded but had the horrible sense that something was wrong with me. "Relax, Em," he whispered. His jaw twitched as he surged forward again, harder still. He was right, it did hurt, but it wasn't working.

He pulled back once more. "Easy now, breathe." He thrust forward again, sharply this time. I felt a hot sting before the pain, and dug my nails into his back, momentarily losing my nerve. He hesitated for a moment, letting me adjust, then pushed into me farther still. A deep moan escaped his throat, flooding me with yearning. "Fuck," he groaned under his breath. He paused then slowly pulled back.

"No," I whispered anxiously, holding him tight. He couldn't stop now. I glanced at his face—his expression looked pained.

He shook his head, as if speech wasn't an option, and curled his hips, pushing back in. I breathed again and he started a slow, steady rhythm in and out. The pain eased and I tried to find the pleasure that I knew must be accompanying his movements. He filled me so completely that I thought I would split in two.

His rhythm continued, steady and gentle, just as he promised, and I waited for the experience I had read so much about to roll over me. My hips met his, matching his rhythm as he moved smoothly, steadily, in and out. I looked down between us and caught a glimpse of his stomach muscles clenching as his hips curled into mine. It was supposed to feel better than this. It was supposed to be something exquisite, and it was just around the corner, if only the sting and the pain would go away.

"Look at me," Jackson demanded. I looked into his eyes—his face was a mask of ecstasy. "I can't hold on." He then used his gift to trap my gaze and push me over an edge I didn't even know I was on. I threw my head back and convulsed my hips, bringing my knees up, pressing them into his sides as a pulsing crescendo overtook me. It came in waves, leaving the pain far behind. I heard myself moan and then he lost the last of his control and stopped being gentle. He pushed my knees forward and slammed into me, pushing deeper again and again. Then it was his turn to shudder and he stiffened then jerked in spasms. He pulled me along with him and even after we had stopped moving, I continued to feel sensational little aftershocks.

He eased out of me and lay on his side, fluttering his fingertips over my arms and torso. "You are magnificent," he said as he bent to kiss me. He couldn't have said anything more perfect at that moment. I was willing to soak up the compliment, even though I was sure he would have preferred a more experienced woman. But just for tonight, I was going to ignore my negative inner dialogue.

"I really didn't know what to expect, but I sure liked the ending," I said, catching his fingers. I felt more replete and content than I'd ever felt before, even though it was taking a bit of concentration to ignore the burning sensation between my legs.

"It won't hurt as much next time," he assured me. *Next time.* I liked the sound of that.

We lay on the sofa, spent and contemplative for a long time. Finally, he stirred. "Let's go to bed." He pushed himself up off the sofa. Taking my hand, he pulled me up into him and kissed my forehead.

We headed below to my former cabin, and he wouldn't let me wear a T-shirt. "I want to feel your skin beside me tonight," he said.

We fell asleep spooning under the thick down comforter.

Chapter Fourteen

I woke with a start and bolted upright, shaking. Jackson jerked up beside me and reached his arm around my shoulder. "You're okay," he said, and gently pulled me back down into the warm bed, pressing my head against his chest.

The nightmare lingered. I felt trapped in the memory, trapped under the surface of the cold water, unable to kick my way free to the top and helpless to stop my body's reflex to inhale. I shuddered at the memory of the icy water spilling down my throat, filling my lungs. Jackson tightened his embrace and kissed the top of my head. He pulled the warm blanket around my shoulders. Gradually, the sweet memory of making love with Jackson eclipsed the horrible nightmare. A smile crept onto my face and I fell back to sleep.

When I woke next, it was to the sight of Jackson standing in the doorway with a tray in his hands. He'd donned a wide grin and a pair of drawstring pyjama pants. "Coffee?" he asked. I wanted to burn that image of him with his sleepy face and broad, naked chest into my memory. Beard stubble looked good on him.

I scooted up, holding the covers tight as I propped a pillow behind me. He'd seen everything there was to see, so I don't know why I was covering myself, but for some reason, I'd never felt so naked.

"How are you?" he asked, holding out a mug. I had the impression the question covered a lot of ground.

"I'm good," I replied, and then winced as I reached for the coffee.

"Really?" he asked, arching an eyebrow. He set the tray on the bedside table and joined me under the covers.

"All right, that's a bit of a lie," I confessed. "My shoulder's sore. My knee too." I offered a weak smile over my mug.

"I'm sorry," Jackson said, "but I'm sure glad you're breathing." We toasted my health with our coffee mugs.

A quiet moment later, he stared into his mug and said, "How are you feeling about the rest of it ... about us ... about last night?"

That very question hadn't been far from my thoughts since I'd opened my eyes. "I'm still smiling," I said, which was true, but in truth, I didn't know how I felt about it.

Would I have given myself to him if I'd not almost drowned? Maybe, eventually, when I knew him better. I was certainly attracted to him before last night. And as far as first times go, this one had to rate somewhere near the top. It was definitely better than some of the horror stories I'd read about. And now it was done with—I didn't have to drag the "virgin" label around anymore.

"How about you—how are you feeling about us?" As soon as it was out of my mouth I regretted asking. After all, what was he going to say? *That was the worst sex of my life—get your sorry butt out of my bed.*

"Me?" He snickered, and gently shook his head. "I'm on top of the world." He ran a hand through his messy curls and reached down to squeeze my thigh. "If I didn't think you'd be too sore to enjoy it, I'd show you right now how good I feel about last night. Truly," he said with a wicked twinkle in his eye, "I can hardly wait to feel good about us again real soon."

I exhaled in a rush and felt a blush of embarrassment that his words were such a relief. He wriggled his dark eyebrows in a ridiculous attempt to be roguish, which made me laugh. And he was right; I *was* sore, inside and out.

Jackson continued in his roguish mien suggesting we share a shower, which brought up intriguing but laughable possibilities; the shower was far too small. So, while I finished my coffee, Jackson headed back to his own head to have a solitary shower.

I pulled on the housecoat that lay draped across the bench at the side of the bed and stood. My muscles ached in protest. I lumbered to the head and stared at my reflection. The face that stared back was the same one as yesterday. I thought maybe I'd look different somehow. I felt different.

I'd let lust have its way last night and there was no going back. I didn't regret it—not at all—but it had been out of character for me.

Letting go of the control that was normally such a reflexive part of my life had left me feeling vulnerable and exposed. Jackson was a man I could fall for. Maybe I already had. That was scary. I barely knew him and now he could break my heart.

I paused to look back into the cabin. My life had changed immeasurably since Jackson first brought me here. It would take time for me to adjust. I knew that. In the meantime, I vowed to enjoy the moment for however long it lasted.

Jackson returned with a towel wrapped around his waist and an electric razor in his hand. "I'm finished with the water now if you want to hop in the shower." He rolled the razor around his jaw and focused his attention on my robe's tie. I loosened it, but long-seated shyness prompted me to turn around before dropping it and stepping into the shower. I felt his eyes on me as I slipped behind the glass. Who knew it would feel so good to be looked at that way?

He was gone when I opened the door to pull a towel from the rack. I dried off and finger-combed my tangled hair. I found my clothes neatly folded on the bed.

He already had a pan on the stove and beaten eggs in a bowl when I showed up in the galley. The smell of bacon made my mouth water. I poured myself more coffee, found Jackson's mug and topped it up. He pushed the toast down and poured the eggs into the pan. I watched him work, as confident and at ease in the kitchen as he was in everything else he did. I could get used to this morning routine. After breakfast, I cleaned up.

Jackson put his cellphone down when I joined him on the sofa. "I've been around Fliers all my life, but I've never seen anyone fly as fast as you last night."

Was he was finally getting around to being angry with me? God knows I deserved it. "I'm sorry. I should never have done that."

"I'm not looking for an apology, Em. I'm just saying ... you're working with some serious speed."

"Speed, perhaps, but not a lot of skill. It was careless of me to show off like that." Embarrassment was the least of it—it had been selfish of me to put us both in danger for such a shallow reason.

"No, it's impressive. It makes me wonder what other hidden talents you might have." His smile trailed off into wistful contemplation.

"Hopefully, I don't have any more hidden talents." The ones I'd already discovered presented a big enough challenge. "And don't worry.

I won't be flying that fast again." At least not until I'd had time to regroup, and a lot more experience flying at regular speeds.

"That's probably a good idea. But you do need to practice. How about this morning?"

"In broad daylight?" I asked with a note of surprise in my voice. "Isn't that too risky?"

"We'll head offshore, far away from casual observers."

"I don't think so." After last night, flying was the last thing I wanted to do today.

But Jackson disagreed, shaking his head. "You need to get back on the horse, Em."

"Come on, Jackson. Last night was a disaster. It wouldn't be getting back on the horse so much as it would be testing the temperature of the Pacific. Believe me, that is *not* something I intend to do again any time soon."

"That thinking is exactly why you need to get back in the air. You're going to be reluctant no matter when you do it. Better you do it sooner than later—before you ingrain false fears into your psyche."

I gave his words some thought. "Maybe you're right." But I wasn't giving in yet. Jackson didn't look as though he was in any rush, so I tucked my feet under me, swallowed a painkiller and got comfortable.

But fly we did, eventually. Jackson steered the *Symphony* far offshore until only the gentle swell of the ocean and the occasional seagull kept us company. I'd lost my earpiece, which left us back to being incommunicado in flight, but that was all right with me. The earpiece didn't exactly hold fond memories for me now.

With trepidation, I stood on the observation deck. I took a deep breath and called forth the crystal, harnessing the power that dwelt within me, and smoothly lifted off. We kept a slow pace, always within sight of the *Symphony* and never too high.

After an hour or so, we landed and sat opposite each other on the sofas. He propped his feet up on the table.

"Thanks, Jackson. I needed that."

"The fresh air?" he asked, with a stupid grin on his face.

"No, and don't look so smug." I turned to stretch out my legs. Jackson seemed at ease. Just looking at him and thinking back to the previous night's lovemaking made me want him all over again.

I was glad I'd taken his advice and gone flying. Truth be told though, I'd found the slow, safe flying boring. I was ready to fly at regular speeds again with all the loops and rolls that made it such fun. My confidence, though shaky, was definitely coming back. Flying was as exhilarating as it was addictive.

The boat gently swayed with the swell of the ocean. I scooched down until my head rested comfortably on the armrest then closed my eyes. The sun warmed me and I let myself drift off.

Sometime later, I woke to find a blanket draped over me but no sign of Jackson. I snuggled under the cover. Finally, my curiosity got the better of me. I stretched in the late afternoon sun then wrapped the blanket around my shoulders, and went in search of Jackson. He was at the computer and looked up when I entered the room. He hit the last key with a flourish then stood and came over, folding me in his arms.

"Thanks for the blanket."

"You looked so comfortable; I didn't want to disturb you. Do you feel rested?"

"Yeah, I feel great. What time is it?" I asked, glancing down at his watch.

"Just after five. Do you feel up to another flight? We have enough time for a short one before we have to head back in for the night."

"I'd love that," I said.

This time we flew at regular speeds and heights. We even added rolls and weaves. It felt good to be back on track, though I wasn't ready to tempt fate with my speed at full throttle.

When Jackson finally anchored the *Symphony*, it was after eight and we were both tired. "Would you like to stay here tonight?" he asked. "We can make dinner, watch a movie if you'd like."

"Sounds perfect," I said, smiling to myself. How quickly things had changed. Just yesterday I'd insisted on sleeping in my own bed. Funny how that didn't seem quite as important now.

We scrounged in the fridge and found ingredients to make chicken fajitas. Jackson opened a bottle of Wolf Blass Yellow Label and poured us each a glass while I set to work chopping vegetables.

I looked over at Jackson, who was bent down, searching for a frying pan, and paused to enjoy the view. How did I get so lucky? I wondered, and then I remembered Sandra. He'd come here to find her, so I guess I had her to thank for bringing him into my life. Had he made any progress on that front? I knew he didn't like to talk about it, but maybe now that we knew each other better, he'd relent and tell me more.

"May I ask you something?"

"I guess that depends," he said, straightening up with the elusive frying pan in his hand. His face was flushed from the effort and he brushed his hair back out of his eyes.

I studied his face. "What is it that brought you here to BC?"

He looked away from me and set the pan on the stove. "Sandra's abduction," he said, his voice barely a whisper.

I would have to be careful or he'd shut me down, as he had last time. "Why here?"

He turned to face me, leaning back against the counter. "Whoever took her still has her and they're headed this way."

"I don't mean to sound insensitive, but how can you be sure that she's still alive?"

"The people who abducted her are making sure that we know it."

"How?"

"They're forcing her to make large cash withdrawals from ATMs. And because the banks digitally record transactions, each time she makes a withdrawal, we get time-stamped proof."

"If that's the case, why don't the police help?"

He reached for his glass. "When she went missing, her family reported her abduction to the police and they investigated. They reviewed the ATM photos but concluded there was nothing in her demeanour to suggest foul play. We tried to convince them otherwise, but they disagreed. In their opinion, she's of age and it's her money, so they refused to pursue it." The disdain on Jackson's face was hard to misinterpret. He gulped his wine.

"But you don't believe that."

"Of course not," he said, raising his voice. "I know Sandra. She would never drop out like this—be out of touch for so long. She'd never put her family through this."

He reached for the Wolf Blass and poured another glass. The anger rolling off him was palpable. "After the police dropped the investigation, we made a deal with the bank. They now send us the photos and the particulars of her withdrawals."

How much money or influence had that negotiation cost? I wondered. "What makes you believe they're headed this way?"

"Her abductors made a mistake a while back and set a pattern. They've either gotten lazy or brazen, but we can tell that they're headed north because the latest withdrawals have been from ATMs along the coast and each one is a little farther north."

I pushed my luck a little further. "Do you have a plan to find her?"

"We think they're travelling by boat now because they're hitting bank machines close to marinas. That's why I had the *Symphony* brought here. I want to be close, ready to go when the time comes. We're tracking them and, eventually, we'll find the boat they're on and then we'll intercept them." His menacing smile sent chills skating down my spine. It was time to change the subject.

"I hope you find them soon," I said, turning back to the cutting board. Sandra's family was lucky to have a friend like Jackson. Her abduction had obviously affected him deeply. I wouldn't want to be on the receiving end of his wrath when he eventually caught up to them— and I had no doubt he would.

"We will," he said, turning the flame on under the pan. He chose a sharp knife and took out his frustration on the chicken. He dialled his anger back as we set the table but didn't relax again until we sat down to eat.

After dinner, we migrated to the sofas with our wine glasses and I settled in beside him. He draped an arm around me. The movie didn't hold my interest. My thoughts drifted. Once again, I found myself grappling with the enormity of the transformation my life had taken. I felt as if I were on the outside looking in at someone else's life rather than my own. I needed time alone, when Jackson wasn't so distractingly close, to think things through. I resolved to tuck my thoughts away until I was home again. In the meantime, I reminded myself: enjoy the moment.

And at that moment, what I wanted to enjoy was Jackson. He'd been trailing his fingers down my neck and across my shoulder for the past few minutes and I sensed him gearing up for more. Such a simple caress, and I was already melting. What was it about this man that felt so damn good? He relieved me of my empty wine glass then turned to face me. I ran my hand through his hair. The soft curls wound around my fingers. I recognized the expression in his half-closed eyes: he wanted me and that felt incredible. He kissed me—softly at first, but soon his kiss became more demanding. He traced his hands over my clothing, exploring my curves, applying pressure with expertise in magical places.

"You are very good at this," I said, pulling away to catch my breath. He held my hand against his chest and leaned his forehead into mine.

"I'm glad you think so, but it has nothing to do with me." He pulled back. "Do you have any idea how you make me feel when I'm with you?" He grazed his thumb over my cheekbone. "To know what you gave me last night and that I'm the only one who has ever been inside you like that? God, Em, you are so beautiful and you don't even know it."

I knew it wasn't true, but I liked hearing it anyway. I felt the blood rush to my face. "I don't know how to respond to that." I turned my face away from him, embarrassed.

He took my hand and ran it down his chest then over the front of his jeans where his erection strained against his zipper. "You don't need to say anything," he said, quivering under my touch. "How about we continue this below," Jackson suggested in a breathy voice as he pressed my hand into his jeans.

"I'm sorry, Jackson, but I couldn't possibly do that again tonight." I felt disappointed that he'd already forgotten about my current, tender condition.

"There are lots of other ways to deal with this," he said, grinding into my hand. He let out a clipped gasp as a horny smirk settled on his face. "Trust me ... you'll like it." He pulled me to my feet and led the way down to my former cabin to continue what we'd started.

I sat on the edge of the bed watching the muscles of his arms and chest dance as he removed his shirt. That horny smirk was back, tugging at the corners of his mouth. I reached up to run my fingers over the fine dark hairs on his toned stomach and he grabbed my hand and urged me to stand.

He lifted my shirt up over my head and kissed me while he reached back to unhook my bra. In no time at all, he'd disposed of my clothes and his hands roamed over every inch of me. The unsure, shy part of me felt self-conscious as I stood naked in his embrace.

When he released me to remove his jeans, I felt the full weight of my exposure. Embarrassment washed over me in a tidal wave. I tried to cover myself, but Jackson stilled my hands. "Don't," he said. "I want to see you." His eyes smouldered over my nakedness, scorching every inch of my skin as he peeled off his jeans. I took a deep breath and wondered what he had planned.

Once again, he played teacher, and as it turned out, he was right—I did like it. An hour or so later, he had me thoroughly convinced that there were, indeed, many other ways to satisfy our arousal. There was not a single square inch of either of us that wasn't thoroughly kissed, stroked or tasted, and I doubted that I would ever again feel embarrassed about being naked with this man. We fell asleep wrapped in each other's arms completely satisfied and relaxed. It was another night of firsts that I would never forget.

Sunday morning dawned bright and warm. I stretched dreamily under the covers, but Jackson was gone. I spotted a mug of coffee beside the bed and recognized the distant sound of the water pump running. Disappointed, I buried my face in the pillow next to me and inhaled deeply of Jackson's scent, recalling the warmth of his body next to mine. I propped myself up on the pillows and sipped the heavenly brew.

After the water pump quietened, Jackson poked his head into the cabin. "Got your coffee I see," he said, towelling his hair. "Sorry for the early start, but I've got some business to take care of today. How about I get you home?"

I tried not to look surprised or disappointed, though I was both. It all seemed rather abrupt, but going back to the cottage, to my safe place, was always all right with me.

Jackson weighed anchor and steered us back to familiar waters. Within the hour, we were in the Zodiac, heading back to the cottage. He walked me up the steps to the patio door and kissed me goodbye. "I'll call you later," he said. Then he was gone.

When the Zodiac was just a speck on the sea, it occurred to me that I didn't even have his phone number. It proved how much the man distracted me. I shook my head and turned away from the view.

I fired up my computer and waited for the emails to download then dealt with them quickly. I sent my mother an email filled with absolutely nothing of consequence and found myself wishing I had a closer relationship with her. Maybe daughters never talked to their mothers about their first loves, but I sure wish I had someone to talk to; I wanted so badly to tell someone all that I was feeling about Jackson. I logged off, closed the computer and went in search of my book and a beach towel. Tucking my phone into a pocket, I headed down the stairs to the beach.

I leaned back against a log and stretched my legs out in the sand. The sun warmed my face. As usual, there wasn't a soul on the beach. I breathed in the salt air and revelled in a moment of pure bliss, thanking the heavens for helping me find my way back to this beach and this cottage that was so much a part of me.

I flipped halfway through *Pillars of the Earth* to find my place. I hadn't picked it up in days and had to reread quite a few pages to refresh my memory. It felt good to lose myself in a book again.

An hour or so had gone by when my phone rang, startling me. Of course, I was hoping it was Jackson, but call display disappointed me. "Hi, Emelynn. It's Dr. Coulter. How are you?"

I set the book aside and pulled up my knees. "I'm not sure how to answer that question," I said, trying to decide just how indignant I should be about the fact that he'd broken a cardinal rule and violated patient-doctor confidentiality.

Dr. Coulter didn't respond right away, but I didn't feel any compulsion to fill the silence. A crow passing overhead cawed a greeting. "You could start with the basics," he said. "You know, 'I'm fine' works, or 'I'm well' is good too."

"Is that right?" I said, continuing with my indignant tone, if not the intent. He might have violated my privacy, but I understood why he did it. I sifted a handful of sand through my fingers.

"Yes, it is. You might even follow up with, say, 'How are you?'"

"I could ... and what would your answer be, Dr. Coulter?"

"I'd assure you that I'm fine. And then I'd take the opportunity to apologize and add that I'd like the chance to explain myself."

"I see." I swirled circles in the sand with my fingers. "I'm not angry," I said, having milked his guilt as long as I could in good conscience. After all, he'd likely done me a service. Jackson had already saved my life in more ways than one.

"I'm glad to hear that, but you had me worried. I thought I might hear from you after Jackson's intervention."

"It's been a busy few days," I said, wondering if the doctor could be that far out of the loop or was he just playing dumb?

"Yes, I'm sure it has," he said, and another awkward moment passed. "Have you had any headaches, blurred vision?"

"No, I'm fine," I said.

"That's good, but I'd still like to see you. I should check your eyes and I'm sure you have questions."

I did have questions, plenty of them—and Dr. Coulter was the perfect resource. "I think that's a good idea," I said, suddenly excited about the prospect. I needed to start making a list.

"How about one o'clock tomorrow?" he suggested. "In my office."

"Yeah, that's great. I'll see you tomorrow."

I wanted to learn as much as I could about Fliers, particularly our eyes and especially about Jackson's little KO trick. Indeed, the doctor and I had a lot to talk about.

I picked up my things and made a beeline for the cottage. *Pillars of the Earth* would have to wait. After my chat with Dr. Coulter, flying was on my mind again, as was the delectable Jackson Delaney. Thoughts of him and the things he could do to me had my libido soaring. I needed to get him off my mind and making a list of questions for tomorrow's appointment with Dr. Coulter would do the trick.

My pen raced across the paper and I easily filled a page and a half without stopping. I got partway through making a sandwich before more questions came to mind and I filled another page.

After lunch, I turned on some music. Eventually, the questions petered out and the thoughts I'd been putting off for days crept in. Thoughts about how drastically my life had changed. I was happy about most of the changes. Glad to have rekindled my friendship with Molly. Pleased about my car and meeting Cheney. And the cottage was so much more than I had ever imagined. Even Charles and Gabby were pleasant additions to my life.

On top of all these positives, I now knew more about the secret that had held me hostage for so many years. I was finally free from the fear of the unpredictable, embarrassing floating episodes. Eden and Alex were turning into good friends and, best of all, Jackson was in my life and working his way into my heart.

So why did something feel "off"? As much as I resisted, my intuition kept taking me back to Jackson, but why? Was it as simple as not being comfortable with having someone in my life on such intimate terms? Perhaps, but if I was honest with myself, it had more to do with me. I wasn't in control when it came to Jackson. Our relationship felt impulsive and reckless, which was a little too much like how I felt when my floating wasn't controlled. The whole Jackson thing put a part of me under the microscope that I didn't like so much: the control freak.

Afternoon melted into evening with no solid conclusions despite all that thinking. However, I had come up with a plan. I would use Dr. Coulter as a resource to learn everything I could about Fliers and their world. I never again wanted to be in the position I was in when Dr. Coulter found me. Naive and vulnerable didn't sit well with me. I favoured being smart and resourceful over being a victim, any day.

Hopefully Eden, who'd proven to be open and willing to share, would have some insight on how to integrate my two worlds. I had a feeling it was going to be important.

As far as Jackson was concerned, I didn't have a clue. He and I had climbed aboard some crazy roller-coaster ride that was exhilarating and fun but scary as hell, and I didn't want it to end. All I was sure of was that I wanted him in my life.

So that was the plan. That's where I would start. Tomorrow.

Right now, a warm bath beckoned. I filled the tub and traded my clothes for a housecoat. After I poured a glass of wine, I grabbed my book and the phone then sank down into the mound of suds.

All told, it had been a good day. I had the cottage to come home to and a plan to move forward. Life was good. The unwooded Chardonnay tasted crisp and clean. I perched the glass on the side of the tub and lost myself in the pages of my book.

The phone startled me but fortunately not enough to upset either the book or the wine glass. Call display read, "Private Caller," which turned out to be Jackson, and my heart skipped a happy beat.

"Are you in the bathtub?" he asked.

"How could you tell?"

"I can hear the echo," he said, chuckling, "and you're splashing." He found that amusing, which made me smile and wish he were here splashing in the other end of the tub.

My pulse raced just talking to him. Did he feel the same way? We exchanged unimportant information about our days and I wondered if this was what couples did. Not that we were a couple—I just wondered.

"I'm taking the *Symphony* in for maintenance in Richmond, day after tomorrow. If you don't already have plans, maybe you could pick me up and we could do something together?" he asked.

"I'd like that." We agreed to talk tomorrow, when he'd have specific details from the shipyard.

"Any more news on Jolene?" I asked.

"No, I haven't heard anything back."

"What about Sandra?" I asked, sensitive now to how important finding her was to him.

"No, nothing there either," he replied.

"You'll find her," I said, trying to be supportive, but he went quiet on me.

"Are you all right?" I asked.

"Sure, I just don't like to think about it."

"Do you keep in touch with her family?" I asked.

"All the time," he replied, sounding exhausted.

I changed the subject. "How can I reach you?" I asked. "Your phone number doesn't come up on call display."

"No, it wouldn't. It's a Louisiana number. I don't suppose you've got a pen or paper there with you in the tub?"

"You suppose correctly," I said. "Why don't you text it to me?"

He said he would, and then he said good night. I read until the water cooled too much to ignore. I got out and dried off. My bed had never felt better. I buried myself in the comforter and slept like a corpse the entire night.

CHAPTER FIFTEEN

The habit of sleeping in was bound to get me in trouble. It was already after ten when I opened my eyes, and Gabby and Charles were due shortly. I jumped out of bed.

My jeans were mid-zip when the doorbell chimed. I ran down the hall, checked myself at the door, and then opened it.

Charles and Gabby waited on the porch. "Come in," I said.

Gabby was her typical chipper self, spilling local news about the neighbourhood as soon as she stepped inside. "The Morrison house over on Fitzgerald Street finally sold," she said. "It was on the market for ... how long now, Charles?"

Charles didn't answer. He was preoccupied, looking through his binoculars out the patio door.

"Don't mind Charles. He's been distracted ever since he got word that there's been a fresh sighting of a rare bird he's been studying."

"Charles," Gabby called again. "I've been telling Emelynn about the Morrison house. How long had it been on the market?"

Charles turned away from the window and joined the conversation. I looked from Charles to Gabby and felt that disconnect again, the same feeling I had with Cheney and with Molly. Their world seemed distant. I used to think of that world as Normal, but the further away from it I drifted, the more I had to challenge my definition of Normal.

They had moved on to talk about their small herb and vegetable garden, and Gabby prodded Charles to write down the names of some perennial herbs they thought might do well in the gardens close to the cottage.

Charles retrieved a spiral notepad from his pocket. I glanced over to the page but he tilted it away from my view. Gabby tsked in admonishment. I looked away to give Charles his privacy and saw Gabby roll her eyes. Who knew birders were so secretive?

Gabby commented on my improved health, which reminded me I had a one o'clock appointment with Dr. Coulter. I stood, hoping to move things along.

"Are you up for a lesson on the mower?" Charles asked, ripping the page from his notebook.

"Sure am," I said. We spent the next hour and a half pushing the mower and Whipper-snipping. Charles finished raking and Gabby showed me how to deadhead the rose bushes beside the front porch. After the tools were stowed in the garage, they refastened their helmets, mounted their bicycles and waved goodbye.

As soon as they'd gone, I headed for my appointment with Dr. Coulter. I was early. I took a seat in his empty waiting room and settled my knapsack on my lap. The room was sparsely furnished with four chairs and two small tables. I reached for a magazine and fanned the pages in a rhythmic slap of paper. No one else came or went.

Dr. Coulter arrived through an inside door, right on time. He looked just as I remembered: fiftyish, tall, blond and casual. Without the white coat, he didn't look like a doctor. Maybe it was the absence of the white coat that reminded me of my father.

"Emelynn, good to see you." Dr. Coulter extended his hand. "I'm so glad you came." He clasped my hand between both of his, oozing charm and sincerity.

He invited me to go ahead of him into the small exam room. I dropped my things on the chair then hoisted myself up on the vinyl-covered table, dangling my feet over the side. The paper covering rustled as I settled. He put on his doctor's face and carefully examined the pink suture lines on my scalp and ankle. A penlight appeared out of nowhere. He flashed it in my eyes, then clicked it off and returned it to his pocket.

"You're healing well. You feeling okay? No nausea, double vision?"

"No. I'm good. Would you mind, though, taking a look at my shoulder? And my knee?"

He had me rotate my arm then my lower leg, examining both in turn. He didn't ask what happened, but after he declared I was only a little the worse for wear, he perched on the edge of an old desk across from me and waited for my explanation.

"I had a tiny mishap the other night and cartwheeled into the ocean," I said. He raised his eyebrows. "It felt more like concrete than water at the time."

"Hmm, kind of cold for a swim this time of year, isn't it?" he said, giving me the same crooked smile he had in the hospital. I found it quite disarming.

I crossed my ankles. "How long have you known about Fliers?"

"All my life," he said. "My folks were both Fliers, but of course they're gone now."

"Are you from here?" I asked.

"No, I was raised in Arizona, but this is my home now. I still keep a place in Chandler though, just south of Phoenix."

"Then you're a member of the local group Jackson told me about?"

"The covey?" he asked. I nodded. "Yes."

Our casual banter ran out of steam at the mention of Jackson's name, and an awkward silence ensued.

"I'm sorry, Emelynn," Dr. Coulter said, coaxing me to look at him. "Bringing Jackson in was the best I could do for you. Your injuries were serious and I could tell you weren't giving me the whole story in the hospital. But I knew if you couldn't tell I was a Flier, you were in real trouble." He really did seem sincere.

"In good conscience, I couldn't abandon you. And when I learned you had no family here, I asked Jackson to get involved. You see, I couldn't help you but I knew he had the perfect set-up."

I couldn't see a trace of deception in his face and I wanted to believe him. "You could have warned me."

"You wouldn't have believed me." He shook his head and straightened up, crossing his arms.

"Maybe you're right. It has been a pretty unbelievable revelation." I looked down at my feet, thinking about the first time I'd watched Eden fly. Words would never have been able to convey what her jaw-dropping demonstration accomplished.

"Jackson called me after he took you to the *Symphony*. I didn't approve, by the way, but he felt he didn't have a choice. He told me how vulnerable you'd been when he approached you on the beach and then, when he learned you didn't even know you were a Flier, well, that was shocking, to say the least. It surprised both of us."

"I can't believe I'm the only one," I said, looking at him again.

"Well, the only one we've come across, anyway." He picked up a pen from his desk and examined the writing on the side of it. "You're flying now?" he asked.

"Yes, and I love it! Jackson's been great. So have Eden and Alex. They've taught me so much. I'm still a beginner, but at least I'm independent now—flying without my 'training wheels' as Eden calls them."

Dr. Coulter laughed. "Given your recent swim, perhaps the training wheels shouldn't be removed just yet."

He asked me to fill in the details and I explained all I'd gone through since my accident in the park. Dr. Coulter listened and the line between his eyebrows deepened, but he didn't interrupt until after I'd finished explaining how I ended up in the ocean.

"You were gifted the flying, then?" he asked.

"Yes, but I never knew the woman who gifted me. Her name was Jolene. She disappeared after she gave it to me." I explained about my father's passing, my subsequent move to Toronto and the unpredictable floating incidents that traumatized me throughout university.

"Interesting," he said. "In all my experience treating Fliers, your situation is a new one. It's fascinating—even though the gift was thwarted, it still seems to have found a way to leak out." He moved behind the desk and sat in the chair.

"That's a different angle," I said, amused.

"You said earlier that Jackson was surprised by your speed?" I nodded. "I'll do some research from my end—see if I can learn anything about Jolene." He opened a drawer and pulled out a pad of paper. "What else can you tell me about her?"

"Not much." I gave him the same details I gave Jackson.

"Jackson's already looking for her," I said. "He thought his San Francisco contact might have some information, but nothing has come through yet."

"It's a start," he said, jotting something down. "We have different contacts. Maybe mine will be able to dig up something."

"Thanks, Dr. Coulter, I'd appreciate that."

"Please, call me Avery. All the Fliers call me Avery."

"Okay, Avery," I said, easing myself off the table. "Then you can call me Em. All the Fliers call me Em." I reached for my bag.

Avery chuckled and looked up from his note-taking. "You're leaving already? We still have some time."

"Oh, no. I wasn't leaving," I said, feeling a bit awkward. "After we talked yesterday, I jotted down some questions. Do you mind?" I asked, retrieving my list of questions.

"Of course not. I assumed you'd have questions." He put his pen down and leaned forward. "Ask away."

I sat in the chair and smoothed the folds out of the papers. He burst out laughing as he caught a glimpse of the extensive list. "Maybe you should prioritize," he said, stifling his laughter.

"All right." I looked down the first page. "Well, I'm curious about the eye thing. Jackson incapacitated me just by locking his eyes on mine. He said most Fliers can do that. Is this your understanding as well?"

"Yes, theoretically." Avery pressed his fingertips together.

"Apparently, I was more susceptible than I should have been to that trick."

"Yes, he mentioned that."

An idea that put Avery into a whole new light struck me. I slowly lowered the list to my lap.

"What is it?" he asked.

"How would you feel about teaching me how to use my eyes like that?"

He leaned back and crossed his arms, staring back at me with pursed lips and furrowed brows. After what seemed like an eternity, he spoke. "It would be a challenge."

"But you're willing to try?" I asked, excited at the prospect.

"Let me think about it—see what I can come up with."

"That would be great!" I said, and then I hesitated. "You, ah, won't tell Jackson about this, will you?" Avery discussing me with Jackson felt like too much of an invasion of my privacy.

"Not if you don't want me to." He leaned forward and grabbed his pen. "How about you and I set up another appointment so we can get started? Wednesday, same time?" he asked.

"That works for me," I said, and started collecting my things, but my curiosity got the best of me and I paused. "How do you know Jackson?"

Avery finished his note and set his pen down. "He got in touch with me earlier this year through a Flier contact."

"So you've not known him for long?"

"No, not long. Why are you asking?"

"Just curious. For some reason, I thought you knew him better."

"No, not well, but enough to know he'd do right by you. We'd talked on the phone when he was thinking about coming up here. Since then, he's met with me and the covey a half-dozen times. He's well connected and people speak highly of him. He's treated you well, hasn't he?"

"Oh yeah, Jackson's been great. Well, at least after I got over our unusual introduction." I paused as I recalled those first few days of feeling like a hostage on the *Symphony*. "I just wondered about him. I don't think I've ever spent so much time with someone I know so little about. That's all. I'm not complaining. He's been unbelievably patient with me, and so have Eden and Alex."

"You know, Jackson was reluctant to take you on." Avery gathered some loose papers and tapped them on their edges to tidy them. "He's quite focused on finding the Flier from his covey who went missing. Sandra, I think her name is. He agreed to take you under his wing, but only until you get a handle on flying." He put the papers inside a file folder. "I'm sure as soon as he finds this woman, he'll leave and take her straight home to Louisiana."

"Jackson told me the police don't believe him about Sandra. They don't think she's been abducted."

"Yeah, he mentioned that early on when I asked him why he hadn't involved the police."

"He also told me about a Tribunal Novem, but that they couldn't help either."

"Why would he bring up the Tribunal?" Avery's features hardened into taut lines.

What the hell was it about the Tribunal that provoked this type of reaction? "At the time, we were discussing the hows and whys of someone wanting to steal the gift, so when Jackson told me about Sandra, I thought maybe this Tribunal could help. He nearly bit my head off when I suggested it and the look on his face was not unlike the look you've got right now."

"I'm not surprised. The Tribunal Novem has a well-earned reputation and not the good kind. You don't want their attention if you can help it."

"That sounds ominous. What does the Tribunal do?"

"They deal with Fliers who break our code of conduct."

What the hell? "We have a code of conduct?" Now I, too, was alarmed.

"Most of it's about not exposing the gift. It's pretty basic."

"Basic? So what constitutes a violation?" I asked.

"The Tribunal only deal with the worst kinds: stealing the gift or using it to break the law. Sometimes, they deal with those who intentionally reveal our gift to the non-Gifted. Their verdict is law and they don't scrimp on the punishment."

There was still so much I had to learn about the Flier world but this particular item seemed like a critical, gaping hole in my knowledge base. "What exactly do they do to them—the ones who break this code?"

"Only one thing. If they find you guilty, they arrange an accident."

"What kind of accident?" I asked, already suspecting but not wanting to hear the answer.

"The lethal kind," he said without inflection.

"That's horrible." I couldn't hide my shock, and I stumbled over my own reaction. Just when were they going to tell me that little gem? After I'd violated their secret code?

"Yes, it is, but rarely do any of us ever have the misfortune to meet them. But enough talk of the Tribunal," he said, waving his hands as if that closed the subject. "Just talking about them sucks the life out of the room. Besides, you're at such an exciting time in your life, Emelynn. Let's not ruin it."

"Yes, let's not," I said, letting my frustration out. "But don't you think there would have been a better chance of my not meeting the infamous Tribunal Novem if someone told me about the damn code of conduct?"

The harshness of my tone took him aback. "No one's worried about you, Emelynn. You already know how to hide your flying activities. Hell, you've successfully kept the gift a secret for years now without any instruction at all. That's the primary rule. Really, Emelynn, you don't have to worry."

I let that sink in, hoping he was right.

"You know, I envy you the thrill of learning how to fly: the newness of it all." A wistful smile crossed Avery's lips. I was relieved for the change of topic.

"Yes, it is all that," I said. "Jackson mentioned to me that you were a rare bird, so to speak. You know—a Flier who couldn't." I paused for effect but didn't have to because his smile told me he'd caught my poor pun.

"Do you feel cheated not being able to fly?" I asked. He frowned, leaving me worried that I'd asked him too personal a question.

"I did when I was younger," he said, "but not now. I'm used to it and I'm needed right where I am. I enjoy the role I'm able to play, 'Physician to the Fliers.'" He made air quotes around the title. "Maybe I should have a plaque made up?" He sported a toned-down version of his crooked smile, but there was a sadness in his eyes that told me my question had bothered him more than he let on.

"I have to go," I said, not wanting to make him more uncomfortable. Besides, after the Tribunal talk, I needed some fresh air. "See you Wednesday?"

"You bet," he said, tucking the file folder away in a drawer.

I said goodbye then headed home. I parked the car in the garage and walked through the cottage to fire up my laptop. My phone rang before the computer sparked to life. It was Eden.

"Hey Emelynn, how are you?"

"I'm good, thanks. It's nice to hear from you." I hadn't realized how much I missed her until I heard her voice.

"I'm still on nights, but I wanted to check in with you to see how you're making out before I head into work."

"I sure wish you were on days." Questions were swimming around in my head: the code of conduct, the Tribunal, this disconnect I felt with one foot in each world. It was too much for a rushed phone call.

"Are you okay?"

"Oh, yeah, I'm fine. It can wait until next time I see you."

"Are you sure? I have a few minutes."

I thought I'd better change the subject before I sprang a leak and started a conversation we couldn't finish. "Do you have time to hear about the dip that Jackson and I took in the Pacific the night before last?"

"What?" she asked, her voice suddenly shrill. "How did that happen? What went wrong? Are you okay? How's Jackson?"

I didn't mean to laugh, but her rapid-fire questioning was touching—no doubt because I was now on the dry side if the incident. "I'm fine. We're both fine," I said. When she got over her anxiety about our health, I filled in the blanks about our cold, wet misadventure. She was particularly interested in the details of my drowning, which I didn't relish repeating but she insisted on hearing.

"That's it. I'm coming over," she said. "You stay put. I'll be there in thirty minutes."

"All right," I said with a laugh. "But honestly, I'm fine."

She was adamant, so while I waited for her, I phoned my mother. We had one of our longer conversations. I filled her in on Charles and Gabby's morning visit and my gardening lesson. Eden's soft footsteps on the deck prompted me to say goodbye.

I sprang to the patio door and let her in. Her spiked red hair looked like a counterpoint to the plain dark jacket she wore over navy scrubs. She carried her stethoscope, obviously ready for work.

"You flew?"

"I left my car on the other side of the park. It was faster than driving all the way here then back. My shift starts in thirty minutes so we'd better make this quick."

"Make what quick?" I asked, confused now about the purpose of her visit.

"Emelynn, you almost drowned. You inhaled sea water. That can leave you highly susceptible to pneumonia. I need to check your lungs. Over here, sit down," she ordered, inserting the stethoscope's earpieces.

"You should have gone to the hospital straight after your accident," she said, kneeling behind me. "Take a deep breath." She slipped her hand under my shirt and held the cold disk to my back. "Again," she said, moving the disk to the other side. "Again," she repeated and then, "One more time."

Satisfied, she stood. "Your lungs sound good. You're fine."

"I've already been to see Dr. Coulter," I said, feeling somewhat sheepish. "If I'd known what you were thinking, I would have mentioned it earlier."

"That's all right. I feel better having checked you for myself." Eden sat on the sofa and relaxed her shoulders. She took a deep breath. "So what happened out there? You've been doing so well."

As best I could, I explained how I wasn't able to handle my newly discovered speed. That, of course, provoked no end of questions.

"Now I'm really looking forward to our next flight," Eden said. "I want to see this speed first-hand."

"I'm not sure that's such a good idea," I said with a laugh, but my smile faded. "Eden, may I ask you something?"

"Sure."

"Do you have friends who aren't Fliers?"

"Yeah, a few. Why?"

"I bumped into someone I knew back before my dad died. She's a schoolmate I hadn't seen in years. We got together the other night. It was fun to talk about old times, catch up." The lightness that I felt thinking about Molly drained out of me as I got to the crux of the issue. "But I felt like everything that came out of my mouth was a lie. It's bothering me way more than I thought it would."

"It's hard sometimes," Eden said. "It gets easier." She sat forward and searched my face. "You can't tell her, Em. It would put you both in danger."

"I know. I wouldn't do that. I just wish I didn't feel like such a fraud."

"Well, maybe you should think about it from a different perspective; you're protecting her, that's all."

"I hadn't thought about it like that." Maybe that was just the thinking I needed to adopt. It sure felt better than thinking of myself as two-faced.

"Good. I hope it helps because the danger is real. The disappearances are real and I can't bear to think about adding your name to the list." Eden shivered despite still wearing her jacket.

"The others who have gone missing," I said. "I got the impression you knew one of them." Jackson had shut down our discussion last time this topic came up, but I was really curious now.

"Not personally, but his story circulated all over the Flier network." Eden rubbed her arms, but offered no more detail.

"I'm one of you, aren't I?" I asked, leaning forward and resting my elbows on my knees.

"Of course," she said.

"Then I should know what's going on."

Eden moved to the edge of the sofa, avoiding eye contact. "I don't want to frighten you."

"And I don't want to be frightened, but Eden," I said, getting up to sit beside her, "when you treat me like a child—keep things from me—that frightens me more."

She held my gaze and sat back. It took her a moment to steel herself. "About two years ago a twenty-four-year-old Flier named David Ashton disappeared. Three months later he resurfaced." Eden looked away. "He'd escaped some kind of lab. It was in San Diego somewhere, or at least that's where he was found."

She looked back at me, her eyes as dead as the expression on her face. "His captors used him like a guinea pig, taking blood and tissue samples. They tethered him and forced him to fly to the point of exhaustion under the most brutal conditions: severe heat, biting cold, even submerged under water. Sometimes they'd handicap him by binding his hands or feet or stripping him naked but that's not the worst of it, Emelynn."

She looked directly at me, and the anger that seethed out of her was palpable. "They took one of his eyes." She swallowed hard. "He hanged himself a few weeks later. He couldn't sleep—couldn't move past the nightmares of what they'd done to him. So his family never did get him back." Her shoulders slumped.

"I'm so sorry, Eden." I reached out and laid my hands over hers. She was ice cold. "What kind of monsters would do that?" I whispered, half to myself. No wonder she didn't want me to know—it was horrifying.

"The inhuman kind." She inhaled a few deep breaths. Just telling the story seemed to age her. "But we're working to find out. We're getting better organized and Fliers are getting less reluctant to involve the Tribunal. Everyone is being so careful, watchful."

"You don't need to worry about me." Now, more than ever, I was committed to keeping our secret. "I'll be super careful."

"Good." Eden forced a smile. "Now I've got to get to work." She stood and walked to the patio door. I joined her.

"Don't let what happened to David rob you of our secret sky, Emelynn."

"Secret sky?"

"That's how I think of it."

"I like it," I said, and offered her a reassuring smile.

"Let's go flying again soon. I want to get a first-hand look at this speed you're talking about."

I leaned in and gave her a hug.

"We'll talk tomorrow, okay?" With a wave goodbye, she took off from the deck, blending into the night as she headed over the trees into the park.

Eden was right about one thing: the horror of David's story felt like an anchor. The negatives of this gift could easily outweigh the positives if I let them. That wasn't me. I lived in the top half of the glass. She'd been blending into Normal for years. I could do it too.

I reached for my phone and dialled Molly.

"Hey, girl," she said, answering. "How are you?"

"Just great," I said, and told her about my day. Eden's words eased my guilt as I skipped over the parts I couldn't share.

"I heard there's a new Brad Pitt movie playing over in Seaside," I said. "Would you like to go see it—maybe go for dinner beforehand?" I couldn't remember the last time I'd gone to a movie. What a refreshingly normal activity.

"I'd love to. Let's pick a day," she said.

We decided on the day after tomorrow.

"It's a date. Do you want to go to the Seafood House again?" Molly asked and I could hear the hope in her voice.

"Sure." Molly probably knew the menu by heart.

And right on cue, she said, "This time I'm going to order the sea bass," which made me laugh out loud. "What?" she asked, laughing at herself.

Later that night, I found the scrap of paper with Eden's scribbled phone number and email, and flattened it out beside the computer. I sent her a brief thank-you and took my phone out to the deck. It was cool, so I pulled a throw around my shoulders.

The phone rang, startling me. "Private Caller." My heart rate picked up.

"Emelynn. How was your day?"

A part of me was not happy about how much the mere sound of Jackson's voice thrilled me. Should he have this much effect on me?

"Productive. I learned how to start the lawn mower," I said, chuckling. "Or maybe I should say, I learned how to pull on the cord and not start the mower."

I told him about my plans with Molly for Wednesday night, but I didn't mention going to see Avery, or Eden's visit. He didn't need to harbour any guilt over my not having gone to the hospital after the accident, nor did he need to know that Eden had told me about David Ashton.

"How about you? How did your day go?" I asked.

"It was uneventful," he responded. "I'm taking the *Symphony* into the shipyard in Richmond tomorrow. Are you still interested in getting together?"

"Sure," I said, feeling ridiculously happy about spending the day with him.

"Good. Why don't you swing by the marina and pick me up?"

He gave me directions and I promised to be there around ten in the morning.

After we hung up I skipped to the bathroom and went through my nighttime routine. I piled the pillows behind me in bed and read my book until the wee hours of the morning.

To say that I was a tad directionally challenged was an understatement. Maps and I didn't get along well, so I left in plenty of time to find the marina and meet Jackson at ten. It was the kind of bright, beautiful day that called for sunglasses. I laid the map optimistically on the passenger seat with a sticky note of scribbled directions on top.

Unfortunately, my directional sense was in fine form this morning. What started off as guarded optimism gradually eroded into full-out aggravation as I slowly got myself twisted around and indeed, lost. I couldn't find the marina to save my life. Finally, in exasperation, I stopped and asked a postman. I was definitely getting myself a GPS.

Finally, I saw the sign for the marina. I was late, but at least the *Symphony* was easy to spot. Her size made her stand out. Jackson met me on the dock with a kiss. He didn't seem to notice that I was late so I didn't cop to my map affliction.

"Let's go for a walk along the dyke," he said. "I could use the exercise after being on board for so long." He took my hand and we started back.

"Have you learned anything about Jolene?" I asked.

"Nothing yet," he said. "And nothing else on Sandra either," he added, pre-empting further questions.

I gave his hand a reassuring squeeze, aware of how distraught the topic left him. "I hope something turns up soon." We got to the top of the ramp and crossed the parking lot to my car.

He circled the MGB with open admiration. "You like?" I asked.

"It's a classic," he said. "What's not to like?"

He fed me directions to the dyke. I parked then we strolled toward the path that ran along the top of it. The gravel trail reached into the distance in either direction. At my hesitation, he suggested we head left. It was a popular spot and we passed bikes, joggers and dogs taking their owners for walks.

We stopped for a leisurely lunch along the water's edge and poked in and out of shops on our way back to the car. Racing goggles in a bicycle rental shop's window caught my eye. "Let's go in," I suggested. The goggles were designed to closely fit the contours of the face. They would go a long way to keep the wind, and more importantly, my hair from getting into my eyes when I flew. I tried on a pair of Ryders with clear lenses.

"Great idea," Jackson said, smiling at me over a rack of Toad and Co clothing he'd been shuffling through. Not for the first time today, I smiled back then shook my head.

Jackson came around the rack and took my hand looking at me quizzically. "What is it?" he asked. "What's so funny?"

"Not funny, at least not hee-haw funny," I said as I looked up to meet his gaze. "It's just so incredibly, oddly, normal. Here you and I are, having a perfectly normal day: walking along the dyke, shopping, eating lunch—just like everyone else." I looked around to ensure no one was close by. "Only there's nothing normal about us. That's what I'm finding so amusing."

"I forget how new you are to this life," he said, pulling me close. "One day this *will* be normal for you. Eventually, flying will seem as natural to you as breathing."

After I paid for the Ryders, we headed back to the car then drove to the marina, where the *Symphony* would remain moored overnight. The mechanics were almost done. Jackson poured us each a glass of wine, and we brought them up to the observation deck. We passed the hour until our dinner reservation watching the sun's golden glare transform into the blue cast of night.

Dinner at Steveston's Jetty was sensational. Afterwards, we split a big, rich piece of cheesecake. And much as I would have liked to have a brandy, I was driving, so reluctantly declined.

It was pitch-black by the time we arrived back at the cottage. I caught myself as I reached for the light switch out of habit. I didn't have to pretend around Jackson. I left the lights off and turned on some music before we moved out to the deck. The water's rhythmic wash over the sandstone played like romantic background music. We leaned over the railing, side by side, making small talk. It was silly banter that didn't take much concentration, which was a good thing because my mind was filling with other thoughts—thoughts that involved seeing Jackson naked and lying in my bed.

The night breeze tossed his dark curls around but his pale hazel eyes were steady and they were focused on me. He wasn't using his gazing gift to get my attention tonight—he didn't need to. By the time our lips met, I melted into him with an intense longing. We teased each other with kisses and caresses to the point of indecency. "Bedroom," he whispered. I nodded and took his hand to lead the way. He stopped dead in his tracks, staring at the trees that lined the cliff to the south.

He pulled me back into a tense embrace. He whispered into my ear as he turned us around. "Look over my right shoulder into the branches of the arbutus tree. Don't make it obvious."

Jackson talked through kisses down my throat and along my collarbone. "Do you see anything unusual?" I partially closed my eyes, trying to ignore Jackson's kisses as I casually scanned the tree. "At about the same height as your roof," he mumbled through more kisses, directing my search.

There weren't a lot of leaves lower down the trunk, and now that I knew where to look, something did stand out. "I see something reflective, maybe about the size of a Red Bull can."

"That's it. Have you ever noticed it before?"

"No. What is it?"

"I can't be sure, but if it's what I think it is, we have a problem."

Chapter Sixteen

J ackson pulled me into the house and slid the door closed. "Do you have binoculars?" he asked, moving us down the hallway toward the front door.

"No. What do you think it is?"

"It looks suspiciously like a camera."

"A camera? What would a camera be doing there?"

"Good question." Jackson paced the hall, dragging a hand through his hair. "I need to get a closer look. You stay here. I'll be back in a few minutes," he said, slipping quietly out the front door.

Through the window in the study I watched, fascinated, as he lifted mere inches off the ground then glided swiftly over the lawn, as if he were wearing skates, before disappearing into the trees on the south side. I hadn't seen that Flier move before.

I dashed to the kitchen window to follow his movement. Moments later, I caught a glimpse of him. He approached the arbutus tree from height on the far side of it and huddled over the device for a few minutes before leaving the same way he'd arrived. I returned to the front door to let him back in.

"Will your computer read this?" he asked, examining a small memory card. He walked briskly toward my laptop as he held out the tiny plastic square.

"I have no idea," I said, once again hamstrung by my lack of computer know-how. "What did you find?"

He planted himself in front of my laptop and pushed the power switch. "It's a camera, but it doesn't look like it's been there for long."

He examined the edges of my computer searching for an appropriate slot. "I think we're in luck," he said, pushing the card in.

After a few keystrokes, a checkerboard of photos appeared: dozens of them. "It's motion activated." He quickly clicked from one image to the next and we got our first look at what the camera had captured. The view was a northward wedge that broadened out from an apex at the southern edge of my property to include the area from my deck to mid-tide. The view also stretched up the beach, encompassing my neighbour to the north.

"They're high-resolution photos. Whoever is taking these can blow up the detail of even the smallest pebble on that beach." Jackson rested an elbow on the table and rubbed his forehead. He moved the cursor over the first photo. "This was taken at six fifteen this morning," he said, pointing to the date stamp in the top-right corner. "The camera isn't wired for remote transmission, so whoever is behind this either set it up or changed the card, early this morning."

He set the photos into a slide show and we watched the images flash by. The majority of them were triggered by birds. Jackson stopped the slide show at eight seventeen, when an image of me in my nightshirt, out on the deck, landed on the screen.

"Oh, my god," I said. The clarity of the evidence frozen on the computer screen shocked me. He restarted it and I watched myself leaning up against the rail, then I was sitting down, a blanket over my legs. The final shot of that series was of my foot as I went back into the house. Countless bird shots followed. Jackson skipped ahead and abruptly sat back in the chair, as if he'd been slapped.

"What is it?" I asked, alarmed by his response to the oddly coloured photo of me peering over Jackson's shoulder on the deck.

"These images are thermal infrared."

"What does that mean?" I asked, wary of his stillness.

"It means that whoever is behind this isn't fooling around. That camera is high-tech ... professional." He looked to me, eyes stone cold, drained of all emotion. "It means someone spared no expense to set up 24/7 surveillance of this area."

I pulled up a chair to sit beside him, unwilling to think the worst. "Could the explanation be as simple as a wealthy birdwatcher? Maybe it's some moneyed organization keeping an eye on a migratory route or a nesting area?"

"If that were the case, you and your neighbours along this beach would have been notified. It's too big an invasion of privacy for it to be legitimate."

He was right, but I didn't want to think about other nefarious possibilities. I'd only been here a few weeks; no one knew me. My pathetic Flier activity prior to meeting Jackson happened south of here, well out of that camera's range. I couldn't possibly be the target, could I?

"How long do you think it's been there?"

"Maybe a week. The thing is clean and the scars on the tree where it's been mounted are still fresh."

"Then Eden, you and I have all been photographed ... flying." I said, as the repercussions of that reality sunk in.

Jackson, lost in thought, popped the memory card out of the computer. "I need to return this to the camera," he said, pushing away from the table. The front door closed behind him.

Despite its small size, the camera was a massive wrecking ball precariously poised and ready to smash my cottage into splinters. I moved to the sofa and pulled my knees to my chest. Jackson was on his phone when he returned and ended the call as he sat beside me. His emotionless stare had been replaced with a nervous energy that was just as disconcerting.

"Who was that?" I asked, taking his hand in mine.

"Alex. I've asked him to bring over a security camera. If you don't mind, we'll set it up in your kitchen window. With any luck, we'll get a look at who's retrieving the memory cards from that camera. If we can ID them, we might be able to figure out what's going on. We should, at least, be able to tell if they're Fliers or not. You okay with that?"

"Sure, anything to help. Do you think that whoever's behind that camera has seen us flying to and from the *Symphony*?"

"Without knowing how long that camera's been there, I'm afraid that's a real possibility."

"Could it be connected to Sandra's disappearance?" I asked, dreading the misery I knew the topic invited.

"It could be." He held steady, not losing his cool this time.

"In that case, I think you'd better tell me the rest of the Sandra story," I said, aware that I was poking a sore spot. He sighed heavily and it was more than frustration—it was sadness. I knew I needed to tread lightly, but I wanted to know more about her and her connection to him, especially now. "How do you know her?"

"She's a friend and one of my covey back in New Orleans," he said.

"I wish you weren't so curious about her. But more than that, I really believe the less you know, the better." He squeezed my hand. "If the people behind that camera are connected with Sandra, you'll be safer if you don't know anything about her."

How much more could there be to know? "I don't mean to upset you. I just want to help."

"You can't at this point. I wish you could but you're too inexperienced a Flier. When we find her, we'll need a team of our best to get her back."

"But I'm fast, Jackson. You said so yourself."

"Fast only helps if you can control it, Em, and you're too green right now. You are fast, the fastest I've ever seen, but your speed would be a detriment to us if we ended up having to pull you out of the Pacific."

He wasn't being unkind, just truthful. "I'll keep practicing. Maybe I'll surprise you."

"Maybe you will," he said, curving his lips into a roguish grin. "It wouldn't be the first time."

"Will you stay?"

"For a while," he said. "I asked Alex to come as soon as he got his hands on a camera. We'll set it up tonight if you don't mind."

"Of course not," I said, but that wasn't exactly what I'd had in mind. I snuggled next to him and he tucked me into his side, under the security of his arm.

I jumped at the doorbell's soft tone. Jackson answered it and let Alex in. "How are you doing?" Alex asked when he saw me. His anxiety showed in the tightness around his eyes.

"I'd be better if there weren't a camera outside watching my every move."

"Yeah, we all would," he said, turning to Jackson. "Where do we need to set this up?" He held a small box. I watched them unpack the hardware, a black plastic rectangle measuring about five by seven inches and maybe two inches thick.

Jackson and Alex collected a few books roughly the same size, then laid the camera in the middle of the stack and set it on the kitchen windowsill. They made it look as if someone had carelessly plopped the books down. It worked; I would never have suspected that a camera was hidden there.

"It's not high-tech," Jackson said, "but it will take a photo of that damn tree every sixty seconds during daylight hours. I've set it up to send the images through your router to my computer, so don't turn your router off."

"Will you feel safe staying here?" Alex asked. "You could come stay with Eden and me. We have a spare room."

His concern was touching. "Thanks, Alex, but I think we'd have a better shot at finding out who's behind that camera if I stayed here and kept up the impression that everything's normal. I don't want to scare them off, especially if they're watching to see when Jackson is going to make a move to go after Sandra."

"Do you think that's what this is about?" he asked, turning to Jackson.

"I don't know," Jackson said. "I can't connect those dots, but I can't rule it out yet either."

Jackson turned to me, placing a hand on my shoulder. "I think you staying here is a good idea, but only if you feel comfortable doing it. If you could carry on like nothing's up for the next twenty-four hours or so, we might get an ID."

Feel comfortable? Right now the only thing I felt was afraid, but I wanted to be brave. The covey needed me to do this—for all of us. "I can do that," I said.

He squeezed my shoulder. "Keep your doors and windows locked. Don't open up for anyone you don't recognize. I'll know the minute someone approaches that camera. Where's your phone?"

I picked it up off the coffee table and Jackson punched a number into it. "That's my phone number," he said, handing the phone back to me. "Call me any time." It occurred to me as he said it that he must have forgotten to text me his number after our bathtub conversation. "Until we know who's behind this, we need to keep a lid on it. So don't tell anyone about our discovery."

"Eden already knows," Alex said. "I phoned her before I left the shop."

"No one else then, okay?" Jackson looked from Alex to me. "We don't know who's involved in this so let's not inadvertently warn them."

"Agreed," I said, and Alex nodded.

"Well then, there's nothing else I can do here tonight," Alex said. "I'll update Eden when I get home." He turned to me. "Call us any time if you change your mind."

"Thanks, Alex." I walked him down the hall then watched until he disappeared into the edge of the forest. Jackson was right behind me when I shut the door.

"I've got to head off too if I'm going to make it back to the *Symphony* without a taxi. Are you sure you're okay with this?"

"I'm not thrilled about it," I said, struggling to keep visions of tortured Fliers out of my head. "But I think it's best."

He leaned down to kiss me. What started off as a brush of the lips quickly rolled into sensual territory, that lovely place we'd been before he'd spotted that camera.

"Lock up behind me," he said, and I reluctantly released him then watched him disappear into the treeline.

My bed felt extra big and cold without him. I curled onto my side and fell into a fitful sleep.

When I woke, it was 10:00 a.m. and my first thought was of Jackson, which provoked a slow smile. Unfortunately, my second thought was of that damned camera. I pulled the covers up around my chin. Maybe I could cocoon here until Jackson figured out who was behind that camera. Ah, but the morning called: bathroom, cuppa, music, computer, in that order.

There was an email from Eden. Predictably, she was concerned for my safety after learning about the camera and once again offered their spare room. She also happily reminded me she was going off nights and wanted to set up a flying date for tomorrow. Her timing was perfect. I needed a diversion. I emailed her back right away and warned her to come to my front porch, which was out of the camera's range. I closed the laptop and steadied my nerves.

With a steaming bowl of cinnamon-laced porridge in my hands, I headed out to the deck and settled into a chair. It was a struggle to not look in the direction of the camera. I used the dull day as my excuse not to linger outside; I didn't even venture down to the beach. Instead, I headed back indoors, cleaned up and dressed.

I might have to maintain the "everything's normal" facade, but that didn't mean I had to spend all day in the cottage. My appointment with Avery wasn't until one o'clock. Until then, I knew just the thing to fill my time. I opened my laptop and dialled Jackson.

He picked up on the second ring. "Good morning. How'd you sleep?"

"Better than I thought I would. How about you?"

"I've been up since dawn monitoring the photos from your kitchen camera, and I've got to say I'm pretty tired of looking at that tree."

"I'm sorry. You must be bored out of your mind."

"I haven't ventured far from the computer, but luckily I do have some work to do so it's not a total waste of time."

"This whole thing is getting to me. I'm going to go out, take a break."

"Okay, I'll call if anything interesting shows up."

"Thanks. Talk to you later," I said, hanging up as I typed "portable GPS devices" into the search engine.

It was time for me to investigate the GPS option. Getting lost yesterday had served to remind me how much I needed one. With Google's help, I narrowed down my choices. The portable one looked handy, but maybe a bigger screen was better? I bet Cheney could give me some pointers. He had offered to help, after all.

I hopped in the MGB and headed to Meyers Motors. At least this visit to Cheney would be without any ambiguity on my part. Jackson being in my life had cleared that up: Cheney was a friend—period. It had been weeks since our kiss and I'd never followed up on his date offer, so if he had any lingering expectations, I would fix that today and hope the friendship survived. After all, I didn't have so many friends that I could toss a good one away.

I parked on Stafford Street and walked toward the open bay doors. Cheney spotted me from his place behind the grill of a beige sedan hoisted in the air. He dropped his gaze and grabbed a hand rag. I took a breath and headed in.

"Emelynn?" He looked up from fidgeting with the rag, his blue eyes narrowed.

"Hi. How's it going?"

"No complaints. I hear I missed you the other day. Dad says you needed a refresher on the ragtop."

"Yeah." I shrugged. "Mind like a sieve, I guess."

A corner of his mouth twitched up and he dropped the rag on the bench. "What brings you by?" he asked, switching to mechanic mode. His expression was open, casual: not suggestive in any way. We'd moved into friendship territory.

"Remember a few weeks back when you showed me your GPS?"

"Yeah. You thinking about getting one?"

"I am, but I'd appreciate your opinion. Would you mind?" I asked, fumbling in my bag to find the fact sheet I'd printed.

"Sure." He took it and nodded his head as he skimmed the list. "I prefer the portability of the small ones, myself. Garmin's a good brand. I don't think you could do much better than this one." He pointed to his choice.

"Thanks," I said. "Molly and I are going to Seaside for dinner and a movie tonight. I thought I'd drop into that electronics store on Campbell Street to see if they had one in stock."

"I might be able to get you a deal at McKay's down here on Fourth. They do some of our stereo work. Want me to call them?"

"Sure," I said. We headed into the cluttered office and by the time Cheney got off the phone, he'd lined me up with a new GPS at a twenty percent discount.

As Cheney walked me back to my car, he asked, "Who's Molly?"

"A friend. She works at Rumbles. It's a bookstore down on the strip. Do you know it?"

"Yeah, a few doors over from Starbucks, right?"

"That's the one."

"Short, dark hair?" he asked, concentrating as if he were pulling her picture out of his memory.

"Yeah, that's her." I arched my eyebrows.

"What? I'm not blind," he said. "And I've walked the strip a time or two."

"So you have," I said, raising my chin. Was he blushing?

"What can I say?" he said. "She stands out."

Grinning, I got in my car, waved goodbye and headed for McKay's.

I could hardly wait to relay Cheney's observations to Molly tonight, and this time it would be without any twinge of regret. What a difference time and a new lover made. The only question was, could I wait until dinner, or would I blurt it out in the car on the way?

The salesman at McKay's was expecting me. I left with my new GPS already programmed with Avery's address. The GPS's audio directions took me right to his front door. I parked and swore my undying love for the friendly man who lived in the GPS.

I was early again, but I had an instruction manual to read and more addresses to enter into the GPS. I brought it all with me into the empty waiting room.

I was engrossed in the instruction manual when Avery cleared his throat. I looked up with a start. "Sorry. How long have you been standing there?" I said, fumbling to gather my things.

"Not long. What's got you so captivated?"

"I bought a GPS today."

"May I see it?" he asked. I handed it to him. "It's so small," he said, turning it over in his hand.

"That little unit is going to save me a lot of directional aggravation. You don't know this about me, but I'm pathetic when it comes to following a map," I confessed.

"It'll be useful when you're flying, too." He handed it back to me. "You know—when you can't see the street signs." I must have looked confused because he clarified. "Signs are designed to be seen from street level, not from height."

Understanding dawned. This GPS was going to be a lifesaver in ways I hadn't even thought of yet. I packed my new toy back into my bag and draped my coat over my arm.

Avery invited me ahead of him into the examination room. "I've got some news," he said, closing the door behind us. He motioned me to the chair and sat on the corner of the desk. "I think I've learned Jolene's identity."

I tensed on the edge of the seat. "Tell me."

"If my sources are accurate, her name is Jolene Reynolds."

"That name sounds familiar, though I can't quite place it. How did you discover her identity?"

"Through Greg, one of my contacts. After you left the other day, I emailed him Jolene's details: her name, the info about your flight speed and the possible San Francisco connection. It didn't take him long to come back with the name."

I pinched my forehead. "How did Greg know Jolene?"

"He didn't, at least not personally. There's a network in place that we're all connected to through our coveys and secure message boards. Someone down the line knew the name Jolene. It's uncommon, so when it was combined with the other details, they were able to zero in on her identity.

"Even in born Fliers, the gift can morph when it's passed on. Not the basic skills—those tend to pass unchanged—but the extras, like your speed or Jackson's ability to incapacitate, those things can change. I took a chance that Jolene's gift was passed on intact and it panned out. Jolene had a similar affinity for speed."

"Jolene Reynolds," I said, as if by saying her name out loud I'd get closer to her. "Did you learn anything else about her?" A major piece of my mysterious life puzzle loomed enticingly close. I was ecstatic.

"I got a few more details. She's an artist, or she used to be. A painter, apparently. Some of her early work sold through an artists' cooperative in San Francisco, but it doesn't look like she was a major player in the art community and there have been no recent sales. I would be interested to compare notes with Jackson."

"Me too," I said. "I'll ask him again." I could hardly wait to talk to him about it.

"Let me know what you learn. Meantime, let's get down to business." Avery went behind the small desk and pulled a portfolio out from under a stack of papers. He opened it as he approached the exam table and laid it down, gesturing for me to join him.

"They say the eyes are the windows to the soul. For Fliers it's a little more than that," he began. The pages depicted cross-sections of eyes, which he used to explain the anatomy of a human eye, and then, in turn, the anatomy of a Flier's eye. They were virtually identical on the outside, but the inside of a Flier's eye had one major structural difference.

"Are you familiar with the red-eye effect in photographs?" he asked.

"Yes," I replied, having frequently seen the red glow that made people's eyes look devilish.

"That's the effect of the flash reflecting off blood vessels at the back of the eye," he explained. "You won't see that with a Flier. We have a second, larger lens at the back of the eye that shields the retina and optic nerve. The second lens develops in born Fliers at about age ten. With gifted Fliers, like you, it would develop shortly after the gifting."

"How does the second lens make us different?"

"Have you ever seen cat's or deer's eyes caught in headlights?"

"Yes. They glow."

"Fliers eyes are something like that. The eyes reflect, but differently. You're more likely to see a white reflection in a Flier's eyes. Sometimes it appears to be grey-white or blue-white, but it's never red."

"I haven't noticed it with the others."

He shook his head. "You won't see it unless you know what you're looking for."

"Why do we have a second lens?"

"It serves as both a shield and a weapon, which we'll learn about later. Today I want to cover something much more basic: communication."

He moved to the far side of the room and stood facing me. "Watch my eyes," he said. He lowered his gaze to the floor. "Are you watching?"

"Yes," I replied.

He then slowly lifted his eyes in a long, slow arc from the floor to the ceiling.

"There!" I saw a white reflection ever so briefly when his gaze passed mine.

"Good. We call that a *flash*. Now watch again." He then swept his eyes from left to right.

"Yes, it was there again, just as our eyes met."

"That's right. We use a flash to identify and greet fellow Fliers. It's subtle, but it's there and unless the other Flier is avoiding contact, you'll spot it."

"That seems a bit of a double-edged sword. If I can only identify another Flier when they're close enough to make eye contact, then won't they just as easily be able to identify me?"

He nodded. "At first, but you'll get better at avoiding or revealing the flash, the more you see it and use it. Trust me, it's second nature to most Fliers—you'll be the same in no time."

"Are all Fliers so secretive?"

"Yes. It's drilled into us from birth, but secrecy is getting even more imperative now that Fliers are going missing. Seems we don't reveal ourselves to anyone not identified through trusted contacts these days. I'm not sure it's any safer, but the introduction makes it seem that way. Our world is changing, Emelynn." From his tone, it was clear that he was saddened by the change.

"I know this is a small step, but identifying Fliers is an important one that you'll need to experience and practice before we move on. What are you doing for the rest of the afternoon?"

"No plans until tonight," I said, thinking about Molly and our dinner date.

"Good. Let's put that GPS of yours to work and go find the Richmond Mall. I've asked three Fliers from our covey to be on standby to meet us there. Of course, you'll have to find them first," Avery said, quite pleased with himself. "I just need to make a few phone calls."

I took a deep breath and rubbed the back of my neck. It wasn't that I didn't appreciate his efforts, but I wasn't sure this was how I wanted to meet Fliers from the covey—our covey. Would I embarrass myself with my newbie efforts?

Probably, but on the plus side, he'd just given me the perfect excuse not to return to the watchful eye of the camera back at the cottage. I'd choose newbie embarrassment over that invasive camera any day.

He made his calls while I set the GPS to find the Richmond Mall, and then we drove off in my little red MGB.

The mall was a sprawling building north of Seaside, a thirty-minute drive away. The GPS worked well. We parked then entered by the food court, where Avery told me to start looking. "They won't be hiding their flash, but I won't make introductions until you find them."

I swept my gaze across the food court. Avery watched but didn't provide any guidance. Evidently, he was a hands-off type of teacher. He soon tired of watching my efforts and led the way through the food court, out into the mall. I followed as he poked into one store after another. Was he shopping? After the fourth store, I let him wander on ahead while I sought out a bench in the large, wide corridor. Shoppers bustled by, looking everywhere but at me.

Avery left the kitchen store with a bag in his hand. He really was using my training exercise as an excuse to catch up on his shopping. For some reason, I found that amusing. I kept him in my peripheral vision as I scanned the shoppers' eyes. He moved out of sight, and as I stood to follow him, I finally caught a flash, but then lost the source.

Farther along the corridor, Avery ducked into a chocolate shop. I caught a flash again. This time, I spotted her. She had long blonde hair and wore a stylish black leather jacket. She turned her back to me and wandered into a shoe store. Maybe it wasn't her after all. Avery was paying for his purchase when I looked back to the shoe store and caught Blondie looking across the corridor into the chocolate shop. That's when I caught her flash again. Avery was right; it was subtle. She looked me right in the eye and winked. Success, at last! Of course, it helped that she was spying on Avery, but I'd found her.

Blondie left the shoe store and crossed the corridor. I rushed to close the gap and Avery saw us both at the same time. He waited for me to catch up then introduced us. "Victoria Lang, I'd like you to meet Emelynn Taylor." She turned and extended her hand to me.

She had a firm handshake, a broad smile and perfect teeth. "So you're Emelynn," she said. "Avery told me about you. It's nice to finally meet you." She was beautiful—model beautiful. Tall, svelte and elegant, she exuded the kind of confidence that comes from old money: the kind that lived on estates and bred horses.

"Likewise," I said. "Sorry it took me so long to find you."

"Don't give it a second thought. I'm sure we'll see each other again, but I must be going now. Avery, I'll see you soon." She kissed him on the cheek. "Goodbye," she said, touching his hand before turning her back and leaving us.

Avery didn't take his eyes off her as she walked away. I got the distinct impression that Avery was smitten. Who could blame him? He wasn't the only man who turned his head to watch her go.

When he finally looked back at me I had a cheeky smirk on my face.

"Yes, well, she's easy on the eyes," he said, sporting a wide grin. "Now, I have some more stops to make and I believe you're still two Fliers short." He turned away and headed in the direction of an HMV store.

I found another vantage point and resumed my search. It was tricky trying to catch someone's eye without coming off as a stalker. After fifteen minutes of trying to spot an elusive flash, it occurred to me that Avery had still not emerged. What was he doing in there? It looked as though he had bumped into someone he knew, a friend perhaps, or a patient. They were deep in conversation.

Avery had his back to the door so I entered the store on his blind side and started flipping through the gaming CDs, all the while stealing glances at his friend. He was slightly shorter than Avery with grey hair and an olive complexion. He was dressed in a business suit and carried a thin portfolio. I couldn't hear what they were laughing about, but they were both distracted, which gave me a few minutes to watch them. My suspicions were confirmed when I spotted a flash, but I waited until I saw it again before I approached. When I had Avery's attention, he smiled and then introduced me.

"Gabe Aucoin, this is Emelynn Taylor." Gabe shook my hand.

"Gabe is a lawyer, but he doesn't like to admit it." Avery chuckled as Gabe rolled his eyes, dismissing the jab.

"It's good to meet you, Emelynn. The doctor here has been telling me about you and your unorthodox arrival here on the coast."

"Yes, seems that story is getting around," I said with a look of admonishment aimed at said doctor. Avery smiled his crooked grin and laughed.

"I'll be on my way then," Gabe said with a nod to Avery. "Good to meet you, Emelynn. We'll see each other again." Gabe tipped his hand to an invisible hat then turned around and left the store.

"Well, that's two down and one to go. Now, if you'll excuse me, I need to pay for this," he said, heading to the till.

He left the store with his growing collection of shopping bags and I trailed him to an Eddie Bauer. I scanned the immediate area then looked up to the second level to watch the down escalator. Avery emerged then moved along the corridor. I continued watching the steady stream of people go by as I slowly made my way to the last store I had seen Avery enter. Unfortunately, he wasn't there. I looked around, but he was gone. Damn it. I'd been at this for almost two hours and though I'd found two Fliers, I hadn't found the third and now I'd lost the one I knew about. I stunk at this game.

Maybe I'd spot him farther along. I continued moving in the direction he'd been headed. There was another escalator ahead and a long curved railing on the upper floor. I looked up and glimpsed a flash in the mix of faces, but I couldn't pinpoint the source. I saw the flash again then got a better handle on the area it had come from. I honed in and with the next flash, I saw the face. It was a young man with dark skin and dreads down to his shoulders. He'd spotted me, too. I watched him make his way to the down escalator. I scanned the crowd again for Avery. At the distant end of the corridor, I saw a flash then another two in quick succession.

The young man with the dreads approached. "Are you Emelynn?"

"I am."

"Danny Thornton," he said, extending his hand. He stood a bit taller than me. "Nice to meet you."

I shook it. "Likewise," I said. "I'm afraid I've lost Avery."

"Oh," he said, and gazed around. "He's down there." Danny indicated the corridor where I'd seen the last flashes. We started in that direction and found Avery walking toward us.

"I see you two have met," Avery said. "Thanks, Danny." He shook his hand then turned to me. "You lost me didn't you?" he said with a laugh.

As the three of us walked back to the food court, I chatted to Danny. He worked at a car dealership close by but was heading home to his apartment in Vancouver. It was well into rush hour and traffic would be thick. He said goodbye and left to find his car.

Avery and I got back into the MGB and he fiddled with the GPS until he had us directed back to his place. Once we were on the road, he asked me how I felt about my first foray into the eye-flash arena.

"It's harder than I thought." We'd hit a patch of traffic. "You wouldn't believe some of the looks I got while trying to catch people's eyes."

"You'll be surprised how quickly you adapt. Did you see my flash when you lost me?"

"Yes! You flashed once then a few seconds later you flashed twice, right?"

"Exactly. Effective, isn't it? I think this went really well today, and you got to meet a few more Fliers."

I agreed. It had been a productive experience. "Thanks, Avery. You don't know how much I appreciate your patience."

"Don't mention it. But we're not done. Will you come by again tomorrow? Same time?"

"That would be great." I let him out in front of his house then headed home to the dreaded camera.

CHAPTER SEVENTEEN

I dialled Jackson from the car in the driveway. "How's the tree-watching going?"

"Nothing yet. Are you home?"

"Yes, but I'm heading out again." It was almost six so I would have to rush to get ready. "Molly and I are going out for dinner in Seaside."

"Good. I feel better when you're away from there. At least until we find out who's behind that camera."

Me too, I thought. "Let me know if you learn anything." He assured me he would.

I hurried into the cottage. In record time, I was showered and dressed. One final mirror check and I was out of there. I didn't relax until I was back in the car.

Molly locked Rumbles' front door as I arrived, and jumped into the passenger seat. She spotted the GPS right away. "You know your phone can do this, right?" she said.

"I couldn't afford the data plan for the amount of use it's going to get."

"You're right," she said, laughing.

We caught up on our respective days during the drive but I decided to wait until dinner to tell her about Cheney's comments. I wanted to see her face when she learned that he knew who she was.

When the waiter left, I settled in to tell her my Cheney story.

"Yes," I repeated. "He knew Rumbles and he knew what you looked like."

"Me?" she asked. "Are you absolutely sure?"

"Actually, he said, and I quote, 'She stands out.'" But as I relayed his words, it occurred to me that she didn't think a man like Cheney would notice her. Her lack of confidence saddened me because it was way off the mark. Molly's dark hair set off her flawless pale skin beautifully, she had a curvaceous figure, and her perky personality sealed the deal. Who wouldn't notice her?

She wanted to know all over again what Cheney looked like, and before long we were in fits of laughter. It seemed the easiest way for her to accept his interest was by turning his striking blue eyes into cataracts, his thick hair into plugs, and those features were in addition to the butt nose and extra appendages she'd given him previously.

Dinner was heavenly, again, and Molly kept her promise to order the sea bass, which she raved about. We skipped dessert then headed to the movie theatre. I guessed Wednesdays weren't big movie nights; we didn't even have to line up for popcorn.

The movie provided a few good chuckles before the credits rolled up. As soon as we got in the car, Molly entered her address in the GPS. Like magic, it guided us right to her door.

"Thanks, Em," she said. "I had fun. See you again soon?" she asked as she got out of the car.

"Sure will," I said, and headed home. It was after eleven when I tucked the car into the garage. I'd successfully put off thinking about the camera, until now. If I could have avoided returning to the cottage, I think I would have, but it was time to do my part and be brave.

Bracing myself, I unlocked the door and stepped inside. I dropped my keys on the hall table and dumped my purse inside the bedroom door. I started toward the deck and froze. My heart jumped into my throat. Someone was out there. Time stopped until my brain kicked in and I recognized Jackson. He had his back to me but turned as I approached and then opened the sliding door.

"What are you doing here?" I rasped. "You scared ten years off me." I pulled at his arm and dragged him inside.

"Oh, *I've* scared *you*?" He bent his reddened face close. "Where's your goddamn phone!" I took a step back. He shot his arms into the air. "I've been calling you for an hour and it's going to voice mail."

I'd never seen him so upset. I rushed to the bedroom to retrieve the phone from my purse. "Oh hell," I said, seeing its black screen. "The battery's dead."

Jackson slowed his back and forth pace in front of the patio door.

JP McLEAN

"I'm sorry," I said. What else could I say? My brain fell out? He already knew that. I plugged the phone into its charger on the kitchen counter.

He finally stopped pacing. "I'm glad you're okay." He pulled out his phone and dialled. "She's fine," he said, looking at me. "No, dead battery ... We'll be there soon." He ended the call.

"What's that all about?"

"We got a couple of photos just before sunset. They're not much, but I want you to come take a look. Maybe you'll recognize him."

So it was a him. "Is he a Flier?"

"No, and he had his face covered, so there's not much to go on."

"How did you get past the camera?"

"I covered the lens. Are you ready to go?"

"Just give me a minute to change, okay?" I rushed back to the bedroom and changed into my standard Flier outfit: black yoga pants, black hoodie and black Rocket Dogs.

Jackson was leaning on the bookcase gazing out toward the water when I returned.

I followed his gaze. "Is that the *Symphony* out there?"

"Yes. It's out of the camera's view. Let's go."

I grabbed my Ryders from the hall table, then stepped outside and locked the door behind us.

We walked into the park. Jackson lifted off from the path and hovered, waiting for me. I composed myself and called on the power that swept me up into the night. We flew out of the tree canopy and Jackson doubled back to remove the branch he'd draped over the camera, careful to make it look as though the wind had dislodged it.

We headed out over the cliff then veered south before making a beeline for the *Symphony*. Jackson circled the boat and landed gently on the observation deck. I landed beside him just as Alex stepped away from the wall. I hadn't seen him and jerked back in surprise.

He put his arm around my shoulder and squeezed me in a half hug. "You had us worried."

"I know—I'm sorry." I offered him an apologetic smile. "I'm not usually this blonde."

He chuckled. "Let's go look at the photos." He released my shoulder and we followed Jackson below.

"I've weighed anchor," he said to Jackson, who was already at the controls. The engines purred below us. Jackson pushed the throttles forward and the big hull pressed ahead.

Alex and I turned our attention to Jackson's laptop. The screen pulsed in a slow heartbeat as it flipped through security images at regular intervals. I leaned in. The screen was divided into quadrants, each an image from one of the *Symphony*'s security cameras. I knew about the cameras, of course—they were hard to miss—but I hadn't known there were this many.

"You can never be too careful," Alex said, observing my interest. That point had certainly been driven home of late. Obviously, Jackson had more than the *Symphony* to protect. I wondered how many of his business associates didn't need the Zodiac to get to shore.

"May I?" Alex asked, turning the computer. He worked the keyboard and moments later had the images from the cottage camera up on the screen.

I sat down and studied each one. They were clear enough, but the man's hood hid his head and a mask concealed his face. He wore a loose bomber jacket, blue jeans and two-tone gloves. The biggest identifying feature was the hardware strapped to his lower legs. "What's that all about?" I asked.

"It's some kind of climbing spur," Alex said. "See here." He pointed to a photo of the man halfway up the trunk. "He's got the spur jammed into the side of the tree."

"I don't recognize him," I said. "But he's so nondescript he could be half the men I know." The figure could easily have been Jackson or Charles or even Cheney. "I'm afraid I'm not much help."

"Neither are these photos. I sent them to Eden too but I don't think we'll be able to ID anyone with them."

"Help yourself to a beer," Jackson called from behind the wheel. "We'll be another ten minutes or so."

Alex headed for the fridge. "Do you want one?"

"No, thanks," I said as he retrieved two bottles. He took one to Jackson, and I moved to the sofa with my back to the big steering wheel.

"I don't think we'll get more photos of this guy until tomorrow or maybe the day after," Alex said, perching on the edge of the opposite sofa.

"I agree," Jackson added. "If he's on a thirty-six-hour cycle, then he'll make a collection day after tomorrow at dawn."

Jackson turned the engines off and finished the shut-down routine before joining Alex on the sofa. "We're in a holding pattern until he shows again."

"Yeah, meantime, Eden's worrying herself sick." Alex rubbed his temples. "At least she's off for a few days after tonight."

"Why don't we go flying?" Jackson suggested. "It'll take our minds off it for a while."

"Speaking of which," Alex said, with a know-it-all smirk on his face. "I hear you have a new trick."

I turned to Jackson. "You told him?" The accusation in my tone was unmistakable.

Jackson feigned hurt feelings until Alex confessed. "Actually, it was Eden who told me."

Crap, I'd forgotten that. "Oh, yeah, I guess I did mention it to her," I said sheepishly. "Sorry." It was the second time I'd apologized to Jackson tonight.

"Let's go," Alex said, guzzling his beer. "I could use a distraction."

"This is embarrassing," I said, standing. I smoothed my pants. "I'm really not comfortable with the show-pony thing."

Jackson gave a half smile and walked ahead of me to the bookcase. "I've got something for us," he said. He pulled a small box off the shelf and opened it on the galley counter. Inside, eight earpieces lay neatly in two rows.

Seeing the devices took me back to the last time I'd worn one, and to how that occasion ended with my nearly drowning. I stiffened in place.

"Help yourself," Jackson said.

"Cool." Alex took one and fit it into his ear like an old pro. "If you'll excuse me a minute," he said, walking in the direction of the head.

"What is it?" Jackson asked, searching my face.

He put his finger under my chin and tilted my head up. "That will never happen again, Em," he said. But we both knew that wasn't something he could promise. No one could promise that.

I shook off my apprehension and reached for an earpiece. "No promises, Jackson. Like I said, I'm not ready yet."

"You might surprise yourself," he said just before Alex rejoined us.

We headed up top and I followed Alex up into the night sky with Jackson close on my heels. The euphoric rush of flying soon overrode my irrational apprehension of the earpiece. We flew a creative circuit around the boat, soaring in high arcs and swan dives. We rolled and twisted, somersaulted and backflipped. Jackson and Alex had a blast trying to outdo each other in the trick department. It was as if I had a front row seat at Cirque du Soleil.

"How are you doing?" Jackson asked, approaching in a hover, taking a break from their antics.

"Great," I answered, but we both knew it was a lie.

"You're holding back—I can tell."

"I told you: I'm not ready to test my speed again, not yet." I was surprised that I had to explain myself to him—again, especially given that he was the one who'd had to fish me out of the ocean that night. He was pushing me. Why would he do that?

"I think you should—just like I thought you should get back up in the air as soon after the accident as possible. Besides, there are two of us to back you up tonight."

Apparently, the look on my face was more effective than words. "Don't look at me like that, Em. Maybe you think it's too soon for me to be challenging you, but you know as well as I do that you have to learn how to deal with your speed. The only way to do that is to use it. I'm not suggesting you commit suicide; just get back in the saddle and test it. Get some more experience under your belt so you can master the speed, instead of the other way around."

I took a deep breath. Maybe I was overreacting. He'd been a great teacher so far, not to mention a patient one. I decided to trust his instincts. "All right, I'll try. But don't expect miracles."

"That's more like it," he said with a suggestive smile. It was a smile I felt all the way down to my toes, and I was thankful Alex couldn't see it. "We'll try to keep up." He winked as he turned and raced off ahead of me. Alex sped off right behind him, leaving me hovering in their wake.

I pitched forward, watching the two of them shoot ahead of me. This time, I wanted to do it right: intentionally and, most of all, controlled. I concentrated on the steady hum in my limbs and reached for the warmth of the crystal. The incredible power was there, always there, coiled and ready. I streamlined my body, slowly increasing my speed. Alex and Jackson continued to widen the distance between us, watching me closely. At least I had two lifeguards tonight, I thought, as I unfurled that tremendous pent-up energy and let it rocket my body forward.

I knew I'd passed Alex when I heard "In-fucking-credible!" over the earpiece.

"And *that's* why I lost her," Jackson said, finally able to justify his part in our watery escapade.

Now his insistence that I perform finally made sense. "Okay, show's over," I said into my mic, letting the speed dissipate as I held a steady trajectory, not daring to move my arms.

When I'd slowed enough to turn around, I flew back to them. Alex's mouth was agape. I reached over and playfully popped his chin up. He recovered quickly, bursting into an unrestrained fit of laughter.

"Wow! Emelynn, that's beyond impressive," Alex said when he'd caught his breath.

"It's embarrassing," I said, unable to keep a blush off my face.

"Nonsense," Jackson interjected. "Let's keep going."

"Gladly," I said, anxious to get out of the spotlight.

We flew another circuit and I took the opportunity to test rolls, spins, dives and weaves at steadily increasing speeds. I constantly needed to adjust my body position to correct my trajectory, but I was definitely getting a better feel for staying in control at higher speeds. Alex and Jackson were happy to offer advice and spot me.

It was late by the time we made it back to the boat. "Thank you," I said. "Both of you. I know I resisted at first, but that was fun. I feel much better now for having done it."

"I'm sure the accident scared you, but Jackson was right. You needed to get back out there and test yourself." Alex yawned. "I'm glad I saw it for myself. That speed of yours—man—that's something all right."

Alex checked the screen of his cellphone. "It's after two. I've got to go."

"If I catch an interesting photo, I'll call," Jackson said, and shook his hand.

Alex lifted off and as soon as he was out of sight, Jackson turned to me and pulled me into his arms. "I've wanted to do this all night," he said, bending down to kiss me.

When he pulled away, I smiled up at him. "So I'm guessing you didn't tell Alex about the happy ending to our swim the other night?"

"Of course not," he said, frowning. "That's no one's business but ours." He gave me another quick kiss. "Will you stay tonight?"

"I'd like that."

We took the stairs down to the galley. "Would you like some wine?" Jackson asked, opening the fridge.

"I wouldn't say no to some white." A drink was just what I needed to quell my nervous anticipation of what I'd set in motion when I agreed to stay.

"White? I thought you preferred red." Jackson pulled a bottle of Corona from the fridge.

"I'm ambidextrous."

"Good to know, but I'm out of white. Will red do?" he asked, closing the fridge.

"Sure," I said. He set his beer on the counter and jogged to the living room. A moment later, Train's "Drops of Jupiter" spilled from hidden speakers. He disappeared below.

No longer a stranger to the galley cupboards, I retrieved a wine glass, scoring a direct hit on the first door I opened.

"You like Malbec, right?" he asked, checking the bottle's label as he returned to the galley.

"Indeed. It's my current favourite red," I said, pleased that he'd remembered. He pulled out a drawer and I heard the tinny rattle of utensils as Jackson searched for an opener. I leaned back against the counter watching him expertly remove the foil then sink the corkscrew.

"I almost hate to say it for fear of jinxing it, but I feel pretty good about tonight's progress," I said. It was a feeling I hoped would last until tomorrow, when Eden and I were going flying.

"You should; you're doing great." He tugged at the cork until it popped, and poured my wine. "Cheers," he said, tapping his Corona against my glass before relaxing back against the counter across from me.

We fell into a quiet lull. After a few sips, I noticed Jackson staring at the floor with a bit too much intensity for casual thought. "What are you thinking?"

He looked up at me, startled for the interruption. "Ah, it's nothing." He tipped the Corona back and took a long drink. "Next time we're flying, I'd like to teach you how to jump-start someone into flight."

His quick subject change hadn't slipped my notice, but I didn't pry. "Why's that?" I asked.

"In case you ever need to help an injured or unconscious Flier ... Say, rescue one from the Pacific?" He had a *did you really have to ask?* look on his face.

"Oh, I get it."

"Kidding aside, it's something all Fliers should know how to do. Like CPR."

Jackson set his bottle down and crossed over to me. He wrapped his arms around me and planted a kiss on my forehead.

"Jump up," he said, boosting me to the counter. He nudged his hips between my knees and I rested my arms on his shoulders. "How about we distract ourselves for a little while?" He reached out to stroke my face, rubbing his thumb over my lips.

His touch ignited my libido and melted my inhibitions. He stepped closer and kissed me, urging my lips apart with his tongue that tasted like beer. His hand, cold from the chilled beer bottle, roamed under my shirt and up my bare back making me shiver. He snapped my bra open in a smooth one-handed move that reminded me I wasn't his first. In a flash, his hand moved around my rib cage and captured my breast, caressing, squeezing. God, I loved the arousal that he teased out of me. How had I lived without this as long as I had?

He broke away from my mouth, pulled off my hoodie and tossed it aside. I loved the greedy look on his face as he tugged the bottom of my tank top up, exposing my breasts. I watched the tip of his tongue dart out between his lips to swirl around the puckered point of my nipple, and closed my eyes, savouring the sensation. His languid devotion spiked my arousal.

"Let's take this below," he said, planting a kiss on each breast before pulling my shirt back in place. I reached down between us and stroked his erection through his jeans. He groaned his approval, taking a moment to enjoy my caress before helping me off the counter to lead the way down the stairs to my former cabin.

Before we'd reached the bed, he'd relieved me of the rest of my clothes. I fumbled with his jeans, hyperaware of my inexperience. He had to finish the job for me. Clearly, I needed practice—lots of practice.

We took our time getting to know each other's bodies again. He used his hands and soft words to guide me, and I knew I was doing something right when I heard him moan and respond to my touch. It's a heady thing having the power to make a man moan. In turn, he showed me how delightful a warm tongue and well-placed caress felt when plied by someone with experience.

He slowly turned me to jelly, but before I dissolved completely, he reached for his jeans to fetch a condom. He was back between my legs in a heartbeat and before I could even contemplate the pain I'd experienced the first time, he pushed himself into me. It felt nothing like before. There was no sting, no pain, just an unfamiliar pressure, and each of his strokes escalated the pleasurable sensation. I liked it. He triggered a craving in me I didn't know I was capable of. With growing urgency, I arched my hips to meet his thrusts. Jackson stayed focused, his rhythm strong and steady, and I couldn't get enough of him.

But he had other things to teach me. Quite unexpectedly, he thrust deep inside then stopped dead, breaking our rhythm while holding me tightly to him. His lips found mine and his lust found a new outlet. He kept himself still, buried deep, resisting my efforts to restart the rhythm. I could feel him pulsating inside me and ached to resume that sweet friction between us.

Finally, giving in, he said, "Roll on top." He pulled me over him, never breaking our intimate contact. We readjusted our limbs and he gripped my hips. "Slowly," he coached, as I moved on top of him and found my rhythm. It was awkward at first. "Slowly," he whispered again as I tried to match my rhythm to the guidance of his hands on my hips. We finally fell into a lusty cadence until his thumb found its way to the knot of nerves between my legs. Jackson soon gave up control to my quickening and increasingly erratic movement. I heard him groan as my orgasm hit, and then we were both riding a wave, my body responding to each of his thrusting spasms. By the time I stopped moving, I no longer had the strength to stay upright. I folded forward, collapsing onto his chest. He rolled me off and we lay side by side, spent.

As I caught my breath, I felt his shoulders vibrate. What started off as a chuckle grew into a huge belly laugh. He turned on his side, still laughing, and smiled down at me. I smiled back, though I didn't know what he was laughing at.

"I never would have thought you had it in you, Em. You surprise the hell out of me and might I say, that was fantastic."

Then I was blushing—naked, sated, but blushing.

We fell asleep in a tangle of arms and legs, the gentle sway of the boat a quiet reminder that I wasn't in my own bed.

When I woke, a dreary day presented itself and the wind howled its accompaniment, causing the boat to rock. Jackson snored softly beside me. I eased out of bed and pulled on a housecoat before padding up to the galley to put on the coffee. While it brewed, I used the small head behind the galley. I splashed water on my face and finger-combed my unruly curls. I poured us each a cup of coffee and returned to the cabin, doing my best not to spill as I made my way back.

Jackson woke when I set his mug down on the bedside table. He looked up at me, a flash of surprise on his face. I could almost see the moment his brain came online and recognition lit his face.

"Good morning," I said, leaning down to kiss his cheek. His stubble prickled.

"Hey." He sat up, rubbing his face with his hands.

The grey day chilled me. I got back between the sheets and bent my knees, holding the comforter close. Reaching to the side table, I picked up my coffee and let the warm mug heat my hands.

We didn't linger long in bed. Jackson had an online conference call scheduled later in the morning, and he wanted to check our security camera's morning photo dump before he took me home. He finished his coffee then quickly showered and dressed. I wasn't far behind him. Our security camera hadn't captured the photographer.

The *Symphony* rocked in the swell as Jackson guided us closer to shore. The Zodiac fought the weather more aggressively than the *Symphony*, giving us a bone-jarring ride back to the cottage, south of the camera's viewing angle.

Once inside, Jackson checked the camera hidden in the stack of books on the kitchen windowsill. Satisfied, he left to inspect the camera in the arbutus.

"No new clues out there," he said when he returned.

"I'm going to be out most of today," I said. "And Eden's coming by tonight." I didn't want him to worry about me.

"All right. I'll call if anything comes up." He leaned in and kissed me goodbye. "Keep your phone charged and with you," he said. "Please," he added, a not-so-subtle reminder of yesterday's phone fiasco.

I nodded. "I will." He turned and jogged down the stairs and across the beach to the Zodiac. I watched him bounce the dinghy over the tops of the waves, back to the *Symphony*.

After I turned on some music, I powered up the computer. Funny, I couldn't remember leaving the laptop open. I habitually closed it after I turned it off. The camera crisis must have upset my routines.

At least I had flying with Eden tonight to look forward to. Unfortunately, the days were so long this time of year that it didn't get dark until late. I wouldn't see Eden until ten o'clock. Thankfully, my meeting with Avery this afternoon would get me out of the house and away from that camera for a few hours.

I went through my inbox, deleting the junk and replying to one from Laura. Hers was full of her usual upbeat, research-related news along with some lamenting about the increasing humidity as summer approached. Though tempted to tease her about it, I didn't have much to brag about weather-wise. In my reply, I told her about my latest night out with Molly, then closed the program and stuffed my hands in my hoodie pocket.

I stood and walked away from the computer to look out to the ocean. The *Symphony* was already out of sight.

An image of Jackson in the captain's chair came to mind. Was I in his thoughts as often as he was in mine? Somehow I doubted that. The notion that Jackson was such a big factor in my life was unsettling. What did I really know about him? About his life?

I'd spent many hours in his company, in his bed, yet he still managed to remain aloof. Perhaps it was the mystery of the man I found so alluring. Maybe my good friend Google could shed some light on Mr. Delaney. I returned to my computer and typed "Jackson Delaney" and "Louisiana" into the search engine and sent the request out to the cyberworld.

Much to my surprise, Google returned dozens of hits. Most of the items referenced Delaney & Son Developments, with the most popular tidbits at the top.

I clicked on an entry about the Delaney family patriarch's recent death. Jackson looked somewhat like the photo of his father. The article described Matthew Delaney as a successful business tycoon. He was only fifty-eight when he died of a massive heart attack last August.

Another entry sketched a brief history of the company. It was founded in 1974 as Delaney Developments. The "& Son" was added in 1982. The original business involved developing strip malls and retail businesses. Delaney Developments had grown considerably since its early days and now developed large high-rise structures and upscale retail facilities.

I moved on to an article published in 2008. It announced a Delaney deal that secured a prime tract of waterfront land slated to be developed into a marina. There was a photo of the senior Delaney shaking hands with a politician, and behind and to the left of them stood a younger-looking Jackson. The photo was proof positive that I was reading about the Jackson I knew.

This article's author was not enamoured of the Delaneys or what he called their "shady business deals." He hinted at illegal and unsavoury business practices but stopped short of outright accusations. The author raised questions about the dearth of alternate bidders for a prime piece of waterfront and about how the developer had secured such hasty approvals for the marina project when similar projects had been scrutinized much more thoroughly by the same government offices.

I continued researching but couldn't find any more information one way or another about that particular deal. It looked like Jackson had quite a colourful history that he had yet to share with me and now I was curious. What else would I learn about the mystery man? But I needed to eat and get ready to meet Avery. I bookmarked the remaining websites and headed to the bedroom to change.

Two slices of toast later I was out the door.

Avery's waiting room was empty but the door to the examination room was open. I glanced in to see Avery sitting behind the small desk in the corner. He looked up when he saw me and beckoned me inside.

"How are you?" he asked, pushing his papers aside. He made me feel more like a guest than a patient. He really did have the best bedside manner I'd ever encountered in a doctor. With the shortage of family doctors in the province, his practice should have been full to bursting, so why his waiting room remained empty was a mystery.

I strode in and leaned back against the examination table. "I'm good, thanks. You?"

"Great, thanks. Jump up, make yourself comfortable." He propped his feet up on the edge of the desk. "I've been giving some thought to how to teach you to use the power of your eyes. It's an interesting problem."

"Why's that?"

"Because we've never tested your gift, so I don't know what to expect—how strong you might be. This is a complex skill and can be quite a powerful tool." He tipped back in his chair. "I'm not sure I'm brave enough to be your test subject."

I was glad he'd said that with a smile on his face. "Come on, don't be a wimp. How bad could it be? I couldn't even fly three weeks ago."

"Yeah, but look at the strides you've made since then. If I let you, you might just knock me on my ass, and how embarrassing would that be?" His smile faded as he dropped his feet back to the floor. "However, you do need to learn the basics."

"Okay, so what exactly are *the basics*?"

"Those are the skills that all Fliers are capable of—even me." He leaned forward. "They're all at the milder end of the spectrum. They include signalling other Fliers with a flash, like we did yesterday, but we can also turn it up and send a wave of energy. Not one that hurts, but it gets your attention—like a shoulder tap. We refer to it as a *spark* when it's at the safe end of the spectrum."

"The safe end?" That was a curious way to phrase it. "What's at the other end of that spectrum?"

"Some Fliers can amp up the spark so it delivers more of a punch. This is the business end of the spectrum, and we call those more powerful waves of energy *jolts*. Think of it like an ocular version of a stun gun, but less predictable. Strong emotions or physical pain have been known to enhance or diminish the skill. We won't know more about how you'll react until we test it." He shifted in his seat.

"As you already know, some Fliers can harness their powers to render a person unconscious. It's what you experienced the night you met Jackson. But most aren't as proficient as Jackson at pulling it off without inflicting pain.

"As I mentioned before, it's a complex skill and how effective the results are depends on the individual Flier. Some Fliers, like Jackson, are very strong. Others are not and never achieve more than flashing. Victoria, for example, can barely get a spark out." Hmm, how would Avery know that? I wondered.

"We also use the lens for defence in the form of something we call *blocking*. Think of it like a shield. The level of blocking one can achieve also depends on the strength of his or her gift. Jackson might not have been able to incapacitate you if you had known how to use your block, though it's unlikely your block would have been strong enough to keep Jackson out."

Avery paused. "There's one more effect you should be aware of. Some Fliers can use the power of their eyes to heighten sexual arousal. We call it *rush*. It falls into the low end of the spectrum. Obviously, it's not something you and I will be practicing, but with the right partner, one day you may experience the wonder of the rush for yourself."

I felt my face heat with the recognition that Jackson had used his rush with me on our first intimate night together. No wonder the sex was so very good. Suddenly, this was an uncomfortable conversation to be having with Avery.

"Okay, moving on," I said, reading amusement in Avery's crooked grin. "Tell me what's involved in producing these sparks and jolts you talked about."

He paused a moment to savour my embarrassment before he got serious again. "It's hard to describe. It isn't so much a physical thing like snapping your fingers. It's more like a determined thought process that's funnelled through your gaze."

"Is it effective on everyone, or just Fliers?"

"To the best of my knowledge, everyone. At least, I haven't come across anyone yet who isn't susceptible. Of course, some Fliers can block the effect if they see it coming." He sat back and took a deep breath.

"Where do we go from here?"

"I think the safest bet is to start with a simple effect. Flashing is the first thing born Fliers learn, so it seems like a logical place to start. You already know how to spot a flash—today I'll walk you through producing one."

Avery explained the process. It wasn't difficult, but doing it without blinking was. I remained seated and Avery moved around the room, changing angles. After half an hour, Avery had me proficient at flashing.

Then we started on blocking. These were two sides of the same coin: the level of effort required to produce the flash was the same as the level of effort required to block it. Blocking came more easily to me, and soon I was ready to move on to the next level, sparks.

Avery seemed a little too happy to demonstrate the concept. His crooked smile held a glint of mischief that I didn't trust. He laughed at my yelp of surprise when he delivered his first spark, and then delivered a few more, purely for "demonstration purposes." His sparks didn't really hurt—they ranged from an annoying tingle to a static shock, all of which I felt only in my head. He got a few good ones in before I was able to strengthen my block, but after that, we were both thwarted.

I called a truce at that point. "Why is it that when I have my block in place, I can't deliver a spark?"

Avery took his seat behind the desk. "It's because the block acts as a shield. It's a physical barrier between you and other Fliers. How strong it is depends on how strong your gift is. Weak blocks can be breached and learning how to quickly establish and remove your block gives you an advantage."

Interesting, I thought, sensing an opportunity to pay Avery back for laughing about those "demonstration" sparks he'd hit me with. "How fast can you block?" I asked, and before he could smell a rat, I hit him with a spark of my own.

He grabbed his head with his hands and squeezed his eyes shut. "Damn it, Em." He inhaled through clenched teeth. "That hurt."

At first, I thought he was playing around because his sparks hadn't hurt me at all, but he wasn't laughing. "I'm sorry, Avery. Are you all right?" I was mortified and waited for him to respond. Eventually, he removed his hands, opened his eyes and straightened up.

"I will be," he said, stretching his neck from side to side. "I thought you might put me on my ass and you nearly did." I was relieved to see the crooked smile return to his face. "And FYI, that was not a spark, it was a jolt."

"I'm sorry," I repeated, feeling terrible.

"I think we'd better work on toning that down."

"You still want to be my test subject?" I asked.

"Only if you don't sneak in any more surprise attacks." His tone told me he wasn't kidding.

"I won't ... and I really am sorry." I hadn't thought I'd put that much juice into it. Toning it down was going to be a challenge. But Avery proved to be quite accommodating and I finally earned his approval when I had the voltage down to a low tingle.

"Now, let's slowly ramp it up so you can learn to better gauge the effect. I'll put up a block so you won't hurt me. Now, give it a go."

I did, and with each subsequent increase in power level, Avery increased his block and assured me he only felt tingles. After half a dozen increases, he stopped me. "That's about as much strength as you want to put into it, Em—much more than that and you won't be making any friends."

He looked at me, his brow pinched in concentration. "Do you have any sense where your top end is?"

"No, not really, I just know there's more there." It was the best way I could describe it. I felt the same way as I had when I was learning to fly—I'd known instinctively that I had more speed pent up. How much more, I had no idea.

"I want to try something." Avery straightened in his chair. "I'm going to put up my strongest block. When I tell you to, I want you to give me all you've got. Just once, okay?"

"No. I don't want to hurt you again." I shivered at the thought.

"You won't. I've got a strong block. I'd like to test your strength, that's all. Trust me, you won't hurt me."

"Are you sure?"

"Yes, I'm sure." He held up his hand and inhaled once, then again. A moment later he signalled the okay.

Unconvinced that I wouldn't hurt him, I didn't give him my all, but I did amp it up a tad hoping to satisfy his curiosity. His resulting glare said it all. "Come on, Em, don't hold back on me—you're not going to get a better opportunity to test yourself." He stood and braced himself then gave me the okay again.

I sighed in resignation. "Well then, I'm not going to watch." I took a deep breath then drew on the power that hummed inside me, concentrating it into a twirling mental ball. He coaxed me to continue, so I closed my eyes then hit him with it. I heard a soft *swoosh* followed swiftly by a solid *thunk* and opened my eyes just in time to see Avery's head crack off the wall on the rebound.

CHAPTER EIGHTEEN

I dove off the exam table and grabbed Avery's shoulders to stop his fall. His body felt slack in my hands. I held him to the wall and eased him down to a sitting position on the floor as best I could. He was barely conscious.

"Avery!" I supported his head in my hands, shouting his name. "Avery!" What had I done? Tears ran unchecked down my face and panic threatened. I held on by the tiniest of threads. He blinked once, twice, but his eyes looked vacant. An eternity passed before he showed signs of returning. I watched his eyes as he tried to focus.

When he was finally able to see, he raised his arms and pushed me away. Slowly, he struggled to his feet and I helped guide him back into his chair. He reached up to wipe a tear from my cheek. It was a gesture meant to comfort, but I didn't want comfort—I wanted him to be okay. I straightened up and backed away.

"You blew through my block. It wasn't my strongest, but it was damn good." He turned his head from side to side, stretching his neck. "You shouldn't have been able to blow through it like that."

Avery rubbed the back of his head, probably feeling a lump. "Thought I was prepared. Clearly, I need to up my game."

"That's not even slightly funny," I said with more vehemence than I'd intended. Tears started rolling down my face again. Avery shot me a look I couldn't decipher.

"Em, this isn't your fault. You didn't hurt me." He reached toward me with a wince and tried to hide it.

I leaned back out of his reach. "Don't lie to me. I can tell you're hurt. Jesus, I thought I'd killed you!" I said in a rush of anger.

"Well, maybe it hurt a little. Sorry. I didn't mean to scare you. Hell, I didn't mean to scare me either, but I think it's best we know. Don't you?"

"Just what do we know?" I asked, my voice rising. "That I'm a freak? Or maybe I should clarify—that I'm still a freak? That I can't even play nice with my own kind? What am I supposed to do now, Avery?" Anger pushed me on. "How am I supposed to deal with this? Damn Jolene! What the hell was she thinking saddling me with this curse?"

He spoke in a soft voice, ignoring my anger. "This is not a bad thing that we've learned, Emelynn. Look at me." I lifted my eyes. "We knew you were a wild card the day you dropped into our laps. We just need to handle you with more care, that's all."

"More care? That's all?" I burst into a hysterical laugh. "With a straitjacket don't you mean?" But even as I said it, my rant petered out. I leaned back against the exam table.

Avery had recovered enough to stand. He came over, grabbed my hand and pulled me to my feet. "Let's go make a pot of tea. I think we could both use a cup right about now." He led me from the examination room, past the ever-empty waiting area, and through an interior door into his house.

We entered a large kitchen that was bright despite the dreary day. He didn't let go of my hand until I was seated at the big round kitchen table. Then he went over to the counter behind the island, filled the kettle and pulled an old Brown Betty from the cupboard. I hadn't seen one of those teapots since my Nanny Fran days.

He made it the right way, warming the teapot before pouring boiling water from the whistling kettle over the tea. As it steeped, he arranged a tray with two cups and a carton of milk.

The clock on the wall over the stove read four o'clock.

Avery poured. I added milk to mine then blew over the top to cool it. We each retired to our mental corners in silence. Avery was busy thinking; I was busy avoiding thinking, at least thinking about what had happened. I envied the ostrich and its patch of sand.

"Why is your practice so quiet?"

"I specialize in Fliers and, as you know, there aren't many of us. I put in my time at the ER to keep my hospital privileges, but I don't generally see patients in my home office."

We retreated to our corners again, sipping our teas, neither of us looking at the other.

Avery finally spoke. "Before today, even though Jolene Reynolds's disappearance coincides with when you received your gift, I thought you might have been mistaken about her name. You were so young at the time, and Jolene sounds a lot like Irene or Jodi."

He paused, gathering his thoughts. "But Greg's San Francisco contact told us Jolene was well known for her speed of flight. He also said she had undocumented 'extraordinary skills.' You have the speed. And now we know you have energy waves that anyone would classify as extraordinary. I think it's safe to say that your gift came from Jolene Reynolds, and that it passed to you intact."

"Why do you put it that way? Intact?"

"Sometimes the gift is diluted when it's passed on, or it morphs into something else entirely. Greg wasn't able to shed light on what Jolene's extraordinary skills were—'skills' plural. So the only outstanding question is what other skills you might have."

"Yes—maybe I can paint, too." I felt entitled to my sarcasm. I had come so far, but fear crawled into my psyche alongside each new facet of this gift; fear that the gift was more dangerous than I'd imagined. The learning curve hadn't even begun to level out when my speed showed itself. Now I faced another steep climb. I hadn't expected it to be easy, but did it have to be so difficult? It was like trying to tame a monster that kept sprouting new heads. At least when the speed facet showed itself, the only one it could hurt was me. This latest facet had the potential to hurt other people, and this weighed heavily on me.

"I'm sorry this is so hard on you, Emelynn. I know you're struggling with it now, but I hope in time you'll come to see this as the gift it truly is."

As he refilled my cup, I wondered if he ever thought about his own stunted gift. How had that happened?

Avery continued. "As it is for all things of worth, there's a price to be paid. For those of us born into it, we know of no other way—the struggles are accepted, the secrets kept. But for those of you who are gifted, I imagine the cost is much higher, the struggles harder to accept, the secret much more of a burden."

The pained expression on his face told me his reflection had resonated with us both. "What price did you pay, Avery?" I asked, daring him to explain the anguish he was unable to hide.

JP MCLEAN

He turned to me and I saw him wrestle with his answer. "I wasn't the one who paid the price." His voice was almost a whisper. I didn't dare speak, afraid to put a halt to his story.

"My best friend was the one who paid for our mistake. Jimmy was his name. We were fifteen when he found an old leather-bound book in his father's home office. I still remember its yellowed, brittle pages. The book was a record of his family's history detailing a two-hundred-year span of births, deaths, marriages and even land ownership. We'd never seen anything like it. It described the other coveys spread throughout the continent, or at least what was known of them at the time."

Avery looked down into the empty teacup. He absently twisted it in circles while he continued sharing his recollections. "We knew it was an old book. Hell, it was hand-made. Hard to miss that. The script was intricate—old English, I think." He concentrated as though he could see the pages before him. "It proved difficult to read and even harder to decipher, but we persisted. Not for any scholarly purpose, of course, we weren't that studious, but a certain section in the book captured our imaginations."

Avery looked up and shook his head. "I don't know why I'm telling you all this. It's not going to help ease you into our world."

"Please don't stop. Tell me the rest of the story."

He took a deep breath and exhaled heavily. "Jimmy and I were barely in control of our own gifts and, being typical teenage boys, we courted trouble from time to time. So when we came across the old incantations in that book, naturally, we couldn't resist. They read like how-to instructions for everything Flier: how to transfer the gift, how to improve flight, how to increase ocular power. We thought it would be great fun to test one out. Of course, once the dare was out there, neither of us could back down.

"We followed the instructions meticulously, right down to the beeswax candles. We assumed the stance, touched our fingertips, and recited the incantation. Next thing I know I'm flat on my back, barely conscious. My folks are in the room, ranting, and Jimmy's white as a sheet. We had never taken it seriously—we were just having a laugh, but I haven't been able to shed gravity since that day."

"What happened to Jimmy?" I asked, sitting on the edge of my chair.

"His flying improved twofold. Turns out the incantation improved his flying skills at the expense of mine, but neither of us knew that at the time. Hell, it was just dumb luck that he was on the receiving end. We didn't know what we were doing. But there was no convincing my father—I'd never seen him so incensed. He was furious with Jimmy's family for giving us access to that book. I remember him comparing it to leaving a loaded gun on the coffee table."

"What did your father do?"

"I didn't know it at the time, but he approached the Tribunal." The oxygen in the room suddenly seemed in short supply. Avery shut down for a few moments and the quiet washed over us.

Avery stared at a scratch on the table, his voice choked with remorse as he continued. "Jimmy's father drove their Oldsmobile into an overpass abutment on the Red Mountain Freeway going ninety miles an hour. Jimmy and his parents were killed instantly. The autopsy report said he'd had a heart attack. The police report said the gas pedal had jammed under his foot. I might have been able to accept it as plausible, if it weren't for the dead dove that was delivered in a red lacquered box to my father the day after the funerals." Avery drained what must have been cold tea from his cup.

"Dead dove?"

"It's the Tribunal Novem's calling card. Lets you know you've been avenged. Of course, times have changed. I understand they no longer send dead birds. I guess they've developed a conscience where doves are concerned."

"I'm sorry, Avery."

"Yeah, me too." He searched the bottom of his teacup as if there were leaves there to read. "It was a tough lesson on so many fronts." Avery stood and began to clear the dishes. "But it was a long time ago." The hinges on the dishwasher creaked open.

"What happened to the book?"

"I don't know."

I watched him finish dealing with our tea paraphernalia. No wonder he'd reacted the way he had when I mentioned the Tribunal.

"Thanks for telling me about Jimmy."

Avery looked up from wiping the counter. "I'd appreciate it if you kept it to yourself. That's not a story I like to share."

"Of course." I needed to get out of there, get some fresh air. I stood, ready to leave.

Avery came back to the table. "I didn't bring you in here just for the tea. I wanted to talk to you about the gift and put it in a positive perspective—you know, the joys of being a Flier and all it entails. Guess I blew that didn't I?"

"Well, I appreciated the tea. And I'd prefer to learn the real perspective, warts and all, not some candy-coated version of it."

"I know it's not been easy for you. Maybe knowing that you're not the only one who's had a rough time coming to terms with the gift will make it easier."

A sad smile settled on Avery's face. It matched my own, and I reached up to give him a hug. He looked as if he needed one.

It was after six when I finally headed home weighed down with the latest in a long line of burdens, courtesy of this wonderful gift of mine. I was glad Eden was coming over tonight. Even if we didn't go flying, I just needed to talk to her.

My head reeled. I couldn't stop thinking about Avery and his horrible history. Worse still, I'd hurt him. The Tribunal's idea of justice frightened me, and that damn camera promised even more trouble ahead. It felt overwhelming. When I got home, I crawled into bed and cried myself to sleep.

The phone's sharp ring snapped me awake. I rubbed my eyes as I answered, momentarily disoriented. "Hello," I said, clearing the sleep from my voice.

"Em?" It was Eden.

"Hi Eden," I replied. I shot upright, suddenly remembering our plans. "Oh god, I'm sorry. I fell asleep."

"You didn't answer your doorbell."

"You're here?" I threw off the covers, annoyed with myself for not having gotten that doorbell fixed. "What time is it?"

"It's ten fifteen. I'm on your front porch—want to let me in?"

I jumped out of bed, feeling grungy and chilled from having slept in my clothes, and ran to the front door. She stood there, patiently waiting. "Sorry, Eden. Guess I was more tired than I thought. And I need to do something about that doorbell. Even when I'm awake, I can barely hear it." I made a mental note to call Charles and Gabby tomorrow to get it fixed.

"It's okay. I just got here." She stepped in, closing the door behind her. We headed down the hall to the living room. "I spoke with Avery." Eden was nothing if not direct.

"He called you?" Knowing they thought I needed special attention took an uncomfortable chunk out of my much-prized independence.

"Yeah, he's worried about you." We sat on the sofa. "He told me about Jolene. That's good news, right?"

"It's another piece of the puzzle. Maybe it'll be enough to find her. I'd like to meet her, if for nothing else than just to know why she chose me. There has to be a reason, doesn't there?"

Eden shrugged. "You'd think so."

I stood, suddenly remembering my manners. "Can I get you something to drink?"

"No thanks, I don't need anything. Sit." She patted the sofa beside her. "I want to hear about what happened at Avery's. He told me you knocked him on his ass, but he wouldn't give me details." She smiled like a schoolgirl on a sleepover and settled back into the sofa, watching me expectantly. She was so open and available that I couldn't help myself. I let it all out.

I recounted what Avery and I had learned. She sat patiently, taking it all in. She didn't offer advice or judge my words or feelings; she just listened.

"Every time I think I've got a handle on this Flier thing, something new crawls out of me and scares me half to death. This gift grows and changes like it has a life of its own, and then it flaunts the aftermath as a reminder that I'm not in control. I don't know how much more I can stand."

She didn't flinch when I told her what I'd done to Avery. It was such a relief to talk about it and the more I talked, the more the tension fell away. When I had finally spilled every last one of my fears, she still didn't jump into the fray.

Instead, she asked, "Have you eaten?"

I had to think about it. "Not since lunch. You?"

"I could use a bite. I also know a great place we can fly to from here. You feel up to it?"

Much to my surprise, I did. We both freshened up and I put my GPS in tracking mode before slipping it into my hoodie pocket.

"When we get up over the park, will you show me this speed of yours that Alex was going on about?" She donned an angelic expression that was so over the top, I couldn't stifle my giggle. She'd just spent an hour listening to me drivel on about my woes—how could I say no?

We lifted off from the darkened front lawn, well away from camera range. After I was up in the air, a startling realization hit me: I no longer had to separate the lift off effort into visualizing the crystal and then calling on the power that hummed just below the surface. Flying was beginning to feel a whole lot more like breathing. Jackson had said that would happen. Guess he was right.

Eden led the way up and over the park and before we got too far, I signalled to get her attention then burst past her in a brief demo of my speed. Thankfully, she kept the "holy cows" to a minimum. We crossed to the western edge of the park then followed along the shore until she pointed to a rectangular clearing. It looked like someone's backyard. Turns out it was a neighbourhood park—not more than one or two lots wide, but it was well treed with no one in sight.

As soon as we landed, she turned to me. "Alex was right ... Wow." And that was all she said about the speed.

"I like your Ryders," she mentioned as we breached the cover of the trees to find ourselves on a dimly lit sidewalk that housed a row of funky-looking shops. They were all closed except for the narrow restaurant wedged into the centre of the row. It was called the Neon Turtle, and even though it was after eleven, it was busy. A dense, exotic aroma rushed to greet us when she opened the door. It made my mouth water.

The textured walls were painted a deep yellow. Half of the dozen or so small tables were occupied. They were crowded close together, forcing whispered conversation, and the vague lighting hinted at the romantic potential of the place.

"Alex and I come here way too often," she said, leading us to a table, where we began perusing the menu. The Neon Turtle specialized in Thai fusion, which was new to me, so I left the menu choices to Eden.

She hadn't exaggerated—the food was delicious and by the end of our meal, I had regained my glass-half-full perspective. But, in Eden's company, that would be hard not to do. She had the kind of personality that burst to overflowing with all things positive. Not in a Pollyanna way but a fun-loving, kick 'em in the pants kind of way. Sparky. That's the word I'd use to describe her. Sparky. Just the kind of friend I wanted in my life. Our light, easy conversation had me once again feeling strong and ready to tackle my now somewhat less daunting gift-related complications. We left the restaurant and wandered down to the beach looking for a spot concealed enough to hide our liftoff.

"This looks good," Eden said, looking around. "Are you going to be able to find your way home from here?"

I pulled the GPS out of my pocket and studied it. "I think so. It looks fairly straightforward," I said, nervous about the prospect.

"Have some faith in yourself. You'll do great. Text me when you get home so I know you made it."

"Yes, *Mom*," I said, rolling my eyes. Eden laughed.

She looked around again to make sure we were alone. "What do you think?"

"Looks good to me," I said, and we both lifted off to a slow hover then waved goodbye before heading in opposite directions.

The tracking program proved easy to follow. I spotted landmarks as I approached the cottage and landed just inside the yard, close to the park's treeline. I'd done it! It was just a little taste of independence, but enough to give me an unexpected high.

Not quite high enough to forget about the camera in the Arbutus, but close.

Once back in the house, I locked the doors and texted Eden. Thinking of her reminded me about the doorbell. It was too late to call Charles so I sent him and Gabby a quick email instead, asking for the name of someone who could repair it.

It had been an exhausting day and I was weary to the bone. I crawled into bed. Sleep came quickly but my evening's nap played havoc with my usual seven- or eight-hour nightly siesta, and I was awake again before dawn.

I stretched out, yawned and then swung my feet out of bed and into my slippers. I pulled on my housecoat and sauntered to the kitchen to make my morning cuppa. The coffee machine gurgled as I watched the first rays of a new day's light poke through the mist that hovered over the water. A quick trip to the bathroom then I was back to the kitchen to pour a steaming cup of coffee. I held it under my nose, inhaling the aroma as I looked out the kitchen window toward the arbutus tree. The sooner we found out who was behind that camera, the better I'd sleep.

Just as I turned away from the window, movement caught my eye. I slowly turned back and watched a dark figure emerge from the park at the cliff's edge. My fear froze me in place. This was the man at the controls of the wrecking ball. He crept along the treeline heading straight for the arbutus. Something about the way he moved seemed vaguely familiar. He didn't waste any time before he started to climb. If I moved, would he notice me here watching him? Oh hell, I couldn't just stand here.

Pushing my fear aside, I slowly backed away, abandoned my coffee

JP McLEAN

mug on the end of the counter and bolted to my bedroom. I grabbed my phone off the bedside table and fought a mind block for Jackson's number. Damn it! My hands were shaking so badly I dropped the phone and scrambled to start all over again. I scrolled down the recently called numbers until Jackson's appeared.

He picked up right away. I cupped my hand over the phone and whispered, "He's here."

"Emelynn?" he asked in a voice thick with sleep. I heard the rustle of his bedding.

"The man," I whispered. "He's in the tree—right now."

"Where are you?" I heard the soft thumping of feet in the background and knew he was headed up the stairs.

"I'm in the bedroom now, but I saw him."

"You need to get out of there."

"I'm getting dressed right now," I said, scooping last night's clothes off the floor.

"Pull yourself together, get in your car and leave. Act casual, like it's just any other day. Don't forget your phone."

"Okay, I'm hanging up now."

"Call me when you can."

I hung up then dressed as if it were an Olympic event and I was going for the gold. Please, I thought, let me get out of here before that man gets out of the tree. I grabbed my purse, threw in the phone and plucked my keys off the hall table as I ran for the front door. I took a brief moment to collect myself before I turned the knob and walked outside on legs that had suddenly turned spastic and threatened to trip my every step.

It felt like an eternity before I got the garage doors open. Once inside, I fought the shakes to get the key in the ignition. The car coughed to life and I pulled out, concentrating on not making my departure look like a bank-heist getaway.

Once out on Deacon Street, with no destination, I just kept driving. Twenty minutes later, on the outskirts of Richmond, I pulled into a twenty-four-hour Tim Hortons and parked. I put my head on the steering wheel and sucked in a lungful of relief, and then another. Sitting back, I pulled my purse into my lap, found the phone and called Jackson.

"Are you all right?" he asked.

"Yeah, I'm fine," I said, finally able to breathe normally.

"Where are you?"

"At a Timmy's just south of Richmond. I'm sitting in the parking lot," I said, looking around.

"We got a great photo, Em. He got careless, took off his mask at the foot of the tree, and we got a clear shot of his face."

"Oh, thank god. That's great," I said with relief. "Do you recognize him?"

"I don't, but I sent the photo to Alex, and Eden recognized him."

"Eden?" I didn't understand. "Who is he?"

"She doesn't know, but he came into her Emerg, night before last. She's already headed to the hospital to dig up his name and address. They're probably fakes, but it's worth a shot."

"What happens now?"

"Alex will go check out the guy's address, see if it's real or not."

"And if it's real?"

"Well then, we'll have to have a little chat with him. Find out what he's up to. See if anyone else is involved."

"I don't know whether to be relieved or not." I wanted that man and his camera out of my life, but I didn't want to think too hard about how exactly that was going to happen.

"Get a coffee, read the paper. I'll call as soon as I know anything."

I locked the car and cut through a lineup near Timmy's front counter to get to the restroom. The mirror told a sorry tale: I looked a mess. I hadn't brushed my teeth or combed my hair. I hadn't even splashed water on my face. After a quick bird bath in the sink, I patted myself dry with a scratchy paper towel then finger-combed my knotted curls. I felt a bit better, but there was no help for my teeth.

The workday grind was in full swing. I joined a long lineup that crawled to the tills. When it was my turn, I ordered a large coffee, grabbed a newspaper and headed to a table to hide.

I'd forgotten how good Timmy's coffee was. I savoured it while I bided my time and read every inch of the paper. An hour had passed when the busgirl made her third trip through my section. I got back in line, ordered a cheese scone and took up residence in a different section.

The shrill ring of my phone had me scrambling in the bottom of my purse. It was Jackson. I abandoned the scone midbite and bolted for the door. "Hi," I said, unlocking the car door and settling inside.

"I think we got him."

"What does that mean?" I asked, breathless from my dash across the parking lot.

"It looks like the idiot used his real address."

"How do you know for sure that it's him?"

"Alex has been watching the address Eden gave him for the past hour. The guy in the photo just showed up. I'm heading over there now."

"Be careful, Jackson."

"Always am. Go on home. I'll be in touch as soon as I can."

I hung up and laid my head back against the headrest. It was barely 9:00 a.m. and already, it had been a very long day.

If I weren't such a mess, I'd go to Rumbles to see Molly and soak up some normal. But she'd know something was wrong. I couldn't hide the fear that still lingered—fear for Jackson's safety and for Alex's, and fear about what they were going to do with the guy. Did I even want to know?

At least I no longer had to worry about that camera. I started the car and headed home feeling numb. The garage doors gaped open, just as I'd left them in my rush to leave at dawn. I drove straight in, not caring enough to finesse my usual back-in, and left the doors ajar.

At times like these, the comfort of the cottage was like Tums for my soul. I opened the front door and made my way down the hall, stripping off my clothes as I went. I got to the bedroom, crawled back between the sheets and let exhaustion claim me.

CHAPTER NINETEEN

It was one o'clock in the afternoon when Jackson's call woke me. "I'm out on your deck—want to let me in?"

"Sure," I said, rubbing my face. "Just give me a sec." I hung up. Was I ready for this?

I pulled on my housecoat and gripped the lapels tight. Jackson was sitting in one of the deck chairs. He didn't get up when I opened the patio door, just held his cold hand out to me. I rubbed it vigorously between my own and sat in front of him.

"Hey," I said. Jackson nodded absently. We sat in silence, letting the outdoor ambience fill the audio void with bird calls and the rustle of the breeze in the trees. The tide was low, the water's edge some fifty yards off.

When Jackson finally spoke, he said, "It's over." He looked off to the horizon. "I can't believe the guy used his real address, considering the trouble and expense he'd gone to in setting up the camera. It just doesn't make sense. I had him pegged for a professional. Guess the guy never thought we'd make the connection."

"What about the camera?" I asked, looking up to the arbutus tree and seeing nothing.

"Gone." I heard a hard shift in Jackson's tone and stepped lightly.

"That was fast."

"Yeah, we had some unexpected help." Jackson's voice turned glacial.

"Oh?" I didn't like the harsh turn of our conversation.

"Apparently, Alex warned the Tribunal three days ago. They had a cleanup crew in the wings just waiting for a positive ID ... so it's all taken care of." He ended that sentence in a flippant sneer.

"Taken care of?" I asked with quiet trepidation. After yesterday's discussion with Avery, I understood what "taken care of" meant. But what if the guy had an explanation?

"Yeah, that's what the Tribunal does." He spit it out as he would a heated insult. "They swoop in, remove the problem and then we pretend it never happened."

"Why didn't Alex tell you about involving the Tribunal?"

"He should have. He didn't know they'd pounce like they did. Alex thought he was organizing backup in case we needed it."

Silence closed around us again. I had a thousand questions. I put all but one aside. "What will the Tribunal do with the man?"

"The man *and* a woman. They took them both, and neither one will be coming back."

My hands flew to my mouth, covering my gasp.

"As bad as that is, it's not the worst of it. The Tribunal's not in the habit of sharing information, so no matter what else they might be able to get out of the guy, we'll never know more than what we learned before they showed up, including who else might have been involved."

"What did you learn before they showed up?"

"He'd been researching us, though I'm almost certain he didn't know what we were. I read some of the stuff he'd written. He thought he was on the verge of a major scientific discovery, like he'd found some modern-day version of a lost Amazon tribe."

"Based on what?"

"Mostly photos from what I could see. Ten or twelve anyway, but not all of them were new. Some were from the mid-eighties, grainy as hell, but if you knew what you were looking at you'd recognize the figures as Fliers. The most damaging photos were clear shots of Eden out on your deck, but there were other Fliers in other locations that I didn't recognize. They were all taped to a wall beside a map that was cross-referenced to the photos. Half of the pins were concentrated along the beach near your cottage."

"Here? This beach?" I asked, shaken.

Jackson nodded. When he spoke, his voice sounded distant. "It'll all be gone by now: the photos, the map, everything."

Quiet settled between us again, but this time I welcomed it. I sat back and pulled my knees to my chest, wrapping the housecoat around me against the fresh breeze. It's an odd sensation looking at your life as if you were a spectator on the sidelines. That camera was in my tree. That man was in my yard. That fear I'd felt at the time was real, but now it all seemed like a bad dream. It had come and gone so quickly that I could almost believe it had never happened. What was wrong with me that I couldn't muster tears for the man and woman whose futures were gone? A chill came over me.

I stood up. "I'm cold, Jackson." I extended him my hand. "Come inside and I'll make us something warm to drink."

He took my hand, but I felt as if I were leading a zombie back into the house.

I opted for hot chocolate and put a warm cup in front of Jackson, then went to get dressed. When I returned, he hadn't touched it. I'd never seen him like this. His eerie calm was unsettling. I sat down beside him wondering if he felt as numb as me.

We looked up as one when Alex landed softly on the deck, followed by Eden. It was a dull day, but day nonetheless—they'd taken a huge risk flying here. When I opened the patio door Eden flew at me and wrapped her arms around me, holding on for dear life.

"Jackson," Alex said, with a nod. He looked over Eden's shoulder at me. "Em."

Eden relaxed her hold then stood back, still gripping my arms. "Are you all right?" she asked.

"I'm fine," but as I said it, tears overflowed her eyes and she dragged me into a hug again. This was not the Eden I'd seen at the Neon Turtle last night. She was a wreck.

"He was after *me*, Em." She sniffled into my hair then pulled back again. "I've never even *seen* the man before. He just showed up in the ER. You know how careful I am. Why me?" Her grip on my arm was on the edge of painful.

"You were just unlucky, Eden. He set a trap and you're the one he caught. It could have been any of us." I patted her hand and she apologized, relaxing her grip. "Who is he?" I asked. "Where's he from?"

"He's local—said he'd fallen from a ladder, but there was nothing broken or contused." She sniffled and I pulled away to grab a box of tissues. "Now I know it was just an act," she said, wiping her eyes. "I keep trying to figure out how he found me, but I'm drawing a blank." She blew her nose and swallowed then looked to Jackson. "I'm so sorry, Jackson."

Jackson got up and hugged her, dwarfing Eden's small frame. "It's over now." He released her to arm's length and stooped to catch her gaze. "You have nothing to be sorry about, Eden. You were the victim here."

"I feel like I've put you all through hell."

"We're covey, Eden." The tone of his voice grew sombre. "We protect one another. It's what we do."

Alex moved toward the kitchen. "Em, I'm going to disconnect this, okay?" He indicated the camera hidden on the windowsill.

"Sure," I replied. I reached for Eden's hand and tugged her toward the sofa, away from Jackson, who'd gone from numb to serious in a hurry. "Here, sit down. Can I get you anything?" Her hands vibrated like tuning forks, reflecting the tension in her body.

"No, I'll be fine," she said, and then her humour peeked out. "Unless you have some sanity on offer?"

I smiled at her, squeezing her hands. "Sanity's overrated," I said. She offered a weak smile. We turned our attention to Alex, who was disconnecting the camera. Jackson had taken a seat on one of the breakfast stools under the counter that separated them.

He spoke to Alex in regretful tones. "I wish you'd given me a heads-up earlier about the Tribunal."

"Sorry, man," Alex said. "I know how you feel about them, but I couldn't take a chance." He looked over to Eden, his protective mantle tangible in his gaze. "Not with Eden."

Jackson's confusion echoed mine as Alex looked from him to me. "You know ... because Eden was here." His hand action indicated the cottage. "The night before you found the camera, she was here—wearing her scrubs—with her stethoscope. Anyone would have been able to see she was a nurse just on or off shift."

"So you thought he'd be able to find her, based on that?"

"He *did* find her based on that, in less than twenty-four hours, so don't tell me I overreacted."

Jackson tensed his brow, speaking his thoughts. "She could have been any medical professional. How could he have searched all the local clinics and hospitals, all the wards and all those shifts and found Eden so quickly? He'd have to have incredible access, and that's even before you figure in the legwork involved." Jackson shook his head. "Something doesn't add up. Think about it. He must have had more information."

Jackson was right. No question. It seemed like a physical impossibility that anyone could have found Eden that quickly without more than the mere fact that she was dressed in scrubs. My mind slid back to yesterday morning. The scrap of paper with Eden's phone number and email address had been sitting right beside my computer. I quietly got up and walked over to the corner of the dining room table, where my laptop lived. A quick flip through the few papers there didn't produce Eden's scrap of paper. My heart crawled up into my throat as I remembered the twinge I'd felt yesterday when I'd discovered my laptop left open. Unable to hide my growing anxiety, I lifted the laptop then ducked under the table to check the floor. Nothing.

"What is it?" Jackson said, but I didn't answer. I was on a mission.

I ran into the kitchen, nudged Alex out of the way then yanked open the cabinet door below the sink and flipped the lid on the garbage. Maybe I'd absent-mindedly thrown the paper in the bin. I tossed the first few layers of paper towels, banana peels and tea bags but found no sign of Eden's note.

The blood drained from my face. I looked over to Eden, stricken, hands coated in coffee grounds. "He was here," I said, feeling sick to my stomach.

"Who?" Eden looked genuinely confused. "Where?"

"The note you gave me? The one with your phone number and email address?"

"Yes?" she said slowly, her mind getting into gear.

"It's gone. It was here ... right beside the computer. I sent you an email and it was right there." I pointed helplessly at the laptop.

Eden's face lit up with comprehension.

"He was right here. In my house. He found you because I left that stupid piece of paper out." I wrapped my arms around myself and swallowed the bile that rose in my throat.

No one moved a muscle while we digested the information.

Jackson broke the silence. "Did you notice anything else?"

"My computer. It was open. I usually leave it closed. That's why I noticed. But things have been so crazy around here ..."

"What about the guy who cuts your lawn?" Eden asked. "He has a key."

"Charles? God no. We've known him for years. He's harmless."

"What about doors or windows? Did you notice anything unlocked or left open?"

I paused to think. "No, nothing that I noticed."

Jackson jumped up and rushed to my bedroom. Alex scurried down the hall. They ran a circuit around the cottage checking all the windows

JP MCLEAN

and doors before returning to the living room. "There are no signs of forced entry. I knew these guys were professional. I knew it!" Jackson shook his head. "I hope the Tribunal knows what the hell they're doing." Jackson paced, rubbing the knuckles of his right hand.

"Jackson, man," Alex said, sitting on the stool Jackson had vacated. "The Tribunal knows what they're doing. No half measures. You know that." Eden moved to stand behind him, her arm around his shoulder.

"I hope so," Jackson said.

But I had questions. "Won't Eden or Alex get the chance to hear what the guy has to say?"

There was a moment of déjà vu with all three of them glaring at me as if my mental faculties were deficient. I felt like an outsider again. Why was I surprised at their reaction? It was, after all, standard Flier response whenever I asked a question about the Tribunal.

"No. No questions; no answers; no witnesses. It's the way of the Tribunal." Jackson said, as though I should have known that. Maybe I should have. He'd mentioned something along those lines earlier, but he'd been angry then. I hadn't thought he was serious.

"Well, go ask them now. Surely they'll understand our concern." Wasn't it a simple matter of getting in touch with them? They couldn't be that inflexible.

"Emelynn, the Tribunal doesn't do questions." Alex frowned. "After they arrived on the scene, Jackson and I were ... dismissed."

Eden wrapped her other arm around him and hugged him close. Alex reached up to her embrace and kissed her hands. "I'm not sorry I contacted them, not with all the other unsolved disappearances. I'm just sorry we'll never know the rest of the story."

Jackson glared at Alex. "That's precisely why I don't want them involved in Sandra's situation. You get that, right?"

"Sure. Sandra's your business. I know that." Alex's expression conveyed sincerity and apology in equal measure. "The Tribunal won't hear about it from me. You and your covey can handle it any way you feel best. You can trust me."

"Good." Jackson exhaled, relaxing his shoulders. "Because what happened here is not the same thing we're dealing with in Sandra's case. Her abductors haven't hurt her and they won't; they're using her to get to her money."

"You can count on us. We'll help you when the time comes. The covey's already agreed to that."

"Thanks. I appreciate it." Jackson dropped the tension another notch and sat on the other end of the sofa.

I addressed all of them when I said, "I'd appreciate it if you wouldn't jump down my throat when I ask this next question, but I need to know. How can we be so sure this is over?"

Alex and Eden looked to Jackson, who took a moment to answer. "Remember how I incapacitated you on the beach?" I nodded ... like I would ever forget that experience. "Well, multiply that threefold then add some extra special effects. The Tribunal's Fliers are the strongest of our kind. They told us they would take out the threat and they will. It's what they do—it's all they do. Then they'll cover their tracks."

I gulped. "Okay. Apparently, it's out of our hands and there's nothing we can do about it."

"Not unless we want to be their next targets," Alex said.

"So, can we put it aside for the night?" I asked, needing a break from the tension.

"Yes, let's do that, or try anyway," Eden said, not loosening her hold on Alex.

Jackson remained on the far side of the sofa. I wanted to reach out to him, but we hadn't yet come out of the closet with our new relationship and this wasn't the time.

"How about we get out of here?" Alex said. "I think we need a change of scenery."

The daylight hour dictated the services of a cab. We went to the Neon Turtle, Eden's suggestion despite our recent meal there. The Tribunal, the camera and its operator weren't mentioned again. Our moods gradually lifted over the course of two bottles of wine, fabulous food and good company. We lingered an exceedingly long time, and afterwards, under darkness of night, we went our separate ways.

Jackson came to my deck but declined my offer to stay over. "Thanks, but I need to get back to the *Symphony*. I can't leave her unattended at anchor." He escorted me safely inside then kissed me goodbye.

I didn't mind. It had been a brutal day and I wanted to tuck into my own bed tonight, safe in the knowledge that the threat was gone.

When I woke, it was late morning. I pointed my toes and stretched under the warm covers, feeling refreshed, content—at least until the words *it's been taken care of* echoed through my mind. My mood sank. I dragged myself out of bed into the bright cloudless day, which would have been a solid ten on the happy-days scale if not for the memory of what happened yesterday.

After making my morning coffee, I made a quick visit to the bathroom, donned my housecoat then stuffed my phone in the pocket and poured the java to go. If anything could bring me back to some semblance of sanity, it was my coffee-on-the-beach routine.

I opened the patio door and a warm breeze blew the hair from my face. This was the first truly warm day since I'd arrived. I dared it to brighten my mood. The stairs to the beach were dew free and the bleached logs were already dry. I sat and tilted my face to the sun.

Seagulls called to one another overhead. As usual, I was alone on the beach. I shut my eyes and relaxed, enjoying the distant sound of the surf and the pungent smell of seaweed.

The therapeutic cottage effect was in full force. The whole camera incident had been reduced to a bad nightmare. The jolting fiasco with Avery seemed inconsequential. Yesterday's worries felt controllable once again, and that made me feel immeasurably better. And there was that word again, "controllable."

A long time passed before the tranquility of the morning was broken by the sound of a boat's motor. I shielded my eyes from the glare of the sun on the water and looked out in the direction of the noise. It looked as if my morning was about to get even better because I was pretty sure the small boat headed in my direction was the Zodiac from the *Symphony* which, I noticed, had also moved into view.

I watched Jackson jump out of the dinghy and pull it up on the rocks. It was low tide and he was a good fifty yards away, which left me lots of time to appreciate his silhouette as he made his way to the cottage. He didn't see me sitting on the beach until I called out to him. His face lit up with a smile and he came over to sit beside me.

He stared pointedly at my housecoat. "I see you're having a leisurely morning." He looked positively scrumptious in an unbuttoned shirt and long linen shorts. I wanted to run my hands across his bare chest, but sighed instead, restraining myself.

"There's more coffee. Would you like me to get you a cup?"

"I'll come with you." He stood, offering his hand. We walked to the stairs and back up to the deck. "I thought you might like to join me for lunch on the *Symphony* today."

"That sounds like a wonderful idea. Help yourself to coffee and I'll get dressed."

I heard him open the cupboard and rattle the mugs. "Do you have any plans for the rest of the day?" he called.

I knew I had a sundress in the closet somewhere. My mother had bought it for me last year to protest the billowing shirts and cargo pants that made up my familiar summer attire. Of course, she hadn't known about the need for reinforced pockets.

"No plans," I said as I pulled the dress out of the closet and removed the tags. The dress had spaghetti straps and the cotton fabric was the palest of blues with tiny white and yellow daisies. The heart-shaped bodice was fitted and the skirt came to just above my knees. I pulled it over my head feeling sinfully wicked about not wearing a bra. With a bit of contortion, I slid the zipper up the back then found a sexy pair of silk panties. The pale amber drop earrings, also a gift from my mother, matched the yellow in the daisies perfectly.

"Good, then we won't have to ... rush." Jackson's words trailed off as I came around the corner into the living room. He looked me up and down. "Wow, you look great. I should invite you to lunch more often." He had the look of a man about to have his lunch and eat it too. His look sizzled me inside and out.

I gave him a sensual maybe-there's-more-where-this-came-from kind of kiss and went to look for my sunglasses while he finished his coffee. I dropped my wallet and phone into my purse before locking up.

We picked our way among the rocks back to the Zodiac then set out for the *Symphony*. The wind felt cooler out on the open ocean, making me wish I'd put on a sweater. But the trip wasn't far and it was much warmer once we slowed down. Back on board the *Symphony*, out of the wind, my goosebumps vanished. Jackson secured the dinghy and we headed up to the galley.

If Jackson was trying to impress me, he'd done a good job. The table, which was already set, included a vase filled with tulips. He removed a quiche from the fridge, put it on a sheet pan then set it in the oven. Two tall champagne flutes stood on the counter. He filled each one half full with orange juice then popped the cork on a bottle of bubbly and topped them up. He handed me a glass, gesturing to the stairs. "Shall we?"

"We shall," I said, and we headed up to enjoy the sunshine.

"You are full of surprises today," I said, gazing at the water over the rail.

"Only today?" he asked with a devilish grin on his face.

We laughed, sipped our drinks and made small talk until Jackson figured our lunch was ready. I hadn't had anything to eat that morning and was already feeling the champagne going to my head. We went below, where he served up a salad with a very cheesy quiche.

"Don't be too impressed; I didn't make it myself," he confessed.

But I didn't care about that part. It was the fact that he'd gone to the effort at all that impressed me. After we'd eaten, he made two more mimosas, and we took them back up top.

I approached the rail looking in the direction of the cottage, which was but a speck in the distance. I felt Jackson behind me. I tipped the flute, draining it before he took it from my hand to set it down on the deck. He wrapped his arms around me, pulling me back snugly against his chest. I rested my head against him, closed my eyes and savoured the sensation of having him at my back and the warm sun on my face. This is what right felt like.

Just when I thought it didn't get any better than this, he brushed my hair aside and trailed kisses from my neck to my shoulder. He had certainly learned quickly how to ramp up my heart rate. I signed with pleasure knowing where this silent conversation was headed.

He slid a finger under each of the thin straps of my dress and pulled them off my shoulders. I felt the zipper slide down, but it was his touch that undid me. He reached around under the fabric and folded the bodice down to my waist. A gentle breeze caressed my exposed flesh. I shuddered when he traced his fingers in lazy circles around my breasts. He pushed all the right buttons and I loved the way he teased the lust out of me. I felt as if I might explode with anticipation. He nuzzled into my neck. There was something unbelievably sensual about being outside, nearly naked, where anyone might see.

He breathed heavily against my neck. I tried to turn around but he pressed me to the railing instead. "Bend forward," he said, his voice rough, demanding. I grabbed the railing and heard his shorts hit the deck. He lifted my skirt and yanked my panties down. "Spread your legs," he said, his breath ragged. I complied, finding his dominant tone curiously erotic. His touch was warm against the inside of my thigh as he moved his hand upward then suddenly pushed his fingers into me. I gasped my surprise as the strength in my knees wavered. He rubbed his erection back and forth in my wetness, and when he finally pressed the tip of it barely inside me, I nearly collapsed. He wrapped an arm around my hips then slowly entered me, pushing deeply.

A moment later, after my body adjusted to the invasion, he picked up a steady rhythm. God, he was so hard and the friction felt indescribably good. He moved his hand lower, brushing his fingers lightly against my hard knot of nerves, driving me to new heights. He brought his other hand around to my lips, pushing his fingers inside. I tasted myself on his fingers. Jackson's breath hitched. His thrusts came faster, more powerful, pounding into me with a wild sense of urgency. I felt an incredible surge of pleasure building from deep inside, slowly spreading out and up through my torso.

My orgasm hit like a tsunami that came in wave after incredible wave. I couldn't think, couldn't breathe, could only sigh in ecstasy and grip the rail for fear my knees would give out. But Jackson wasn't yet ready to end his own pleasure. He continued, thrust after thrust. A second orgasm cascaded through me and this time he unravelled, moaning as he stiffened and jerked. Finally spent, he draped over my back.

"God, that was good," he whispered. I couldn't yet talk. Making love with Jackson was never dull. How did I ever manage so long without sex? When we finally straightened, we locked in an embrace, both of us reluctant to end the moment. Eventually, we gathered our clothes and headed below.

"You go shower," he said, heading toward the galley. "I'll clean up lunch."

I revisited my former cabin and stripped off my dress. The shower felt soothing after the vigorous lovemaking, which had left my tender skin bruised. Then the shock of something else hit me. We hadn't used a condom. The happy, sated feeling quickly melted into one of dread. I towelled off, re-dressed and returned to the galley.

"Did you leave any hot water for me?" Jackson asked with a grin, a tea towel draped over his shoulder. He landed a kiss on my head. "I'll be quick." He turned and dashed for the stairs.

I watched him go. The no-condom discussion could wait until he finished his shower; it wasn't going to get any worse for the delay. Walking toward the sofa, I noticed his computer screen glowing, and wandered over to see that he'd left his email program running. That was a first—Jackson must have forgotten it was open.

Unable to dismiss my curiosity, I glanced down the list of emails in his inbox. The subject lines referenced updates or reports on development projects. Exactly the type of correspondence I'd expect given the little bit of research I'd done. I didn't open the emails, but I did use the mouse to scroll down the screen, glancing at the subject lines.

The water pump kept up a steady pulse indicating Jackson was still in the shower, so I kept scrolling despite an overwhelming sense of guilt. This was unbelievably bad girlfriend behaviour. I took my finger off the scroll button, ready to reset the page to where I'd found it when the subject "Jolene" jumped out at me. I let go of the mouse as if it had bitten me and froze. Seeing Jolene's name on the screen shot a rush of adrenalin through me. I bent down to double-click on the message. The water pump shut down. I quickly read the contents, desperate to get through it before Jackson returned. The email was short. It read:

Jolene Reynolds, b. 1961
Watercolour artist, Sun Meadow Cooperative, SF
Disappeared from SF/CA area fall of 1999
Known contact in Vanc area
Renowned for speed and undocumented special skills

It was dated Monday, May 30. Over a week ago. That was just after Jackson first brought me here to the *Symphony*. This didn't make sense. He'd known Jolene's identity practically since the day we met. Why was he keeping this from me? I'd asked him about Jolene repeatedly ... hadn't I? The knowledge left me cold. What else had he learned? Unfortunately, I didn't have time to look. I quickly closed the email and returned the screen to where it had been when I found it.

I rubbed my arms, which were now covered in goosebumps, and turned away from the computer. Had Jackson forgotten he'd received that email? Perhaps he'd been so preoccupied with his work that it had slipped his mind. Maybe he hadn't even read it. No, if that were the case, it would have been displayed in bold on the computer screen. Whatever the reason, I couldn't very well ask him about it, having found it by snooping.

I heard Jackson moving around below and returned to the galley. He arrived with a bounce in his step. One look at me though and his smile faded. "What's wrong?" he asked as he approached.

Apparently, I needed to work at hiding my emotions. I hesitated. I wanted to ask him about Jolene, but I wasn't ready to fess up to trolling through his email like a boil-the-bunny girlfriend.

I ended up blurting out, "We didn't use a condom."

His face fell. "You're right. I'm sorry." He reached out and I let him pull me into his arms, but I couldn't bring myself to return the embrace. A disturbing uneasiness had settled on me that had little to do with the condom and a lot to do with the email about Jolene. I pulled back from his embrace.

"Are you angry with me?" he asked.

"No, of course not. It takes two, right?" I forced a smile onto my face while my insides churned. The cottage pulled at me: my safe place, my sanctuary.

I asked Jackson to take me home, making excuses about errands I had to run. He accompanied me up the beach to the foot of the stairs, but I didn't give him the opportunity to linger. I kissed him in a manner that made it clear I was going up alone, said goodbye then turned and climbed the stairs. If Jackson noticed my dismissal, he didn't let on.

When I got inside the cottage, I locked the door behind me and headed to the bedroom. It was after three o'clock. I kicked off my sandals and flopped on the bed.

Why hadn't Jackson told me what he knew about Jolene? Avery had told me right away when he learned Jolene's identity. Jackson received that same information a week ago, yet still hadn't mentioned it. Would there be any purpose in keeping it from me? The answer had to be no. He must have just forgotten. After all, Jolene was a far more intriguing part of my life than his. Maybe the information had gotten lost in the midst of the whole camera fiasco. I thought I'd asked Jackson about Jolene a number of times, but perhaps it was only Sandra I'd asked about?

I was probably making too big a deal out of it. Next time I saw Jackson I'd raise the issue and find out what he'd learned about Jolene. He just needed a gentle reminder, that's all. And then he'd likely be embarrassed and fess up that he'd had the info earlier and had forgotten to tell me about it. That's got to be what happened. It made perfect sense. I really was thinking it to death. Right?

So why was my intuition prickling? Surely it wasn't fair of me to think the worst of Jackson. He'd never given me any reason to doubt him, had he? Maybe it was my need to be in control that was throwing me for a loop, and why wouldn't it? I was on a roller-coaster ride with no indication it was slowing down. My intuition just needed time to recalibrate.

And the cottage was the perfect place to do it. No matter what turmoil howled in my life, this place always calmed me. It was yet another reminder that this was home—the place where I belonged.

Feeling decidedly better, I slipped off the bed and went in search of a snack. I poured a glass of milk and took it and some oatmeal cookies out to the deck. The sun beamed and the air was warm. I brushed crumbs from my lap and looked out to the *Symphony* on the horizon.

Jackson. Seemed he was always on my mind. And since he was evidently going to dominate my thoughts, I might as well do something about it. I took my empty glass back to the kitchen and turned on the computer. While I waited for it to start up, I turned on the stereo and hummed along with Taylor Swift singing about her Romeo.

I pulled up the bookmarks from my last search and clicked on an article published in 2007 by the *Times-Picayune*, which speculated on the future of a prime piece of waterfront that had hit the market. This was the land that Delaney subsequently developed into the marina I'd read about yesterday. Another company, Touchstone Enterprises, was mentioned in the article.

The Touchstone name rang a bell. I went back to the Chamber of Commerce website and found the company amongst the list of New Orleans developers then followed the link back to the company's website.

Touchstone Enterprises was founded in 1978 by Richard Des Roche and, like Delaney & Son, it was family owned and operated. Also like Delaney, Touchstone had started with small developments and had grown over the years to develop bigger, more prestigious projects. These two old companies were, in all likelihood, long-time rivals in the local development business.

I typed Touchstone Enterprises into Google's search engine and groaned when I saw the dozens of results it garnered. This was going to be a bigger chore than I had thought. I started sorting through the entries.

It looked like Touchstone was more involved in the residential end of things, but both companies had the appearance of success. At least, that was how it looked until I dug deeper. A number of articles written in 2009 hinted at financial problems within Touchstone. More troubling articles appeared in 2010, but I found nothing newer.

I typed Richard Des Roche into the search engine. There were a few photos together with some complimentary pieces written about him and his philanthropic endeavours. A recent family photo, taken at a fundraising event, identified Richard, his wife Bronwyn, and their son

Cole. I clicked to enlarge the photo. They were a handsome family. Richard had a full head of grey hair. Bronwyn looked somewhat younger. Cole was fair-haired, like his mother. He looked strangely familiar. Perhaps I'd seen his photo in one of the other articles I'd run across.

I revisited the bookmarks I'd tagged on the Delaney search and clicked on an article about the opening of the marina in 2010. The amount of concrete and steel that had gone into the development was staggering, as were the estimates of tax and rental revenue the project would generate in future years. If Delaney had any stake in that revenue stream, the company would do very well indeed.

Then I clicked on a footnote that took me to another article in which the author quoted an unnamed source at Touchstone, who indicated that Delaney & Son had been investigated for corporate espionage. The alleged espionage had apparently resulted in Touchstone's losing the marina deal and millions of dollars in revenue. The author was careful to note that no charges were ever brought against Delaney & Son.

As interesting as this was getting, I'd had enough computer research for one day. I checked my email then logged off and closed the computer.

My mind wandered back to my afternoon with Jackson. The lust he was capable of stirring in me was such a pleasant discovery. Regardless, it was stupid of us to skip the condom, especially considering I didn't know Jackson's history very well. I suppose I should be grown-up about the situation and get my butt to the pharmacy to pick up a morning-after pill. At least the pregnancy worry would be taken care of. That much I could fix.

CHAPTER TWENTY

I t was nearing six o'clock when I pulled into the empty Shoppers Drug Mart parking lot. Relief washed over me at the sight of the bright neon Open sign. I rushed in and sprinted to the pharmacy counter at the back of the store. The pharmacist was a dowdy woman who looked as if she'd never cracked a smile in her life. I steeled myself and spit out what I needed. She didn't say a word. Her expression as she looked over the top of her glasses at me said it all.

She turned her back and disappeared. When she returned, she held the pill captive while she explained the dangers of unprotected sex. It was humiliating, but given my current predicament, I supposed I deserved that and more. I paid an astronomical price for the pill then raced out of there.

I tossed the white paper bag into the back seat and drove to Rumbles. Molly was still behind the counter. She looked up when she heard the bells jingle over the door, and smiled a hello when she saw me. She was actually bagging a book for a customer. It was a Miracle on Deacon Street moment.

I stood quietly while she finished the transaction. My look of astonishment followed the man and his bag out the door. When I turned back to Molly, she rolled her eyes.

"Yes, occasionally people actually do buy books here," she said with a chuckle as I approached the counter. "How are you?"

"Great thanks." I hoped she'd agree that some girl talk was overdue. "Are you off at six thirty?"

"I am," she said, and a Cheshire Cat grin spread across her face. She looked particularly sharp tonight in a sleeveless, bright green dress. Molly always looked good, but this was special—not her usual retro-casual look but a retro-dressy look.

I grinned back at her infectious smile. "Want to go for a drink?"

"Well, usually I'd jump all over that offer. However, tonight, I've got a date. He should be by any minute now to pick me up."

"Oh Molly, do tell," I asked, and then the bells over the door jingled. We both looked to the door and watched Cheney come waltzing in looking very handsome indeed in black jeans with a white shirt and tweed blazer.

"Hi Emelynn," he said as he approached. "Molly, am I too early?"

Molly reached for her purse. "No, I just have to lock up."

"Molly, we'll talk later." I made sure she saw my face and the wide-eyed glare that left no doubt I would be following up for all the details. "You two have a good time," I said, heading for the door.

Molly's date left me at loose ends for the night. Maybe I'd look for a movie on TV and order pizza. Once home, I turned on the flat-screen and scrolled through the guide. Saturday night and here I was, home alone, watching the tube. A positively boring evening compared to my activities of late.

My phone rang from the depths of my purse. I sprang up to find it. "Hello?" I answered.

"Hi Em. It's Avery. How are you making out?" His tone was cautious.

Not surprising, I suppose. I'd been pretty shaken last time he'd seen me. I still felt the guilt from slamming him into a wall with my jolt.

"I'm doing okay. And thanks for talking to Eden. She was a godsend." Eden was just the kind of older sister I would choose if I could. The thought made me smile. "She's turning into a good friend."

"I'm glad. You needed a friend after what I put you through."

"I think you've got that the wrong way around," I said. "But never mind. It's behind us."

"You sound great, so I'm going to trust that you're being honest and what happened really is behind us."

"It is," I said, and then searched for something else to talk about. "Eden and I went to the Neon Turtle for dinner. Have you been there?"

"No, was it good?"

"It's Thai fusion, whatever that means, and it's just a small place, but the food is great."

"I'll have to check it out sometime." Avery paused and I waited for him to tell me the real purpose of his call. "Are you ready to continue your training?"

"Ready as I'll ever be, but shouldn't I be the one asking you that question?"

I heard him chuckle under his breath. "You know me, I'm a masochist in training," he said, the laughter still in his voice. "Why don't you come by tomorrow morning? Better still, why don't you come for breakfast?"

"Are you sure? Tomorrow's Sunday. You know ... the day of rest."

"I trade my bran flakes for bacon and eggs on Sundays."

"In that case, yes. What time?"

"Nine o'clock work for you?"

"Great."

"I'll see you at nine then," he said, and we hung up.

Now I had something to look forward to tomorrow, even if I was looking forward to it with a tinge of trepidation.

I found the phone number for the Flying Wedge and placed an order for a medium Greek then settled on the sofa. I muted the TV so I'd hear the doorbell when it announced the arrival of my dinner.

Instead, the phone rang. It was Jackson, and my heart skipped a happy beat.

He rushed through his hello to ask, "Have you ever played paintball?"

Where did that come from? "No, why?"

"I was going to set up a game with the covey. What do you think?"

"I don't know. I've never played."

"Oh, you'll love it." Jackson explained the concept of the game with enthusiasm.

Guns and paintballs didn't catch my interest, let alone drop it into the "you'll love it" category, but I didn't want to be a spoilsport.

"Best of all," he said, excitement animating his voice, "the whole park is ours after dark so we'll be able to incorporate flying into our game."

"Now *that* sounds like fun," I said, revising my earlier opinion.

"Great. I'll set it up and let you know the details. And Em, just so you have a heads-up, I'm going to use the opportunity to brief the covey on the incident with the camera. They need to know what happened so they keep their eyes open, stay vigilant."

"Okay. Thanks for the warning," I said, not really wanting the reminder. And thinking of reminders ...

"Jackson," I said, catching his attention before he could hang up. "Before you go ... have you learned anything about Jolene?" I waited with my heart in my throat.

"Ah ... yes ... there was something."

I exhaled. I was right. It had just slipped his mind.

"A Flier by the name of Jolene disappeared from the San Francisco area around the time you received your gift. If I'm not mistaken, her name was Jolene Raymond."

My relief left me weak in the knees. All my worry, I thought, for absolutely no reason at all. Now I felt embarrassed about all the negative notions that had flitted through my mind to explain what had turned out to be a memory lapse. Bad girlfriend.

"Thanks, Jackson. That's great. At least now I have a name. Maybe I'll be able to learn more about her."

The chime of the doorbell nearly blew me out of my seat.

"What was that?" Jackson asked.

"The doorbell." Apparently, my new doorbell. "It'll be my pizza."

"Pizza sounds good. You'd better go get it. Good night," he said, and we ended our call.

I met the pizza delivery girl at the front door and pushed the door-bell twice more, just to be sure. It was definitely new and loud. Before I dove into the pizza, I emailed Charles a quick thank you.

Once again, the Flying Wedge did not disappoint. As I ate, a stray thought hit me. Jackson had said "Jolene Raymond," but her last name was Reynolds. He really had forgotten.

After stashing the leftovers in the fridge, I ran a hot bath. I read in the tub until the water cooled then headed to bed with my book and read until the wee hours of the morning.

Sunday's brilliant sunshine woke me relatively early. At least early for what had become my usual late-night, late-morning routine. But today, I had a breakfast date with Avery that I didn't want to be late for. I dressed casually in a T-shirt and capris then threw on my jean jacket as I headed out.

I knocked on his door just after nine and he answered it with a tea towel in his hands.

"Come on in," he said, ushering me into the large, bright kitchen, where his faithful Brown Betty awaited with a belly full of steeped tea.

He poured us both a steaming cup then got the breakfast fixings out of the fridge, chatting the whole time. He was meticulous in his methods, so it was fascinating to watch him cook. I set the table with lots of "where's this and that." He served up both our plates and we sat down to toast our good health with our teacups.

In addition to perfectly cooked crispy bacon, we had eggs, hash browns, toast and sliced hothouse tomatoes. It was heavenly. I cleaned every crumb off my plate, and then we sat back and sipped our tea.

"I asked Jackson about Jolene again last night."

"What did he say?"

"He's uncovered the same information you did." I didn't mention the fact that he'd forgotten to give me the info last week or that he'd actually gotten her name wrong—Jackson would be embarrassed about that for sure.

"That's good news. Has he learned anything more about Jolene's 'extra' skills?"

I thought back to our conversation. "No, he didn't mention the details of her gift at all. Just her name and that she was from San Francisco."

"That's too bad. I was hoping we might learn more from Jackson's sources. Something to help us uncover the extent of your gift would have been nice."

Come to think of it, the email on Jackson's computer had listed Jolene's speed and her undocumented special skills, neither of which he'd mentioned. Not that it mattered; we already had those details.

I set my cup down. Something else was on my mind. "Avery, do you talk to Jackson about me?"

"Not since you torpedoed into the park," he said with a snicker. "Of course, I did talk to him again the night he took you to the *Symphony*. He thought I might notice you missing. Frankly, I was just glad he'd taken you under his wing."

He continued, more solemn. "I won't share more than I already have with Jackson or anyone else. If you want to tell Jackson about our discoveries, or what I've learned about Jolene, I'll leave that up to you."

"Thank you," I said, insisting he sit while I cleared the table and loaded his dishwasher. I wiped the counters before we headed back through the waiting area into the exam room.

Avery sat in the chair behind the small wooden desk and I hopped up on the exam table.

"Avery, I need to tell you something." I hesitated, a bit unsure of myself.

"What is it?" he asked, offering me his doctor's face, a blank slate, ready for anything.

"I've started seeing Jackson." Then, because I wasn't sure I was being explicit enough, I added, "In the biblical sense." It was an awkward moment, but I didn't want to have secrets with Avery. He'd been too good to me.

He looked surprised. "He works fast. When did this start?" he asked.

"The night of my impromptu dip in the Pacific."

He sat back, staring at his steepled fingers. "It's a big step."

If you only knew, I thought... oh crap. My face flamed red. I'd forgotten that he'd examined me for sexual assault in the hospital a lifetime ago. He probably knew I'd been a virgin. I prayed for the earth to swallow me up.

Avery asked, "So, how's it going?"

I shifted and the paper on the exam table crackled. "Good... I think. It's all pretty new to me."

"Are you taking precautions?" he asked. If the blood hadn't already taken up residence in my face, it would have with that question.

"Yes." Or most of the time, but he didn't need to know that detail.

"You don't know him very well."

"I know. I don't usually jump in with both feet like this. I'm a bit of a control freak, as it turns out. Guess I'll just have to add Jackson to the growing list of things in my life that are a little out of control right now."

"You can always slow things down—take it easy with him until you get to know him better." He looked down at his feet. "Take your time, Emelynn. There's no rush." He recrossed his ankles. "Be careful with your heart. You've only got one."

"Thanks, I'll try." He really was a gem, and his concern warmed said heart.

Avery looked at me for the longest time, then slapped his thighs and sat up. "I guess we'd better get down to business."

We continued where we'd left off. He put up his block and I practiced my sparks. I didn't dare test my full power. I wasn't sure I would ever do that again. We kept at it for about an hour and, by the end of that time, I felt fairly good about my ability to spark consistently at varying but nonlethal levels.

When we were both confident that I was ready, Avery lowered his block to let me test how other Fliers would feel my spark. He was a good sport, and it was a relief to pass that nerve-racking test without incident.

It was getting close to noon and I didn't want to take up all of Avery's day. I made motions to call it quits. "What's next on our agenda?" I asked as I got up to go.

Avery's phone rang, and he motioned for me to hold on while he answered it. "Jackson, good to hear from you." I started to excuse myself, but Avery gestured for me to stay. I felt awkward eavesdropping on their conversation, but there was no avoiding it, considering the small size of the room. Avery talked for a few minutes then hung up.

"Do you know anything about this update that Jackson wants to share with the covey?"

It pained me to replay the whole camera incident, but Avery's stare down left me little choice. "I'm afraid I do," I said, and reluctantly recounted everything I knew, from our discovery of the camera to the details about the Tribunal Novem's involvement.

"Does Jackson think the guy picked your property because of its proximity to the other sightings?"

"That, and its location. The park was great cover for him."

"This is getting way too close to home," Avery said, rubbing his face. "How is Eden?"

"She was pretty upset, but she bounced right back. I think it helps that she knows it could have been any one of us. You know, for a tiny girl, she's one tough cookie. She's also got Alex watching her back and he's a pit bull when it comes to her. It's sweet really."

"Jackson can't be happy about the Tribunal's involvement."

"You got that right, but how did you know?"

"I know he doesn't want them involved in his covey's business. Having them this close must have him on edge."

"You're right. He made Alex promise not to involve the Tribunal in anything Sandra-related." Avery nodded as though he understood.

"Does anyone know who's on this Tribunal?" I asked. "Jackson made it sound like they were some kind of Super Fliers."

That prompted a quiet chuckle from Avery. "Super Fliers." He shook his head. "I guess they are that."

"So who are they?"

"The Tribunal Novem draws its members from the nine founding coveys, though at any given time only five members are active. The odd numbers ensure decisive votes."

"So every Flier in each of the nine founding coveys is a Super Flier?"

"I don't know that. I doubt it. But when the Tribunal has to carry out decisions, their enforcers have to be highly skilled and powerful."

"I've got to tell you, this Tribunal Novem scares the pants off me."

"I'm sure they'd be happy to hear that. Deterrence is a far better solution than dealing with infractions. Unfortunately, they're the only thing standing between us and those who would expose us, or otherwise harm us."

"So you think they're a good thing?"

"No, I don't. But without a judicial system, we don't have a better option."

"Well, they still scare the pants off me."

"Yeah, me too." Avery exhaled a heavy breath. It seemed he needed an end to this conversation, and I was happy to oblige.

"Did Jackson give you a time for the paintball game?" I asked.

"Tonight. Ten o'clock."

"Are you going?" we both asked at the same time.

I answered first, with a stupid grin on my face. "Yeah, I think I will. I've never played before."

"It's fun. Sounds like most of the covey will be there too. Do you know where it is?"

"No, but I'll find it. Do you want me to drive you?" I asked, remembering that he didn't fly.

"Thanks, but how about I drive you instead. I'll be driving regardless."

We agreed he'd pick me up at nine thirty. I thanked him for breakfast then said goodbye.

On my way home, I drove past Rumbles. It was Molly's day off and I was itching to know how her date had gone last night. I dialled her number as soon as I got home.

She answered my call out of breath. "Hey, Em."

"Hi. Sounds like I pulled you away from a marathon."

"No, I'm just heading out from my yoga class. What's up?"

"Nothing much. I wondered if you wanted to get together this afternoon."

"What did you have in mind?"

"It's a beautiful day; we could go for a walk on the beach or maybe a hike in the park? I could pick you up."

"Either one sounds good, but you don't need to pick me up. The yoga studio is on Deacon. I'll just hop a bus. Be there in thirty minutes."

She arrived in twenty. We decided on a hike through the park after Molly reminded me about the old lighthouse. I had vague recollections of picnicking out there with my parents when I was a kid.

The lighthouse wasn't on the GPS. I set it on tracking mode then put it in my fanny pack along with my phone and a bottle of water. "Do you know which trail to take?" I asked when we got into the park.

"I don't remember. It's been so long since I've been out there."

When the trail branched off, we chose the path to the right.

"So, how'd it go with Cheney last night?" I asked, hoping I wasn't being too nosy.

"I wondered how long it would take you to ask," Molly said, looking theatrically at her watch. "You waited twenty-two hours by my calculation."

"Oh, go on." I laughed. "You're dying to tell me all about it. I can tell by that dreamy smile on your face."

That was all it took to burst her dam. "We had a wonderful time. He took me to a trendy restaurant in Yaletown called Brix. We had a fabulous dinner then we went bar-hopping. Yaletown is such fun. Have you ever been there?"

"No, but back to you. When did you meet Cheney?"

"He came into the shop last Thursday." We were on a particularly treacherous section of trail where the tree roots twisted across our path. Molly stopped her narrative to watch her footing.

"And ..." I asked, impatient for more information.

"Well, he wandered around the stacks, but I could tell he wasn't paying mind to the books. He kept looking back to the front counter. Finally, he picked up a magazine and came to me—you know, to pay for it. But ..." She stopped again to cross a fallen sapling. I feigned frustration, motioning for her to carry on.

"But what he really wanted was an introduction. Of course, as soon as he said his name was Cheney, I knew who he was." She stopped and her lips curled into that dreamy smile again. "Good thing he told me his name." She caught my eye, shaking her head. "When you get around to looking for a job, you can cross sketch artist off your list."

"My description wasn't that bad."

She continued to wag her head. "I was looking for a lumberjack with greasy hands and the real possibility of a monumental nose. And that's before I got around to looking for the extra appendages."

After our laughter died down, we got back to hiking.

"He is so nice, Em. We like the same music, though I can't say we're in sync on movies, but that's okay. We both have Sundays and Mondays off, which is awesome. And he's so handsome." Molly's face took on a contented glow as she talked about him. "We're going out again this week."

The shrill ring of my cellphone interrupted us. I fished it out of my fanny pack, apologizing. "Hold that thought," I said, and took the call. It was Jackson. He gave me the same details about tonight's game that he'd given Avery earlier. I told Jackson I would find my own way to the facility and would see him tonight. When I ended the call, it was Molly's turn to look at me with that "spill it" expression on her face.

"What?" I asked, pretending innocence.

"Who, may I ask, is Jackson?" After my digging into her date with Cheney, she wasn't about to let me off the hook.

"Just a guy I met on the beach." It wasn't even a lie.

"When was this?" Now I was the one on the pointy end of the stick and the inquisition was on.

"About ten days ago," I said, after doing the mental math.

"And ..." she said, rolling her hands.

"And ... we've been to lunch." I paused, but Molly wasn't letting it go. "And dinner ... and a breakfast or two," I added, with the good grace to look abashed as Molly absorbed the implication.

She stopped dead in her tracks. "What!" She looked truly stunned. "Here I was thinking you were such an angel. All this time you've been a closet tart." She laughed. "You're making Cheney and me look positively boring."

"No. I think I just jumped the gun a bit with Jackson."

"I don't think it was a gun you jumped." A look of surprise lingered on her face. "I think I'm a little jealous," she said, and started walking again. "Any chance of meeting the mysterious Jackson?"

"Eventually," I said, but didn't elaborate further on Jackson or our relationship, though I did tell her about the *Aerial Symphony*. She was quite intrigued about the boat and asked me all about it.

When we finally found the lighthouse, the path to the area was chained off. A posted notice advised that the grounds were now closed to the public. It was a disappointment after our long hike out. Ignoring the sign, we hopped the chain to check it out. The grounds looked well maintained despite being closed and the lighthouse looked as white as ever, almost glowing in its brightness.

We headed home speculating about the lighthouse and dug up more childhood memories of time spent on the beach and playing in the shade of the trees in our front yard. The GPS's tracking feature guided us flawlessly back to the cottage.

Molly let me drive her home and I promised to call or stop by Rumbles again next week.

After I got home, I input the paintball park's address into the GPS and let it do its thing. A review of the directions told me the park was thirty-two minutes away, directly east.

With a few hours left to kill before Avery showed up, I brought my laptop out to the deck to resume my research on Jackson.

I reviewed what I'd learned so far about Jackson's father, Matthew Delaney, and their family business. A reread of the article on the marina development reminded me of the name of their business rival, Touch-stone Enterprises, and its owner, Richard Des Roche. I pulled up the photo of the Des Roche family and was struck again with a sense of déjà vu on seeing the son, Cole.

An older item in the search results made reference to the Des Roche's lavish wedding in 1979. I followed a link and found a photo of the newlyweds, Richard and Bronwyn Des Roche. I went down the rabbit hole and clicked another link. It was a snippet from what looked like the society section of a 1978 edition of the *Times-Picayune*.

How very interesting: Bronwyn was formerly married to Jackson's father, Matthew Delaney. Even more interesting was that their marriage ended in a storm of speculation surrounding Bronwyn's infidelity and the questionable parentage of her son, Cole, who was born in 1978.

It must have stung for Jackson's father to learn of his wife's affair. And with a business rival no less. Seems he got over it, though. The next society piece described the second marriage of Matthew Delaney to Leigh Morisette in 1981. Leigh was a beauty but I couldn't help noticing how much she resembled Bronwyn, at least physically with her fair hair and high cheekbones. Matthew Delaney's company name was changed to reflect "& Son" in 1982, the year Jackson was born.

I returned to the photo of Cole and then it struck me—the reason

Cole looked so familiar was because he looked a lot like Jackson but with fair hair.

I sat back. Could Cole and Jackson share the same father? If Bronwyn's infidelity in her first marriage caused speculation about Cole's parentage, then was there a possibility that Mathew was his father? If he was, that would make Cole and Jackson half-brothers. Jackson had told me he was an only child, but the resemblance between he and Cole was striking.

Then again, Cole's last name was Des Roche, not Delaney. And Jackson's father hadn't added the "& Son" until Jackson was born ... but still, I couldn't get over how much they looked alike. I put up photos of Matthew and Richard side-by-side on my computer screen. No question—Cole and Jackson looked like Matthew, not Richard.

Did Jackson suspect he had an older half-brother? Even if he didn't, he must have known about his father's former wife. After all, they had to run in the same circles. At a minimum, they would bump into each other at society functions.

My head spun. I shut the computer and tried to sort through it all. Jackson likely had a half-brother that he either didn't know about or didn't acknowledge. Cole's very existence made the rivalries between the two companies more than just business as usual. Sparks had to fly when these two families crossed paths. I wondered if I'd ever hear the story from Jackson's perspective.

CHAPTER TWENTY-ONE

The evening was already deep in the bluing shadows of dusk when Avery arrived at nine thirty in a sleek black Porsche.

"Nice wheels," I said with genuine appreciation. I didn't know much about cars, but even I knew the cachet of this particular vehicle.

"Thanks, it gets the job done," he said, smiling proudly.

"The job of picking up women?" I asked. "Guess I should feel pretty lucky tonight then."

"Indeed, you should," he said, rolling his eyes. "Are you ready?"

"Yup." I already had my knapsack over my shoulder and my keys in hand. I locked the cottage then he escorted me to the passenger door and opened it for me.

I carefully lowered myself into the seat and reached over to fasten the seat belt. The interior smelled of leather and Avery. The seat rested so low to the ground, I thought my butt would scrape the asphalt. When he started the motor, it purred smoothly. No uncouth puff of smoke coming out of this precision machine.

We headed to the main drag then turned up the cross street connector to King Street, which was a major artery heading east. I turned on the GPS to follow our route. Avery took a sharp right turn and was gearing up before we hit the top of the ramp. By the time we merged, the speedometer's needle was taunting the speed limit and Avery's grin was as wide as his face.

He shifted gears and headed to the passing lane. "I think you'll meet everyone tonight. Jackson said the entire covey would be there."

"Is it unusual for all of you to get together?" I asked, curious about the concept of a covey.

"For us it is. We rarely met as a group until recently. We didn't need to. They all came to see me for medical issues on a regular basis so I acted as the covey's conduit. But it wasn't enough."

"Wasn't enough? What do you mean?"

"When Jackson arrived, he didn't come alone. He brought a whole boatload of worry with him. Excuse the pun." He did a shoulder check and pulled back into the travel lane. "I knew he was coming of course; he'd been in touch through our mutual contacts—that's the norm—it's expected. But what none of us knew or expected was the news he brought about Sandra's disappearance. He also has suspicions that other organized groups are looking for our kind. It shook us up. If he's right, we'll all be putting out welcome mats for the Tribunal."

"That's a scary prospect," I said.

"Jackson felt it was important for the covey to be able to act swiftly, as a cohesive unit, in the event one of us is ever threatened. The others agreed. So, for about two months now, we've been meeting more regularly and keeping closer tabs on one another. We've pledged to help rescue Sandra if we get the chance. As it happens, the paintball games are good fun but they also serve as a training tool. I think you'll like it."

"I think I will too." And I did, but a part of me felt unsettled. The very suggestion that the covey could be threatened was frightening and I couldn't avoid the reality that, like it or not, I was a part of this covey. That meant I, too, was not safe. The thought chilled me.

I stared out the window watching the city lights give way to farmland. The GPS advised us to take the Highway 10 exit northbound to Pinecrest. Avery geared the car down as we exited, and accelerated around the curve. The big grin returned to his face as we glided smoothly around the corner.

Pinecrest was a narrow street that hadn't seen fresh asphalt in years. One street light lit the exit ramp then the road ran off into darkness. It was rural here with vast fields of some type of grass crop on either side of the road. We drove for another five minutes before Avery slowed down, and turned at a fence post that bore a faded placard marked Pinecrest Paintball Park. If Avery hadn't pointed it out, I would have missed it.

We drove down a long, gravel driveway at a painfully slow speed, and even at the snail's pace, Avery winced each time a piece of gravel bounced off the undercarriage. He pulled into an empty parking area and turned off the ignition. With his headlights out and no other lights around, darkness took hold. A group of people milled around the door to a large dilapidated barn about fifty yards away.

Avery walked around to open my door. "Don't forget your knapsack," he said as he helped me out. I unfolded myself and slung the bag over my shoulder. We headed toward the group and I felt an old but familiar sensation. Throughout my life, my circle of friends had always been minuscule. This relatively large gathering intimidated me.

As we got closer to the group, I picked out Jackson from the crowd. He saw us and broke away from the others.

"Avery," he said, extending his hand. Jackson put his hand on my shoulder and squeezed. "Em, glad you made it." He smiled warmly but stopped short of displaying any acknowledgement of the real nature of our relationship. I was grateful not to have the additional pressure or the attention.

When we joined the group, Avery wandered off to greet the others. Jackson guided me around making introductions. Eden and Alex were among the first people we came across. Their welcoming smiles eased some of my apprehension. They were talking with Victoria, who remembered me from the mall. Her long blonde hair was tied back into a tight twist. She wore black from head to toe—the Flier uniform, I was coming to realize.

Jackson interrupted a woman named Kate midsentence. Kate was thirtyish with shiny chestnut hair cut in a precision bob. She put me in mind of my grade nine home ec. teacher. She'd been enthusiastically extolling the virtues of organic wine to Deidra, who, from a distance, looked like a lollipop with her apple-shaped body perched atop spindly legs. Like the rest of us, they were dressed in dark tones.

"Nice to meet you," Kate and Deidra said in unison, and I heard them chuckle at their vocal harmony as we moved on.

Danny saw us approach and tapped Gabe on the shoulder. Gabe's face lit up. "Nice to see you again, Emelynn," he said, extending his hand. He wore a thin wool cap pulled down over his grey hair.

"You too," I said, and then turned to Danny, who shifted anxiously from one foot to the other. "Danny." I offered my hand. He awkwardly reciprocated after extracting his from the pouch of his multihued hoodie. He then turned to introduce me to Steve Elliott and Sydney Davenport.

Steve looked to be about the same age as Danny. Steve had a similar build but the kind of nondescript looks that would easily allow him to blend into a crowd. The same couldn't be said about Sydney; she would definitely stand out. I couldn't determine her ethnicity, but the Asian influence was undeniable. Her coal-black eyes matched the shoulder-length hair that was razored in layers and moved like silk when she shook her head.

After introductions were made, Jackson looked around the group like a tour operator, counting heads to check for stragglers. "Has James arrived yet?" he asked the group. No one had seen him yet, but Alex assured Jackson that they had spoken and James would be coming.

Jackson then took the lead, getting everyone's attention. "Before we get to the game, I need to brief you on a recent incident." He summarized, hitting on the high points: finding the camera, setting up the countersurveillance, and Eden identifying the man. He also mentioned the research they'd found and, finally, the Tribunal's involvement, which was the only point that garnered reaction—a collective gasp that no longer surprised me.

"Avery has the man's photo and he'll email it to you." He looked to Avery. "Or have you already?"

"I'll send it tomorrow."

"As far as we know, only three of us were exposed, so let me know if anyone else recognizes him. We've been assured that the matter has been dealt with, but this incident is a reminder. Everyone has a camera phone these days so be vigilant."

Hushed whispers threaded through the group and a number of Fliers offered Eden their comfort, which she graciously acknowledged. When the murmurs petered down, Jackson moved on.

"It looks like we'll have the whole contingent tonight—that is if James ever shows up. You've all met Emelynn now. She's the only one who's never played paintball before, so let's go over the game for her benefit."

I loathed being the centre of attention and felt a blush rise in my cheeks, but there was nowhere to hide.

"There will be twelve players tonight, so we'll break into two teams of six: a red team and a green team. Each team will be outfitted with coveralls, face masks and paintball guns loaded with your team's coloured paintballs. The goal of the game is to try to eliminate all the players on the other team. A player will be deemed eliminated if he or she gets hit by the other team's paintball. If you're hit, you have to land immediately and you can't fire any further rounds unless or until you make your way to Avery.

"Avery is neutral so he won't be armed. He'll be in the centre of the barn under the canvas with the red cross marked on it. If you make it to Avery, he will put you back into the game by neutralizing your paint mark with his blue dauber. He can only void two paint marks at a time. If you have more than two paint marks, you're out, so you might as well take a seat in Avery's tent until the game is over.

"We've got the park to ourselves until dawn, so we'll get in a few games if we're lucky."

Jackson looked over to me. "Any questions?"

"Not yet." I lowered my head, acutely aware that all eyes were on me at that moment.

"Great. Let's split into groups then. Who wants to lead?"

Danny stepped forward right away. "I'll be green leader," he said.

Alex then stepped up to claim the red leader position.

"Great. Danny, you start first. Pick your teams."

Then, as if on cue, another man walked out from the cover of the barn. Jackson called to him, "Hey, James, glad you made it. You're just in time. We're picking teams."

James was as tall as Jackson and lean. He wore his long dark hair pulled back in a ponytail. Nothing about him looked at ease. He held his head bent slightly down and kept his hands in the front pockets of his dark jeans. He nodded greetings to a few people and looked over the rest of us, one at a time.

He stopped his sweeping gaze at me and raised his head. He approached, extending his hand. "James Moss," he said.

"Emelynn," I responded. I couldn't tell if his pale eyes were green or blue. He tilted his head as he shook my hand, holding on longer than a handshake required. Abruptly, he lowered his gaze and stepped back.

Danny quickly got us back on track. "James, you're with me."

Alex called out next. "Eden, you're on my team." He wiggled his eyebrows, drawing a smile from her.

They took turns choosing their players. Thankfully, after a nudge from Eden, Alex picked me, so I wasn't the last one chosen. That would have been too much like high school all over again. Our team had Alex, Eden, Jackson, me, Sydney and Steve. I felt marginally relieved being on the team with the three Fliers I knew best. Hopefully, my inexperience wouldn't cost them the game.

Danny's team had James, Kate, Deidra, Gabe and Victoria. James stood apart from the others. His eyes darted around, missing nothing. It left the impression he was wound tight, expecting trouble. And his demeanour left the impression he could deal with whatever trouble he found.

We headed into the barn through a wide door directly beneath an open loft. I glanced around at my new friends. For better or worse, this was my covey. *My covey*. I was getting used to the sound of that.

Gabe helped Avery hand out the coveralls, matching us up with appropriate sizes. The coveralls were not the heavy canvas type that mechanics wear, which was what I'd expected. They were made of a nylon fabric that fit snugly, was quilted for padded protection, and zippered up the front.

Next, they handed around the face masks, which looked like something out of a space movie. The portion that protected the eyes was made of a clear material while the rest was solid black with a row of thin slots for air exchange.

The paintball guns resembled machine guns, something Bonny and Clyde might have used. They had shoulder straps and weren't as heavy as they looked.

Avery and Gabe finished handing out the equipment then made the rounds ensuring everyone had what they needed and knew how to use it. We all took a few practice shots just to make sure.

Alex handed out red vests to our team. Without them, it would be difficult to distinguish friend from foe. The green team, of course, wore green vests.

When we were pretty well suited up, Avery got our attention. "I'm headed over to the tent now. Take ten minutes to reacquaint yourselves with the space. The barn doors at the other end and the loft on this end are both open so you've got good access to the great outdoors. When I sound the horn once, you'll have five minutes until the next blast. At the second horn, it's game on. If you hear the air horn twice in short succession, the game is over and we'll meet back at the tent." He turned then and headed off.

Excitement flitted through the group. Alex wasted no time. "Okay team, let's plan our strategy." I saw Danny's green team retreating through the door we'd come in.

Alex marched briskly down the centre of the floor pointing out stacked hay bales on either side. In some areas, the bales were so high you couldn't see over them. The barn might have been dilapidated, but it was huge in height and breadth. Along the entire length of the building on both sides was an open loft with more hay bales. Alex gestured to the loft. "There's good cover up there."

Throughout the main hall area was a series of both partial- and full-height walls combined with hay bales and sheets of canvas. "That's a maze," Alex said. "If you go in there, be careful. It's easy to get lost." We made our way toward Avery's tent. Avery ignored us as we trotted around him and moved on toward the back end of the structure, where the large double doors of the barn stood open. We had to skirt the maze to get there.

Alex rose above us and motioned for us to follow. As we did, he took us on a slow cruise along the interior loft line through the barn, back the way we had come. Flying inside a building was a lot different from flying outdoors. I found myself constantly checking my flanks, thinking I was going to whack into a beam or another Flier. We assumed horizontal positions and moved cautiously through the space. Passing over the maze below, I spotted a number of dead ends that could prove problematic for players on the ground. But there were also areas of cover, where canvas stretched out to provide line-of-sight protection from above.

When we reached the front of the building again, Alex flew out the loft door into the night sky. We followed in single file. He led the way around the exterior of the barn. A lean-to ran the length of the north side. It housed some rusted farm equipment and more carefully placed hay bales. Additional canvas walls and partial covers were set up at the back end of the barn, but the long south side was clear of obstructions. The green team was nowhere to be seen.

Alex gathered us together. "Sydney, you're stealthy and a good shot. When the game starts, I want you to take up a protected position in the loft, close enough to Avery's tent to pick off players trying to get back into the game. Jackson, take a position outside, close to the loft door to get anyone coming in or out that way. Emelynn, you and Eden take the barn doors and do the same. Steve and I will take offensive positions. We'll start here and work our way into the building, taking out as many as we can along the way." Clearly, this wasn't Alex's first paintball game.

The first horn blew.

"Okay, move to your positions and be careful—Danny will have his people heading for the same targets. Don't shoot before Avery blows the horn, and good luck out there."

Eden startled me, grabbing my hand and pulling me straight up. Way up. We hovered ten storeys above the barn then drifted around until the big barn doors were in our line of sight. She whispered close to my ear, "From up here, we'll be able to see whomever Danny positions near the doors. We won't be able to hit them from this height, but it will give us a strategic advantage."

Jackson had a similar idea in mind. I saw him hover not above but parallel to the loft door at the other end. I couldn't see Sydney at all but thought I caught a glimpse of Alex and Steve flying around below us, close to the roofline.

The second horn blew: the game was on.

Immediately, I heard paintballs splatting. I looked with trepidation at Eden. "Hope they didn't get Sydney."

She shook her head. "Sydney's pretty good at this game."

We kept an eye on the barn doors. Soon enough, we saw a green player drift up the side of the building, hugging the wall, and steadily move toward the barn door. Eden motioned for me to stay put. She shouldered her weapon, waited until the player got closer, and then she smoothly drifted down. She put her eye to the gun's sight and I heard a short staccato burst then a splat, followed by a female voice grunting. The green player dropped to the ground then out of sight.

Eden sped back up to me and flashed a wicked grin. "Got one." We resumed our lookout positions, listening to the erratic splat of paint-balls.

Before long, another green player made his way around to the barn doors. This one was more careful to keep a lookout all around, but he didn't look up. Eden motioned for me to take him. I copied her moves and slowly closed in, careful to keep myself above him. When I thought I was close enough, I sighted him in the gun's scope and pulled the trigger. The gun's kick sent me backwards a few feet, eliminating any chance at a second shot, but I hit my target. It was a lucky shot; I'd missed his torso entirely, hitting his forearm instead, but a hit was a hit. As I darted back to Eden, I caught a glimpse of him searching for the source of the shot. She gave me a silent high-five then it was my turn to grin. This was fun.

Another green player popped his head up, this time from inside the barn. He stayed inside and left of the door, undoubtedly taking up the

JP MCLEAN

position to catch our team coming and going. Eden signalled that she was going to take him out. She kept high and to the left, dropping low then keeping tight to the building, creeping slowly toward the door. She had her gun sighted. I heard the pop of air signalling she'd pulled the trigger. Her target was down but before she could retreat, another green player came up behind her and got her. She cursed as she drifted down, but she didn't look back up to give my position away.

I sighted the gun on Eden's shooter and raced in, hitting him twice in quick succession. I retreated just as quickly then watched him gaze around, a look of confusion on his face. He hadn't seen me. At that point, it occurred to me that I'd been using my speed unawares. It didn't even feel uncomfortable. It felt natural. I liked it.

But I didn't much like hanging around up here by myself. I hoped that Eden was able to make it to Avery so she could get back into the game.

The sound of splattering paintballs slowed. The game wasn't over yet, but I was curious as to what was going on and debated whether or not to venture from my post. Before I did, another green player popped into view. He'd come around from the side of the barn and was trying to get back inside. I sped in and let off three shots, only one of which hit him, then quickly retreated. He was out with a grunt, looking bewildered. I smiled. The players I hit couldn't tell where I'd come from or where I'd gone. My speed was turning into a pleasant, if unexpected, bonus.

Of course, Eden got credit too; she'd had the good idea of perching way up here to pick off players. I kept to my post and swooped in once more, successfully putting another player out of action. Turns out, I was a lousy shot. I adapted, making up for my lack of accuracy by pummelling my opponents with quantity. The game had been going on for forty-five minutes before I heard the two short blasts that indicated the end of the game. Our team must have won because I was still out here. I beamed in delight—I hadn't cost the game after all.

I pulled the gun's strap across my shoulder and headed up and over the barn roof, then in through the loft. When I spotted Avery's tent, I drifted down to the outside edge of the group. Everyone was already on the barn floor, talking excitedly, rehashing every hit and miss. Most of them wore paint splatters, some both red and green, which I found amusing. Eden saw me and came running over.

"Did you get back to Avery?" I asked as she approached.

"No, they had Deidra close to Avery's tent, and she took me out."

"What happened to Sydney?"

"She hung in there until the end, but Danny finally got her. Then Jackson hit Danny and that was the end of the game. You know, I don't think they even knew you were still outside." She looked at me and we smiled as only co-conspirators could.

Avery jumped up on a hay bale outside his tent to get our attention. "We've got lots of time for another game. Is everyone up for it?" A resounding affirmative echoed all around.

"Okay, come see me so I can void your paint marks. Then you can regroup. Alex, you're at the east end this time, Danny you're at the barn doors. You've got ten minutes. The game starts on the first horn blast." Avery jumped down to the floor and started daubing blue over everyone's paint marks.

Most of the players had three or four paint splats, but Kate with the shiny precision bob was absolutely covered in red—someone from my team was channelling Rambo. Victoria had more than one green splat that had already been covered with blue, which made me wonder just how many times she'd made it back to Avery's tent. Maybe there was more to that smile they'd shared in the mall.

Jackson made his way over and casually draped his arm across my shoulder. "Looks like you and I are the only two who didn't get hit," he whispered. He squeezed my shoulder and that little crumb of attention sent my heart fluttering. I looked over his shoulder and saw James scowling at us. I glanced behind me, thinking he was looking at someone else, but there was no one there. When I looked back at James, he'd turned his attention elsewhere. Maybe I'd imagined the menacing scowl.

We split off into our teams and I followed Alex to the east end of the building. When we were out of earshot of the green team, he started strategizing. "Sydney, great job. Why don't you take the loft door this time—use Eden's strategy. Go high, but be careful, they might be expecting that now. Eden, take Sydney's place and stay inside to pick off Fliers heading to Avery's tent. I'll take Steve and cover the barn doors. Jackson, since you and Emelynn made it out of that last round unscathed, how about you take the offensive leads. Work as a team to pick off as many green players as you can. Steve and I had a lot of success last game moving from the outside in, so you may want to use that strategy again. Does that cover everyone?" he asked. We all nodded.

We moved off to take our positions. Jackson came up beside me and took my elbow. We headed out of the loft then down and around the corner under cover of the lean-to. "How do you think we should approach this?" he asked.

"I like Eden's approach, but instead of high, how about we stay low and way out there?" I pointed to the field surrounding the barn.

"Okay. Let's go before someone sees us and figures out our strategy." We raced about a hundred yards away then settled low into a horizontal hover close to the ground.

After we were in position, I said, "I'll move left, you move right and we'll meet on the other side. We may have to do a few sweeps before we can move inside."

He nodded his head in agreement. As we waited for the horn, Jackson whispered, "I heard James and Gabe talking in there. I think you hit them both because Eden was already inside by the time they snuck back in."

"Did I?" I couldn't tell who was who out there.

"Interesting that both of them said they didn't see who hit them. I still don't think they know." He took his eyes off the barn and looked over at me. "Did you play with your speed by any chance?" he asked, a smile dancing around the corners of his mouth.

"I might have," I said, and then the horn blew. We were back in the game.

Almost immediately, we heard action within the barn and saw two players speed out of the loft in unison. Sydney was guarding the loft by herself. The green team was undoubtedly going to try to get her. Instantly, I signalled Jackson my intention to go after them and bolted from cover. With a little help from my speed, I reached them before they got to her. I sighted the Fliers midflight, shot at one player then sighted and shot the second. I couldn't tell if I'd hit either target, and I was flying too fast to change my trajectory. I flew right past Sydney before I could slow enough to drift back down behind her. I looked around for Jackson. He was thirty yards away giving me a big "okay" sign.

The two players I'd hit were on the ground, sauntering toward the barn. I gave them a wide birth as I made my way back to Jackson.

"Way to go, Em," he said, laughing. "They didn't have a chance to react before I got them twice more. They're out of the game. I don't think we should split up. We're better as a tag team." He smiled mischievously. "Let's see who else we can find."

We resumed our low, horizontal position, moving slowly around the perimeter of the barn. We spotted another green player, but he got under the cover of the lean-to before we could get him. A second green player followed suit and we lost him as well.

Jackson reached out and grabbed my arm, stopping our movement. He leaned in to whisper and I had to resist the urge to kiss him. "Let's sit tight for a few minutes. See if they make a move." Our patience paid off. They emerged from behind a high stack of hay midway down the side of the barn. They flew out at a forty-five-degree angle, one following closely behind the other.

"We've got them," Jackson whispered. "They're heading to the barn doors to take out Alex and Steve. Looks like they're going to sneak in behind them." He looked over at me with a crafty glint in his eye. "But they didn't see us—and they certainly won't be expecting your speed. You ready?"

I positioned my gun and nodded then took off, letting my speed loose. I missed with the first shot as I slowed to aim, but tried again and landed a hit. Luckily, Alex was alert and turned to see what was happening. He and Steve quickly shot them both out of the game before Jackson caught up. I winked at Alex then sped away as quickly as I'd arrived.

I returned to my low-hover position, waiting for Jackson. "That's two more," he said when he got close. "The others will be hiding inside. We should head in. If Sydney is still guarding the loft, then we have at least five Fliers still in play. Green team is down to two."

We headed toward the loft to find Sydney still there. I flashed my eyes to make sure she saw us. Jackson went in ahead of me and a series of splats followed. Someone had blasted him from just inside the loft door. He was hit and headed down. I saw him land then dash under the lean-to. I pulled up, nodded at Sydney then sped toward the barn doors.

I paused until Alex and Steve acknowledged my flash, and then went in. They moved in closer. No one guarded the barn doors from the interior. I dropped inside, whisked around the corner and quickly sought cover among the hay bales. I moved into a vertical hover just inches above the floor and moved silently, keeping watch above and in front of me. Slowly, I made my way toward Avery's tent looking for Eden. I scanned the loft and saw a flash. A smile of relief spread across my face. I'd found her—she was still in the game.

A burst of activity followed. The green player who'd been protecting the loft shot at Sydney, hitting her, but Alex and Steve had teamed up with her. They took the green player out then stormed the barn. The last green player made a valiant effort to take them out, but she didn't see Eden and me: we converged, peppering her with red splats. She held up her hands in surrender and we relented. The horn sounded twice. The game was over.

The player we'd hit ripped off her face mask. "That hurts you know!" It was Kate of the precision bob, the player who'd been hit so many times in the first game. I guess she had good reason to be miffed. Eden and I offered our apologies.

Avery prompted everyone to come out from under cover. Victoria emerged from Avery's tent again. I looked pointedly from her to Avery. He shrugged as if to say "What?"

We gathered amidst loud laughter and excited conversation. Avery handed out waters and sodas, moving around to talk to everyone. Jackson did the same. Eden and Alex, arm in arm, came to find me. "I see you're putting your speed to good use," Alex said.

Sydney overheard the comment and came to join us. "That was you, Emelynn? You fly remarkably fast."

"I guess," I mumbled, and lowered my head to pick at the label on my water bottle.

I looked up to see James glaring at me from a distance. This time there was absolutely no doubt. What was that about? I diverted my gaze.

Avery jumped up on a hay bale and got our attention. "Looks like that's it for the night. Red team wins 2–0, which means green team buys the first round. Jackson will organize a night out this week. Good night, everyone," he said, and jumped off the bale.

Jackson came over and touched my elbow. "I have to stay to lock up. Do you want to hang around for a while before you head out?"

"Only if you'll help me get home—I don't know if I can find my way from here."

"Yeah, sure," he said, then moved away to say goodbye to the others.

I searched for Avery and found him talking quietly to Victoria. "Excuse me," I said, interrupting. "If you don't mind, I think I'll fly home."

He nodded. "Of course—go ahead. It's good practice for you." I thanked him for the ride over then turned to find Jackson. I overheard Avery ask Victoria if she wanted a ride home. I didn't hear her response but I hoped it was yes and that Avery's car would live up to its reputation.

The Fliers headed toward the door, removing their coveralls and depositing them in the bins. Jackson put the guns back in the racks and the facemasks in the cupboards. The last ones out the door were Eden and Alex. Jackson and I waved goodbye before heading back into the barn.

Finally, we were alone. Jackson put his arms around me and kissed me so thoroughly my toes curled. It was enough to send tingles shooting down my torso. When he finally broke away, it wasn't to take me to the hay stacks as I'd hoped. "How would you like to do some more flying around in here?" he asked.

"All this comfortable-looking hay and you want to fly?" I looked up at him with the most sensual expression I could muster.

Apparently, it wasn't enticing enough. Jackson stepped away from me with a laugh. "*That*, little girl, can wait. *This*"—he gestured around us—"we only have for a few more hours."

Reluctantly, I shifted mental gears and followed his lead, flying up into the rafters.

CHAPTER TWENTY-TWO

We flew every square foot of that cavernous barn and, once again, Jackson was right. It was fun to fly indoors, especially in such an interesting space. We chased each other in and out of the loft and up and down the length of the barn. We played hide-and-seek manoeuvring through the tight confines of the maze, over and under cover. I crashed more than a few times and was grateful to be hitting hay bales and nothing more substantial. It was a blast. I even poured on some speed when I had the space. Jackson watched with interest, egging me on, wanting me to show him what I could do.

We finally called it quits and headed outside. Jackson locked up behind us and deposited the key in a lockbox on the power pole.

"Remember what I said about jump-starts being like CPR? How about I show you how to do one?"

"Now?" I hesitated. "With you?"

"Why not?"

"You've got about sixty pounds on me for starters."

Jackson laughed. "More like seventy, but it's not like lifting dead weight. Come here," he said. I approached, looking skeptical. "Get behind me," he said, tugging me behind him. "Put your arms around my waist." I did as he said and he put his hands over mine where they joined at his belt buckle.

"Good," he said, talking over his shoulder. "Now think about your liftoff—that surge of energy you feel when you break free of gravity."

"Okay." I knew exactly what he was talking about.

"You'll have to ramp up the energy a little as you lift me."

A little? I was thinking a lot. "You ready?" I asked.

"God, I hope so," he said, patting my hand.

I widened my stance, pressing the side of my face into his back to brace for the lift, and then channelled the thrumming energy that lived in my limbs. When it peaked, I reached into my mind's eye for the crystal and gave it my all. I pulled up on Jackson and we were airborne in a flash ... but then gravity's bungee cord snapped, hurtling us through the air at frightening velocity. Jackson's laughter reverberated through my embrace as if he'd expected this. He kept his hands tight on mine while slowing us down, controlling the ride.

When we'd slowed, he pulled my hands free and dragged me around to face him. "Not bad for a first attempt," he said, smiling widely. "Want to try that again?"

The next time, I didn't hurtle us into outer space. I'd figured out the critical element was getting his feet off the ground. After that, it required no more effort than flying alone. On the fourth jump-start, he declared me emergency ready.

Jackson convinced me to spend the rest of the night on the *Symphony*, but it wasn't as though he had to twist my arm. All it took was a promise to take me home in the Zodiac in the morning.

Jackson showed me on the GPS the route we'd fly, then led us away from the lights that signalled population and out over the ocean. Once over water, we flew a straight line to the *Symphony*. We landed gently on the observation deck and stopped to catch our breath.

Jackson took my hand and led me down to the galley. "How about a drink?" he asked, already reaching for the glasses.

"Sounds good," I said, and headed to the white sofas.

Ice clinked against glass followed by the soft glug of liquid being poured from a bottle. He turned the music on low and brought us our drinks. "Rusty nail," he said, handing me a glass, his eyes intense.

I returned his gaze, trailing my fingers from his wrist to the cold glass. "You know, you don't need to feed me booze to have your way with me."

"I'm glad to hear that," he said, moving away to take a seat on the sofa opposite. He settled back and put his feet up. He took a long, slow sip of his drink while his pale hazel eyes melted me.

His gaze started at my toes, wandered leisurely up my legs, glanced at my hips then paused at the swell of my breasts before finally resting on my lips. His lips had my return attention. He tipped his head, compelling me to meet his eyes. When I succumbed, he quickly locked on and took hold of my hormones from the inside, sending electricity skittering across my body. A smug smile crossed his face as he released me.

Damn, he was good. He already had me in the palm of his hand and he hadn't even touched me yet. I wanted to learn that rush trick.

But even without it, two could play this game. I tucked my legs under me, sat back and sipped my drink. The smooth liquid warmed my throat. I licked the rim of the glass then used my tongue to jiggle the ice cubes.

His lips parted and I upped the ante. I set my drink aside then reached down and pulled my hoodie up over my head, ditching it behind the sofa. I reclaimed my glass and threw him a sultry look.

Without missing a beat and without taking his eyes off mine, he put his glass down and ever so slowly unbuttoned his shirt. He took his time, teasing me with the flick of each button. When he finished, he left the shirt gaping open, revealing his muscled chest. He then casually picked up his glass.

My gaze travelled his whole length, enjoying the new view. I slowly sipped my drink, letting him see the smile he'd put on my lips. Setting my glass aside again, I pulled my tank top over my head and discarded it. I picked up my drink and leaned back, happy that I'd worn a pretty, low-cut bra.

If Jackson's hooded eyes were any indication, he was enjoying this game. His gaze took a return trip around my body. He made sure I was looking, then slowly removed his shirt and threw it aside. Just to make it more interesting, he undid the button on his jeans. He found his glass without taking his eyes off mine and slowly savoured another sip.

Anticipation proved a very sweet aphrodisiac. I wanted him as much as he wanted me, but I wasn't ready to end our sensual game—not yet. I took another sip, letting the amber liquid roll around my tongue before I swallowed. I set my drink down, rose to my knees and slid my thumbs under the top edge of my yoga pants. Ever so slowly, I pulled them down. When they were at my knees, I lowered myself to the sofa and let them fall to the floor. I tugged off my socks, one at a time, and dropped them on top of the pants. I retrieved my glass and stretched out my legs to rest on the coffee table.

Jackson took leisurely sips of his drink. His gaze, focused and intense, wandered to my body, stirring my lust. After what felt like an eternity, he set his drink aside, unzipped his jeans and stood. He took his sweet time pushing them down his long legs before kicking them away. He too removed his socks then sat back down, collected his glass and took another sip.

My gaze slid down his sculpted chest and rested on the bulge pushing at the front of his Jockeys. This game was going to be the end of me. I put my glass aside again, reached behind to unhook my bra then shimmied the straps down my arms and let it drop to the floor. I settled back into the sofa and retrieved my glass. I dipped a finger in my drink and trailed the cold liquid around one nipple and then the other.

Jackson's breath hitched and he tipped his drink back. He lifted his butt off the sofa and removed his Jockeys, releasing his magnificent erection. I was so distracted that the condom he produced seemed to appear out of thin air. He slowly opened the crinkly packet then more slowly still, rolled the condom down his stiffness, stroking himself while he watched me. The sight of him touching himself like that sent a shiver through me. Finally, he held his arm out to me. "Get over here," he said, breaking the silence of our erotic game.

I downed the rest of my drink and sauntered over to stand in front of him. He leaned forward and licked across the skin along the top edge of my panties, then made short work of removing this last barrier. This man knew no end of sensuous moves. I reached out and tangled my fingers in his dark curls.

He nudged my legs apart and looked up at me, watching my face as he slid a hand toward that part of me that begged for attention. He found the pulsing nub, rubbed it with his thumb and slid his fingers inside me. I inhaled sharply as he replaced his thumb with his tongue and sent sparks shooting up my torso. His fingers played a well-practiced tune that pushed a moan from my lips.

"Don't stop," I begged, feeling that sweet release building. When it rolled over me a few moments later, Jackson teased it out all the way. He put his hands on my hips and pulled me forward so that I was kneeling on the sofa, straddling him. I slid my hand down between my legs and wrapped my fingers around his erection. He shuddered, but the time for teasing was over; I wanted him inside me. I swiftly lowered myself, engulfing the length of him, and was rewarded with a strained expletive. Bracing my hands on the sofa behind his shoulders I started a slow, steady rhythm. He leaned forward, took a nipple into his mouth and sucked hard, which put a kick into my pace. Sweat beaded between my shoulder blades.

JP McLean

His mouth sent shimmers of delight dancing around my body and the slow, steady pace I'd set was no longer possible. Another release was just ahead and I increased the urgency of my rhythm. A few seconds later, it hit. I moaned fiercely while it shook me right through to my bones.

Now it was Jackson's turn to mumble, "Don't stop." His hands pushed my hips, forcing my shaky legs to keep going. Moments later, he stiffened and jerked, moaning his own completion. I kept him tightly inside while his spasms subsided. He relaxed in increments, breathing deeply. When he opened his eyes, he looked up at me with a satisfied grin. He reached up and cupped my breasts, and I felt the familiar ebbing aftershocks in both of us.

"This keeps getting better and better," I said, leaning down to kiss him. Reluctantly, I lifted myself off and settled beside him. He draped his arm around me and pulled me close, kissing the top of my head. He seemed quiet, caught up in his own thoughts. We cuddled for a few more minutes, but the heat of the moment had dissipated and I was getting cold. He rubbed my arm, but it wasn't enough.

"Let's go shower," I said, sitting forward. But I froze midbreath at the sound of a soft thump on the deck above us. Jackson heard it too, and became deathly still. We looked quizzically at one another until the sound of footsteps jarred us to action.

He bolted up, grabbed me roughly and pushed me toward the door. He whispered urgently, "Go to your cabin. Lock the door." He raced to a drawer under the computer and pulled out a gun. I panicked at the sight of it, tore out of the room and down the stairs. I slammed my cabin door and locked it.

Fuck! He had a gun.

Footsteps came down the stairs on the floor above and angry voices followed. I cringed in terror behind the door. Jackson shouted furiously and a second man shouted back, matching Jackson's anger. I ran into the head and threw on a robe before dashing back to the door, straining to hear. I took a breath to calm my shaking.

The violent shouting match escalated, but I couldn't make out their words. Steadily, slowly, I turned the lock until I felt it release. I silently opened the door, held it ajar and pressed my ear to the crack. The second voice belonged to James. I slipped out the door, down the hall and behind the stairs, where I could hear without being seen.

"What the fuck is this, Jackson?" A glass smashed and then heavy

footsteps thumped around the room. "Whose are these?" Then it was quiet for a moment. "This is just great. You are one first-class fuck-up," he shouted, and then something solid hit a wall.

"This isn't your concern, James! Stay out of it."

"Like hell it's not." Loud steps rumbled across the floor. "You selfish bastard!" This was followed by the unmistakable sound of fists hitting flesh.

"Jesus Christ!" Jackson yelled. "Back off, James."

"This is beneath even you—who is she?" he demanded. Without waiting for Jackson's answer he ploughed on. "It's Emelynn, isn't it? Does she know about Sandra?"

"Yes, it's Emelynn and yes, she knows Sandra's missing."

"So, she's the *Ghost* you've been researching?" His footsteps paced above. "This is not good. She's going to distract you." The footsteps stopped. "I knew something was up when I saw you watching her fly tonight."

"She is not going to distract me." Jackson matched the vehemence in James's voice.

"You're already keeping secrets, Jackson. We can't afford to lose our focus now. We're too close."

"That won't happen. We're going to find Sandra and take her home." Jackson's voice sounded calmer.

James's didn't. "You'd better hope so." The pacing started again. "Alex's contacts got close to the boat last night. They're sure it's the one they're holding her on. They followed it to a marina south of Seattle. They don't know how many men are on board, but they're watching it. We'll learn any time now. You have to be ready."

"We *are* ready. You saw us tonight."

James sighed heavily. "You'd better put your team together and do it quickly. I'll phone the minute we know the numbers." I heard him race up the steps and then it was quiet again.

I slipped back to my cabin, locked the door and sat on the bed waiting for Jackson. Moments later, he knocked. After I unlocked the door, he came in with our clothing in a heap in his arms. He put the pile down then took my hand, pulling me down beside him on the bed. He had an angry red welt on the side of his face.

"Did you hear that?" he asked.

"Some," I said, because I was sure I'd missed a lot of it. "Are you all right?" I asked, gently touching the side of his face.

"I'm fine," he said, brushing away my concern. "It was James. He's angry." Jackson shook his head. "He's so focused on finding Sandra that he's not thinking straight, and he knows you were here."

"He's gone?" I asked, praying I was right.

"Yeah, he's gone." He rubbed his jaw. "He thinks our relationship is going to distract me." Jackson tilted his head and smiled. "You certainly are that, but I won't lose my focus."

"I don't understand. Why is James even involved?"

"He's with the New Orleans covey. We're working together."

I inspected the welt where James had hit him. "But why is he motivated to these extremes?"

"It's just James. He's intense and he takes covey seriously. The sooner we find Sandra, the sooner he can get back stateside."

James's reaction still seemed wildly off-kilter to me.

"James tells me our contacts are close to finding her. That means we have to be prepared to move quickly. I need my team ready to go."

"What's your plan?"

"The people who snatched Sandra take her to a new port and a new bank machine each night and force her to make a withdrawal. Two or three men accompany her each time, leaving some of their men behind to guard the boat. Our plan is to grab her on the way to or from a bank machine, when we'll only have two or three men to deal with."

"Who's on your team?"

"There'll be six of us, including James and me. We're using Alex's Seattle contacts, so he'll be there, and I'm going to ask Danny to join us. I'd like Eden to come, in case Sandra needs medical attention, and Steve Elliott's my backup if any of the others can't make it. But Em, I want you with us. Your speed might be the edge we need." He squeezed my hands as he said it.

"Me?" I looked at him as confused as I've ever been. "Just a few days ago you told me I was too inexperienced. You said I wasn't skilled enough with my speed to be any help to you at all."

"That was before I watched you in action earlier tonight. I misjudged you. You are ready. You're more than ready."

"I'd like to help, Jackson. Truly, I would, but I'm so far out of my depth here." I couldn't see how I'd be more than a hindrance to them.

"You and Eden will be our secret weapons. They may be expecting a rescue attempt, but they sure as hell won't be expecting women. At a minimum, you can distract them. And they won't have a clue about your speed, Emelynn. You might be able to do things we can't. Please say you'll help us."

It was pretty hard to resist Jackson, especially when he was so desperate for me to say yes. Maybe I could help. Besides, Eden would be there. I'd certainly want them to help me if I were the one who'd gone missing.

"What do I need to do?" I asked.

"Keep your passport with you. We might not use official channels, but it's best to have it anyway. Keep your cellphone charged and within reach. And bring street clothes in case you need to act as a decoy. I'll organize a float plane to take us close to our target, but be prepared to fly home on your own."

Jackson's words to Eden after the camera incident echoed in my mind: *We're covey, Eden. We protect one another. It's what we do.*

"Okay, count me in," I said, and Jackson reached his arms around me and held me tight.

"Thank you," he whispered. "Now get into the shower. You have to go home to get ready, and I have a team to organize."

I showered and dressed then caught up with him in the galley. He was on the phone, still in his robe. When he disconnected, he came up top with me and kissed me goodbye.

It was near dawn. The solo flight home was both nerve-racking and exciting, and I was exhausted by the time I landed. I dropped my bag inside the patio door and headed to bed. I pulled the blanket around my shoulders and curled into a ball. Sleep came quickly.

When I opened my eyes again it was noon and a dull day. I fired up the computer and carried it to the living room while the emails trickled in. It was my lucky day. I had emails from my mother, Molly and Eden.

My mother had exciting news—her latest research would be published. I wrote her back with my congratulations and a quick hello. Molly was anxious to update me on her and Cheney, and wanted to set up another get-together. That was an update I couldn't wait to hear and wrote back to say so. Regrettably, I couldn't give her a date because my life was going on hold until the entire Sandra mess was cleaned up. Eden was still high on our paintball game and said she'd see me soon. I deleted the junk mail, closed that program and opened Google.

With Sandra's rescue mission imminent, and me a new, if somewhat reluctant, participant, I wanted to uncover all I could about Jackson and the history he had yet to tell me. I pulled up the bookmarks and after a couple of hours, I'd finally found enough of the puzzle pieces to make some sense of his family history.

What didn't make sense was Jackson's father not acknowledging Cole. You would have to be swinging a white cane not to see the family resemblance, and that made Cole Jackson's older half-brother, whether he acknowledged it or not.

The rivalry between Delaney & Son and Touchstone must have been vicious. Both companies were successful until the time of the marina deal. After that, Touchstone's fortunes plummeted in direct proportion to the skyrocketing fortunes of Delaney.

Last fall, when Matthew died and left the multi-million dollar family business to Jackson, the press rehashed the bitter feud between the families, including the old accusations of espionage and payoffs.

Despite all my searching, Sandra's name never popped up. Of course, I didn't know her last name, and I supposed, even though she was in Jackson's covey, it didn't necessarily mean she was connected to the business or even ran in the same social circles.

It was after three when I closed the computer and stood to stretch. I needed a distraction. On a whim, I phoned Avery. I wanted to talk to him about what I'd learned. Maybe he knew Sandra's last name or something more about her. He answered on the third ring.

"Emelynn, are you checking up on me?"

It took me a moment to connect the dots. "Yeah," I said with a chuckle, "I'm calling to see if your Porsche worked its magic last night. Actually," I said, on a more serious note, "I wanted to drop by if you have some time."

"Sure," he said. "I'll go unlock the door."

I packed my knapsack, making sure I had my cellphone, passport, wallet and GPS tucked inside, and headed out the door. I had to be ready when the call came.

Thirty minutes later, I walked into Avery's waiting room. He invited me back to his kitchen and filled the kettle. "Did you enjoy the paintball game?"

"I sure did."

"We've got a great covey, don't we?" He sported a contented smile, and I wasn't sure if it was the covey or just one particular blonde that had put the smile on his face.

"Yeah, we do. Speaking of which, don't forget to email that surveillance photo to everyone. They're expecting it."

He frowned. "I already sent it."

"I didn't get it."

"Sorry, Em, I assumed you'd already seen it. I'll send it next time I'm online."

He pulled out the Brown Betty and made a pot of tea while I updated him on my findings about Delaney & Son and their business rivalry with Touchstone.

"I had no idea," Avery said. "But I knew Jackson's name was in the business news last year when he inherited the company. My contact told me about it when he made Jackson's introduction."

"Has Jackson ever mentioned a half-brother to you?"

"No. He's never mentioned any sibling," Avery said as he poured us each a cup.

"To me either, but I'm not so sure he's an only child anymore." Taking pains with the details, I relayed the story as I understood it, about Jackson's family. Something I said caught Avery's attention.

He cocked his head. "What did you say Jackson's half-brother's name was?"

"Cole Des Roche."

"It might be a coincidence, but I'm sure Jackson dropped that name a few months ago. I'm almost certain he said he suspected the man responsible for snatching Sandra was named Cole."

His words left me cold. "That's too big a coincidence. Is Cole a common name in the South?"

"I wouldn't have thought so." We sat in silence mulling over this unexpected twist.

"Has Jackson ever told you anything about Sandra?" I asked.

"Other than that she was snatched, no. She was a friend of the family, as I recall."

"Yeah, that's all I know too. How awful for Jackson. If he suspects his brother snatched her, that's probably why he wants to keep the Tribunal out of it. He wants to handle it himself."

"Do you know her last name?" I asked.

"No, I don't."

"How about James? What do you know about him?"

"Less than I know about Jackson," he said. "Why do you ask?"

"James dropped in on us aboard the *Symphony* last night—uninvited. He and Jackson had words—heated words."

"About what?"

"Me, for starters. Seems James isn't too happy that Jackson's seeing me. He thinks our relationship is going to distract Jackson from finding Sandra."

"That sounds a little harsh."

"He told Jackson they're close to finding her. He wants Jackson to be ready to go quickly."

"It sounds like the situation is coming to a head. James must be worried. I know he's just as interested in getting Sandra back as Jackson is."

"Did you know that James is from the New Orleans covey?"

"Not exactly, though he did come to us through Jackson. It was a few weeks after Jackson settled in. He introduced James as a friend, but they don't seem close. James is a loner, ex-military. Has some impressive skills—I've seen him in action during our paintball games."

"I don't like him." He'd put out strong vibes at the game last night, and he'd been positively volatile on the *Symphony*. "He frightens me. And something else ... Jackson has a gun."

Avery's mood darkened, but he didn't look surprised. "I'm not happy to hear that."

I reached for the teapot and a lighter topic of conversation. "How did things go with you and the beautiful Ms. Lang last night?"

He took a deep breath. "She let me drive her home." As he exhaled, his face melted into a slow, contented smile.

"Are you going to ask her out?" I asked, hoping I wasn't being too pushy.

"I might. Maybe I'll take her to that Thai fusion place you told me about, the Neon Turtle." He grinned at me over his cup of tea.

I grinned back. "That sounds like a good start."

My thoughts drifted back to last night, and something else I'd overheard. "Avery, have you ever heard of a Flier being referred to as a Ghost?"

He frowned. "Where did you hear about Ghosts?"

"It's something James mentioned last night. He referred to me as the *Ghost* Jackson's been researching. It just sounded like an odd way to refer to me. It made me curious."

"What exactly did James say?" Avery sat up and leaned forward.

"Just, 'She's the Ghost you've been researching.' That was the extent of it." Suddenly Avery was paying close attention. "What's got you so interested?"

"Ah, it's nothing. I haven't heard anyone mention Ghosts in a long time—that's all. Ghosts are the stuff of legend amongst Fliers, but they don't exist. At least there aren't any documented cases. I guess the fairy tales are still alive and well."

Avery scraped his chair back and walked to the cupboard. Something was on his mind. I could tell by the crease between his eyebrows. He dug out a bag of cookies, dumped some on a plate and brought it back to the table. "Help yourself."

I reached out and nabbed one. It was one of those maple-leaf shaped sandwich cookies. I hadn't had one in years, and the maple flavour tasted as good as I remembered.

"I have some time right now. Do you want to do some more work?"

"What did you have in mind?" I asked, lazily nibbling at the cookie.

"Let's work on your sparking."

"You really are a bit of a masochist, you know."

"Not today," he said, and a much-too-smug grin twisted his lips. "I was thinking we should practice speed blocking and low-end sparks. It'll be good practice."

"You're smiling because you already know you're faster than I am. You're trying to get me back for that nasty spark I pulled on you last time." I cocked my eyebrow at him, and he laughed.

"Guess we'll find out. And that wasn't a spark, by the way," he said, standing. "Clear the table, if you wouldn't mind. I'll get my computer."

I did as he asked, and he returned a moment later with his laptop. He sat down opposite me and worked the keyboard. "This program sends out audio tones at irregular intervals. We'll take turns. The first tone is yours. When it sounds, you spark and I'll block. Low-end sparks only. The second tone is mine. Keep that in mind when you're deciding how much juice to use. You ready?"

I nodded and he reached over and started the program. A second later, I heard the tone. But Avery was quick with his block and I didn't land a spark. He got me though, and his sparks were an excellent motivator for speed blocking.

We repeated the exercise until the novelty of the game wore off. Avery leaned back in his chair and stopped the program. "I'd like to try something, Em."

"Oh, no, I think I've heard that line before. Wait a minute, yes, now I remember—it was right before you asked me to hit you with my best shot." I delivered the lines with animation and was delighted to see that I'd made him laugh.

"Okay, so that one wasn't such a good idea, but I'm serious." He stopped laughing. "I'd like to try something but I need you to trust me."

"That sounds mysterious ... and ominous." I sat back and studied his face. His expression was dead serious. "What's this about?"

"Trust me?" he asked, again.

"All right, I guess I can do that."

He scooted his chair closer. I watched him straighten and expected an explanation. Instead, he blindsided me with a powerful jolt I had no chance of blocking. Excruciating pain exploded in my head, crippling me. I squeezed my eyes shut. My brain felt as if it were on fire. When the burn eased off, I opened my eyes a crack.

Then I realized something was wrong with Avery: very wrong. He was white as a sheet, frozen in place, and staring oddly past me. I forgot all about the pain in my head. "Avery, what's wrong?" I asked in a panic. "Are you okay?" What a stupid question. Of course he wasn't okay. Was he having a stroke? My mind raced to remember the signs.

I reached out to put my hand on his shoulder but something was off. My balance felt strange—kind of like it had when I had no control over my floats. I looked down at my lap, and blinked, puzzled. My eyes were playing tricks on me. My thoughts no longer focused on Avery because I couldn't quite comprehend what was driving my own strangeness. I held my hand out in front of my face and wiggled my fingers. I knew my hand was there, but I couldn't see it. I looked down at my lap again and saw only the fabric that covered the seat of the chair. I looked over to Avery. His eyes had grown wide.

"Avery," I whispered. Fear clawed its way to the surface. "What's happening?" I said, touching my non-existent hand to his shoulder. I felt the fabric of his shirt, and the warmth of his skin beneath, but I couldn't see my hand. Then I watched him start to fade into thin air, starting at the place where I held my hand to his shoulder. I couldn't take my eyes off the growing empty space that was quickly erasing Avery.

"Em, lift your hand off my shoulder." Avery's voice quivered.

I removed my hand and Avery slowly reappeared. He shivered and then stood and tested his limbs. "Where are you?" he asked into the room.

"Right in front of you. You can't see me?" I asked, confused.

"No." Avery's gaze darted wildly.

"What did you do?" I asked, my fear escalating.

"Nothing that can't be undone. Em, listen to me. Focus on your breathing: slow, deep breaths. Try to relax, calm yourself. You're going to be fine—trust me."

I heard his words and focused on his instructions. Closing my eyes, I concentrated on my breathing. In ... out ... in ... out. I felt the tension ease and worked on relaxing my shoulders.

After what seemed an eternity Avery touched my hands. "How do you feel now?" he asked.

I opened my eyes and saw his hands on mine. The relief of seeing my arms overwhelmed me. I couldn't stop the tears that streamed down my face. Avery gathered me up into a big bear hug. He held me close until I stopped crying, then pulled away and looked down at me with a mix of relief and apprehension.

"You want to explain any of that?" I asked, my breath still hitching from my tears.

"That, dear Em, is ghosting."

CHAPTER TWENTY-THREE

Ghosting?" I repeated. "Are you referring to the, and I quote, 'stuff of legend' or to the 'fairy tales' that you told me about less than an hour ago?"

"Looks like we may have a documentable case," he said with a flash of chagrin. He released me and sat down.

"Please, tell me you're kidding," I pleaded, absolutely horrified.

"Afraid not," he said, deep in thought. Then he looked up at my stricken face and quietly amended his tone. "Not about the ghosting. But I won't be documenting any of this. We can't tell anyone about it. Not a soul."

"You need to tell me everything you know about this ghosting thing," I said as I sat down.

"I don't know much. I wasn't kidding when I said it's the stuff of legend. I don't know of any first-hand accounts, but you can bet I'll be doing some serious research now."

"Did you know that hitting me with that big bloody jolt would trigger it?" I asked, not as calmly as I'd intended.

"No, not for sure, but I had my suspicions. Strong emotions are common triggers for such phenomenon. That's why I asked you to trust me even though I knew you'd kick my ass if I was wrong. It may not have been the best way to find out, but it was the only one I could think of on short notice. And now we know."

"Yeah, now we know." I slouched and stared at the ceiling.

He leaned forward, closing his hands over mine. "What did it feel like?"

"Disorienting. It reminded me of when I was young and would float off without warning. But I wasn't really floating. It felt more like I was off balance, drifting. I could feel your shirt under my hand and your shoulder. I could even feel the chair beneath me. It was the oddest sensation."

Avery hung on my every word. He eventually shook himself and sat back.

"What did it feel like for you?" I asked, sitting up.

"Similar. I know exactly what you mean about the strange sense of balance. It took everything I had to sit still. It felt surreal to watch my arm disappear, but when my legs evaporated, I lost my nerve."

"It all happened so quickly."

"I know. A split second after I hit you with that jolt, you faded. It was fast—not instantaneous—but within a second or two, you were gone."

"Avery," I said, hesitating, "Do you have anything stronger than tea in this house?"

"Yeah, good call. Do you like Scotch?" he asked as he got up and moved to the far side of the kitchen. He removed two glasses from a cupboard.

"Beats me, but I'll let you know."

He chuckled softly and held the glasses under the ice chute on the door of the fridge. The hard cubes rattled in the bottom of the glass. He poured an amber shot over the ice and returned, handing me a glass.

"Let's go to the den," he said, leading the way out of the kitchen into an adjoining room. We sat in leather chairs on either side of the fireplace. Bookcases lined the walls and a richly coloured Persian carpet covered the floor. A big desk sat a few feet in front of large French doors that opened out to the backyard. It was a comfortable room and very much a man's room. We sipped our drinks.

"So, do you like Scotch?" he asked, breaking the silence.

"Yes, I think I do," I said. "It's strong." It tasted like an unsweetened version of Jackson's rusty nail.

He swirled the golden liquid around the ice in his glass. He spoke softly. "We can't tell anyone about this, Em." He waited until I caught his gaze. "Absolutely no one: not Eden, not Alex, not even Jackson." I didn't respond.

He sat forward. "Do you understand?"

I frowned, too dazed to have thought the situation through.

"If word gets out that you're a Ghost, Em, you'll become a target. What you have is priceless. It's the kind of thing that some people are willing to take big risks to get their hands on."

I felt the weight of the world pressing down on my shoulders and closed my eyes.

"I'd sure like to know what led Jackson to think you might be a Ghost. Obviously, you got it from Jolene. Maybe I've got to look further back—find out more about Jolene's family and her heritage."

He continued. "I'll engage my network, put some feelers out, but I'll have to be careful not to set off any alarms. Meantime, you have to be vigilant. Don't breathe a word to anyone. Do you think you can do that?" he asked.

I drew in a ragged breath. "Regretfully, it's one of my core competencies." I remembered all too painfully the secrets that I'd shouldered for years: the secrets Jolene had laid at my feet. The very same ones that had put me in this cage I couldn't seem to get free of. I was back on that damn wheel again, going round and round.

"Good," he said, his voice soft.

Tears welled up, but I didn't let them fall. If this was fate, then she was one heartless bitch. Just how many land mines did I have to step on before she put me out of my misery?

It proved impossible to carry on any semblance of conversation after that point. We sat in distracted silence, finishing our drinks.

Sometime later, I returned home.

I ate cold pizza then changed into my nightshirt and climbed into bed. It was only eight but I fell asleep, exhausted. In my dreams, I ran and ran. Something had frightened me and I knew if I stopped running, it would kill me. At three fifteen I woke. I got out of bed, poured a glass of water and wandered to the windows. The sea shimmered under the moon's pale light: a heavenly, calming influence. When I crawled into bed the second time, I slept a dreamless sleep.

It was nine before I woke again. I'd slept for thirteen hours.

I staggered to the kitchen to make a pot of coffee then plodded back to the bathroom. With my housecoat around my shoulders and a steaming cup in my hands, I walked out to the deck and down the stairs to the beach. I sat on the sand, leaning back against a beached log. It was overcast. I closed my eyes and lifted my face to the clouds.

My morning ritual wasn't helping ease my mind today. Neither the coffee nor the setting did much to quiet the elephant stomping around in my head. I pushed the pachyderm away and concentrated on the breeze and the call of the seagulls. Sea fleas and flies buzzed around my feet. An hour passed but the melancholy didn't. I headed back up to the deck and curled up in a chair.

Depression lapped like a current just below my surface. I thought about Jackson. At least thinking about him was still pleasant. I wished he were here. I wished I could talk to him about this. I wished he'd make love to me so I wouldn't have to think at all.

I wondered what else Jackson knew about Jolene. Would he tell me if I asked? Then again, after yesterday, maybe I didn't want to know. And Jackson didn't need me adding to his trouble. He had enough crap on his plate with a wacko half-brother kidnapping their family friend and James breathing down his neck about me. What I could do, though, was help him. Given all he'd done for me, it was the least I could do.

The doorbell rang. I looked down at my housecoat. It was eleven in the morning and I wasn't even dressed. This was so embarrassing. I pulled the tie of the robe tight and walked down the hall to answer the door.

It took me a moment to put names to the faces of the two police constables who stood on the porch. Constables Tao Wong and Chris Mendel reintroduced themselves.

"I'm sorry, I haven't been feeling well," I lied, making excuses for my late morning attire. "Would you like to come in?" I asked, hoping they wouldn't, but no such luck. They accepted my offer and I followed them down the hall to the living room.

Their gait was officious, their footfalls heavy on the hardwood. They held their arms out from their bodies, away from the paraphernalia that crowded their belts. Their demeanour felt vastly different from their last visit. They glanced into each of the open doors along the hallway with more than cursory interest.

"Please, have a seat," I said, gesturing toward the sofa. They sat down in a creak of leather and got right down to business.

Constable Wong pulled out a notepad. "Your name came up in connection with a case we're investigating."

"Oh?" I said, baffled, and just a little bit intimidated by their formality.

"We understand that you're a client of Charles and Gabby Wright?"

"Yes," I answered, frowning. "Why do you ask?"

Constable Wong ignored my question. "When was the last time you saw them?"

I walked quickly to the kitchen and pulled their schedule off the fridge, running my finger down the dates. "Last Monday, June the sixth," I said. "Will you please tell me what's going on?"

Once again, Constable Wong ignored my question. "When is their next scheduled appointment?"

"Every two weeks. They come every two weeks and have done so regularly for ten years. Will you please tell me what this is about?"

The constables looked at one another as if weighing whether or not to answer me. Finally, Constable Mendel relented. "The Wrights have been reported missing."

"I don't understand ... missing?" I asked, my mind not quite grasping the concept in relation to Charles and Gabby.

"Other regular clients of theirs became concerned when they didn't show up on schedule, and reported it. Have you ever known them to miss an appointment? Perhaps go on vacation or visit family without notifying you?"

"No, never, but I can check with my mother in Toronto to be sure."

"Yes, please do that." Constable Wong handed me his card. "Call us if the Wrights show up or you learn anything different from what you told us today."

"They ride their bicycles everywhere," I offered. "Did you find their bikes?"

"Yes, but they also own a car, which is unaccounted for," Constable Wong said.

Constable Mendel added, "There was nothing at their home to indicate foul play, and though we understand for this couple it's unusual behaviour, it's not unheard of. Emergency situations do crop up and sidetrack even the staunchest routines."

"Have you talked to Jack Meyer?" I asked, remembering Cheney's dad.

Constable Wong flipped through his notes. "No. Who's he?"

"He's a long-time friend of Charles's. He owns Meyers Motors on Fourth Avenue."

"Thanks. We'll talk to him," he said, making a note. "In the meantime, if anything comes up, please let us know." He indicated his card, which I still held in my hand.

"Of course," I said. They stood and I escorted them back down the hall.

They left in their cruiser and I returned to the kitchen and put Charles and Gabby's schedule back on the fridge, along with the constable's business card. I phoned my mother. On learning of Charles and Gabby's disappearance, she was in as much shock as I was, but she had no additional information to offer.

It didn't feel real. People like Charles and Gabby didn't just disappear. What could have happened? Where could they be? As I tumbled the questions around in my mind, another thought struck me with a sickening blow: *a man and a woman*. Oh, my god.

But no, it simply wasn't possible. Calmly, I stood and slowly walked to my laptop. I looked for Avery's email in my inbox. I clicked on it and held my breath as I double-clicked on the JPEG attachment.

And there it was: a sharply focused, black and white photo of Charles, looking into the camera, fresh off his descent from the arbutus tree. I remembered thinking the man's walk had looked vaguely familiar. *It's been taken care of* echoed in my head.

I barely made it to the bathroom before I threw up. When I had nothing left to vomit, the tears came. Who was this man I'd befriended and welcomed into my home? How long had he been spying on me, rummaging through my things? I didn't want to believe he'd knowingly hurt me. And did Gabby know about any of this?

When I ran out of tears, I laid my head on the cool bathroom tiles and grieved. I grieved for the kind couple I'd thought were my friends; grieved for everyone who would miss them; and then I grieved for myself and the profound sense of betrayal I bore like a brand.

The shock took a long time to pass and when it did, I dragged myself into the shower and scrubbed at my skin as if the cleansing would remove the dark film of despair that stuck to me. I towelled off and dressed, feeling like a numb, empty shell of my former self.

I pulled the lawn-maintenance schedule off the fridge and ripped it into tiny pieces. I started a load of laundry. I needed more dark clothes. Hadn't Eden said she knew of a good place? Had Jackson asked her and Alex to join his team yet? I needed more milk.

My scattered thoughts reeled off in disarray, but it was safer than letting myself think about Charles and Gabby again. Not yet. It hurt too much.

I grasped at mindless chores. I pulled the vacuum out and ran it around the house. I scrubbed the bathroom then dusted every surface. I washed the windows and straightened the closets. I finished the laundry then folded everything and put it away.

Taking care of the cottage settled me. Calm slowly crept back where it belonged. I flopped into my chair on the deck and looked out to the empty horizon.

Charles and Gabby drifted back into my thoughts like foul perfume. I couldn't reconcile my feelings about the malicious man behind the camera with my memories of Charles. But the proof was irrefutable: it was Charles. He'd betrayed my trust and had been prepared to do even more damage. Had he given a damn about me or the others whose lives and freedom would have been compromised if he'd exposed us? What about Gabby? Had he considered her?

The hurt he'd inflicted wasn't instantaneous like the sting of a slap. It was a more gradual pain, an ache that filled my chest. He hadn't even had to break into the cottage to get Eden's contact information—he'd just used his key. That realization felt like a punch in the gut—I'd trusted him.

My emotions were a tangled mess. One moment, I'd be fuming at Charles for making me sink so low as to feel relief that he and his photos were no longer a threat to me. The next moment, I'd be angry with the Tribunal for their rash and irreversible action. I felt a new affinity with Avery and what he'd gone through years ago with his friend Jimmy.

The guilt I felt over Gabby ate at me. I wallowed in the "what ifs," but eventually the futility of it sank in. They were both gone and nothing I could do would ever change that. Maybe once I'd processed the enormity of Charles's duplicity, I'd be able to shovel some of my guilt and regret onto him. Meanwhile, it was mine to live with.

The sharp ring of my phone dragged me back to reality. I jumped up to find it. It was Jackson, and my heart was in my throat.

Without preamble, he said, "It's time. Are you ready to go?"

"Yes, of course," I said, already racing around to find my knapsack. The rescue mission was the only distraction weighty enough to change my focus, and I was thankful for it.

"Can you be ready in twenty minutes?"

"I'm ready right now."

"Good. Alex will be by to pick you up. He'll take you to the float plane. I'll meet you there," he said in a rush. "I've got to go. See you soon, Em."

After disconnecting, I paused. This was it. I'd put myself in the game, so now, no matter how ill-prepared I felt, I had to step up. *We're covey; we protect one another; it's what we do.* Jackson's words reinforced my new steely determination.

I rechecked my knapsack then locked the front door and walked to the end of the driveway. A grey van crawled down Cliffside. I waved when it got close enough that I recognized Alex. Eden sat in the passenger seat. I jumped in the back and closed the door behind me.

"Buckle up," Alex said, accelerating. "Danny's at work. We're picking him up on the way." We collected him from the boulevard in front of the Dodge dealer in Richmond.

Alex turned north again. It was a quiet trip, the four of us tense and contemplative. We turned into the south terminal parking lot of the Vancouver airport and parked. Each of us carried a small bag. We crossed back over the road and headed toward the float plane docks alongside the Fraser River.

Jackson and James were waiting for us. Jackson stopped pacing when he saw us. James stood with his arms crossed, scowling. I was beginning to think angry was his modus operandi. Our two groups exchanged hellos. I quickly looked away from James; he made me uncomfortable.

"We're heading to Lake Union to do some sightseeing," Jackson announced. "Is everyone ready?" We nodded our agreement and went inside. There was no chit-chat: anxiety rode the air. Alex and Eden held hands, and Danny was as antsy as he'd been before the paintball game. James avoided me and generally behaved himself. I got the sense it was only because Jackson was keeping him in check.

We were on a chartered flight, so we didn't have to wait. After we passed through the security check, we carried our own bags down the ramp to the dock. The co-pilot waited outside the Turbo Beaver float plane to help us negotiate the ladder-like steps over the floats. James and Danny claimed the front seats. Eden and Alex boarded next. I sat at the back. Jackson talked to the pilot for a moment then came to sit beside me.

"You okay?" he whispered.

"Yes," I lied. My father had been killed in one of these planes. Perhaps I should have tested my luck before today. Too late for that now.

Eden reached behind and patted my knee. "Lake Union is just outside of Seattle. It'll take us about an hour to get there." Jackson hadn't told us why we were landing at Lake Union, but it wasn't for sightseeing. It had to be close to where Sandra was being held. Alex looked back and winked. They knew about my father and I appreciated their efforts to reassure me. Jackson reached his hand over and squeezed my shoulder. He was doing a good job of keeping our relationship private.

The co-pilot deftly leapt on board while the pilot reviewed a laminated checklist, which didn't boost my confidence. Satisfied with his review of the gauges, he jammed the laminated sheet beside his seat, pumped a lever on the dash and turned a small red switch. I clenched my jaw. The propeller on the front of the plane whirled to life. It was loud. I followed Jackson's lead and pushed the disposable orange earplugs into my ears to dampen the noise.

The plane moved away from the dock and headed down the Fraser River toward the ocean. The ride got rougher the farther into the choppy waters we went, and we taxied a long way out. I balled my hands into fists. The noise level rose to deafening when the pilot pushed the throttle, and the plane surged forward and then up. As soon as the floats broke free of the water, the roughness dropped away, but the noise continued unabated.

We banked steeply before levelling out then climbed higher still, giving us a panoramic view of the shoreline and the mountains on Vancouver Island. The pilot circled us away from the airport and headed south with the engine droning loudly, making conversation all but impossible.

I looked out the window. Below, land and water intersected like lace. Jackson split his time between watching out the window and thumbing through the seat-pocket magazine, but I'm not sure he saw either one. Eden and Alex shared a set of earphones plugged into an iPhone. Danny was straining to see inside the cockpit. I avoided looking in James's direction.

Fifty minutes later, I heard the engine being throttled down. The co-pilot's Charlie Brown voice crackled over the speakers, unintelligible. I assumed he was telling us we were nearing our destination.

The plane banked sharply, heading down into a narrow waterway that opened up over what had to be Lake Union. The pilot levelled the plane out and we landed with a slight bump. It was a long taxi to the dock, where a man with a boat hook pulled our plane alongside and secured us.

The co-pilot jumped down and helped us out then guided us up the ramp where we were quickly ushered into a small US customs booth. We cleared customs without a hitch. Jackson turned to James. "Let's go pick up the rental van." The rest of us waited in silence outside the terminal building, anxious and fidgeting.

When the van pulled up, James sat behind the wheel. Jackson jumped out and Alex took his place in the front passenger seat. We settled in and buckled up. James pulled out, heading north, following Alex's directions. It was almost seven thirty and still daylight.

Jackson reached forward to tap Danny and Eden on the shoulders. "We're going to rendezvous with Alex's contacts, get a bite to eat, and then coordinate our plans."

Eden looked over to me. "Stell's Burgers," she said, licking her lips. "Fantastic! And the best sweet potato fries." Being from the Seattle area, she and Alex would be familiar with the neighbourhood.

I dug around in my bag until I found my GPS and added Stell's as a waypoint. We made our way down Third Avenue. Lake Union peeked out on our right as we headed northwest along the shore.

James found Stell's Burgers and cruised around the perimeter of the building to the lot behind. We slowed to a stop beside a black van parked at the edge of the asphalt, away from the other cars. Alex jumped out and greeted the two men inside. He didn't make introductions.

"Come on," Eden said, tugging at my sleeve. We got out and headed to Stell's restroom. "How are you holding up?" she asked when we were alone. We walked to the stalls and continued our conversation through the partition.

"I'm nervous. How about you?"

"I'm feeling the pressure," she said.

"Do you know Alex's friends?"

"Not well, but I've met them before. Gary's ex–law enforcement, the others are Gary's friends. They're good guys, tough, but they have our backs. You should know, they're not going to pull their punches tonight. It could get rough. Gary's probably armed but he knows what he's doing. They're pretty pissed that these guys took a Flier. The fact that she's a woman has only added fuel to the fire."

Eden was washing her hands when I joined her at the sink. Another woman walked in, putting an end to our talk. We walked out to the restaurant to find Danny juggling a few bags of takeout with a drink-laden tray.

"Need a hand?" I asked.

He passed me the tray. "Thanks."

Eden opened the doors for us and we joined the others in the parking lot, between the two vans. Danny handed out the burgers and fries and while we ate, Jackson updated us.

He didn't touch his food. "Sandra is being held on a forty-five-foot dump of a ship named the *MayBell*." He gestured to a man who didn't look particularly big or tough but was built as though he could throw a punch. His nose certainly looked as if it had taken a few. "Gary has been following the *MayBell* the past three nights. She docked at the Stabbert shipyard late last night."

Gary continued where Jackson left off. "Unfortunately, Stabbert is less than twenty-five miles from the Puget Sound Naval Shipyard. The naval yard has eyes on the sky so that limits our movement.

"The *MayBell*'s been operating with a five-man crew, but we couldn't watch them last night. We'll have to reassess once we spot them again. They're armed and at least three of them are Fliers."

Jackson jumped back in. "We'll start at Stabbert's shipyard and scout the shoreline north from there to pick her up again. Gary has two men stationed about three miles north of Stabbert, but they haven't spotted her yet. When we locate the *MayBell*, we'll keep her in our sights until she docks. If they follow the pattern they've set so far, they'll be hitting another ATM tonight."

"You gotta like those odds," Alex interjected. "Five of them to eight of us, not counting our two distractions." He winked at Eden.

"Let's just hope they're not expecting us," Jackson said. "I'd prefer to drop in on them unannounced, if you know what I mean."

We finished eating and tossed the garbage in the bin. Jackson said, "We'll be less conspicuous travelling in one vehicle. Gary, you and Tony can ride with us." It was the first time I'd heard Tony's name. He was shorter and stockier than Gary and had the ruddy weathered skin of someone who worked outdoors.

James got in behind the wheel again, while Alex resumed his position as navigator. The rest of us piled in. We continued north. I glimpsed water out to our right and checked my GPS. I found the Stabbert shipyard in its directory and added it as a waypoint. The Ballard Bridge over Salmon Bay was just ahead.

After we crossed the bridge, we headed back toward the coast. This time, the water was on our left. The neighbourhood was a mix of residential and retail, but the residential sections thinned out in favour of industrial the farther north we travelled. Traffic was light. We found the Stabbert shipyard at the end of a dead-end street.

James drove into the yard as if he owned the place. He passed a hut with a billboard-sized sign advising all visitors to report in, and kept going. He turned left behind the next building and headed toward the docks. The shipyard was huge, and judging by the sound of machinery all around us, it was still on the clock.

When the road gave way to dock and he could go no farther, James wheeled the van around and parked alongside a rambling aluminum-sided structure. I held my breath, expecting someone to kick us out, but no one approached. It wasn't fully dark yet, but the blue cast of dusk was setting in nicely.

"Eden, Em, stay here to guard the van," Jackson said. "We'll be back as soon as we've located the *MayBell*, then we'll head north to rendez-vous with Gary's men."

"Is everyone with me so far?" he asked, looking around to make sure we all nodded. "Danny, hand out the earpieces, would you?" He gestured to a box at the back of the van. "They're good for about a five-mile radius." Gary whistled, impressed with the gadgetry. "Gary, take two for your other men."

I took one and fitted it into my ear then flicked it on. At least this was a part of the plan I was familiar with. I was completely out of my depth with the rest of it.

Jackson said, "There are a lot of us on this channel, so keep chatter to a minimum." Danny slid the side door open and the men jumped out, dispersing into the shadows. I slid the door closed behind them and Eden climbed into the driver's seat. I claimed the seat beside her.

I shielded the mic with my hand. "This place gives me the creeps," I whispered, looking out over the docks with their creaking aluminum sheds and the distant cranes groaning high in the sky, dangling counter-weights and chains under bright lights.

Eden covered her mic. "Yeah. I sure hope the guys find her fast and get back here." Eden pulled the hood up on her jacket and I followed suit.

Moments later, my earpiece sparked to life. The surprise of it wrenched a squeal from my throat. "*Jackson here. Answer me when I call your name.*" He then ran through all our names, and each of us answered in turn.

"Good. We're splitting up. James and I are checking the slips. Gary and Tony are headed to the dry docks. Danny and Alex are already sussing out the outlying anchorages. We haven't found her yet."

Eden held her hand over her mic and muttered "Hurry up" as we continued to huddle in the front seats waiting for the bogeyman to show up.

Time dragged its feet as we waited in the growing dusk, vigilant of our surroundings. Ten minutes turned into fifteen and still, we waited, not daring to break the unnerving quiet as darkness fell around us.

Eden's arm shot out to draw my attention to the passenger-side mirror. *"Please tell me that's one of you."* Eden spoke quietly, her voice coming to me in stereo—live and simultaneously through my earpiece. The man wore dark clothing and moved without a sound, sweeping his head from side to side.

I recognized Jackson's voice. *"Not us."*

"Nor us," Gary said.

Alex's voice sounded tight. *"It's not us."*

"Damn ... we've got company," Eden said, keeping a keen eye on my mirror.

Alex said, *"There's a map in the glovebox. Tell whoever it is that you're lost."* I reached to open the glovebox and retrieved the map.

The dark figure sidled up on my side of the van. Eden gasped. I stole a glance and watched the man raise a gun. It was the second time this week I'd seen a gun and I liked the experience now even less than I did when it was wielded by Jackson.

"What's happening?" Alex asked.

Eden's wide-eyed expression reflected my fear. *"A complication,"* she said, and covered her mic. "What do you think?"

I shielded my mic and fumbled with the map. "We don't have a lot of choice," I whispered, ever hopeful that the man would see the map and buy our story. What would happen if he didn't? Would he shoot us? What a stupid question. He was a security guard. The gun wasn't a decoration.

I turned off my mic. "Be ready to boot it."

Eden white knuckled the keys in the ignition and I made a show of flattening the map on my lap.

The guard approached my window. "If he doesn't buy our story, we have only one other option," I said. My hood hid my face as I lowered my head and ran through the exercises Avery and I had spent so much time on. I drew on the power that hummed deep inside and concentrated it into a twirling mental ball of energy.

Eden choked out, "*That's no security guard.*"

Her mic picked it up and Alex's anxiety kicked up another notch. "*Eden? Talk to me.*"

The man rapped on my window with the barrel of his gun. My heart lurched, but I held on to the ball of energy. I whispered to Eden, "Start the van," and then I whipped my head toward the window, hitting the man with the biggest jolt I'd ever delivered. I heard the van fire up as I watched the man fly backwards, limbs splayed out, until he hit the side of the aluminum structure with a resounding twang. His gun flew out of his hand and skittered across the pavement as he crumpled to the ground.

Eden froze. Jackson's voice crackled over the earpiece. "*What's happening?*" His voice shook her out of her inertia.

"Go!" I screamed. Eden slammed the van into gear then hit the gas.

"*How the hell do we get out of here?*" she shouted as we sped forward, barely missing the guy wire of the power pole in front of us. The van's tires squealed as we careened off the raised curb.

I fumbled in my pocket for the GPS. It had been tracking our route. I tapped the screen to reverse our course and shouted directions. "Left here," I said, "and slow down. Straight ahead," I directed as we rounded the left turn back toward the entrance. "Turn right at the hut and don't stop." I could see the entrance up ahead. "That's it, slow down," I said, not wanting to draw attention to our departure.

I continued to call out directions until we were well clear of the shipyard. We bolted up 24th Avenue on a green light and kept going for several blocks before Eden took a sharp right onto a residential side street. She pulled over and put the van in park, then turned it off. She pushed herself fully back against the seat and only then did she take a deep breath.

Alex's worried voice broke the silence. "*Are you okay?*"

Eden exhaled. "*Yeah, we're fine,*" she said. "*It was a close call, but we made it out of there.*" She looked over at me and mouthed, "Are you okay?"

I nodded then turned my mic back on. "*Someone needs to go check on that security guard,*" I said, already feeling remorseful. I'd seen the damage one of my jolts had done to Avery, and he'd been prepared for it. This man hadn't been, and I'd had panic behind me to amp it up this time. The jolt itself would have been bad enough, but the whack against the wall wouldn't have been a picnic either. I hoped he was all right.

"*He was dressed like a Flier,*" Eden said. "*And he had his gun drawn.*"

"*But he didn't have a block up,*" I said.

"*What did you do to him?*" Jackson asked.

"*Let's just say you don't want to get on Em's bad side,*" Eden said, looking at me askance.

CHAPTER TWENTY-FOUR

I'*ll check on the guard—make sure he doesn't warn the wrong people.*" I recognized the voice of the volunteer: James. I didn't want to think about how he was going to accomplish that.

Gary broke in. "*The MayBell just passed our position at Golden Gardens Park.*"

"*Is Sandra on board?*" Jackson asked.

"*Can't tell yet. The same goons as last night are on deck.*"

"*Okay Gary, ask your guys to stay with her. We're on our way. James, when you're done with Mr. Security, catch up with us. Danny, Alex, you're with me. We're heading up the coast to find Gary's men. Don't forget who's watching the skies. Fly close to the ground and keep your air times short. Eden, Em, start up the coast and let us know when you pass Golden Gardens Park.*"

Eden looked at me and reached out. I took her hand and squeezed it in a very Thelma and Louise–esque moment. She covered her mic. "You ready?"

I nodded and mouthed, "Let's go." She started the engine and we pulled out. I propped the GPS on the cupholder and set Golden Gardens Park as our destination. Thank god for that electronic marvel—if we had to depend on my sense of direction, we'd already be hopelessly lost. We drove in silence, catching updates from the men in our earpieces as they made their way north.

With no traffic to hamper us, we arrived at the park ten minutes later. "*We're at the park,*" Eden announced, slowing to a crawl.

"*Okay. We're following the MayBell and she's not slowing down.*

Continue north and check back in another ten minutes," Jackson said.

Eden followed the GPS as we continued up the coast. Ten minutes later, we reported in. "*We're south of Carkeek Park now.*"

Jackson responded. "*You're ahead of us. We're keeping pace with the MayBell so we won't be able to keep up with you. They might pull in at Richmond Beach. There are a few ATMs there, but I think the better bet is Edmonds; it's bigger with more options. Why don't you head there and find a spot where we can meet? I'll let you know if anything changes from this end.*"

"*Okay, we're on our way,*" Eden said. I reached over and punched Edmonds into the GPS.

Twenty minutes later, we drove over the railroad tracks down to the Edmonds waterfront. Old-fashioned light standards lit up a picturesque boardwalk. Eden and I searched for a dark corner where we could all meet. We drove to the north end of the parking lot adjacent to the boardwalk. Only two other cars were parked at this far end. We locked up then headed for the trees at the edge of the boardwalk.

"*We're here,*" Eden announced. "*We've found a heavily treed area at the north end of the boardwalk that's almost deserted right now.*" There was no response.

"Maybe we're out of range," I suggested, pointing at my earpiece.

"Of course," she said, sounding relieved. "My phone's in the van." We headed back, and she called Alex and put him on speakerphone to update him.

He was with Jackson, who did most of the talking. "Hang tight. The *MayBell* has just rounded Richmond Beach and is headed your way. Let's hope she pulls in there."

"We'll wait to hear from you," Eden said. We settled in for the duration, keeping an eye on the foot traffic. To the south, distant lights of seaside restaurants twinkled. It was a beautiful night with only a light breeze coming off the water. Our timing was good. Later in the summer, this place would be swarming with people.

Twenty restless minutes later, our earpieces sputtered to life as the men came back into earpiece range with broken, static-laden reports.

The first clear communication came from Gary. "*Looks like she's headed for the public dock. Mark, stay with her and keep us updated. We want to know when she docks, and see if you can get a head count.*"

I assumed Mark was one of the two men whom Gary had sent on ahead.

Jackson spoke. "*Everyone else rendezvous at the van as soon as you can. James and I are on recon. We'll be there soon.*"

We turned off our mics and waited. Soon Alex stepped out from the cover of the trees at the edge of the parking lot. Eden jumped out to greet him and he folded her into his arms. They kissed as if they hadn't seen each other in a week. I watched them with envy. I wanted that in my life.

Danny emerged next, followed closely by Tony and then a man I didn't recognize. I got out of the van when they approached. "This is Jin," Tony said. Jin nodded but didn't speak.

Gary arrived and then we milled about, waiting for Jackson and James, whom we heard speaking to each other through our earpieces as they scoped out nearby structures and landscape.

When they finally joined us, Jackson ushered us all into the van. James took the driver's seat and Alex once again climbed in beside him. We headed out of the parking lot and turned south, back toward the marina.

We drove over a speed bump at the entrance to the marina complex. Jackson drew our attention to the left. "That's a public restroom." He indicated a squat cinder-block building that backed onto a treed green space.

We drove a short distance then he pointed to the right. "That's the Loft." It was a bar adjacent to the marina building. We continued south to the end of the marina's parking lot and stopped. Jackson pointed toward the waterfront. "The *MayBell* will moor somewhere in that area." He indicated a maze of slips beside the pier.

Jackson continued. "If they follow the pattern they've used in the past, two or three of the men will take Sandra to an ATM between eleven and midnight. The banks are all located in a two-block area around Dayton Street, north of here. They'll come down that pier, pass by the bar and take the path that goes past the public restroom. The Amtrak fencing you can see over there will funnel them through this parking lot."

James restarted the van, turned around and slowly drove north along the route that Jackson had described. I pulled out my GPS. Dayton was the major east-west artery for traffic between the waterfront and downtown Edmonds.

"They won't risk taking her along Dayton because it's too busy, too bright," Jackson said. We crossed back over the speed bump. "Once they're past the restrooms, they'll have to continue through this park area"—Jackson pointed to our right—"then across the Amtrak rail." We continued to the first intersection and turned east before crossing the tracks. "They'll continue up this road, past these empty lots and up to the corner." James pulled over and parked just past the empty lots. "We can't be sure what route they'll take beyond this point."

"Our best bet is to snatch her before she gets to that corner," Jackson said, pointing ahead of us to the far end of the street. "We need to make our move at some point between the pub and these empty lots, preferably without an audience." He looked through the van windows all around. "I see a few street lights at the Loft, but none in the park or the Amtrak area. James, let's go."

James pulled out. We continued east to the next corner then turned north on Edmonds Way. We hit Dayton a few blocks later and turned right. Two blocks along, Jackson pointed out a U.S. Bank, then in quick succession a Bank of Washington and a Horizon Bank. They all had ATMs. We continued east on Dayton for another five minutes until it morphed into Main Street. James slowed down and turned left into Pine Ridge Park, which was deserted. He parked the van in the shadows and turned off the ignition.

My earpiece squawked to life. It was Mark who'd been left to watch over the *MayBell*. "*They're docked, but not for the night. They've taken a two-hour slip. I haven't got a head count yet.*"

"*Stay on it, Mark, and keep us posted,*" Gary responded.

Jackson spoke. "Eden, Em, we need you on the ground close to the targets. Go to the Loft and change into your street clothes. You'll guide them into position for us. Okay?" We both nodded.

"Gary, Tony, we'll meet up with Mark to watch the *MayBell* and follow Sandra from the air, when they make their move. Alex, James, Jin, Danny—meet up behind the public restrooms, keep out of sight and wait until we tell you they're on the move. You'll position yourselves in the air in front of them.

"When they get into range, we'll extract Sandra and take out the targets. We'll have the advantage of surprise and with four of you in front and another four of us behind, we'll also have the advantage of numbers. Those are damn good odds." Jackson exuded confidence and the men nodded and high-fived each other in approval.

"When Sandra's secure, we'll splinter off. If the targets are disabled, and I sincerely hope that'll be the case, they won't be following us, but if any of you pick up a tail, call for backup. We'll meet back here at the van. The keys will be in the ashtray. If you can't make it back to the van, then get yourself to Lake Union. The float plane is scheduled to take us back tomorrow at noon. If you miss that flight, get yourself home and I'll reimburse your expenses."

Jackson checked his watch. "It's after ten. We need to get into position. Any questions?" When no one responded, he asked Mark if he'd heard and understood the plan.

"Yeah, sounds good, but I think our odds just got worse. It looks like the MayBell picked up a man in Stabbert's yard. I count six of them and I haven't seen the woman yet."

"Damn it. Let's hope the increase in numbers doesn't change the rest of their routine. Gary, Tony—we're out of here." The three of them left the van and Jackson called out, "Be safe. I'll see you back here soon." They walked out into the shadows of the park then faded out of sight.

Moments later, James stashed the keys in the ashtray. As he reached over, his jacket rode up, and I caught the flash of a gun tucked into his waistband. No doubt it was the guard's gun. You'd think I'd be used to seeing them by now, but my Canadian sensibilities railed against the sight and sent my pulse racing.

We cleared out of the van. Eden and Alex kissed goodbye and Jin was gone before I turned around. The rest of us spread out, heading into the shadows. I saw Alex lift off and kept him in sight as I called on my own power, then surged upward to follow him. Eden was close behind. I'd already lost track of James and Danny, though they had to be near.

We flew high and drifted slightly north to avoid the brightest lights. It took us another ten minutes to get back to the coast. Jackson announced that his group was in position.

Eden and I signalled our intent then broke away from the others. We drifted down to land close to a majestic shade tree at the grassy edge of the marina parking lot. I had the eerie sense someone was watching. Turning, I looked behind then up. James hung back, eyeing us. That man gave me the creeps.

"Em and I are headed to the pub now," Eden said as we emerged from under the cover of the big tree and started walking through the parking lot. We turned down the road toward the docks and the Loft's sign, and went inside. The tables by the windows were mostly occupied. Eden leaned close. "I'll head to the restroom to change. Get us a table?"

I nodded. She moved toward the restroom and I claimed a table away from the door. I pulled the GPS out of my knapsack to enter the Loft as a waypoint.

My earpiece squawked. "*James here. We're in position.*" We had all reported in. I removed the menu from its holder and waited.

Eden came out of the restroom and scanned the room, spotting me. She'd taken the distraction part of our job to heart. Her snug off-the-shoulder shirt didn't quite touch the top of her short skirt. The high-heeled gladiator ankle boots pushed her into smouldering territory—sure to draw attention.

She dropped her shoulder bag, stuffed with her dark clothing, onto an empty chair. "Your turn," she said.

I reached for my knapsack and headed to the restroom but knew my transformation wouldn't be quite as distracting. All I had to offer were a pair of capris with a handkerchief halter top. I stepped into ballet flats and checked the mirror. Yup, positively frumpy stared back at me—at least compared to Eden. When I had the last of my things tucked into my knapsack, I returned to the table.

A glass of Coke awaited me. "Thought you might like the caffeine," Eden said, rhythmically rotating her own glass by the rim. Eden turned to the window and adjusted her mic. "*Eden here. We're in the pub and all set.*" I heard her voice in stereo again, live and in my earpiece.

The rescue was in motion. All we could do now was sit and wait and hope it turned out as well as it had been planned.

We both flicked off our mics. I picked up the glass, but it shook in my hand. I set it down again knowing the longer we waited, the more nervous I'd become.

An unsettling quiet fell over us. I couldn't read Eden's expression. "Are you feeling as out of your element here as I am?" I asked.

"I've got a lot of confidence in these guys. They'll keep us out of the thick of things. I'm just counting on it being over in a hurry."

"I hope you're right."

"I am. With these odds, the kidnappers will be out of commission before they know what hit them. They probably won't even get airborne."

Eden's confidence was reassuring. I traded my apprehension in favour of the positive energy that flowed from her.

The waiter refilled our drinks and then a voice shattered the quiet. It was Jackson. "*I can see Sandra. They're leaving the boat. Eden, Em, head outside and stay in front of the pub until you see them.*"

Eden dropped ten dollars on the table. We turned on our mics and walked outside.

I heard Mark speaking. "*Five of them left the boat. I see three with the woman and two others a few paces behind.*"

Gary responded. "*Jin, you better get back here. We're going to need you.*"

"*On my way,*" Jin replied.

I covered my mic. "James, Alex, and Danny are still ahead, right?"

"I think so," Eden said. I crossed my fingers.

Jackson spoke. "*The two stragglers have split off from the main group and are headed south toward the boardwalk. We need to cover them.*"

Gary directed his men. "*Jin, Mark, Tony: follow them but don't engage unless they try to join up with the others.*" This unfortunate turn of events meant we'd been pared down to Gary and Jackson at the back end. Our rescue team had just dropped from eight to five.

Would it be enough? I wrapped my arms around myself and looked to Eden for reassurance.

Eden covered her mic. "The numbers are still in our favour," she said. "And we still have the element of surprise." I tried but failed to look more confident than I felt.

"Try to relax, Em." She donned a smile as she painted a picture for me. "We've just left the pub after drinking too many margaritas." She hiccupped for my benefit. "We're celebrating ... let me see ... my promotion. Yes, and now we're looking for more action because ..." She frowned in concentration. "Because the new vice president of Margaritaville," she said with a grin, pointing at herself, "would like to go dancing."

I smiled at her. "You're good at this."

Jackson's voice interrupted. "*They're heading your way, Eden. Three men and a woman just left the pier and are now on the board-walk.*"

We saw a clump of people approaching, still a hundred yards away, closer to the marina office than us. "*We see them,*" Eden said.

"*Good. Position yourselves in front of them and let them get close.*"

Eden and I strolled into the middle of the walkway and started up an animated conversation. Sometimes the words didn't make sense, which sent us both into manic bouts of laughter. The nervous energy proved hard to control, especially as our targets neared.

I heard Jackson. "*Okay, good. Keep them close. We need to move them across the tracks and into the park.*"

Eden and I started across the parking lot all the while keeping up the drunken ruse, slurring words as we wobbled toward the path across the tracks. The group followed behind.

"*That's right, a little farther then start slowing them down,*" Jackson said, guiding our actions.

We escalated our laughter, and then stopped abruptly on the pathway. Eden reached over and pushed my shoulder. "No way," she shouted, and staggered backwards, exaggerating her laughter. I echoed her escalated voice and joined in. We occupied as much of the pathway as we could, forcing them to stop behind us. There were four of them. The man in front darted beady-eyed glances left and right.

Copying her move, I reached over and pushed her shoulder. "Yes way," I retorted as we continued with the fake drunken laughter and exaggerated movements.

"Excuse me, ladies," the lead man said as he hustled past us.

I heard Jackson again. "*Perfect. Better than we could have hoped for. Now keep them separated and move forward, slowly.*" I took comfort in the fact that he was keeping a close watch on our procession.

I wrapped my arm around Eden and we kept up the stupid banter while we staggered forward, alternating between tripping each other and holding each other up. The man behind us mumbled irritably under his breath. I took a chance and turned around, walking backwards to get a better look. The man escorting Sandra towered over her and looked as if he ate women like us for breakfast.

"So sorry," I said, slurring my words. He slowed his pace. "My friend went and got herself a promotion today. We're celebrating." I caught the glimmer of something I couldn't make sense of. I used our drunken charade to stumble toward the couple, catching myself at the last moment. It was enough. My stumble forced the big man to pull back. The movement caused Sandra's jacket to gape open. I turned back around and gripped Eden's waist even tighter.

Sandra was beautiful, even with the shadows under her eyes and her hair a tangle. She wasn't walking entirely under her own steam and her eyes were wrong—not focused. She had to be drugged. Her wrist was handcuffed to her bodyguard, but that wasn't the worst of it; the glimmer I'd caught a glimpse of was a chain around her waist that I suspected was also secured to her guard. How on earth was I going to pass that crucial tidbit on to Jackson? The goon was too close—he'd hear anything I said.

My earpiece burst to life, and everyone talked at once. *"James, you're with me. We've got dibs on the filth holding Sandra."* It was probably Jackson, but the voice was broken up and interspersed with someone else saying *"Alex ... with me,"* and then there was something about *"the prick out front."* Gary's voice broke in talking trash about the one in the caboose of our slow-moving train.

Eden tightened her grip and jerked us to a sudden stop. We froze in place, as all hell broke loose.

Fliers dropped out of the sky all around us. I heard the smack of fists hitting flesh and explosive grunts. We were facing forward, so we saw when Danny kicked the legs out from under the guy in front and landed a punch to his head. The guy went down, but he was tough and elbowed Alex in the neck, taking him down too. Alex hit the sidewalk hard and Eden flew from my grip and rushed into the fray. She got her arms under Alex and pulled him out of Danny's way.

Danny continued his assault in a blur of dreads, fists and feet. In all the confusion, I didn't see the stray kick that hit my thigh. The force of it spun me around on a sharp inhale, but it didn't knock me down. I tucked in my arms, shrinking away from the chaos all around me.

Jackson and James had tackled the mountain of a man holding Sandra, but they weren't making much headway. The man held Sandra in the grip of his formidable left arm and flung her around like a ragdoll to block James, who was attacking from that side. James danced around trying to land a blow without hitting Sandra. His lips were pursed, his nostrils flared. He was close enough to see the cuffs and hopefully the chain that secured her. She was barely coherent.

Jackson attacked from the opposite side, taking shots at the big guy's head while dodging the man's blows. His anger swirled around him like a black cloud that prevented him seeing the real problem—the hardware.

Meanwhile, Gary's fight with the man at the back of the group had moved to the far edge of the parking lot.

I refocused on the fight closest to me. Man Mountain stepped back, away from an onslaught of Jackson's fists and reached into his pocket. His thick hand came out wrapped around the barrel end of a gun.

"He's got a gun!" I shouted seconds before he swung his arm and smacked Jackson hard across the face with the butt of it. Jackson went down hard, stunned. His foot caught mine on his way down and I lost my balance and stumbled forward. A shot rang out and I landed heavily on my knees, right in front of Sandra's dangling feet.

A burning sensation lodged in my left side and quickly flared into mind-numbing pain. Everything went quiet inside my head, as I watched the scene in front of me unfold in slow motion. That strange off-balance sensation overcame me as I sank lower, oddly detached from everyone around me. I recognized the feeling and knew that I had ghosted. Despite the fog of my pain, I also knew that I had to take Sandra with me. I reached out for her, gripped her leg—and watched as she too blinked out of existence.

Once she'd disappeared, the chain that had been secured around her waist dropped, rattling as it settled along Man Mountain's leg. He stepped back with a puzzled look on his face and stared at the empty end of the handcuff that now dangled from his wrist. James paused. I heard him mutter "*Jesus Christ*" just before he threw a fist and possibly a jolt into Man Mountain's head, stunning him.

James then turned his attention to Jackson and got him up and hovering. Jackson was not steady and held his head in his hands.

I watched it all happen as if it were a foggy dream. I floated inches off the ground, pulling Sandra close to me with a firm grip around her waist. I could feel her but couldn't see her as I tugged her upward. She was as light as the air she resembled.

The pain in my side made it hard to breathe. I headed higher, looking for a safe place to go, and glimpsed the activity below. Sandra's guard lay unconscious on the sidewalk looking like a broken G.I. Joe. The fighting hadn't stopped, but I couldn't stay to see how it ended. I had to get out of there.

In a voice that sounded far away, James said, "*We've got Sandra. Let's go. Disperse.*"

I was high enough to spot the tree that Eden and I had landed behind when we'd arrived and aimed for it. Our team spread out and scattered in all directions. Gary and Danny flew right by me, bloodied and tattered, unaware of my presence.

My earpiece crackled. "*Em, where are you?*" It was James.

"*Heading to tree ... parking lot.*" It was all I could manage with the limited air I could get into my lungs. James had watched Eden and I land there earlier—surely he would know which tree and which parking lot.

I floated over the tree and drifted down behind it. James closed in from the side, landing ten feet away from us. I set Sandra down and released her then drifted a few feet farther away and curled into a ball. The pain was unbearable.

James was close. "What the hell ..." he said, though it didn't come through my earpiece. "Sandra? Oh, thank you, god," he whispered. "Jackson, over here," he said, and I closed my eyes. Relief washed over me. "Take her—get her out of here."

I inhaled another ragged, shallow breath and waited for Jackson to wrap his arms around me and take the terrible pain away.

But he didn't.

I opened my eyes and focused, but he was gone. Confusion overwhelmed me. Where was he? James crouched close by. He whispered, "Em, where are you?" I watched him scan the area around the base of the tree. "Em," he repeated, more urgently. "Tell me where you are. Let me help you."

The pain was not subsiding. I needed help. "Here," I called to him, but it came out in the breath of a whisper.

He moved closer. "Where?"

"Here," I repeated, but the effort was too much. Darkness fell around me, thick and heavy.

CHAPTER TWENTY-FIVE

I woke in a fevered sweat. The brief moment of vague lucidity repeated itself a number of times over the course of god knows how many hours. I was aware of being moved, and unfamiliar voices drifted on the air, but none of that broke through the blackness that held me in its clutches.

Consciousness returned slowly. I gazed around an unfamiliar room. The paintings and furniture suggested it wasn't a hospital despite the equipment that beeped softly beside me and the needle dripping something into the back of my hand. Heavy curtains hung on either side of a window beyond the foot of the bed, but I couldn't tell if it was dusk or dawn; it was that in-between time. I couldn't see a call button and I didn't have the energy to shout. I closed my eyes.

The next time I woke, sunlight streamed across the floorboards. I teared up when I caught sight of Avery. He snored softly, slumped in a wingback chair with his feet propped on an ottoman, a magazine across his lap. The moment I laid eyes on him, I knew I was safe.

He must have sensed that I'd woken, and he stirred. He looked over and smiled that crooked smile I'd grown to love. He slowly shook his head. "What are we going to do with you, Em? The last time I patched you up the worst of it was a few stitches and a concussion."

He got up and stretched, then made his way over to the bed. "I guess that wasn't traumatic enough for you. It seems you've graduated to gunshots." He checked the beeping machine and the IV drip line. "What do you have in store for us next time?"

"Next time?" I rasped, managing a weak smile through my tears.

Avery rested his hand on my shoulder and gave it a gentle squeeze. "How's your pain?" he asked.

I cleared my throat. "I know it's there, but it's not too bad."

"You should still be feeling the effects of the morphine I pumped into you last night. Let me have a look." He pulled the blanket down, moved the hospital gown away from my side, and peeled back the edge of a large bandage. He then rolled me onto my side to check another dressing on my back before replacing the covers.

He took my hand. "You are one lucky woman. The bullet went right through. It missed your large intestine but damaged muscle. It'll heal, but it's going to take a while."

"Where am I?" I asked.

"My house." He held out a cup with a crooked straw. "Drink," he said, holding the cup. "Are you hungry?"

"I don't think so. I'd love a coffee though," I said, and he chuckled. He pulled my hand to his face and pressed his cheek into my palm, holding it there for a moment. There was something beyond tender, almost fatherly, in that gesture, and it brought fresh tears to my eyes.

"I'll make you some tea. It'll be easier on your stomach." He turned for the door, closing it behind him. The room felt cold in his wake.

I thought of my father and for the first time in years, I ached with the grief of missing him. I let my tears fall, unchecked. They weren't just tears of grief; they were tears of relief, tears of gratitude. They pooled under my jaw and ran down my neck.

The tears were under control when Avery returned a short time later with two cups. He raised the back of the bed to a steeper incline then removed the wires that were stuck to my chest and turned the machine off. He left the drip in my arm and handed me the cup of tea.

My hands shook as I brought it to my lips. It was just a small cup but it felt too heavy to hold. I rested it on my lap.

Avery cleared the magazine off the chair and resumed his seat. "You had an adventurous night, Em."

"Is Sandra all right?" I asked.

"I think so. I haven't seen her myself."

"She's beautiful," I said, recalling her fragile, haunted features.

"Where's Jackson?" I asked.

"On the *Symphony* at the moment," he replied, watching me closely.

I tested my shaking hands and once more brought the tea to my lips. "Was it James who brought me here?" I asked.

"Yes, two nights ago, and he's been checking on you ever since."

"I'm feeling ashamed now about my earlier opinion of him. I guess he saved my life."

"You guess?" Avery said, raising an eyebrow.

"How do you thank someone for something that significant?"

"I don't know, but you'll get the opportunity tonight when he visits again."

There was a bump at the door and Victoria pushed a big tray in the room ahead of her. Avery jumped up to give her a hand. I sat there with my mouth open, looking from him to her and back again.

"You can close your mouth now," Avery whispered under his breath as Victoria passed behind him. He hid a grin as she walked to the far side of the bed, avoiding the IV trolley, and positioned the tray's legs on either side of my lap.

"I thought you might be hungry so made you some oatmeal," Victoria said, draping a napkin across my lap.

"Thank you. It looks good—I guess I am hungry." The oatmeal was topped with brown sugar and a splash of milk.

She chatted with Avery while I ate. A few spoonfuls filled me. When I couldn't eat any more, she lifted the tray. "Is there anything else I can get you?"

"No, but thanks."

She topped up my tea, then did the same for Avery, and left.

I let the silence settle in then asked Avery, "How was the Neon Turtle?" He'd taken up residence in the wingback chair again.

"Just wonderful." His contented smile said it all.

After a few sips of my cooling tea, sleep once again tugged at me. Avery took my cup then lowered the head of the bed. I closed my eyes and let sleep drag me under.

I slept for a few hours and felt more like myself when I woke again. Victoria had taken over the wingback chair and looked up when she heard me stir.

"How are you doing?" she asked.

"Stiff and sore, but better," I said.

"I'm glad. I'll go get Avery. Would you like a bowl of soup?"

"Thanks, yes," I said. "Soup would be great."

Avery was up in a flash and checked me over again. He inspected under the bandages and checked my heart and temperature. Satisfied, he went to help Victoria.

They returned a short time later, and while I unfolded the napkin, I asked Avery if Jackson had been by.

"Eat first," he said as Victoria set the tray down across my lap. The aroma made my mouth water. It was a thick chicken gumbo that tasted as good as it smelled. I dipped a piece of French bread into the broth.

"This is really good," I said to Victoria.

"Oh, I didn't make it," she said with a laugh. "I'm afraid oatmeal is the extent of my talents. Avery made it. He's been cooking for two days straight. You should taste the lasagne he made last night. *Delicio*." She kissed the tips of her fingers in an Italian-inspired gesture.

"You're too kind," Avery said from behind Victoria, his hands on her shoulders. I heard a doorbell chime and Avery started for the door. "I'll be right back."

That's probably Jackson, I thought. I couldn't wait to see him and quickly finished my soup. Satisfied that I'd had enough to eat, Victoria collected the tray and returned to the kitchen.

I lay back against the pillows, rested my head and closed my eyes. The pain was making a comeback.

The door opened and James entered.

I was at a total loss for words. I tried to find the menace in his eyes that I'd seen before, but it was gone.

"Emelynn—you're looking better." He looked about as awkward as I felt.

"Yeah, turns out Avery has some pretty good painkillers here."

He walked around to the foot of the bed. Dark shadows under his eyes suggested he hadn't slept very well.

The silent gap stretched on. I looked up at the man who'd saved my life and saw him in a whole new light. My thoughts did not fit easily into words. "I'm not sure how you thank someone for saving your life," I said, barely holding back tears.

"You saved Sandra. I think that makes us even." He fidgeted with the blanket at the bottom of the bed, avoiding eye contact. "I'm very happy to have her back. My family is indebted to you." After a brief pause, he looked at me. "I'm not sure you knew, but Sandra is my sister."

His words dropped like a bomb, stunning me momentarily. "No, I wasn't aware of that." I didn't quite know what to make of the revelation. James was preoccupied with the bedding again. "No wonder you were so worried that Jackson was going to get distracted by me."

James snapped his head up and looked at me, puzzled.

JP MCLEAN

"Is she all right?" I asked, ignoring his odd reaction.

"Yes, she's on the *Symphony*. My mother flew up yesterday to help out. She brought a specialist with her. Sandra's been pumped up with drugs for so long she's having a hard time coming off them."

"I'm sorry."

"Yeah, me too," he said, softly. "But I'm glad you're doing well." He forced a smile.

"Yes, and thanks to you ... and Avery, I'll be fine. I'm already feeling better," I said. "The only thing I'm missing is Jackson, but I'm sure he'll visit as soon as he can."

That wiped the smile off his face in a hurry. "Jackson won't be visiting, Emelynn, soon or otherwise."

I searched his face for the meaning behind his words. He wouldn't look me in the eye. Then I remembered his words to Jackson that night on the boat. He didn't approve of Jackson's seeing me, and apparently not just because of Sandra's impending rescue.

"James, I know you saved my life and I'm grateful to you for that, but you don't get to decide whether or not Jackson and I see each other." I kept the anger I felt out of my voice. I owed this man my life so I would be reasonable. "You don't even know me."

"No, I don't." He sighed heavily. When he finally looked at me, I saw the struggle in his pale blue eyes. "But I do know Jackson and I'm getting the distinct impression that he's not been honest with you."

The intensity of his gaze scared me. "What do you mean?"

"Did Jackson tell you he was married?" He didn't need my answer. He read everything he needed to know from my face. "I didn't think so."

The ensuing silence rang in my ears.

"I don't believe you. He can't be," I said with defiance.

"I wish that were true." He hesitated, and then added, "Sandra is his wife."

His words rendered me numb. Time stopped. I felt as if I were floating outside of myself. I raised my palms to stop any more words from tumbling out of his mouth.

But he kept speaking and my ears kept hearing. "I'm so sorry, Emelynn. He should never have done this to you or to Sandra. He sure as hell shouldn't have left it for me to tell you."

I squeezed my eyes closed and pressed my hands to my ears. "Please, I don't want to hear any more. James, just leave—please."

He watched me, hesitating at the foot of my bed.

"Please," I pleaded. "Leave."

He turned and left.

I tuned out the raised voices outside my room. I pulled my knees to my chest, hugging them close, ignoring the stabbing ache my wounds broadcast. I rocked back and forth. And then the pain hit my heart and blew it apart.

Avery came running in. I shoved him away, flailing my arms, punching out at him. The IV trolley toppled over, clattering to the floor. I was inconsolable, unconcerned with who or what I hit. The physical pain felt good.

But I was no match for Avery. He caught my arms mid-swing and tucked them between us. He held me tight until the fight died out of me. Soon, all that was left were heaving sobs.

"How could he do this to me?" I repeated, over and over. Avery rocked me gently, stroking my head. He called to Victoria, who then took his place cradling me. I looked over her shoulder and watched Avery plunge a needle into my IV line, and drifted into oblivion.

When I woke, for about thirty seconds, my world was okay. Then it hit me anew: Jackson's betrayal—and I was undone all over again. He didn't care about me. He'd used me and then tossed me aside without a backward glance. The ache burned in my heart as tears rolled down my cheeks. Physical pain didn't even register next to the train wreck that was my heart.

I didn't notice Avery until he came over to brush the tears from my face. I looked up at him through weepy eyes.

He handed me a tissue. "You pulled your stitches and started bleeding again. I've given you some more pain med. It'll kick in soon." He stood over me until I closed my eyes.

I stayed with Avery for three more days. On the morning of the third day, he came to my room and sat on the bed. "There are some things you need to know, Emelynn," he began, gauging my reaction. "At the risk of opening fresh wounds, I'm going to tell you because I think it's important you know. I think knowing will help you move past this."

I didn't interrupt him. "James and I have had many conversations these past few days. I needed to understand what happened—not just with Sandra and Jackson, but with you.

"James knows you're a Ghost—there's no denying it. He saw it with his own eyes. But he's convinced me he's genuine in his intention to protect that secret. He feels he owes you, given all you've gone through to bring his sister home. I believe him. He doesn't think Jackson has figured it out, and Jackson's too preoccupied right now to pursue it."

I should have felt some relief at that, but I didn't. Over the past three days, I'd moved on to a place beyond hurt and my feelings were now, thankfully, comfortably numb.

Avery continued. "Jackson learned of Jolene's identity the day you told him her name. I suppose fast service is one of the perks of having well-paid contacts. He suspected you might have her speed, but he didn't know for sure until the night you cartwheeled into the ocean. That's when Jackson got curious about the possibility that you might be a Ghost. After that, he targeted you. He wanted you on his rescue team and didn't let his morals get in the way of garnering your trust.

"James doesn't know if Jackson had a source for the ghosting rumour or if he was just speculating. He tells me that Jackson's not mentioned it since Sandra's rescue and James is certain that Jackson didn't see what happened that night. I hope he never finds out."

He searched my face for a reaction, but I had none to give him.

"You were right about Cole," he said. "He is Jackson's half-brother. Cole went after Jackson's inheritance following the death of their father. He tried to force a DNA test, but Jackson wouldn't allow it. Cole then tried blackmailing him—said he had proof of illegal corporate espionage. But Jackson didn't budge. When Cole ran out of options he took the one thing he knew meant something to him: Sandra."

He sat with me a while longer. I smoothed the bandage on the back of my hand; it covered the needle puncture from the IV he'd removed yesterday.

I stared out the window revisiting the steady stream of blows I'd endured: the accident in the park, almost drowning, Charles's duplicity, getting shot, and now Jackson's betrayal. How much, I wondered, could one person endure before they were irreparably broken—irretrievably lost? I was the chimney left standing after the fire, my life a smouldering, blackened ruin lying all around me.

Avery and Victoria took me home the next afternoon. Eden and Alex joined us at the cottage, arms full of groceries.

Physically, I was on the mend, my wounds healing, but my heart still ached. I didn't know who knew what about what had happened, but no one asked me any questions, and I was grateful for that.

Eden fed me and stayed over that first night I was home in the cottage. It was comforting to have her there.

The next morning dawned sunny, and Eden left after breakfast. It felt odd, being alone—finally and completely alone. For the first time in a long while, I wrapped my housecoat around my nightshirt and carried my coffee down the stairs to the beach. I leaned against a log and tilted my face into the sun. I let the perfect day wash over me, inhaling the briny air and listening to the steady rhythm of the water at the ocean's edge.

Over the course of the past few days, I had come to a sobering conclusion: I was never going to make it back to Normal. That place didn't exist for me anymore, and letting go of it would be the hardest part of my recovery. In my heart, I knew I had to leave Normal behind if I was ever going to move forward. I was a Flier, whether I liked it or not. I had to accept it and move on.

I took solace in knowing that although I hadn't found Normal, I'd found freedom—a very special kind of freedom that only flight made possible. But that realization didn't make the letting go any easier. I got weepy just thinking about it. Normal was where my father lived, and I couldn't help feeling as if I were leaving him behind.

I knew it wouldn't happen today, maybe not for a long while yet, but eventually, my heart would heal—it wouldn't always hurt this much. Eventually, I would allow myself to feel good things again, the way they were meant to be felt, not through the filter of a damaged heart.

I looked around at the majestic vista before me and felt the enormity of it, the possibility of it, and smiled, just a little. In a few days, I would be well enough to fly again. At least I had that. My secret sky. Just thinking about it had that hum of power flowing through my body.

Soon, I would reconnect with Molly and hear all about Cheney. I looked forward to that, but not yet. My emotions were still too raw, too close to the surface and I had secrets to protect: dangerous secrets. You needed to be strong to guard secrets.

I returned to the kitchen to refill my cup. I cradled it in my hands, smiling at the familiar act while I wandered around the house as I had on that first day, letting the comfort of the cottage wrap me in its embrace.

I would have to touch base with my mother today. She would be wondering by now why I'd been out of touch. At other times in my life I might have wished for a closer relationship with her, but right now, the relationship we had seemed perfect. We were distant enough that she didn't worry about me every day and that was a relief. Her worry was a burden I didn't need to add to my already heavy load.

I retrieved the mail and sat down in my father's study to sort through it. There was only one interesting piece in the pile. It was a handwritten envelope personally addressed to me. It looked like a card. I set the rest of the mail aside and slid my thumb under the back flap. It was a beautiful get-well card. I flipped it open and a piece of paper flitted to the floor. I read the card as I absent-mindedly reached down to retrieve the paper. The card was from James and immediately, pain flared around my heart. I read his note.

> *Get well, Em. I think of you more often than you know. My family and I are so very grateful to you for rescuing my sister. You weren't aware of it at the time, but a reward had been offered for her safe return. That reward is yours. Perhaps one day our paths will cross again.*
>
> *Fondest regards,*
> *James Moss*
>
> *p.s. Your secret is safe with me.*

I looked at the slip of paper. It was a cheque, made out to me, for $250,000. I sank back into the chair, too stunned for words. Life really was full of surprises. As I contemplated that, I found myself staring at my father's favourite seascape painting. It had hung on the wall behind his desk for as long as I could remember.

I got up and stood in front of it and really looked at it, the way my father had a thousand times before. The artist had a talent for catching the light as it danced along the crest of the wave and then reflecting that light deep within the water below. The light had a life of its own, shimmering through the thin upper edge of the wave, making the towering wall of water translucent. I looked for the artist's scribbled signature along the bottom edge of the frame. And there it was, just as I'd seen it a thousand times before ...

J.Reynolds, '86

Thank You

Thank you for reading *Secret Sky*. If you enjoyed it, please tell a friend or consider posting a short review where you purchased it. Reviews help other readers discover the books and are much appreciated.

—JP McLean

Excerpts

Emelynn Taylor's story continues in Book 2, *Hidden Enemy*. An excerpt follows.

Lover Betrayed is Jackson Delaney's story. His role in *Secret Sky* was controversial, pivotal and demanded to be told. Love him or hate him, you won't forget him. *Lover Betrayed* is *Secret Sky* Redux. An excerpt follows.

Hidden Enemy

Emelynn survived her painful initiation into the world of Fliers, but are her secrets safe? Were the whispers true? Are powerful people searching for proof of their existence and do they know about Emelynn? Can she guard her secrets and her life now that she knows how easily either could be lost?

Read on for an excerpt ...

Someone was in the house. My eyes shot open. I strained to hear the noise repeat, but I couldn't hear a thing over the pounding of my heart.

The bedside clock projected the time on the ceiling: 2:55 a.m. I kept absolutely still and concentrated on my breathing. Damn! I thought I'd gotten over this, weeks ago. My nerves were now officially fried.

I pushed aside the covers. Living alone meant it was up to me to check the cottage for intruders. Sweat trickled down between my shoulder blades as I tiptoed the perimeter of the bedroom then slid into the hall.

My search of the small cottage revealed nothing out of place. The doors and windows remained locked—just as I'd left them when I went to bed. Was I losing my mind?

The covers were still warm when I crawled back into bed and curled into a ball, holding my knees tight to stop the shakes. I squeezed my eyes closed and tried to push away the fear. God, I hated this feeling.

Tonight was just like the previous times. I could have sworn I'd heard footsteps out on the deck or shuffling up on the roof, yet not once had there been any evidence. Not a single footprint in the dew; not a single finger smudge on a windowsill.

The lack of evidence suggested my imagination was playing tricks on me. I didn't want to believe it, but maybe a little paranoia was normal when you'd been shot. I just needed more time to adjust. Besides, this cottage had always been my sanctuary, and I'd be damned if I was going to let fear, imaginary or not, drive me from it. This cottage was my home.

Tomorrow I had an appointment with Avery. This time, even if I had to beg, I would convince him to prescribe sleeping pills. A couple weeks of undisturbed sleep would fix me up and then I'd be back to my usual upbeat, glass-half-full, self.

The next day, at my eleven o'clock appointment, I learned that Avery wasn't quite as convinced as I was about the whole sleeping pill solution.

"It's a bad idea, Emelynn." He frowned over the top of his ebony-framed glasses and released the blood pressure cuff with a rip of Velcro. "I'm not surprised you're feeling somewhat vulnerable and anxious, but sleeping pills aren't going to fix that."

He walked over to the small wooden desk and scribbled a note on a scratch pad then turned to lean back against the desk. Avery was tall and fit. He kept his blond hair short and the only thing that gave away his fifty-plus age was the greying at his temples, which you had to look closely to notice.

Avery Coulter was my doctor, but he was much more than that. He was my friend and confidant and he'd saved my life—twice. For that alone, I would always be grateful, but that wasn't what made him so special to me. It was because I'd come to think of him as my stand-in dad.

My father died in a plane crash when I was twelve years old and though ten years had passed, I still missed him. Dad had also been a doctor. His name was Brian Edison Taylor. He was forty-two when he died, so he and Avery would have been about the same age. They also shared a similarity in their casual manner and confident styles. I could talk to Avery about absolutely anything and I liked to think that if Dad were alive today, we would have the same kind of relationship.

"We'd be further ahead if we addressed the underlying cause of your anxiety instead of masking the symptoms with drugs." Avery, as usual, was maddeningly logical, but I'd already heard this particular speech.

"That's what you said last time, Avery. All I want is to sleep through the night. Is that really too much to ask?"

"The pills will help you sleep, Em, but as soon as you quit taking them—*if* you don't become dependent on them and *if* you can actually quit taking them, you'll be right back to hearing noises in the night." He crossed his arms over his chest. That was never a good sign.

"Well then, what would you suggest I do?" I huffed in exasperation.

"Last time we talked about this, your new fitness regimen was helping. What happened? You're still working with Malcolm aren't you?"

Malcolm Perreault was the personal trainer I'd hired after Avery cajoled me into it. Well, actually, that wasn't the entire truth. In the early days of my recovery, I started having these late night wake-up calls. Avery, working from the theory that an exhausted body rested better, suggested a fitness regimen.

At the time, it was hard for me to disagree. I was physically weakened from the damage the bullet had inflicted, and still reeling from the naïveté that led to my involvement in a situation I was ill-prepared for. What on earth possessed me to think I could come out on the winning side of a physical confrontation, let alone one that involved guns?

"Yes, Malcolm's great. We're up to 8K now. It gets easier every time, but it's still a challenge." I chuckled to myself thinking of my first runs with Malcolm. Between my calf cramps and side stitches, he must have thought he'd taken on an albatross. "Poor Malcolm."

"Don't feel sorry for Malcolm—that's what you pay him for. Besides, trainers like Malcolm run that distance just to pick up the newspaper."

Malcolm Perreault was almost six feet of flawless, dark skin melted over smooth muscle. I'd met him at the local YMCA after paying drop-in fees at half a dozen gyms in my search for a trainer. He was a refreshing change from the others I'd met, most of whom were Lycra-clad, muscle-bound men and women full of themselves and self-congratulation.

Malcolm was different. Within moments of our introduction, I knew I'd found my man. Well, not my man in that sense, though he could easily be a contender if I ever got into that frame of mind again.

Avery finally uncrossed his arms, but that put him back to staring at me over his glasses. "What's changed to set off your anxiety? Why the uptick in cold sweats in the night?"

"I have no idea. When it's happening, all I can think is that someone's trying to get into the house. It's terrifying, but by the time I'm able to think straight, the noises are gone and I never find any evidence that someone's been lurking. I can't keep doing this."

Avery walked behind the desk and pulled a phone book out of the drawer. He flipped to the back and ripped out a page. "Home Alarms." He pointed to the column of ads he'd handed me. "Maybe it's time you invest in a security system. It'll take the guesswork out of these noises you hear in the night."

"This is your solution?" I said, underwhelmed, as I looked at the flimsy sheet of yellow paper. He was the only one I knew who used the phone book rather than the Internet.

I considered his idea for a nanosecond before I started ticking off counterpoints. "Sleeping pills are quicker ... less complicated ... smaller," I said, touching my third finger, though that last one was a stretch.

Avery shook his head and smirked. I knew that look well enough now to know he wasn't about to give in. "A sleeping pill won't scare away intruders or alert the police," he said, having a good chuckle at my stubborn stance. "Ah, come on—being a victim doesn't suit you, Em. Take the reins and get back out in front. Let's give the non-chemical approach a shot first and if that doesn't work, then we'll talk about alternatives."

Avery bent to put the phone book back in the drawer, but changed his mind and set it aside. He twisted his mouth and flipped through the drawer's contents. "That's odd," he said, puzzled.

"What's odd?"

"I could have sworn I brought your chart down here this morning, but it seems to have grown legs and walked away." He replaced the phone book and came around in front of the desk again. "If only they made a pill that could cure absent-mindedness."

I stared at him and blinked, just once. "Surely you're not suggesting chemical intervention?" I said, barely hiding my amusement. Avery arched an eyebrow. My bid for sleeping pills was lost.

Perhaps a home alarm was a good suggestion. As his idea settled in, I allowed it some merit. "I suppose I could look into a security system. Maybe Cheney could recommend a company?" I brightened at the thought.

Cheney Meyer was the twenty-five-year-old mechanic who'd resurrected my father's old red convertible. I'd discovered the abandoned MGB in the garage when I returned here to our family's cottage on the west coast a few months ago. Cheney and his dad, Jack, restored it so it spewed exhaust like the day it came out of the factory. Cheney had contacts. He'd know someone in the security business.

"I bet he could," Avery said. "Lie back."

This was our Tuesday routine. First, he took my temperature. Then he checked my eyes and reflexes. Next, he took my blood pressure. The last step was checking the bullet wounds. The paper crackled under me as I lay back on the red vinyl exam table and hiked my shirt. The bullet hole that caused such terrible pain just seven weeks ago was now a dime-sized shiny pink circle of skin. The exit wound wasn't as pretty, but it was on my back so I didn't have to look at it. He examined the wounds with gentle fingers, palpating all around them. We did the, *does this hurt; how about that*, routine and then he pulled my shirt back down and I sat up.

"The night sweats, the sudden waking—they're typical symptoms of anxiety," Avery said. "You've been through a lot these past few weeks, physically and emotionally. You need to process it." Avery pushed his glasses up into his hair. "Let's give it more time. If your symptoms persist, we'll discuss it again, but my preference will still be to try behaviour modification therapy before chemical intervention."

I frowned. My preference was still the quick fix of pharmaceuticals.

"But we're getting ahead of ourselves. Your work with Malcolm has already helped heal your body. A home alarm will put your mind at ease and don't forget about Eden. She knows what you're dealing with and she wants to help. Besides, she's one of us—discreet is in her DNA."

Avery was right about Eden. She started off as one of my teachers, but the intensity of our time together had turned our bond into a close friendship. Eden Effrome was four years my senior and five foot nothing to my five foot seven. Her spiky red hair looked nothing like my long, curly mop, and her eyes were bright blue, whereas mine were green. The physical differences made it impossible to mistake us for real sisters, but she's exactly who I'd pick for my sister if I could. I hopped down from the exam table and straightened my clothes.

"Do you think Jackson was telling the truth?" I asked. "You know—about the military or organized crime, knowing about us? Looking for us?" Jackson Delaney's integrity had been obliterated in the wake of a deception by him that left us questioning if anything he'd told us could be trusted.

"Honestly—I don't know. We're all asking the same questions. Everyone with contacts has put feelers out searching for more information. I just hope we're not stirring up a hornet's nest with all the speculation. Just a few days ago, one of my contacts had his computer hacked. His first thought was that someone was on to him. It's worrisome."

"Everyone's feeling the pressure," I said, gathering my things. I walked out of the small exam room into the empty waiting area. Avery's home office was in a converted garage attached to his Victorian-era home in an old-money neighbourhood. The stately old house filled out nearly every square metre of a large city lot. It was a beautiful home with a small back garden. Avery and I had shared numerous mugs of coffee and pots of tea in the kitchen, and it was upstairs in one of the bedrooms where I'd recovered after the shooting.

Avery put his arm around my shoulder and walked me to the door. "Don't wait too long to look into an alarm. The sooner we address the anxiety, the faster you'll get over it. And call Eden," he said as he opened the door for me. "Are we still on for Thursday?"

I sighed heavily. "Yes, of course." I stepped into the bright August sunshine. Tuesdays were physical checkup days but Thursdays were when the real work happened. On Thursdays, we challenged my gift, the source of so much pain and angst. *The gift* was the secret we all kept, but only three people knew that mine was different. That difference would cost me my life if my secret got out.

LOVER BETRAYED

When his wife leaves him for his half-brother, Jackson Delaney flies into high gear to find them. He dives headlong into dangerous intrigue involving the feared Tribunal and unscrupulous thugs from his past, in a quest for justice at any cost. When that quest leads him to a mysterious young Flier with no knowledge of her arcane gift, Jackson's vengeance gets the better of him and may cost him something worse than his life.

Read on for an excerpt ...

The oppressive heat was unavoidable, omnipotent, like the man in the casket. We followed dutifully behind, our steps out of time with the rhythmic clops of the black hearse horses. White lilies hugged the casket, quivering to the drum roll of a jazz band's lively rendition of "When the Saints Go Marching In," an absurd funeral favourite. Tourists in waist pouches and flip-flops, unsure of the show, whispered behind finger curtains and stole glances under furrowed brows and baseball caps. I understood their uncertainty. The father I'd loved and loathed died without warning, too soon to recognize his mistakes, let alone fix them.

"This is a goddamn freak show," I said. "I'd never have agreed to it if it wasn't spelled out in his will."

"But it was," Sandra said. "You and your father may have had your differences, but you're a good son, Jackson."

"Was. I *was* a good son."

"You always will be," Sandra said. My wife's fingers felt cool in my hand, despite the heat. She looked up at me, her blue eyes hidden behind sunglasses and a loop of black netting that covered her face. I eased the pressure off her hand with an apology, ignoring the bead of sweat that crawled down my spine.

It took thirty minutes for my father's slow funeral procession, wafting the cloying scent of flowers, to wind through the streets of New Orleans. We'd walked an unpleasant mile behind the coffin before passing under the iron arch of the cemetery. Like a shrimp trawler with its net out, our parade snagged tourists and curiosity-seekers in its wake.

The music took on a sombre tenor only when we mounted the slight rise, which housed the Delaney tomb. The last time I'd seen the tomb open was fifteen years ago when we'd laid my mother to rest. Following long tradition, her coffin had been discarded and her remains dumped into the bone heap below to make way for the new arrival. One day, my coffin would displace my father's in a similar ritual. Would I also succumb to a stroke before I'd finished living my life?

I was a teenager when my mother died. There were times now when I had to see her picture to remember her face, but I had no trouble remembering her love. She'd bathed me in it, cooking my favourite crawfish boil, which my father hated, and baking pecan pies he wouldn't touch. She liked that I'd inherited her hazel eyes. Dad had said she coddled me, or at least that's the excuse he used to justify his tough-love approach to parenting. I doubted I'd ever need a photograph of my father to remember him.

The priest raised his voice over the crowd while photojournalists captured video of the mourners. Tomorrow, they would justify the intrusion in the name of news. Equally unwelcome tourists snapped cellphone photos they'd later show their friends at home in some macabre recollection of their good fortune in stumbling upon a genuine City of the Dead funeral.

I looked out over the perspiring faces. Tourists aside, my father would have been pleased to see the calibre of mourners who'd braved the August heat to pay their last respects. Top-echelon politicians and business people mopped their brows and donned sombre expressions, hopeful that the priest was nearing the end of the ritual. Half of the men gathered were better candidates for a casket. My father wasn't yet sixty. It shouldn't have been his time.

After the casket was laid in place, I bid him a final farewell and then nodded to the cemetery workmen, who kept their wheelbarrows at a respectful distance. As soon as they moved in to seal the tomb, the mourners began to scatter.

Jimmy Marchant was the first to approach. Sweat was beading on his red face and dribbling down ample jowls that melted into a thick neck. His jacket was soaked through, but he hadn't loosened his tie. He'd be a proper southern gentleman for my father one last time if it killed him.

He pecked Sandra on the cheek before offering me his hand. "Sorry for your loss, buddy. Your father's left a big hole on half the boards in

Louisiana." Jimmy was born and raised in New Orleans. He spoke with a Yat accent, pronouncing "boards" with a barely perceptible *r* and "Louisiana" as "Loo-ziana."

"Thanks, Jimmy." In his younger years, Jimmy could have passed for John Goodman's brother. My father respected Jimmy Marchant for his legal counsel and even more for his discretion. Jimmy understood my father's definition of doing business. It entertained him, and earned his firm a lot of money, especially when my father bent the law. I was in Jimmy's debt for making sure no one knew how often that had happened. "I hope you'll join us at the Omni tonight. Let Dad buy you one last drink."

"Wouldn't miss it. Matthew Delaney knew how to throw a party and I intend to honour my promise: your father's wake will be one to remember." He leaned close. "And well lubricated," he added with a conspiratorial wink.

I forced a smile and shook Jimmy's hand. One final spectacle to endure.

Dad had made a good and loyal friend in Jimmy. I'd known Jimmy all my life and had my own reasons for liking the man. It was through him that I'd met my wife, Alexandra, or Sandra, as she preferred to be called. Like Jimmy, her father was a lawyer, and Redmond Moss was well connected. After Katrina, Redmond used those connections to generate funds to help rebuild. Sandra Moss distributed her father's funding out of Jimmy's donated office space. When Jimmy recruited my father's development expertise, I was the lucky son of a bitch who got to work with her.

I took Sandra's elbow and turned toward the first in a long line of idling limos.

"Kyle, Anthony, you'll ride with us, of course," Sandra said, addressing my old Stanford classmates who'd flown in for the funeral. Kyle Murphy lived in Dallas so knew enough to wear a light coloured suit. Anthony Dimarco was New York through and through. His navy Brooks Brothers was a choice I suspected he now regretted.

The driver opened Sandra's door, and we followed her into the blessed air conditioning.

"Jackman—how the hell do you live in this heat?" Anthony said, using my college nickname as he mopped the sweat from his brow with a limp pocket square. He tugged his tie loose.

"Northerners," Kyle quipped.

The driver pulled out, leading the train of limos to the hotel.

"I'm serious," Anthony said, supplementing his pocket square with several tissues he'd yanked from the limo's complimentary supply.

"You get used to it," I said, sparing a glance at Sandra. She'd smoothed her hair into some complicated knot the heat didn't seem to touch.

"Will you be staying long?" Sandra asked.

"Only if you dump that lousy husband of yours," Kyle said with a lecherous smile. Anthony swatted him. "What? We all know she's out of his league."

"Oh, and you think she's in yours?" Anthony said, raising his eyebrows.

Sandra looked down at her folded hands, fighting a smile. They'd met her on our wedding day. The last-minute introduction had been unavoidable, but Kyle and Anthony had taken the piss out of me about it. They insisted she would have chosen either of them over me if they'd been introduced earlier. The truth was, if Sandra and I hadn't wed quickly, and quietly, her family would have tried to stop us. It wasn't just that she came from old money and I came from new—it was that her father didn't approve of the way my father had amassed his fortune. Redmond Moss was not a religious man, but he was a judgmental bastard who held firmly to the belief that the sins of the father should be visited upon the son. Thankfully, Sandra had a mind of her own.

The driver pulled up in front of the Omni hotel, where a black-capped doorman hurried to open Sandra's door. The limo's cool air dissipated in a suffocating wave of heat. We hurried inside.

"We're going to freshen up," Sandra said, removing her sunglasses. "We'll see you in an hour or so?"

"For sure," Kyle said. Anthony already had his jacket off and his tie in hand.

Sandra took my arm and we headed to the elevators. Back in our suite, she kicked off her shoes. "That went well, don't you think?" she said.

I removed my jacket and flopped on the sofa. "A few more hours and it'll be over."

"Don't wish it away too fast." She stood in front of a mirror untangling the netted hat from her hair. "After all, the Delaney board will be there and so will most of the city's politicians, not to mention the governor."

"And your father?"

"He'll be there. Mom as well. Etiquette dictates, as you know." Etiquette and old money went hand in hand. Sandra should know; she'd been raised on both.

"Have you told them about my plans for Delaney & Son?"

She dropped her hat on the coffee table and sat beside me. "No. I want them to hear it from you."

After the initial shock of Dad's death had worn off, Sandra and I talked through the night about what came next. I didn't keep secrets from Sandra—her discretion was impeccable, so she knew about Dad's *strategic donations*, as he'd referred to them, and his propensity to *eavesdrop* when he thought it would win him an advantage. I was ashamed of that. I told her I wanted to be a better man, to behave respectably and with honour. To do things right.

"Cleaning up Delaney's reputation will take a long time. Years probably."

She turned in her seat. "The fact that you want to is what matters. And soon you'll be the one making the decisions, not your father. Dad will see the difference. He'll come around."

I took her hand and brushed my thumb against her wedding band. "I hope it's not a mistake. My father may have been short on scruples, but he knew how to make money."

"And so do you, but you know how to do it without compromising your integrity."

I lifted my head in a flash of annoyance. "My father had plenty of integrity."

She stiffened. "Of course. That was careless of me to say."

I dropped her hand and stood. "I'm going to shower."

"I'm sorry."

"I know. It's been a tough week." I squeezed her shoulder in passing. "We'll get through it."

After changing into fresh clothes, we took the elevator back down to the ballroom. The scent of flowers nearly knocked me over. I doubted there was a lily in Louisiana outside of this room. Was this the measure of a man? Personally, I'd never understood the flowers. A man had died. He'd lived and breathed business, not flowers. Flowers were something his guilt trotted out on Valentine's Day. Why not a genuine tribute to the man when he was still alive? A fine bottle of bourbon? Midfield seats at a Saints game? A favour he didn't have to pay for?

My arrival dimmed the raucous laughter. Jimmy, finally free of his jacket, raised his glass in a silent toast from across the room, and held it aloft. One by one, everyone in the ballroom did the same. Say what you want about my old man, he made an impression. A rocks glass landed in my hand. I stared at the amber liquid and fought the lump at the back of my throat.

Slowly, I raised my glass. "To Matthew Delaney," I said. "A formidable businessman, a generous benefactor, and my father. May he rest in peace." A collective shout rang out and then bubbled away.

Conversations resumed, backs were turned and bursts of laughter rose above the ambient noise. Sandra stroked the back of my arm. "That was lovely."

Lovely? Anger crawled up my chest, prickling my neck. I scanned the crowd. Every gluttonous supplier, every slippery politician, every Barbie Doll wife, and every major charity bold enough to send a representative had benefited from my father's acumen and generosity. They still were, sloshing back the best the bar had to offer. What had Dad gotten? Flowers he would hate and a toast from a son who couldn't even say he loved him. He'd taught me everything he knew, and it wasn't enough. My love for him was rough around the edges. In time, it may have softened, but we had no more time.

I quaffed my drink and another magically appeared. Condolences flowed, abundant as the liquor, and one after another, Dad's impressive circle of influencers, friends and rivals approached me to pay their respects. Marcel Cadieu, a Louisiana senator and early convert to my father's way of doing business, was one of the first to slither up.

"My wife, Claudette," he said, making an unnecessary introduction. "Please accept our sympathies, Jackson. Louisiana has lost a great man." Marcel hid his animosity behind a politician's smile. He'd never figured out how my father had learned of his affair with a sandy-haired gentleman half his age. Marcel had been so careful; he and his lover had never acknowledged one another in public, not so much as a wayward glance. They'd checked into separate but adjoining rooms on the forty-second floor of the Sheraton in New Orleans. Yet my father knew the sandy-haired gentleman had spilled his flute of Cristal out on the balcony that fateful night. Dad had a photograph to prove it. And if he knew that detail, then he knew everything.

Marcel immediately became a staunch supporter of Delaney & Son. But while he championed Dad's development projects, he quietly initiated and then backed the strongest anti-drone legislation in the country. If only he knew that a drone had not been necessary.

Carl Prudhomme, also a convert, waddled up with a hearty handshake. He was head of Industrial Rod and Steel in Lafayette. My father had ensured his loyalty and a favourable pricing structure after Carl heard a recording my father played for him. Apparently Carl and two other major steel suppliers had taken a midnight trail ride into the wilds of Carl's eight-hundred-acre ranch outside of Vidalia in Concordia Parish to discuss their new pricing scheme. My father had been eager to point out that collusion in any form would likely be frowned upon in Louisiana's legislative circles. Carl had had little choice but to tip his hat, but soon afterwards, he fired his ranch hands and hired new security. Not that any of that would be an obstacle to one of our kind.

With Sandra on one side and Jimmy on the other, we received the mourners. They dropped their smiles to shake my hand, and offer condolences. Sandra's father, Redmond, and her mother, Diana made their obligatory appearance and soon after disappeared. But not all the guests wore fake smiles. My father was a generous man who loved a good party and treated his friends well.

The line of grievers marched on and my father's acquaintances crawled by, kissing my wife and patting me on the shoulder. I grew tired of repeating what felt like my mantra: "Yes, I am proud of my father's legacy." And to those few who needed to hear it, I added, "Yes, I look forward to taking Delaney & Son in a fresh, new direction."

After the handshakes and back pats subsided, Jimmy headed to the bar and Sandra excused herself. I searched the room for Kyle and Anthony. They had been welcomed into Jimmy's clutch of insiders at the bar, many of whom were Dad's closest friends. I joined them and we put a dent or two in some of the finer bottles on offer and listened to my father's friends tell ribald stories of Dad's exploits.

My father had chosen to lead a public life, and some of the tales were ones he'd leaked himself. He'd manipulated the media as handily as the men he'd kept markers on, cashing them in when it suited his game. And it didn't suit his game to have the public know his other persona: the man who grieved when my mother died; the man who stayed by my side until I conquered my deadly fear of heights; the man who helped me bury Razz, short for Razzmatazz, the crazy black lab he'd bought me for my fifth birthday. Sadly, his tender moments had been as rare and fleeting as a *loup-garou* sighting in the bayou.

This game he played ensured that, to his face at least, people referred to him as a maverick, a shrewd negotiator, a visionary. But in the backrooms and bars, they called him manipulative, contemptible and crooked. That was my legacy. I was the *& Son* of Delaney & Son, and now I had to clean up the mess.

Standing in the midst of the huddle of men at the end of the bar, I watched Sandra work her way through the mourners. She clasped a hand here, stroked a shoulder there, smiled a blessing with a nod of her head. She charmed every man in the room and befriended every woman, and she was mine, my oasis in the quagmire of grief and guilt my father's death had stirred.

A little after midnight, Sandra approached the table where Jimmy had been reminiscing about Dad and the early days, when it was still just Delaney Developments. He'd been developing strip malls back then and married to his first wife. I loved those stories best. Dad hadn't yet felt the sting of betrayal or learned to like the feel of dirt on his hands.

The wake was just warming up and wouldn't end until dawn. Sandra offered the men a shy smile and then leaned down to my ear. "I think we've done our part, Jackson. Let's go."

Her sweet vanilla scent pulled me out of my chair. It always put me in mind of my mother's bread pudding, something else I could never resist. My father once told me Sandra was too good for me. His callous comment had angered me at the time, but not because he was right. He considered her a feather in the Delaney cap, but he never once acknowledged it was me, the *& Son*, who'd won her.

I excused myself and followed her to our suite, freeing the mourners to drain the bar and speculate about what would happen to the dirt Dad had on most of them.

Acknowledgements

Secret Sky was originally published as *The Gift: Awakening*. The title change is a result of overwhelming feedback from the books' readership. My gratitude goes to Elinor Florence, who was instrumental and supportive throughout the rebranding process.

This book could not have been completed without the guidance, input and feedback of innumerable supportive friends and family. Thank you all for showing an interest and cheering me on.

John, thank you for believing in me and this project. Thank you, Will, for your early encouragement and guidance—it helped immensely. Karen, your boundless enthusiasm warms my heart and you'll recognize your input. Thanks, Mom, for not crossing out the dirty words. Dad, thanks for the comic relief—your unconventional support lightens my day. Thanks, Gee, for the expert medical advice and sisterly support. To Sally, Denis, Colleen, Lorna, Cathy and Sue, the time you've given and the bravery you've shown in reading the early drafts is much appreciated, and your input helped shape the final version—thanks so much. To Jasna, thank you for your input with the new summary and the cheerleading.

Thanks to the design team at JD&J Designs for *Secret Sky's* enticing book cover design.

My gratitude goes to my editor, Nina Munteanu, who is also a writing coach and author (https://ninamunteanu.me). *Secret Sky* bloomed and twisted wonderfully with your insightful critique and skilful edits. Thank you.

And finally, thanks to Rachel Small, Rachel Small Editing for a thorough copy edit that added a beautiful polish (www.rachelsmallediting.com).

All errors in the research and writing of this novel are entirely my own.

GLOSSARY OF TERMS

Covey: A group of Fliers who are geographically connected. Older coveys were and still are connected by family rather than location. All Fliers belong to a home covey and are expected to check in with coveys in areas they are visiting. Coveys are a source of information and are trained to protect their Fliers.

Crystal: All Ghosts need a crystal to achieve ghosted form. The two exceptions to this are Emelynn Taylor and the woman who gifted her, Jolene Reynolds.

Flash: Fliers can use the second lens in their eye to produce a flicker of light within the eye that other Fliers recognize.

Flier: A human either born or gifted with a mutated gene that allows him or her to shed gravity and take flight. The gene can also manifest with additional facets, such as memory reading and telekinesis. The mutation produces a second lens in the eye.

Founding families: The nine founding coveys are comprised of the oldest and strongest families within the Flier community. Centuries ago, these family coveys founded the Tribunal Novem to police the Flier ranks.

Ghost: A Flier with the ability to dissipate into molecules too small for the human eye to see. Ghosts are rare. The process of turning into this form is called ghosting. All members of the Tribunal Novem are Ghosts.
The Gift: The mutated gene that allows a Flier to shed gravity. The mutation produces a second lens in the eye. The gene can also manifest with additional facets, such as memory reading and telekinesis.
Gifting: The process of transferring the gift, in whole or in part, from one Flier to someone else. The receiver can be any human. The process strips the donor of the element gifted. When the entire gift is given, the

process weakens the gift-giver and is fatal half the time. Giftings are strictly controlled by the Tribunal Novem. A Flier who has been gifted is considered a second-class Flier.

Jolt: Fliers can use the second lens in their eye to produce a wave of energy along a spectrum from sparks, which are like static shocks, to jolts, which are painful and can even be fatal. The degree of energy produced depends upon the Flier's particular gift and varies from weak to strong. A fatal jolt causes a brain bleed (hemorrhage or aneurysm), which is medically classified as a stroke.

The Redeemers: A group of Fliers who feel they have been wronged, or are not represented, by the Tribunal Novem. Their goal is to replace the Tribunal Novem. They are led by Carson Manse.

Rush: Fliers can use the second lens in their eye to produce a stimulative energy that falls within the low-end of the spectrum of energy they are able to produce. It's sexual in nature and used to heighten sexual arousal. Referred to as the/his/her rush.

Spark: Fliers can use the second lens in their eye to produce a wave of energy along a spectrum from sparks, which are like static shocks, to jolts, which are painful and can even be fatal. The degree of energy produced depends upon the Flier's particular gift and varies from weak to strong.

The Tribunal Novem: Judge, jury and executioner in the Flier world. They are comprised of one representative from each of the nine founding coveys. They are always Ghosts. Their identities are not known within the Flier community. The Tribunal's leadership rotates every five years. At any given time, five Tribunal members provide day-to-day investigation and enforcement.

DISCUSSION QUESTIONS

Spoiler alert: These questions contain spoilers that will ruin the story for those who haven't yet read the book.

1. Emelynn's relationship with her mother is markedly different from the one she had with her father. What are the clues to those differences? What impact does her father's death have on Emelynn's relationship with her mother? Are there other family traumas that could produce the same result?

2. Emelynn was twelve years old when Jolene gifted her. At that time, Emelynn promised Jolene she wouldn't tell a soul about the gift. What might cause a child to misplace their loyalties by making such a promise? Is there something parents can do to prevent a child from making this kind of error in judgment?

3. Even as an adult, Emelynn maintains the secrecy of Jolene's gift. Do you think this is a mistake? How might her life have been different if she'd divulged the secret of Jolene's gift a) immediately? and b) after she became aware that she could shed gravity?

4. Lonely versus alone; how do Emelynn's circumstances isolate her, and what are her coping mechanisms. Are they effective?
5. If you were Molly and learned that Emelynn could fly but had kept that secret from you, how would you react? What if you were her mother, Laura? Do you think Emelynn is doing the right thing in keeping her gift a secret?

6. In some regards, Emelynn is naïve, and in other regards, she is mature beyond her years. What are some examples of her naïveté/maturity?

7. The author does not treat Emelynn with kid gloves. In *Secret Sky*, Emelynn suffers a catastrophic fall, a near-drowning and an devastating betrayal. How does the severity of these events impact Emelynn's character? How do these events impact your impression of Emelynn?

8. Knowing Jackson's personal situation at the end of *Secret Sky*, what clues did Emelynn miss that might have informed her? What, if any, motherly advice would you offer her?

9. Dreaming you can fly is one of the most common dreams humans have. "In almost every culture, flying dreams represent freedom or a release from daily pressures." —Jeffrey Sumber, MA, MTS, LCPC. In the Victorian era, Sigmund Freud was of the opinion flying dreams released sexual tension in an age of sexual oppression by society morals. Do you agree with either of these opinions? Do you dream you can fly? If so, do you fly face down, or upright? Indoors or out? If you could fly, where would you fly to?

10. If you were casting Emelynn's character for the big screen, who would you choose? Who would you choose for Jackson's character?

11. If you could ask the author one question, what would it be? Would your organization or group like to arrange an author appearance in person or online? If so, please contact the author at jpmclean @jpmcleanauthor.com.

A printable version of these discussion
questions is available at www.jpmcleanauthor.com/extras.

ABOUT THE AUTHOR

JP (Jo-Anne) McLean is best known for her contemporary fantasy series, The Gift Legacy. Reviewers call the series *addictive, smart and fun.*

The first book of her Gift Legacy Series, *Secret Sky* (originally titled *Awakening*), received Honourable Mention at the 2016 Whistler Independent Book Awards. In 2016, JP's body of work was included in the centennial anthology of the Comox Valley Writers Society, *Writers & Books: Comox Valley 1865–2015.* Her writing has appeared in WordWorks Magazine, Wellness and Writing blog, Mystery Mondays blog, and many others.

JP holds a degree in commerce from the University of British Columbia, is a certified scuba diver, an avid gardener and a voracious reader. She lives with her husband on Denman Island, which is nestled between the coast of British Columbia and Vancouver Island.

She enjoys hearing from readers. Contact her via her website at www.jpmcleanauthor.com or through her social media sites. Reviews are always welcome and greatly appreciated.

 Sign up for her newsletter ~ www.jpmcleanauthor.com

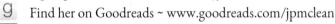 Find her on Goodreads ~ www.goodreads.com/jpmclean

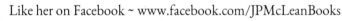 Like her on Facebook ~ www.facebook.com/JPMcLeanBooks

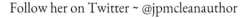 Follow her on Twitter ~ @jpmcleanauthor